THREADS OF HOPE

Quilts of Love Series

Christa Allan

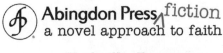
Abingdon Press fiction
a novel approach to faith

Nashville, Tennessee

Threads of Hope

Copyright © 2013 by Christa Allan

ISBN-13: 978-1-4267-5266-7

Published by Abingdon Press, P.O. Box 801, Nashville, TN 37202
www.abingdonpress.com

Library of Congress Cataloging-in-Publication Data
has been requested.

Printed in the United States of America

1 2 3 4 5 6 7 8 9 10 / 18 17 16 15 14 13

Threads of Hope

Other books in the Quilts of Love Series

Beyond the Storm
Carolyn Zane
(October 2012)

A Wild Goose Chase Christmas
Jennifer AlLee
(November 2012)

Path of Freedom
Jennifer Hudson Taylor
(January 2013)

For Love of Eli
Loree Lough
(February 2013)

A Healing Heart
Angela Breidenbach
(April 2013)

A Heartbeat Away
S. Dionne Moore
(May 2013)

Pattern for Romance
Carla Olson Gade
(June 2013)

Pieces of the Heart
Bonnie S. Calhoun
(August 2013)

Raw Edges
Sandra D. Bricker
(September 2013)

The Christmas Quilt
Vannetta Chapman
(October 2013)

Aloha Rose
Lisa Carter
(November 2013)

Tempest's Course
Lynette Sowell
(December 2013)

Scraps of Evidence
Barbara Cameron
(January 2014)

A Sky Without Stars
Linda S. Clare
(February 2014)

Maybelle in Stitches
Joyce Magnin
(March 2014)

Other books by Christa Allan

Walking on Broken Glass
The Edge of Grace

To the families and friends
of the men, women, and children whose lives
will be forever stitched together
on The AIDS Memorial Quilt.
Remember. Understand. Share the lessons. Act.

Acknowledgments

Much like the varied and various panels stitched together to compose a quilt that is unique and a reflection of all those who participated in its completion, so too is this novel. Because of the contributions of others, each offering a special talent or wisdom, this novel is in your hands.

Thanks to Abingdon Press for their continued support: to Senior Acquisitions Editor—Fiction Ramona Richards and Teri Wilhelms, who edited the novel, and to everyone there whose dedication makes publishing possible.

I deeply appreciate my agent Sandra Bishop, who tirelessly stitches me together every time I unravel. I probably should enroll her in Thimble-of-the-Month Club (not that there is one, but if there was, she'd be a charter member).

Jenny B. Jones . . . how can I thank you except to give you a few weeks of peace between novels. I've leaned on you (okay, maybe sometimes poured concrete and used you as a foundation) through texts, telephone, tweets, e-mails, and gchats. I've exhausted every means and method of communication in seeking your help, and you still haven't (yet) moved to an unknown location on some unknown planet.

Thanks to Shelley, whose plotting skills save me, and to Carole and Carrie for calling me to make sure I've not impaled myself on a red pen. Thanks to the lunch bunch for laughter: Michelle, Meredith, Tammie, Jennifer, Kim, Tracey, Adam, and Andrew.

Without my brother John and my brother-in-law Ricky, every meal would be Coke Zero, popcorn, and chocolate. It's incredibly reassuring to know that, every day, I'm only twenty-three steps away from encouragement, food, and love.

My children, Michael, Erin (and Andrae), Shannon, Sarah, and John (all now old enough to be adult-ren), continue to claim me as their mother even when I'm at my craziest. And, of course, my forever love and gratitude to my husband Ken, who has learned the art of self-preservation during my writing and of us-preservation when I'm not.

Thank you God for making all of the above possible.

1

After three years, it finally happened.

Janie Bettencourt announced her promotion. She would be moving from Houston to New York to become Senior Editor of *Trends* magazine.

The promotion Nina O'Malley had hoped would be her own.

And, as if that news wasn't enough to justify Nina adding banana splits as main dish items on her diet, ice cream became its own food group after Janie added that joining her would be staff photographer Brady Lambert.

The Brady who, years ago, promised her the moon. The Brady who, later, spun out of her orbit and splashed down in Janie's. The Brady Lambert whom Nina had hoped would be her own.

When was she going to learn to wait for the other shoe to drop before assuming she could celebrate?

Earlier that morning, when she'd spotted an email message from Elise Johnson, the Executive Editor, Nina allowed herself the luxury of dreaming. Elise's personal emails were infrequent, at least in her in-box, and generally, no frills, as if she'd be charged by the word count. So, she wasn't at all offended when she read the brief request: "My office. Nine o'clock. Important matter to discuss. EJ." In fact, she was elated. And she remained so for the next fifty-four minutes, not counting her elevator time to the seventh floor where she was ushered into Elise's office.

In less time than it took for Nina to arrive in the starkly modern office of the executive editor, disappointment introduced itself. Later, when the elevator door swished open to reveal Janie, Nina felt like a contestant on a game show who'd guessed wrongly and seen what she might have won.

The weight of Elise's remarks might have pushed Nina to the second floor almost as efficiently as the elevator: *Structurally correct writing, but lacked style and passion. More initiative and less predictability. Network. Move out of your comfort zone.* Elise challenged Nina to convince her that she'd be making a mistake not to promote her. "We're considering other markets like Atlanta and Nashville, perhaps Los Angeles. One of those could be yours. Show me what you can do."

By the time Janie gathered the staff and squealed her news, Nina had power walked to Starbucks and returned caffeinated and composed. She smiled in Janie's direction, grateful Janie couldn't read her thoughts to know her angelic face came from imagining a subway door closing on one of her size 6 Ferragamo shoes.

Just as the image was becoming crystal clear in Nina's mind, a tidal wave of a voice in her head crashed over that picture and left behind the sound of her mother's words: *"You're being so petty, my dear. God doesn't like ugly, you know."* Nina mentally shushed her mother who, even more than twenty miles away, could still inject an admonition into her daughter's nerve center of guilt.

Sheila Hudson O'Malley married Nina's father Patrick not long after they graduated from high school and then stayed home to mother two children into semi-adulthood. What would she know about fickle boyfriends and dashed career dreams? "Sure, mother. Easy for you to say," Nina muttered as she diverted her attention from the fawning frenzy over Janie to rearrange the clutter on her desk. She hoped to unearth her iPad from underneath what looked like an office supply store explosion of paper that had landed there.

"Were you talking to me?"

Nina paused between lifting legal pads to turn toward her cubicle-mate, Daisy Jeffers, who had scooted her desk chair past her partition, and now stared at her. As usual, her dark hair sprouted from the top of her head like sprinkler arms. She was always one strong wind short of being propelled above ground level.

"No. I was talking to my mother." Nina resumed her excavation.

"Well, I'm assuming the one in your head since I don't smell Chanel No. 5 in the vicinity. And, anyway . . ." she bit into her apple.

Now that Nina found her iPad lurking in her desk drawer under a stack of folders and three expired restaurant coupons, she focused on Daisy. "Are you aware how absolutely annoying that is?"

Daisy swallowed. "You mean her?" Still holding her half-eaten apple, Daisy bent her arm over her head and motioned in the general direction of the newly promoted.

Nina flipped open the leather cover to find her interview notes. "Not Janie. You. Can you wait until before or after your thoughts, not between them, to eat? It's so maddening waiting for you to finish chewing . . ." She paused.

Her mother's voice. She heard her mother's voice, the one that forever seemed marinated in exasperation, spill out of her own mouth. She looked up at Daisy. "You just got a whiff of

Chanel No. 5 didn't you?" Nina gave way to the defeat and disappointment and flopped into her chair.

Daisy pinched her nose for a moment and grimaced. "A serious overdose." Not an unexpected reply from someone who smelled as if she'd spritzed herself with bottled spring rain, newly mown summer grass, and a hint of an autumn bonfire. She tossed her apple core into her stainless steel eco-lunchbox, wiped her hands with her cotton napkin, and rolled herself closer to Nina. Almost ten years younger than Nina, Daisy exuded a wisdom beyond her age. As a child, she slept in a car for weeks until her single mother found a homeless shelter for them. Daisy figured living on the streets was poverty's answer to accelerated learning. Nina suspected Daisy's minimalist approach to the externals in her life—clothing, furniture, car—balanced the burden of her emotional life.

"It's just not your time," said Daisy. "There will be a season for you, too."

Nina felt as if she'd just been patted on the head and told to run along and play. "I'd like to wallow in my pity party a bit longer before you start breaking it up with your New Age-y philosophies," she responded.

Daisy smiled. A reaction Nina found more annoying than the smattering of applause earlier that followed Janie's news.

"Well, I wouldn't be a worthy friend if I didn't at least try to save you from yourself. And, anyway, how much of a party is it if you're the only one with an invitation?"

"Speaking of invitations . . ."

Nina was as startled to see Janie materialize as Daisy appeared to be when she heard her voice. Daisy slowly swiveled her chair and looked up at the leggy blonde who leaned against the gray dividing wall separating their desks from the receptionist's. "Whoa. How did you do that? Is magically transporting yourself part of the new job description?"

Janie tilted her head, placed her forefinger on her cheek, and became a perfect model for "deep in thought." Except for the smirk. She dropped the pose and looked at Nina. "I suppose having my finger on the pulse of the magazine is a requisite for effective management. Wouldn't you agree?"

Daisy and Nina exchanged eye contact then stared at Janie.

"So . . . anyway . . . back to invitations." Janie reached into the pocket of her flouncy skirt and silenced the pinging on her cell phone. "I'm having a cozy going-away dinner at my condo in two weeks. Of course, you're both invited. Bra and I are hosting it together."

"Bra," which she pronounced like "hey" was her special name for Brady, used only when not in his presence. The first time Janie uttered it in the office, it sliced through any thread of expectation Nina held for a future with him. She suspected the affectation was Janie's unseen electric collar around Brady, but instead of confining him, it zapped a warning to any women on the prowl contemplating new territory. Or one like Nina, who hoped for an open gate.

Over time, most of the staff became adept at avoiding eye-rolls when Janie blathered on about Bra. Though Daisy refused to abandon the idea that she might one day write a story about Bra and Janie's relationship. She hoped Victoria's Secret would think it a grand tale of a woman who referred to her lingerie in third person.

Now, faced with the prospect of swallowing food while enduring Brady and Janie, Nina rifled through her mental file of excuses. She barely had time to consider the choices when Daisy said, "We wouldn't dream of missing an opportunity to send you off on your new adventure." She glanced at Nina. "Would we?"

What Nina wanted to do at that moment was send Daisy twirling back across the partition. Instead, she mumbled something about making sure she'd be free, grabbed her iPad, and hoped when she swiped her calendar she'd find an event so monumental it would be impossible to attend the dinner. But no. No White House interview, no late night talk show appearance, and no undercover expose planned. Just a reminder to drop off her clothes at the cleaner and buy a case of dog food. *Pathetic. My life needs a makeover.* She stared at the socially vacant month of April. "Well, I do have two things I'm committed to that day . . ." Nina avoided looking at Daisy and told Janie she didn't see any reason why she shouldn't be able to finish in time to attend the dinner.

Janie clapped her hands. "Wonderful! Check your emails because I'm sending e-vites with all the information and directions—" A piano riff sounded from her pocket. She pulled out her cell phone, then excused herself with an, "I have to answer this one." The rhythm of her stiletto heels click-clacking on the wood floors accompanied her departure.

"Commitments? Since when did you have commitments?" Daisy could have replaced "commitments" with "children" and sounded no less surprised.

It was, after all, a word Nina had iced, figuratively speaking, along with others like *engagement, marriage, wedding gown,* and *honeymoon.* If only Nina could remember to forget some commitments in her life as much as she forgot to remember others, she wouldn't have to place her dreams in the freezer.

"I consider feeding Manny and wearing clean clothes important responsibilities. Especially since they both cost more than I ever anticipated." She had adopted her hybrid dog with the dachshund body and poodle hair from the local animal shelter almost a year ago. When she brought him home, she named him Manhattan and thought it clever and optimistic. Today, it just seemed ridiculous. The little runt developed severe food allergies and now required a special diet. She didn't expect him to be so high maintenance. Expectations did not seem to be working in her favor lately.

"If that works for you, then stay with it," said Daisy as she scooted her chair back to her desk. She closed her laptop, gathered her environmentally-safe assortment of bags, and wiggled her metro-nylon backpack out of the bottom drawer. "I have two more people to interview for the yoga feature, so I'll let you get back to that one-woman pity party I interrupted."

"Thanks." Nina clapped, Janie-like. "It saves me from sending an e-vite."

"You actually smiled. One small step—"

Nina grabbed a sheet of paper out of her printer and waved it in front of her. "I surrender. I surrender. No more words of wisdom."

Daisy laughed. "Okay, but the terms of surrender include walking to the stairs with me. You've been sitting so long I'm surprised you're not numb. But, the bonus is you'll make sure I actually leave. And leave you alone."

"That, my dear, is motivation enough," said Nina. She waited until the glass doors of the office shut behind them before she asked Daisy if she noted Brady's conspicuous absence from the Janie show.

"Probably not as much as you did." Daisy's eyes swept over Nina's face, and Nina knew desperation hovered there. "You need to let go of him in both places," Daisy said as she pressed her hand first to her forehead and then to her heart. "Remember, 'There's a season for everything.'"

Nina sighed. "Is that some mantra you chant?"

Daisy pushed open the door to the stairwell. "No, but that's not a bad idea." She paused, shifted her backpack, and said, "By the way, it's not new age-y talk. It's old age-y. Very old, as in Old Testament. King Solomon."

"So, you're telling me I'm in a very long line of people who know what it's like not to get what they want? I suppose that's some comfort," said Nina drily. Comfort and God hadn't been synonymous for her since before her brother was hospitalized. It wasn't so much that she gave up on God. She just chose not to give in to Him.

"The real comfort is, the line didn't end there," said Daisy. "See you tomorrow. Take care of yourself."

Nina watched Daisy and couldn't help but notice that, despite the baggage she carried, Daisy floated down the stairs as if she carried no weight at all.

2

Do you know the origin of the word *deadline*?"

"Hmm. Let me think. Does it have something to do with cutting off service to the cell phone of your friend who persists in calling you when she knows you're working?" Nina's eyes stayed focused on the screen while her fingers continued their waltz over the keys of her laptop. The few paragraphs she needed to finish the piece tapped their feet in the waiting room of her brain. If she didn't concentrate, they'd fly out the door and, from experience, she knew coercing them to return was almost impossible.

"You have me on speaker phone, don't you?" Aretha's accusation was as loud as it was unmistakable. "That's it. I'm buying you a Bluetooth device for those perky ears of yours."

Nina bit her bottom lip, typed in a few key words to pacify the paragraphs, and picked up her cell phone. "You're off now," she mashed the speaker button, then held the phone to her ear as she plowed through the contents of her purse hoping to excavate a buried Snickers bar. "And I have no idea where deadline originated, and I don't need to know at this moment because I'm less than an hour away from meeting mine." She pulled out an empty Twix wrapper, two smashed

15

cheese crackers, and an aging peppermint. Her stomach rumbled in disappointment. "What's up? And the microwave version." They'd been roommates a little over a year, and Nina learned Aretha couldn't tell someone the time without detailing where, when, and why she bought her watch.

"Well, if you'd bother to listen to your voicemails you'd know what's up. The fact that you're so cranky ought to remind you we're waiting for you at Carrabba's. It was your idea to eat Italian this month. Remember?"

Girls' Night Out. She forgot. Again. "It can't be seven o'clock already . . ." Had it been that long since Daisy left? She stood and looked around the room. With the exception of a few interns huddled around *Grey's Anatomy*, she was the lone staff writer left in the office.

Squinting to check the clock in the corner of her computer screen, she heard Aretha's voice, "No. It's almost thirty minutes later."

Nina figured by the time she finished checking and rechecking the article before sending it off to Elise, the girls would already be ordering or eating dessert. Doubtful they'd want to wait for her to catch up. Not that she could blame them. And if she wasn't already holding her breath to button her jeans, she'd go straight for the tiramisu and skip dinner altogether. With enough misery threaded into her voice to gather a bit of sympathy, Nina said, "I'm so sorry. I have to get this story in on time. Especially after today . . . but I'll tell you more about that later. Please ask the girls to forgive me for making them wait."

She truly meant the part about being sorry. In college, Nina chose not to rush for a sorority, mainly because she never received an invitation. It wasn't until she and Aretha became roommates that she began to let loose of the notion that all women her age were younger versions of her mother, eager to provide a list of her shortcomings in the name of helping her become the way God meant her to be. Nina felt comfortable with this group, and she didn't want to jeopardize that friendship by being the lone no-show every month.

"You're just lucky we all like you or else we'd have voted you off the dinner table by now," said Aretha. "I suppose you want an order to go."

Nina thought she felt her stomach applaud. "Yes, please. Pasta Weesie."

"You know you order that every time? I think you just like saying the name," she said and sounded less frustrated and more amused. "Let me hang up or else they'll start thinking I'm redecorating the kitchen or something."

Aretha, in her last semester of interior design school, had a "fabulous idea to make this room pop" almost everywhere they went. At the last dinner, the group threatened to blindfold her just to have a conversation not focused on window treatments or paint colors.

Knowing she'd be met by fettuccine Alfredo with shrimp motivated Nina to push herself through the article, assembling what remained like puzzle pieces, snapping them into place until the picture was complete. Not that profiling candidates for local county elections made for riveting writing. And that was exactly the problem. Nina hoped there was a story waiting for her to find it. A story that would prompt Elise to maybe send a two-line email. A story that would begin to pave her way to the Big Apple.

"Miss O'Malley?"

Startled, Nina's body hiccupped. She took a deep breath and recognized the lilac perfume Shannon, one of the interns, typically wore. Nina turned to face her. "Now that I know it's you, what scares me more is your using 'Miss.' It ages me five years."

"I'm sorry." A smile flickered across Shannon's face as she slid her pearl drop back and forth on her necklace chain. "We're all leaving. Do you want us, me, to wait for you?" The other interns, three young women who looked like they shopped in each other's closets, hovered a cubicle away.

Nina stretched back in her chair, mowed her fingers through her entirely-too-short hair, then stared at her monitor. "Not much more to go." She looked at Shannon and realized she didn't even know her last name. Or even what she did for the magazine. Have I been that cocooned in my own life? Earlier, Elise encouraged her to network. Nina realized at that moment she better begin in her own office. But clearly not now.

"So . . . um . . . does that mean it's okay for us to go?" Shannon asked as if she had dropped Nina off for her first day of kindergarten and needed the teacher's permission to leave.

Distracted by her own shortcomings, she'd created another by not answering Shannon's question. "Oh, of course, of course," she replied and sounded perkier than she meant to. "I shouldn't be long, and Nelson can walk me to my car."

"Well, I'll see you tomorrow," said Shannon, and she trailed after her friends as they headed out the door.

It didn't register until after Nina had clicked "send" that she forgot to thank Shannon for thinking about her. How inconsiderate.

Nina didn't know if she heard her mother's voice just then or her own.

Did her mother always have to be right?

Nina had asked herself that question, she supposed, since she could first express a coherent thought. The answer didn't change. Sometimes Sheila wasn't 100 percent right, but on some weird pie chart of probabilities, there would always be a slice for her mother. Little wonder her father spent so much time shrugging his shoulders and shuffling into his mancave when his wife's pronouncements fell like stinging rain.

In sixth grade, Nina became friends with Elizabeth Hamilton, and Sheila told her she should stay away from her because "that girl's nothing but trouble." With every trouble-free year that passed, Nina reminded her mother what she had said about her friend. Four years of trouble-free, until the tenth grade when Elizabeth had a "stomach virus" that eight months later was named Andy. And Sheila reminded her daughter what she had said about her friend.

During her junior year of high school, Nina started being invited to parties given by girls who wore shoes that cost more than all of her clothes. They didn't seem to mind picking her up in their sleek cars, the ones that didn't have names, just initials. They even let her wear their dresses to school dances where the beautiful girls met the handsome boys, and they moved inside their own force field that kept everyone else away. One day, on the way to the women's Bible study at church, her mother said, "Those girls are just buttering you up to use you. One day, they're going to drop you like a hot potato."

Nina laughed. "What could I possibly have that those girls would ever want? Is it too hard for you to believe popular kids could like me?"

Some days after school, Nina would be invited to one of their houses, the ones kept behind gates. They'd ask their maids to fix them something to eat, escape to the kids' den where they would listen to music, watch television, and complain about homework. They were so very impressed with Nina's ability to understand calculus, analyze poetry, and write essays. They asked for her help, flattered her. It felt good to be needed. She noticed, though, as weeks passed, that the more she did to help them, the less they did to help themselves. When Nina refused to write Courtney's research paper because she could barely complete her own, she faded from their sight a little bit every day. Until one day, she was completely invisible. And Sheila reminded her daughter of what she had said about her friends.

Her first relationship in college ended when, after almost a year of dating, Adam informed her he wasn't "ready to commit to anything more serious." Sheila said "he was up to no good." Three months later, he married her roommate.

Nina spent her life walking through the mine field of her mother's judgments, and no matter where she stepped, something was going to blow up. Tonight, forgetting to thank the intern? Not even a minor blast.

Nina shut down her laptop, slipped her feet back into her not-at-all sensible suede peep-toe shoes, and decided fettuccine and an upcoming story on the new ambulance service weren't compatible. All she needed for home was herself. She hoisted her purse onto her shoulder and headed for the door when she remembered she forgot to email Daisy about a possible interview with one of the preservationist candidates she profiled. Since she was only a few steps away from Daisy's desk, Nina pulled a blank sheet of paper out of the printer, jotted the information, and set it on her calendar pad next to a screaming yellow sticky note. Certainly, Daisy couldn't miss that. Neither could Nina because what Daisy had written on it shocked her: "Ask JB about the opening in NY."

3

As soon as she put her key into the lock, Nina heard Manny's canine symphony of yelps, barks, and squeals on the other side of the door. She scooped him up after she walked in because, if she didn't, he'd be doing figure eights around her legs until she did. "Okay, okay, little man, I'm happy to see you, too," she said as she petted Manny and calmed his enthusiastic, cold-nose nuzzling greeting.

Aretha stood at the kitchen sink filling a teakettle with water. She looked over her shoulder at Nina and smiled. "You know, I hope to find a husband who's as excited to see me come home as that dog is to see you."

Nina laughed and released the wiggling puppy who headed to his water bowl, his stubby legs causing him to toddle on the oak floors like a canine Charlie Chaplin. "I'd be willing to sacrifice some of the excitement if he didn't have doggy breath." She hung her purse on the hall tree and felt her body sigh in relief as if it had just been permitted to acknowledge it was tired. Nina pulled off her shoes and left them at the foot of the stairs before sitting on one of the kitchen barstools. "I'm so glad we ended up living here in the city; otherwise, I might have had to spend the night at the office."

"You're so welcome," Aretha told Nina and smiled, knowing they shared the memory of that decision. Nina, with the exception of college dorms, grew up in neighborhoods where the ranch style homes differed only by their brick color and front door placement. After college, she moved into an apartment complex that wasn't much different. Coming home at night required close attention to make certain the door you attempted to unlock was your own. But, it was close to her job then and, even after she was hired by *Trends*, she grew accustomed to the long drive.

Her choice of rentals was one of the few intersections of belief that Aretha and Brady, the then Brady, had. When he asked if she planned to move closer when the lease expired, Nina had shrugged and said, "I'm not sure. It's not that bad."

The two of them had driven to Baldwin Park to let Manny, just months old then, experience grass and sunshine and other wonders of nature he couldn't see from his kennel in Nina's kitchen. Brady had stopped the game of fetch he played with the puppy to look at Nina. "Don't you want more from life than, 'it's not bad'?" She sensed, by the way he averted his eyes so quickly, that he could see she'd never given it a thought.

Aretha had been dating Franklin, a friend of Brady's, when they met. The four of them would often meet for dinner or brunch on Sunday mornings. At first glance, the two women seemed the unlikeliest of friends. Nina was as fair as Aretha was dark, as tall as she was short. While Aretha kept her wits about her, Nina scattered hers everywhere. They became fast friends, the kind of comfortable that allowed them to be quiet or rowdy in one another's presence, and knowing which one the other most needed. Their relationships with the men in their lives ended, one sputtering to a close, the other screeched over the finish line. Instead of feeling abandoned, the two young women picked themselves up, dusted themselves off, and started all over again.

When they'd first committed to become roomies, Nina had thought she and Aretha should consider renting a garden home in one of the upstart suburban communities miles outside of Houston. Manny would have a yard, and they wouldn't have to worry about crime. Aretha countered that since Manny was smaller than a five-pound bag of sugar and would spend almost all of his time inside, a yard the size of a beach towel would be sufficient. "And you will have to deal with crime," she'd told Nina, "because if I have to drive back and forth to school and work fighting that traffic, I'll want to kill you myself. Plus, a woman with cornrows named Aretha has no business being anywhere but the city."

But now her cornrows were long, loose braids whose movements reflected an energized or subdued Aretha at any given time. She placed a bag of Earl Grey tea in one of the vintage cups from her collection, this one decorated with delicate violets and sprigs of greenery. "Guess my evening ritual will include nuking that dinner of yours," Aretha said and took a lemon for her tea and a to-go box out of the refrigerator.

Nina ran her bare feet along the bottom rung of the chair trying to restore her cramped toes to life. "I had one of those horrible, no good, terrible, awful days. I felt like Alexander in that children's book. And it started this morning." Elbows on the counter, cradling her face in her hands, Nina might have fallen asleep except for the lush smell of garlic and butter and rosemary escaping from the microwave. And Manny barking at his empty food bowl.

"Mister, I fed you earlier. Don't pretend you've been neglected just because your momma's home." Aretha always translated his barks, growls, whines, head tilts, and chirps into words, and he almost always ignored hers. He circled the bowl as if to reassure himself he'd not missed a nibble, eyed Aretha, then Nina, and settled himself in his dog bed. "He's pouting," Aretha concluded. "He'll get over it."

Knowing Aretha took this conversation seriously, Nina just nodded her head and tried not to smile. Especially since, after hearing Aretha's voice, Manny turned his head away from them and faced the wall.

She transferred Nina's dinner to a plate, "Take this, you can tell me your sad story while I do my homework." She nodded in the direction of the den where a mini-library spilled over the sofa cushions.

Nina sat in the worn leather chair next to the sofa. She draped a placemat across her lap and balanced her plate as she propped her feet on the glass-topped coffee table. Between bites, she narrated her dreadful day, ending with the cryptic note on Daisy's desk.

"Give her the benefit of the doubt. Maybe all those initials are wildly incidental," Aretha said in that voice she used when she complimented someone's rather ordinary-looking baby. She didn't sound convincing then either. Her legs tucked under as she sat on the sofa, Aretha had formed a moat of books and magazines around herself in search of historical photographs for her upcoming design assignment.

"You couldn't even make eye contact with me when you said that. If you don't believe it, why do you want me to?" Nina ate the shrimp she'd stabbed with her fork and waited for Aretha's response.

"Look at this stunning Louis XIV armoire," said Aretha, her brown eyes lit with a reverent awe as she held up a picture of a massive wardrobe with a star of Bethlehem carved on each door. "Sorry." She closed the magazine. "Got distracted." She rearranged an almost toppling stack of art books, unwound her legs and stretched them out on the ottoman. "I doubt if there's an inner office conspiracy at *Trends*. Just ask Daisy tomorrow."

Nina looked up from her pasta-twirling. "Sure. I'll ask her what the note on her desk, not mine, meant. She wouldn't at all think it might be an invasion of her privacy. And, anyway, she's not once expressed an interest in going to New York. Wouldn't she have said something when I told her months ago that I wanted that position? Do you think . . ." She stopped, her voice shifted into worrisome. "Do you think maybe she wanted to go? But not with me?"

"If you were any more neurotic, I would have to take you to work and pray someone would take pity on me and commit you. Those county mental health specialists don't fool around," said Aretha, her words edged with just enough seriousness to pinch Nina's ego. "Maybe it's time for you to reassess." She looked over Nina's shoulder. "And take Manny for a walk."

Nina looked down to see her dog, holding one end of his leash between his teeth, the rest of it snaked behind him.

"See, even he knows, sometimes you just have to be upfront about what you want," said Aretha.

4

Nina pulled away from the drive-through at Starbucks when her mother's phone number flashed on her navigation screen. Did Sheila O'Malley feel a shift in her frugal universe because her daughter just bought a latte for the price of a pound of coffee? Nina decided to stay on the feeder road and not attempt merging into the early morning Houston freeway. Verbally sparring with her mother while negotiating the traffic version of dodge ball—could it get any worse? *Probably not. Get the worst over with now, and the rest of the day will seem like the set of a Disney movie.* She had the cloud waiting for her to answer; the silver lining couldn't be far behind.

She took a deep breath, pressed the call button, and prepared herself for battle. "Good morning, Mother."

"Are you in your car?" It sounded like an accusation, not a question.

"I'm on my way to the office," said Nina and wished she could close her eyes during their conversation. For some reason, shutting out the world in the soft blackness inside herself made her feel less anxious during these painful volleys. "Is there something you need?" She used her best chirpy voice even after she pushed her brake hard to avoid smashing the car in front of her. Her purse toppled onto the floorboard and burped out its contents.

"Need? Do I need something? Why would I need something to call my daughter? I just wanted to remind you about Sunday dinner," she said. "That's all. You know how much it means to your father to have you there."

"So, what are you saying? That my being there isn't important to you? And how could I forget about a dinner you call every week to remind me about that's been a standing appointment so long my car would drive there without me?"

But, of course, Nina asked none of those questions. She simply said, "I'll be there."

Nina took the stairs instead of the elevator, a sort of aerobic decompression to move the tightness in her chest down her body and out through her feet, leaving the tension behind with each pounding step. *Why do I let her get under my skin like a splinter?*

She knew the reason. She'd known for decades. She was her parents' only child. Their only surviving child. When Nina was nine, her older brother Thomas came home after his second year at the University of Miami. At first, her parents told their friends Thomas wasn't sure he wanted to return, that he might want to attend college closer to home. Nina remembered running to hug her brother, excited about the possibility of his being close. But when the summer ended, he didn't enroll at a Texas university or any other one. Thomas started helping his friend Rick, a housepainter, which annoyed and disappointed their mother who accused him of wasting his intelligence, his potential to make something out of his life. He told her, "It's what I put in to life that matters. Every day I get to make something fresh and new. That is enough for me, for now."

That was the only part of their conversation Nina heard that day when she walked in to the kitchen after the yellow school bus lurched away from their street. Thomas looked tired, which, as she headed to her room as per her mother's orders, she understood on some level even then. The emotional tug-of-war with their mother required endurance training. Sheila continued to tug, but eventually Thomas let go of the rope. Nothing to fight for when there was no one to fight with.

Less than a year later, Sheila picked Nina up from school, an act in itself a signal that something was awry in the O'Malley home, to tell her that Thomas was gone. At first, Nina thought she meant he'd left the hospital where he'd been, but her mother told her that he wasn't coming home. Ever. After Thomas's funeral, her father retreated into his wordless shrugs, and her mother donned the armor of the self-righteous because, as she told anyone with an ear, "I told him that he wasn't meant to waste his potential that way."

Twenty years later, Nina still couldn't penetrate the shield of her mother's emotional defenses. And, like her brother, the pain of trying became much greater than the fear of not. But now she needed to sharpen her own sword, fight her own battles. And two of those battles sat in offices on the other side of the *Trends* door that she now opened.

She stepped into the lobby, and the aroma of hazelnut coffee greeted her before Michelle, the new receptionist, had a chance to. She started a month ago, replacing a twenty-something who wore clothes on the verge of vintage and kept an iPod bud in one ear and the receptionist's headset in the other. The day Elise overheard her tell a client to hold on, "my song's almost over," she fired her. Two days later she interviewed Michelle, who looked like she could have been

Elise's older sister though she was probably old enough to be Elise's mother. The perfect combination of maturity and chic. Michelle was on the phone, but she mouthed "hello" to Nina when she passed and pointed to a tray of scones and muffins on the hospitality table next to the coffee. Nina stopped to fix herself a cup of coffee and carried it and a cinnamon scone to her desk, whispering "Thanks," to Michelle on her way.

Nina hadn't yet decided how to approach Daisy about the cryptic note, so walking down the hall to the offices, she felt a pinprick of anxiety. *Ridiculous. Daisy is a friend, not your mother. She's not out to sabotage you. This could be your silver lining after the storm.* She took a breath and summoned a smile.

But Daisy wasn't sitting in her chair eating her predictable breakfast of yogurt, blueberries, and walnuts; in fact, the desk looked just as it did the night before when Nina left. After setting her coffee and scone down, Nina walked around the gray partitioned wall and asked Carole, in charge of ad sales, if she'd seen Daisy or heard if she was out on assignment somewhere. Neither Carole nor her sales reps knew anything. She was about to call Michelle, when her phone buzzed. It was Michelle telling her that Daisy had left a voicemail that she wouldn't be in the office for a few days. "She said she had unexpected family business to take care of, but she'd be back on Monday."

"Did she mention where she was going?" Not that her destination was any of Nina's business, but Daisy wasn't known for doing disappearing-from-the-office acts. Most of the time, convincing her to disappear from the office was the problem.

"Hmm. No. No, she didn't. But you have her cell number, right? Maybe you could call and find out, see if she needs us to do anything."

After Michelle hung up, Nina made it through half her scone and still the "family business" angle confused her. Daisy never mentioned her father in any of their conversations, and all she ever said about her mother was that they had made peace with each other. She knew she didn't have any siblings because they'd had the "only child" discussion soon after they met. And why didn't Daisy call her? They didn't spend too much time together outside of the magazine, but they did text and phone chat at least about office business. So, if Daisy wanted to contact her, she could. Nina checked for a text message, a voicemail. Nothing. She opened her laptop to check her email. Nothing from Daisy, but what she did see there could be a silver lining or another cloud in waiting.

Elise had sent her another email. "Please see me as soon as you arrive this morning."

5

Nina stared at the email from Elise, then started to roll her chair back to tell Daisy. Only there was no Daisy. No Daisy to demand that she not focus on her unmanicured hands, go-to faux-wrap dress and overdue highlights. No Daisy to reassure her that every communication from Elise was not an invitation to disaster.

She closed her email, checked her makeup using the mirror she kept in her top desk drawer, and wished praying did not seem like a foreign language. Too late to wish an Elise-summons didn't go directly to her inner child—the one biting her nails as she sat by the telephone and listened as it didn't ring.

The office stirred around her, awakened from its overnight sleep by phones that rang like alarms, doors that yawned open, and desks that claimed their owners. Still, she hadn't heard Janie's voice, so if she just pushed herself into action now, she wouldn't have to endure the knowing glances as the elevator doors closed.

Nina walked up and found Shannon, the intern from the night before, at the elevator. She held two venti-sized Starbucks' cups and wore a discombobulated expression. When she spotted Nina, she smiled as if she'd been rescued from a bad blind date.

"Are you going up, too?" Shannon rolled her eyes. "Well, that was a stupid question. Why else would you be standing at the elevator. Right?" She looked at the cups in her hands. "Guess I should've bought a caffeine jolt for myself. But I couldn't figure out how to juggle all that."

"Can I help you with one of those?" Nina stepped in the elevator first and pushed the button to keep the doors open.

"Thanks. But if you could just press seven for me, I can handle these."

"Is one of those a skinny soy chai tea latte no foam?"

"Actually, they both are," Shannon answered.

"So, you're on your way to Elise's office," said Nina, ashamedly relieved that at least she wasn't the person asked to make the coffee run before the visit.

"Right again." She held up one cup. "Elise." The she hoisted the other. "Whoever orders for Elise. How did you know?"

"She's the only thing the 7th floor and chai tea have in common," Nina said as the elevator doors opened. She nodded in Shannon's direction. "Go ahead. I'm getting off here, too." And she hoped not for the last time. "Wait. I can deliver those for you."

Shannon hesitated, and Nina imagined she weighed the awkwardness of being the coffee waitress against the possible payoff of being willing to serve. Not that she blamed her. "You know, maybe it's better for you to bring them. I should stop by the bathroom first."

"Oh, okay. Then I'll see you downstairs." Shannon headed to Elise's office, while Nina veered in the direction of the bathroom that she didn't really need, but spared the intern from having to make a decision.

"Shannon said you were on your way," said Tammie, Elise's assistant. "She's expecting you."

"Thanks," Nina said and smiled when she saw the Starbucks cup by Tammie's keyboard. She wondered what came first, the order or the boss?

Nina opened the door and heard Elise's voice as she entered, but she wasn't at her desk.

"Behind you," said Elise.

Nina looked back to her right and saw Elise standing over a table in a small room off her office. She'd never noticed it before, but then she had never been in Elise's office long enough to know where the doors led. Laid out on the long table were flat-plans of each page of the next issue.

"I could do this digitally, but there's something about being able to see it, large, this way that appeals to me so much more," said Elise, who continued to look at the pages in front of her. She was one of the few women Nina knew who could pull off a red pleated skirt and silk cream T-shirt without looking as if she was returning to high school. The gunmetal gray suede pumps probably helped. The metal toe seemed perfectly suited for Elise.

Nina didn't know if a response was expected, since Elise hadn't even made eye contact yet. She knew what Elise meant because sometimes, especially when she felt stuck, Nina outlined and wrote drafts of her stories on her yellow legal pads. Moving a pen across something tangible connected her to whatever she was working on at the time. But before she could move the words from her brain to her lips, Elise picked her coffee cup off the table, finally looked at Nina, and said, "Let's go to my desk."

"Sure," Nina replied. *Oh, brilliant, Nina. What a sharp response.* But whatever Elise's reason for this particular summons, Nina felt confident it wasn't another cloud. Elise seemed too relaxed. When it came to terminations or demotions, Elise was a guillotine. Fast, sharp, and irreversible.

She reached in her desk drawer and handed Nina an envelope. "Here are two tickets to the We Care benefit next Friday."

The swish of panic zipped through Nina's chest because her lack of an immediate response stood between them. Nina knew that Elise knew that she didn't know enough about the benefit to reply. She watched the realization move over her face as if a window blind had been lowered to block the light.

"The We Care benefit? The fund-raiser for The AIDS Memorial Quilt?" Elise filled the quiet with a question meant to shovel enough mud out of Nina's brain to unearth the answer.

The shovel hit paydirt. "The quilt in Washington, D.C., right?" Nina unwound her fingers from the chair arm. She'd been holding on like she was preparing for an airport landing.

"Yes, that one. Local support groups donate quilts for a silent auction as a fund-raiser. The money goes to support local projects and the NAMES Project Foundation that preserves and cares for The AIDS Memorial Quilt."

She took the envelope from Elise and wouldn't have been surprised if she snatched it right back. Now that she'd saved her head from being chopped off, Nina wondered why she was covering an event so meant for Daisy. Feature writing was definitely not her forte, and schmoozing with Houston's gilded made her uncomfortable. Daisy could handle being out of her element, especially if it involved such an important cause.

"I know you're working on the story about that local politician and questionable contracts, so you're going to have to add this one to your list. Janie will be in New York looking for an apartment. If Daisy's out longer than we or she expects, well, I don't want to take that chance." She took a sip of coffee, then looked at the cup as if someone had just handed her the wrong baby in delivery. "What is this?" Elise set the cup aside. "How difficult is it to order coffee?"

Nina assumed that was a rhetorical question, but rather than risk a conversation about Shannon being the orderer of the coffee, she asked about Daisy. "Michelle told me this morning that Daisy wouldn't be in for a while. Do you know how she's doing?" Nina tread cautiously, unsure how Elise would react to being asked information about another employee.

Elise stopped tapping her pen on her desk. "Daisy, from what I could tell by her message, is fine." She resumed the pen's previous beat, but Nina was grateful she drummed her desk pad this time. "She wasn't very forthcoming about her situation, so we'll just have to wait to see how it unfolds." Elise turned toward the Houston skyline where glass, brass and mirrored high-rises pierced the clouds. "If only we could figure out a way to grow roses at this height."

The sadness in Elise's voice surprised Nina. And the fact that she took time to muse about flowers when she seemed so like those buildings. Imposing, impressive, and impenetrable. She looked at Nina. "So, all the information is on the tickets. If you have no need for the extra ticket, I'm sure someone in the office would be happy to take it."

"No . . . no, I have someone in mind for the other ticket," she said. Aretha would love a free night out. "And thank you." She hoped she sounded genuine. Nina might be disgruntled, but she didn't want to be impolite. Seeing the worn heel on her shoe when she crossed her legs while she spoke reminded Nina she was not only going to be a stranger to covering benefits, her present wardrobe would surely mark her as a misfit. She returned both feet to the floor, hid her untidy cuticles in her lap, and exposed her fashion-sense handicap. "Is what I should wear on the ticket? Because if it's not, what do you suggest—"

"It's Black Tie Optional." She leaned in closer. Elise must have noticed her expression of confusion. "For you that means a cocktail dress or dressy separates. Some women wear long dresses, but they look like they were lost on the way to their high school prom."

Note to self: Ask Aretha if my one long dress can be shortened to cocktail length.

She stood and shuffled a stack of papers, "If you have any questions, let Tammie know."

"Yes, yes I will." Nina stood and felt the flap of her dress turn east instead of west. She smoothed it back into place. "Thank you, again. And I'm sorry that you won't be able to attend that night."

Elise looked up from her iPhone, and her eyebrows lifted as if Nina had just said something amusing. "Oh, Peyton and I will be there. But I certainly wouldn't attempt to cover the event."

6

You know, you're not the date of my dreams."

Hearing Nina's voice, Manny whined from inside his portable pet carrier. If Aretha had been along, she could have translated. But Nina was pretty sure he'd be complaining about not riding in one of those hot, new car seats where he could sit high and view the road.

"I can't wear a pet booster seat to a fancy party, so your ride will have to wait. Besides, spending my Saturday taking you to Dr. Alvarez isn't what I had in mind for an outing either." Nina looked in her rearview mirror as she spoke, though all she could see was a pair of wet brown eyes through the netting of his carrier.

No comment from Manny. The more Nina talked to him, the more she understood the conversations between him and Aretha. Manny made for the perfect chat mate when all she needed was to not feel crazy speaking out loud when she was alone or to be able to vent because she didn't want someone to solve her problems, just to listen to them. She wasn't so sure he was as thrilled with the arrangement, but the fact that he couldn't tell her whether he was or not made him such a great non-conversationalist.

She found a parking spot on the dog side of the veterinary clinic. When she first opened the clinic, Dr. Alvarez had one common waiting room. Some of the cats would practically leap on their owners' heads when the dogs howled and growled and barked. Over time, her dog and cat clients were becoming as antagonistic as their pets. So, for everyone's safety and sanity, each now had a separate entrance. The reception desk in the center of the clinic with a swinging door on each side provided, as Dr. Alvarez said in her newsletter, " . . . just enough space for the two and four-legged creatures to get along."

After checking in, she found a corner away from the sneezing Pomeranian and the Labrador Retriever that wanted to smell every inch of her body. Nina didn't mind the wait so much. The clinic smelled like lemon oil and appeared freshly scrubbed every time she came in. In fact, the one negative about it was that it made her feel guilty about the state of the dust bunnies at her own home.

A few pages into the latest issue of *People*, it was Manny's turn. Nina always smiled when the assistant called out, "Manny O'Malley." She wasn't sure Manny was impressed by his lyrical name.

After weighing Manny and showing them to the examination room, Wendy explained to Nina that they'd be seeing the relief veterinarian because Dr. Alvarez's husband surprised her with a weekend getaway for their anniversary. "The entire office helped him plan it. He's such a romantic." Wendy hugged Manny's file to her chest and looked off into some Maui sunset. "And it doesn't hurt that he looks like a younger version of George Clooney."

"I'd be happy with the present version. Does he have an older brother?" Nina attempted to pry Manny's paws from her shoulder. He'd draped himself across her chest like a sash, and his too-long toenails dug through her sweater and into her skin. "Preferably one who doesn't mind neurotic pets." Aretha might have added "women" to that question, so it was probably good she had a hair appointment and couldn't make it.

Wendy tapped her chin and narrowed her eyes as if the answer to Nina's question might materialize if she squinted hard enough. "You know. I'm not sure. I don't remember Dr. Alvarez—"

"I was kidding, really," Nina reassured her in case she left in search of the family tree.

"Oh, I figured you were," she said and laughed like someone who just realized they'd missed the joke. She slid Manny's folder on the examining room table. "Here, let me help you with him." She gently tugged Manny from Nina. He fought valiantly and, though he ultimately lost, he snagged Nina's sweater in four places and scratched her shoulder.

But Manny was not to be denied. He squirmed out of Wendy's arms, landed on the floor, and tried to make a run for it. He almost succeeded, except a man wearing a white lab coat happened by, crouched down, and nabbed him just as he reached the doorway. "Well, you must be terribly excited to see me." He picked up Manny who, in the arms of someone tall and broad-shouldered, looked small and somewhat fearful to be held at such a height.

"I'm so sorry, I was just trying to . . ." Wendy gestured toward Nina and Manny.

"I understand," he said and actually sounded as if he meant it. "What's . . ." he peered under Manny's belly, "his name?"

"Manny. And she was helping in the tug-of-war he was playing with me," Nina explained wanting to reassure both Wendy and Dr. Whomever of the knife-pleated khaki slacks and starched buttoned-down shirt that she wasn't upset, even with four sizable pulls in her almost new, almost cashmere sweater. Make that Aretha's sweater.

"I'm Dr. Hernandez, the relief veterinarian for Dr. Alvarez." He handed a dutifully ashamed Manny to the assistant and asked her to keep him company on the examination table. "What a relief, right?"

Nina suspected he used that line often, but she smiled anyway as if it was the most charming statement she'd heard all day. He seemed so familiar, but, after years of interviews and going through photos, everyone looked like someone she knew. Or everyone she knew looked like someone. "Nina O'Malley. Manny's mother. Of sorts."

Dr. Hernandez shook Nina's hand, but it was one of the most distracted handshakes she'd ever experienced. He might have been mentally reviewing his agenda for the day because he didn't so much look at her as he did past her, and he seemed to run out of energy. A strange slow-motion handshake. But it did have the advantage of giving her time to notice that even with a polite smile, a dimple appeared in his chin. And directly underneath it, as if drawn for emphasis, was the thin line of a scar.

"Nice to meet you," he said, but he spoke as if coming out of a brain fog.

He walked over to the table and started by checking Manny's teeth and gums. Nina hoped he wasn't going to suggest flossing because brushing his teeth required a Sumo-wrestler hold. Manny didn't mind the vaccine, but he resented his blood being drawn for the heartworm test. Nina knew this because he made the same low rumble in his throat when she'd take his squeeze toys away. Dr. Hernandez handed the blood sample to Wendy, who left the room to pass it off to someone else, Nina assumed, because she returned before Manny had finished having his temperature taken. Mortified by the indignity of the thermometer, Manny curled himself into a circle on the table. Nina scratched his head, but he didn't move. *Probably giving me the silent treatment*, Nina thought.

Dr. Hernandez checked Manny's throat, and Nina waited to see if he'd model the open-mouthed "Ah" when he used the tongue depressor. He didn't. "Dr. Alvarez noted he's allergic to beef, so he's on potato and duck food. How's that working out for him?"

"For him, great. For me, not so much at over a dollar a can," Nina said.

He asked Wendy if the clinic had samples of the food Manny ate while he appeared to be pummeling Manny's chest and stomach.

Nina cringed. She hadn't meant to sound as if she needed a subsidy. "Wendy, don't worry about samples. I'm not struggling. Really. It's fine. I've never owned a pet before, so I didn't even know dogs had food allergies."

"Wow. Your first pet," Wendy said, politely not saying the "at your age" that was clear in her tone. "Were your parents allergic to them?"

No, they were allergic to emotional attachments. Nina shrugged. "I doubt it. My brother always wanted a Yellow Lab. He probably would've been a great vet."

"Really? So what does he do instead?" Wendy held Manny still while Dr. Hernandez poked and prodded.

Nina hated this moment because she knew her words would smack people on the blindsides of their hearts.

"Um, nothing. He died ten years ago." As she anticipated, Wendy and Dr. Hernandez exchanged those glances of shared awkwardness. She expected, when he started to speak to her that it would be the standard apology. She'd learned it helped to ease their discomfort if she preempted. So, she said, "It's okay. You didn't know. I understand."

He looked confused, not appeased. "Wait. I thought I had seen you before or at least met you someplace, but I couldn't get the memory to connect. You're Thomas's sister?"

Nina flinched. She hadn't been called Thomas's sister in over ten years. In fact, she barely knew or remembered any of his friends. "Yes. How did you know?"

"He worked with a friend of my father's who owned a construction company, Rick Higgins. I didn't know him, really, just knew he painted for Rick because they did some work around our house and the medical office." Dr. Hernandez sat on the stool near the counter, scribbled in Manny's chart, then looked at Nina as if she'd just walked in to the room. "And, I guess you don't remember me from high school, though, until now I didn't totally remember you either."

"I'm going to check the inventory for those samples now," Wendy said and darted out the door.

High school? The worst four years of her teens? Nina pushed up the sleeves of her sweater and wished paper fans were still popular. But she'd have to swallow it to cool off the flush she felt radiating from her self-consciousness. All she wanted was a simple trip to the veterinarian for Manny's check-up, not a family reunion or any reunion, especially high school. She rifled through her high school yearbook in her brain, but she didn't remember graduating with anyone with his last name. "No, I'm sorry. The best part of high school was graduating."

He closed the manila file, slipped his pen in his top pocket, and rubbed the top of Manny's head. "I was three years ahead of you. That day in the cafeteria near where my friends and I sat, we weren't very nice—"

The memory exploded, sending images showering through her brain like shrapnel. "You're right. You weren't." She forgot her lunch at home, so she ate in the cafeteria that day. She hated eating there because where you sat defined your social status, and she had nowhere to go but the corner of the room. Which meant passing everyone she was invisible to. She had walked fast, so fast that she didn't see whatever was on the floor until she was on the floor with it. She had managed not to fall flat on her back, but the red divided tray dumped its entire contents into her lap. From the waist down, her jeans were splatter painted with mashed potatoes, gravy, meatloaf, and a smattering of corn. And she had just provided front row entertainment for the basketball team table.

And Greg Hernandez was their center.

7

As most significant events in Greg Hernandez's life, this too began with a phone call. This one from his sister. And, like most phone calls from his bossy older sister, this one began with her attempting to make up his mind for him.

"You need to move to Houston."

"Why? We're fine where we are. Plus, I don't have a job in Houston. I'm too young to retire and too old to live with my sister." While he talked, Greg finished loading the dishwasher, turned off the kitchen light, and stretched out on the sofa.

"You're incredibly stubborn. You must have inherited that from your father's family," Elise said.

Technically, Elise was his half-sister. She was not yet five when her father died in an oil rig accident and almost eight when her mother Beth married Greg's father, a pediatrician. Elise's pediatrician. Between the settlement from the oil company and Sidney Hernandez's income, they lived more than comfortably. Elise lived on the side of "more than," while Greg stayed content in comfortable. When their parents died on American Airlines Flight 11, the plane flown into the North Tower of the World Trade Center, Elise and Greg were forever changed. They came to realize that without one another and without the promises of a loving God, they might not have survived the tragedy themselves.

"No, I'm thinking it's a maternal trait." The sofa cushion seemed lumpier than usual. Greg reached underneath and rescued two cloth dolls, one of which was in dire need of clothes. "Look, you find me a job, and I'll start packing."

"Game on," she said.

He should have known better than to challenge Elise. A slow economy and his resistance weren't going to intimidate a woman who built a magazine from the ground up. He turned the volume back up on the television and, before he fell asleep, made a mental note to start looking for boxes.

———

"I'm not sure I can leave this house," Greg said, his voice heavy as he stood in his bare family room. The only evidence of a life there was the indentations in the carpet from the legs of their couch and tables.

Amelia, his next-door neighbor, held his daughter's hand and reached up with her other arm to hug him. She had been a mother to him and a grandmother to Jazarah, especially this last year. "I know, sweetie. But your memories go with you. And think how much love resonates in those walls that will bless whoever lives there."

Six years of love seeped through the pores of these walls. The arguments, he hoped, fell through the cracks of the concrete floors. Last night he walked through every room before going next-door to spend the night at Dale and Amelia's house. Lily, taking a cake out of the oven, her freckled face dewy and smiling. Lily, walking through the back door after weeding the garden, grass and dirt still visible on her bare knees. Lily, painting the nursery, her denim overalls and hair sprinkled with every color she rolled on the wall. Lily, on nights he'd work late, waiting for him, turning back the covers on his side of the bed and inviting him in with, "I missed you."

Sometimes her scent would catch him by surprise, and he would turn to look for her, his heart racing at the thought of her softness in his arms. Nights that Jazarah awoke, her screams throbbing in his chest, he rocked and cried silent tears with her. Lily was never coming home.

The next morning, Greg buckled his daughter in her car seat, hugged Amelia and Dale one more time, and looked out his rearview mirror until their waves and his home became specks and disappeared. He stopped only once on the way out of New Orleans. When he did, he unbuckled Jazarah and handed her the bundle of lilies he'd cut from their garden. "Let's go talk to Mommy," he said and took his daughter's hand.

Together they walked into Lakelawn Cemetery.

⸻

In the six months he'd been back in Houston, Greg had more requests for relief work than there were hours in the day to fill. At first, adjusting to different veterinary practices was challenging, but as his reputation grew, the doctors who hired him knew exactly what kind of service he could provide. He had the freedom to set his own schedule, be selective about the jobs he chose, and get a feel for where he might want to settle in at a practice one day.

Today he was headed to Tessa Alvarez's clinic early, since it was his first time to work there. Houston traffic, he learned, had a life all its own, and until he could take its pulse, he didn't want to risk being late.

Greg pulled into the parking lot with more than thirty minutes to spare, but since her clinic was at the front of a new residential community, he'd have time to check out the neighborhood.

He grabbed his briefcase, locked the car door, and walked around the outside of the clinic. The white-planked building with its dark green shutters and its wide wraparound porches reminded him of an Acadian home. Even the landscaping avoided the appearance of a commercial building, with curved walkways and bench areas. If the exterior of the practice was this meticulously groomed, then Greg felt sure the interior would be as well. Always reassuring because he'd worked in practices that truly had gone to the dogs.

He'd just taken a few steps when he heard the xylophone ring tone on his cell phone, which meant Paloma, the nanny was calling. Elise hired her to start the day Greg and Jazarah arrived in Houston. "She needs to be a part of your daughter's life here from the beginning. Otherwise, that's one more adjustment Jazarah needs to make." She was right. Having Paloma's help with all the logistics of moving made the transition so much smoother. Greg did tell Elise that she had to find a two-unit condo because he didn't want Paloma living in the same house, setting up an awkward and potentially problematic arrangement.

It took a great effort to not stop breathing when Greg saw her number on his cell phone. He was so afraid that she would be calling with terrible news. It was never that. This morning she called to ask if she and Jazarah could go to the zoo and the Children's Museum. "On one condition. You have to take pictures," he answered, knowing Paloma already made every event a photo op.

"She asks if she can talk to you."

"Sure. Put the princess on," he said and smiled picturing his daughter's little apple-round face, her corkscrew curls dancing when she nodded, and her bright eyes that seemed to hold their own laughter. Lily had insisted they keep her Ethiopian name, which meant "beloved princess" because, she'd said, "Isn't that what she is to us already?" How could Greg argue with that?

"Da-de? I going to the zoo," she said, her voice rising and falling with each syllable. "See what I wear?"

They'd have to start making face-to-face calls because she thought holding the phone in front of her outfit would be enough for him to see it. At first, he'd tried explaining to her that he couldn't, but it only served to frustrate her. Incredibly, she did what most adults would do in the same situation. She repeated, "See!" louder and louder, until he would finally tell her she looked adorable.

"You are beautiful," he told her, and he didn't need to see her to know it was true.

"Tank you. Talk to P now. Bye!"

Greg heard Jazarah giggling as she handed the phone off to Paloma.

"Do you want I should feed J her supper?"

His daughter and her nanny were on a first initial basis since they met. He expected his name might change to D at any time. "Yes, go ahead and do that since the clinic doesn't close until six. I'll call as soon as I'm on my way in case I don't make it home before her bedtime."

"You have a good day. We will see you later."

After every conversation with Paloma, Greg uttered a silent prayer of thanks for this young woman being in his daughter's life. Over the past year, his prayers were not always of gratitude. Actually, some of his conversations with God were rants of anger and despair and pain. He learned, though, that he could find comfort in the arms of a God who knew grief. He didn't subscribe to the theory that God took Lily away from them. A drunk driver, with two previous arrests, took Lily on her way home from shopping for Jazarah's birthday party. God was giving her back to him, in memories, and his daughter, and the promise that he would see her again.

—◦◦◦—

Manny, now on his leash, high-stepped out of the examination room with Nina following close behind. Neither one of them looked back. He wouldn't have either in her shoes.

Thomas O'Malley's sister. What a random collision in the universe of coincidence. Especially since she was the first person he'd seen from his high school since returning to Houston, and she was the last person he would have paid attention to when they were students. He had been a different Greg Hernandez then. Privileged and popular. He and his friends thought they ruled the school. They barely noticed girls like Nina. Girls who paid attention to the teacher and not them during class. Girls who did their homework and passed tests because they weren't partying all weekend. Greg and his friends pitied their sad lives.

Nina had looked familiar in that way that a stranger appears, but your brain can't access the file of recognition. Sometimes, days later the connection happens, sometimes, not at all. Had Nina not mentioned her brother's name, Greg was certain the connection would have short-circuited before ever leading to her. He'd seen her only a few times in the hall before that day she landed on the floor and became a human food tray. Had there been a class superlative for Most Ordinary, Nina would have won. Her hair must have been long because she wore it pulled back from her round, clean-scrubbed face. She wore jeans and sweats, shirts that might have even been Thomas's. Instead of disguising her figure, the baggy clothes just magnified it.

One of his friends remarked that she might not have fallen if she hadn't been waddling so fast. That day and for days after, he and his friends would quack when they passed her in the hall. Greg knew her brother had died. He knew her family lived more than modestly. But why would he have told his friends that? They'd think he was soft. His friend Lance said she must really be a duck because all their torments seemed to roll right off her back. They grew bored and moved on.

Now, all these years later, Nina was no longer a lump of coal in a room full of diamonds. She had become a gem herself.

But Greg also knew that transformation happens only one way.

Under extreme pressure.

8

Shouldn't Mr. Manny be the one barking and growling coming back from the veterinarian? Sounds like you should've had a shot yourself. Distemper, maybe?" When Manny spotted Aretha, blockaded on the sofa again, he dashed across the room and tried to jump through the wall of magazines. "Of course you're glad to see me. What happened to Miss Grumpy, huh?" She set one of the stacks on the floor, so Manny would have just enough space to land on her lap.

"I won't even mention the traffic," said Nina as she set the case of special diet dog food on the counter. She dropped her purse on the floor, opened the refrigerator and slid food around looking for a bottle of water. "Do we have any—"

"In the door. Always in the door," Aretha said. "So, what happened? You look like you tangled with somebody."

Nina found two aspirins at the bottom of her purse and washed them down. "And how's that?" She moved to the bookshelf and poured some of her water in the exhausted-looking ivy plant.

"I won't even mention the aspirins," Aretha noted in an almost-perfect mimic of Nina. She nudged Manny off her lap and settled him next to her. He thanked her with a hand lick.

"You know I hate when you do that," she said and wiped the back of her hand on her jeans. "Back to you." She pointed at Nina. "I know by now when you're in a snit. Your whole face is wound tighter than Lady GaGa's clothes, your eyebrows bear down on your eyes, and your mouth does this funny fish thing." She demonstrated a pucker that made her look like a wild-haired guppy.

For a moment, Nina attempted to maintain her indignant demeanor. But the expression on Aretha's face broke her resolve, and she laughed so loudly that Manny barked at her. "If only I'd taken a picture of that, I'd have leverage for life," Nina said. "But, thanks, I needed to laugh." She cut the plastic wrap off the dog food and as she put the cans away, started telling Aretha the story of meeting Greg Hernandez, omitting what most infuriated her: the fact that the lanky high school teenager with the toothpaste-commercial smile had grown into an even more attractive version of himself.

"What a fool . . . how can someone so mean be taking care of . . . what is the matter with him?" A flustered Aretha was an incoherent Aretha. Nina learned to fill-in-the-blanks as she spoke.

"Good questions. I didn't know him in high school. I just knew of him. I mean everyone did. Everyone knows the kids with money, and everyone wants to go after the ones who are eye-candy. He was both, and he played sports. A triple play or threat depending." Nina moved to the chair in the den. "Next to losing Thomas, that day in high school was one of the worst days of my life. I wished I could have stayed on that cafeteria floor until the bell ended lunch and everyone left for class." Her mind rewound to that teenaged Nina, moving in slow motion as she stood, scraps of food clinging to her jeans. She'd bent down to pick up the tray, and her glasses slid off her face into the mess on the floor in front of her. "Getting out of there was like trying to get out of a net. The more I struggled, the deeper I sank."

"Didn't anyone try to help you?"

Aretha's outrage only magnified for Nina now how pathetic a figure she must have been then.

"No. Well, I don't know for sure because I didn't turn around. I walked straight out through the delivery entrance."

"I bet your mother wanted to beat every one of them," said Aretha.

"I'm not sure. I never told her what really happened." Nina slipped her feet back into her ballet flats. "You're the first person I've ever shared this story with."

"You could come with me. Manny would be fine in his crate for a few hours." Nina looked down at her dog, and she didn't like what she thought she heard. "Like you know the difference between Sunday and Monday," she said to him.

He pranced off and jumped on the chair opposite where Aretha sat, using a pillow as a laptop desk, her legs crossed underneath. "I have to finish this paper, plus I have that meeting tonight."

Nina tied her neck scarf. "Meeting? On Sunday?" She looked in the mirror, muttered, and re-tied it.

"I told you about it, but you don't listen to anything that involves the word 'church.' Our women's group is deciding on our community outreach. We're just yakking over dinner." She winked at Manny, then said to Nina, "You could come with me."

"Not any more likely than you doing the same." She loosened the scarf. "Do I look like I'm wearing a neck brace? Tell me now because if you don't, she will."

"I like it. It softens you."

"So, are you saying my face looks hard?" Nina looked in the hall tree mirror, turning her head side-to-side. "Is my eyeliner too severe?"

"Sister, you are exhausting. That's not what I'm sayin' and you need to get over yourself. Just because you've revved up your career engine doesn't mean you start rolling over your friends."

"Sorry. Sorry. I have Sunday-dinner anxiety."

Aretha eyed Manny as she opened her laptop. "Well, now that's your own fault for saying 'yes' when you mean 'no.'"

———

To avoid thinking about the torture that awaited her, Nina shut off her usual driving music and started planning the stories that would land her in New York. The one she was putting together now had potential. If a local county official was sabotaging how contracts were being awarded, that had legs. And, with some digging, maybe even arms. When it came to graft in government, she had to follow the roots and figure out who was on the other end. And if the ambulance service contract truly did turn out to be a political favor, that meant the mayor was willing to risk the lives of everyone in the county to stay in the good old boy network.

She'd have to be careful with documenting, verifying sources, and corroborating evidence. If the hard-hitting story came back and hit the magazine hard because of sloppy work, Elise would not be happy, and Nina could stop worrying about New York because her career would be in the dumpster. *No kids, no husband, not even a hint of one. Now's the time to make the push.*

Still no word from Daisy, which continued to concern her. That and knowing if she didn't return, Nina would be stuck going to that benefit. She had Daisy's number. It's not like she couldn't call her. But if she wasn't contacting Nina because that "it" was serious, then Daisy didn't need to be fielding calls either.

Nina exited the freeway that led to her parents' neighborhood. At least they moved to a town outside of Houston that didn't have a weapons buy-back program every other month like where they used to live. They bought a garden home, about which her mother complained to the point of calling the real estate company and threatening to sue for false advertising. "Six bushes and a tree aren't a garden. I have a throw rug bigger than the back yard," and on and on and on. When the real estate agent offered to send over boxes, movers, a for sale sign, and promised they could have them out in under twenty-four hours, she stopped the phone calls. After that, she blamed her husband and her daughter for moving her someplace she couldn't plant a decent-sized shrub.

By the time she parked in the driveway, there were enough knots in her stomach for a hammock, which, clearly, would not fit in the backyard. As always, she rang the doorbell. It sounded more like a cattle prodder on steroids. Nina fiddled with her scarf, dusted off the threat of something she might not have seen on the front of her emerald green silk dress, and checked the toes of her platform shoes for scuffs. She swiped her front teeth with her finger in case of lipstick bleed and hoped she'd brushed her teeth without leaving anything behind.

She heard her mother's, "I'll get it," as if battling her father to open the door was ever an issue. Sheila O'Malley peered out like she might be expecting a deep cover agent for an exchange.

"Oh, it's you. Well, come on in. But you're early. Dinner isn't ready yet. Just make yourself at home."

Right. It's what she'd been trying to do her entire life.

9

Nina wondered if all grown children, when they looked at their parents through adult eyes, tried to find what first attracted them to one another. She'd seen all the old photos paraded around the house that captured smiles meant for the camera. But it was what happened before and after the picture that intrigued Nina. If she could travel back in time to show the young Patrick O'Malley, the one with the dimples and broad smile, whose eyes signaled mischief and zest, a photo of what he would become in forty years, might something in his life have changed? Maybe so much so that the Patrick O'Malley, who now waved his remote like a king's scepter from the throne of his recliner, the one whose downturned eyes matched his downturned mouth, whose hair was gray and disheveled, might have been someone else? Or perhaps Nina might not have been at all?

"When did you get here?" He made motions as if he was going to disengage himself from the comfort of his chair.

Oh, almost thirty years ago. "Don't get up," she said and walked over to kiss him on his forehead. He smelled just like the closed-up insides of an unhappy house. "How are you?"

"Good. Good." He spoke to the cast of *Gilligan's Island* on the television screen. "You?"

Awful. My career is off-the-tracks, my social life consists of taking my dog to the veterinarian, only to meet the one jerk I've tried to forget for the past ten years. "I'm great. Everything's great."

"Glad to hear that, honey." His eyes flickered in her direction for a moment. "Your mom need some help in the kitchen?"

Sheila didn't need help in the kitchen, the house, the country, the universe. Had he forgotten Nina trailing behind him during those years when he spent more time vertical? She'd hand him tools when he fixed the leaky something or other under the car, tape when he bundled the outside pipes against the cold. He didn't need help either, but he at least let her think he did. And Nina loved him for that.

"Doubt it, but I'll check." She wasn't sure he knew she left.

Nina walked through the hall to the kitchen where she would be of no help whatsoever. For someone whose idea of an emotional moment was sneezing, Sheila created lovely meals. Given the choice, Nina would have preferred peanut butter and jelly sandwiches if that meant her mother could invest more time in her.

Sheila hated hovering, so Nina leaned against the doorway between the kitchen and the dining room. Aretha would be in designer heaven if given the chance to makeover the industrial look of the kitchen with its stainless steel appliances, gray tiled floors, and white cabinets. But her mother puttering around a French country kitchen wearing a cornflower blue apron edged in lace was as likely as Madonna showing up an award ceremony wearing a cotton housedress and slippers. "Smells great in here. Anything I can do?"

Her mother sprinkled sliced almonds on top of a salad. "No. Not now. Everything's almost finished." She sighed. "I've been in here all morning making lasagna while your dad's been in there," she nodded her head toward the den, "wearing out the batteries in the remote."

"I would have been glad to be here sooner to help you," Nina said and hated that she felt like a child uninvited to a party.

"All you had to do was offer." Sheila lifted that one eyebrow that signaled "so there," as she added olive oil and vinegar to the salad.

Nina shoved her indignation away before it jumped right out of her mouth and splat itself on her mother's forehead. Instead, it coursed through her body and, if someone had struck a match, Nina would have exploded on the spot.

     ❦

After Thomas died, the fourth chair at the dining table screamed his absence. It screamed so loudly that for months and months and months, Nina and her parents took refuge in the den where they balanced their plates on television tables and finished their meals in communal silence. Nina looked across the table now at Thomas's empty chair and between the clicks of forks against the thick white plates, wondered what he would have been like at almost forty. Would they have expanded their table for Thomas, his wife, their children? She almost hoped he couldn't see them all now. See how they all went on living, but died inside.

"So, how's that writing job of yours?"

Even with one eye on the television, at least her father pretended an interest in her career. However, when her mother figured out that her daughter wasn't going to be Houston's version of *Entertainment Tonight*, Sheila thought Nina had just

wasted her college education. After Janie's promotion, it frightened Nina that, once again, her mother might be right.

Nina started to explain the story about the mayor and his
cronies when her mother interrupted to ask if she had a life
outside of that job.

"Yes, of course." She didn't add that it mostly centered
around Manny. "In fact, Elise, my editor gave me tickets to the
We Care benefit. The one that's held at the St. Regis Hotel."

"That fancy one the Houston society people go to? Isn't it an
AIDS thing? And who are you going with?"

Her mother hadn't asked her that many questions in the
past four dinners they shared. "Since the tickets cost $400
each, I imagine it's going to be an upscale crowd. As for the
'AIDS thing,' the money raised at the benefit goes to local hos-
pices. There's also a silent auction of quilts made by different
support groups in Houston. I read online there's going to be a
display of a section of The AIDS Memorial Quilt."

"Seems like if everyone's paying that much money to attend,
you'd be able to see the whole quilt," her father observed and
served himself another slab of lasagna.

"Well, I've done some research. The quilt is not very portable anymore. It weighs fifty-four tons. The article said if you
spend just a minute on one panel, it would take over thirty-
three days to see the entire thing. I don't think anyone can stay
that long," said Nina.

Neither of her parents laughed. Her mother's lips twisted
to the side, which Nina learned in her teens was a prelude to
a lecture on being sassy. Her father's head bobbed and a thin
thread of cheese hung from his lips. He looked like an aging
redfish that had just swallowed a hook. *And just think, Thomas,
you missed all this.*

Sheila handed her husband a napkin. "You need to
take care of that," she said and pointed to her chin to

demonstrate. She looked at Nina. "What are you going to do with that extra ticket? Have someone in mind? Because if you don't, Lola across the street told me she has a son who isn't married yet. He owns three fast food restaurants, and he makes a good income." She stretched the word "good" to two syllables.

"Then why is he still single?" Lola must be the new neighbor her mother mentioned last month. The one whose furniture didn't arrive via a moving van, but through a convoy of local furniture store delivery trucks.

Her mother patted her mouth with her napkin as if her lips would shatter if she pressed them too hard, cleared her throat, and smiled too deliberately for Nina's comfort. "Well, funny you should ask that because Lola asked the same about you."

Not staying for the key lime pie her mother had made shaved about thirty minutes off Nina's torture time. She rarely ate dessert there anyway because it was usually something she didn't like. Since her mother's eyes seemed to focus on Nina's hips each time she offered her something sweet, she guessed her refusing it was her mother's plan all along. Either that or her mother purposely provided her an easy escape.

The sound of Nina's key in the deadbolt flipped an internal barking switch in Manny that didn't shut off until he spotted her walking through the door.

"I need to remind your human grandmother there's at least one man in my life who can't contain his excitement when I walk through the door." Manny's tail wagged like a windshield wiper as he wiggled out of his crate and into Nina's arms. "Though you really do need to chew a few breath mints before you tell me hello."

Manny trotted up the stairs after Nina. He gnawed on a rawhide bone he found under her bed, while she changed into her sweats. She rifled through her closet hoping to find something she already knew wouldn't be there: a dress to wear to the benefit. Nothing even close to benefit-worthy. That dress she hoped Aretha could modify would set off the fashion police alarm.

"Aretha doesn't know it yet, but there's a shopping trip in her future," Nina told Manny as she grabbed her laptop from her dresser. He paid no attention to her until she mentioned going downstairs for food. He pushed the bone under her bed and led the way to the kitchen.

After Manny had been fed, watered, and escorted outside for his nightly routine of fertilizing the flower bed, Nina settled in her chair to read the online news and compose questions for the council member she'd soon be interviewing. She opened her email to find a message from Daisy.

"Just wanted you to know I'm fine, and I should be back in time for Janie's party. Not much to talk about right now. I'll call you. Hugs, D."

That was all the online news Nina could handle for the night.

10

The day after Greg's unexpected reunion with Nina O'Malley, he left Dr. Alvarez's clinic and drove straight to the support group meeting he first attended four months ago. Elise, of course, found Threads of Hope even before he moved back to Houston. What she neglected to tell him was not only was this HIV/AIDS support group primarily women, they spent almost every meeting sewing quilt panels. The group, of course, knew everything about him, including the little known fact that he dabbled in photography, pencil sketches, and watercolors. All talents the group welcomed with enthusiasm, especially as they prepared their quilts for the We Care benefit.

He told his sister later that he might not have ever returned to the group had a little girl named Tabitha and The AIDS Memorial Quilt not led him and Lily to their daughter.

"Well, that worked out nicely then, didn't it?" Elise purred, and Greg saw the look of triumph blaze in her eyes.

Tonight, thinking of that exchange between himself and his sister, Greg smiled at her ability to transform what some might see as manipulative into something serendipitous. Lily would have been delighted by the group considering her gratitude to the NAMES Project Foundation for all it did to preserve and care for the quilt that they'd viewed in Syracuse, New York.

Originally, Greg hadn't planned for his wife to join him at the Syracuse veterinary conference. But when she had her third miscarriage weeks before, Greg insisted she go with him. The second day there, Lily sent him a text asking him to meet her after his sessions at the Oncenter Convention Center. He found her sitting on a bench when he arrived, writing in the small leather-bound journal she carried in her purse. Though she smiled when she spotted him and her eyes were dry, he knew she'd been crying because of the faint, uneven black smudges under her lower lashes.

"I want to show you something," was all she'd said when she'd reached for his hand and led him into the center where huge quilts rained from the ceiling. Lily could barely thread a needle, so he couldn't understand what might have attracted her to a quilters' convention display. Reading the question his face asked, Lily explained the quilts were all panels from the larger AIDS Memorial quilt, on display there because the first day in December was World AIDS Day.

Without offering any more in the way of explanation, she said, "Come see this," and brought him through the exhibit to a quilt on the far right end. She pointed to a cotton-candy pink panel, edged in white lace and seeded all over with beads that looked like pearls. A buttercup yellow crocheted bonnet, a smocked dress that looked as if it had been dipped in the sky the blue was so delicate, a silver teething ring that bore the tiniest of indentations, and a lace bib that barely showed signs of use were all attached to the panel. In the center of the quilt, the name Tabitha was embroidered in white thread. Underneath, in the same embroidered script, was "Age: 5 months when she went to the Lord in peace."

Continuing to stare at the panel, she said, "Do you know that about one thousand babies are born with HIV every day?"

"No. I didn't know that," he responded, sure that until today, Lily probably didn't know that either. Greg looked down at his wife and wondered if this experience was healthy for a woman mourning another failed pregnancy.

She turned to him. "And half of them will die before their second birthday without treatment."

"That's a staggering number," he said. Instead of unsure, Greg now felt uneasy. Lily's plane was coming in for a landing, but he still couldn't locate the runway. When she informed him that 90 percent of the world's HIV infected children live in Africa, Greg knew the wheels had hit the ground. A year later, Greg and Lily traveled over eight thousand miles, and this time when the plane landed, they were the parents of a solemn-eyed baby girl.

Later, Lily would tell anyone with ears that losing three babies due to miscarriages brought them to another one. She never doubted that God meant for them to be Jazarah's parents. And Greg never doubted Lily's absolute conviction. He already felt blessed to be loved by Lily. Knowing their little daughter would be loved so fiercely and generously, how could he say anything but yes?

Tonight, that little girl was tucked into bed under her princess blanket, her head on her princess pillowcase, and slept unaware that 99 percent of the HIV in her body was undetectable. And while she slept, Greg and the rest of the support group he'd be meeting at the Fellowship Hall planned to put the finishing touches on the two quilts they would be donating for auction at the benefit.

Nina showed Aretha the email from Daisy. "What do you think this means?" In the time she waited for her roommate to return, Nina exhausted every possibility she could think of.

"You really want to know?" Aretha sipped her tea, set her cup down, and eyed Nina. "It means she's fine, you're not, and when she's ready to tell you something, she will. Oh, and she'll be back for Janie's party."

"Wow. What did you eat for dinner? Nails?" Nina closed her laptop.

"You asked me. So don't start playing your mother by asking me questions that you already have the answer to."

"That was harsh, too. What's going on?" Nina regretted ever beginning the conversation.

Aretha tossed the rubber ball that Manny just nosed in her direction. "I'm telling you this because I care about you—"

"Stop right there. It's late, and I'd rather you just get to the point instead of dancing all around whatever it is you want me to hear."

"Then, here it is, girlie. Ever since Brady stopped calling and Janie announced her promotion, you've dragged your face around here. Then, when Daisy didn't show up for work, your first thought wasn't about her well-being. You dove into the conspiracy theory and barely came up for air. Now, you're determined to break the political story of the year to get Elise's attention." Aretha added more hot water to her tea. "I guess if you believed that God had another plan for you, you might not be so bitter."

Nina snickered. "God has another plan for me? Why? Did He finally figure out this one wasn't working? Let's see, my only brother died, I spent all of high school trying to make my lumpy self invisible, the only relationship my mother and I share is our mutual disappointment in me, and my father is buried so deep inside that shell of himself I don't know if there's a shovel long enough to reach him." Manny jumped on the chair and draped himself across her lap. "So, are you telling me God's not in favor of my wanting to make a career move?"

"I don't pretend to know what God knows. What I do know is that you see New York as some geographical cure for your life. Maybe God's giving you what you need right here, but you just can't see it."

"Enlighten me," said Nina, exasperation evident in her voice.

"Elise could have given those benefit tickets to someone else in the office. Really, how difficult is it to cover an "ooh-la-la" event with all the beautiful people? Someone could probably look up the one last year, change a few names, and—*voilà*—instant coverage. Maybe Elise wants to see what you're going to do with something you believe is mundane."

"Oh, so you're thinking this is some kind of test? God's or Elise's?"

Aretha placed her cup and saucer in the sink. "That's exactly what I think, and whose test it might be doesn't matter. So far, you've not even shown up for it."

11

Dr. Hernandez is here. Hide the cookies, Miss Martha."

"You mean you haven't eaten them all already?" Greg tousled Jacob's hair on the way to the coffee pot in the Fellowship Hall. Not yet twelve, Jacob and his six-year-old sister Helen were adopted from Ethiopia four years ago. When his parents died, Jacob was seven and, until social workers came to their home, he had been taking care of his sister Helen by himself. Now the siblings live with their adoptive parents, Pam and Eli, and their three biological children. "Where's your Mom?" Jacob pointed over Greg's shoulder where Pam sat with three other women at a table bearing a mountain of fabrics.

"They told me to find more scissors. Guess they think I'm old enough to handle them." Jacob shook his head. "I think they're just tired of doing all the cutting themselves," he observed, then shuffled off in the direction of the supply room.

Greg smiled and looked around for Martha, the group's matriarch and founder. From the time he first met her, he felt an instant connection. She reminded him of Amelia, his neighbor in New Orleans who meant so much to both him and Jazarah. Martha walked out of the storeroom with a pair of scissors before Jacob even reached the door. "Here ya go, baby," she said as she handed him the scissors and another bag of fabric. Close to eighty, Martha told everyone she'd earned the right to call everyone else "baby." No one dared disagree, mostly out of respect. Then again, at almost six feet tall, her silver hair cropped close to her face, she made quite the imposing figure.

"Hey, Doc," she called out to Greg. She gave him a quick hug when she reached him. "Saved ya some cookies of your own to take home." She winked, then asked him to give the two quilts they were donating a final look.

"I see you're already starting on more," Greg said. "Those for next year?"

She shrugged. "We thought we'd try to get a few ready for the county fair. Plus, Becca asked if we could make one for a patient of hers. And, I know we all like to have a say in the ones for the benefit every year, but I thought it couldn't hurt to have some pieces ready. Crystal works at the Goodwill store, and she had the idea of bringing some clothes from there. We're just cutting big squares and whatnots for now."

Becca, a hospice nurse, joined the group a few months ago after seeing a quilt they'd made that belonged to one of her patients. "I may not be a seamstress," she said when she introduced herself, "but I can operate a pair of scissors and thread a needle."

Crystal and her mother Kelley were members of Living Faith church and helped the group secure the Fellowship Hall for their meetings. Crystal's twin sister, Carlys, after several trips to rehab, still couldn't stay clear of drugs. She died of AIDS when she was sixteen from a needle share. Kelley said the quilting group and just pushing a needle to create something good were all the therapy she needed since her daughter's death more than five years ago.

Greg set his coffee down before walking to the tables where the finished quilts awaited final inspection. Last year, the group had decided to make one quilt for children and one for adults. The children's quilt was designed using a pattern called Cupcake, but they nixed using a cupcake fabric. Greg thought it might be too limiting, and despite all the gender neutral talk, he didn't think cupcakes would appeal to parents of boys. Instead, they used a fabric featuring apple green, orange, and aqua colored giraffes against a bright yellow background sprinkled with cherry red hearts. The quilt's border was a polka dot fabric of complementary colors, and edging the border were strips of yellow gingham. Greg thought he might have to bid on this one himself because his daughter loved seeing the "stretchy" giraffes as she called them, and he could already picture her giggling and pointing to the diamonds of the happy-colored animals.

Greg flipped over the bottom right corner. "Aren't we sewing one of the 'Threads of Hope' labels on the back?"

"Oops. See, you really are helpful. I'm on my way to get one, and I'll be right back," she said. She took a few steps then turned around. "Doc, best check the other one."

"This one's ready to go," he said seeing the circle logo of their group carefully stitched to the back of the double pinwheel spin patterned quilt. Though the quilt used only five different fabrics, the nine pinwheels were all sewn over the same lime green firefly-designed diamonds, which stitched over nine snow-white squares of fabric. Two of the pinwheel arms were sewn from a hot pink fabric with red-and-lime green paisley prints. The other fabric featured a white background with hot pink added to the paisley print. Greg thought the almost retro-colored fabric and design might attract some of the younger attendees at the benefit.

Martha returned with a threaded needle and a label. "We need to write Elise a thank you note for donating all this fabric," she said as she held the quilt corner, her thumb holding the label straight while her needle flashed through the fabric.

"She doesn't expect that," Greg said.

Martha paused, cocked her head to one side, and narrowed her eyes. "Now, Doc, we're not doing it because she expects us to. We're doing it because we want to. And it's the right thing to do, to tell people you appreciate them for helping you get somewhere you need to be."

"Guess I needed to be reminded of that," he said, thinking of the backlog of thank-you notes he should've written. Beginning with Nina who, all those years ago in high school, started him on his journey toward compassion. And Lily who traveled the road with him. And Jazarah for bringing it to life.

Nina stepped into the elevator and stared straight into the eyes of Brady Lambert. "What . . . how . . . why are you here?" *At least I'm incoherent when no one else is here.* Before she could step aside, he reached around to press the button for their floor. His arm grazed hers and she caught a wisp of his familiar Dolce & Gabbana woody-citrus scent.

"Hmm. I still work here, right?' He shifted his black leather camera bag just as Nina attempted to sidestep him. But, too late. The bag hit her cup, and launched a spray of foam and coffee. Some of it splashed on Nina's pumps, but Brady's grey cable-knit sweater soaked up the rest.

"Thanks. What a great way to start my day," he said and glared at the half-dry napkin Nina offered him as if she just pulled it out of a baby's diaper.

She was just about to tell him that he should be glad the cup was half full, and he needed to be more careful swinging heavy camera bags in small spaces when the doors opened on their floor. Brady had a foot out the door before it had opened all the way. He pulled his cell phone out of his pants pocket and, as he left the elevator, turned to Nina and said, "Elise must be saving a bundle in dry-cleaning bills keeping you off the big stories."

Stunned into muteness, Nina rode the elevator right back down to the parking garage again. Fortunately, no one got on, so she had time to compose herself and think of places she could have finished off what was left of her coffee on Brady. And when did he become so snarky? And why?

When she finally made it through the office doors, Nina knew the latte aroma did as well.

Michelle raised her eyes over her reading glasses. "I've been wondering when you'd surface. Mr. Happy steamrolled in here complaining about your lack of gracefulness. He might have mentioned something about a dry cleaning bill . . ." She smiled at Nina. "Have a nice day, dearie. Ignore the malcontents."

Nina dropped her cup in the wastebasket by Michelle's desk. "The thrill is gone . . ."

"Speaking of thrills, I emailed you a few messages. Seems you're stirring the nepotism pot in that county election."

Maybe Aretha was wrong about this one. How can a quilt auction compete with election fraud? Readers want corruption exposed, not benefit dollars. Nina decided she'd postpone a discussion with Elise about her idea for an ongoing feature story about the We Care benefit and auction. If anyone understood the importance of news that mattered, it was Elise.

Nina planned to meet Aretha after work so they could shop for something to wear to the benefit. After spending most of the day talking to county officials, the District Attorney's office, more research into how contracts were awarded and to whom, Nina was ready for an afternoon that involved nothing more than, "love it/hate it." She thought they were going to start at The Galleria, but Aretha's text said to meet at a shop on Richmond.

"Why are we here?" Nina whispered to Aretha as they walked over to a rack of cocktail dresses. "I thought we were going shopping for new dresses, not used ones."

Aretha laughed. "Look at this store. Does this look like a used clothing shop?"

Nina swiveled her eyes from one end of the store to the other. Chandeliers, Oriental rugs, period furniture. "No, it doesn't. But I still don't understand what we're going to find here."

"Look, we can't compete on the same playing field as some of those divas who'll be sashaying around at that benefit. We're so not on the same playing field, we couldn't even be the water girls." Aretha scoped out the cocktail dress rack, flipping price tags as she talked. "So, we're not even going to try to play their game. Vintage clothes are classics. Just because they're old, doesn't mean they're outdated. We'll make a statement, but in a way that's unique and sophisticated. I promise."

Several racks and hours later, they each found the dress of their dreams. Aretha bought an off-shoulder, wine velvet dress with a scallop trim on the neckline, shoulders, and back. Nina's dress from the 1950s seemed to have been designed to fit her. The black taffeta dress had a polka dot illusion net bodice, cropped sheer sleeves, and a tulle skirt lining.

Nina had heard Brady might be there. She hoped so. Maybe seeing her in this dress would cause him to redefine *clumsy*.

12

"Peyton and I are about to leave. We wouldn't mind swinging by to pick you up," said Elise. "Would we?" She directed the question to her husband, who must have been in the room when she called. Peyton answered loudly enough for Greg to hear him, "I think Greg trusts that you're telling the truth."

Greg laughed. "Ask him if he wants me to pick him up instead."

"The two of you deserve one another," she said, the smirk apparent in her voice. "But the truth is, he looks so great in a tux, I think I want to walk in with a trophy husband on my arm."

"Thanks for the offer, really. I'm leaving as soon as I tuck Jazarah in."

"Give the little princess a hug and kiss from the two of us. See you soon," said Elise.

Greg tucked his phone in his pocket and headed upstairs to his daughter's room. He knew his sister wanted him to ride to the benefit with them to spare his having to walk in alone. And he appreciated, not only that she offered, but that she didn't say the obvious. But for Greg, it wasn't just the arriving by himself that magnified Lily's absence on nights like tonight.

He missed her little rituals, like when she'd lift her hair so he could zip her dress, and he'd always take the opportunity to softly kiss the back of her neck. Or when she'd spray a new perfume on the inside of her wrist, then hold it up to him to ask if he approved. And before they'd walk out the door, she'd make him stand perfectly still while she adjusted his tie, smoothed the lapels on his jacket, and declared him presentable with a soft kiss. Then she'd laugh that she'd just given him a lipstick cheek, and she'd smooth it over with her hand that was as soft as her face.

Will someone ever love me that way again? And, as he opened the door to Jazarah's room, he wondered if someone would ever love her again with Lily's fierceness and abundance. One thing he knew for sure. They were a package deal. And that was his prayer, always, that God would open his heart to a woman who would accept them both. A woman after God's own heart.

Greg tapped lightly on the partially closed door. "Is there a special little girl here?"

"Daddy, Daddy, come see!" His daughter's excitement reached him before he stepped into the room.

Paloma sat, Jazarah on her lap, in the pink-and-white ticked armchair that Jazarah called her reading chair. The small crib quilt that Lily had sewn for her while they waited for word they could finally fly to her was an uneven ball of fabric bunched in her arms. Every night Greg tucked her in with the quilt, always showing her the square that Lily stitched with, "I'll love you forever," and his daughter's sleepy eyes would blink as she'd clutch the quilt to her chest and whispered, "J woves you, too."

Jazarah waved him over and pointed to the page in Max Lucado's *You Are Special* where Eli, the woodcarver, explains to the wooden Wemmick Punchinello that the stickers the others use to label him only matter if he lets himself care about them.

Greg loved the story's message, that joy comes from what God thinks of us, not others, and that in His eyes we are all special, regardless of how we look.

When he and Lily bought the book years ago, they knew their daughter would face all sorts of issues and not just because of her race. Being an HIV-positive child would not be a ticket to popularity. But what made Jazarah special was what made her different, and what made her different would make her later question her self-worth. As her parents, Greg and Lily were determined their daughter grow with the conviction that nothing could sway God from loving her. *You Are Special* became a book that they gave to their own families and many of their adult friends, some of whom apparently either forgot or were never told the message.

His daughter pointed to Paloma's face, then his, then her own. "No 'tickers!" She grinned as she clapped her hands.

"Come hug me, no sticker girl." Greg held out his arms, and she reached for him. He gathered her close with her familiar just bathed, lavender soap smell and still damp hair. "Paloma will tuck you in tonight because daddy is going to Aunt Elise's party."

Jazarah loosened her arms from around his neck and leaned back against his arms, her brown eyes targeted on his own. "Why?" Her expression, so solemn and yet so parental-like, made him want to laugh.

"Remember Daddy told you about the party to raise money so more mommies and daddies can bring home beautiful little girls like you?"

She glanced up at the ceiling, then back at him. "Uh-huh."

Greg kissed her forehead, then settled her in Paloma's lap. "Well, that's where I'm going. I'll wake you up in the morning, and we can have pancakes for breakfast."

She grabbed her quilt and wiggled comfortably back in her reading spot. "Like me?"

He laughed. "Yes, I'll make 'J' pancakes just for you." One morning he made pancakes in an assortment of alphabet shapes, and they hadn't been round since. Unless they were the letter "O."

"Both doses, right?" Greg asked Paloma as he smoothed his daughter's hair.

She nodded. "Yes, sir. Both on time."

Even though he asked the question daily, and even though she answered the same daily, Greg appreciated that Paloma responded each time as if his daughter's required regimen of drugs was new. She knew, because of the drugs she took herself, that missing a dose of antiretroviral therapy or even juggling the times the drugs were administered were the biggest threats to HIV-positive kids. A disruption in the schedule either way could mean chancing the virus would become resistant to the therapy.

"Great. Thanks." Greg kissed his daughter one more time. "I love you, my special Wemmick."

She smiled and mashed her quilt against her chest. "Me, too. Forever and ever."

When Nina entered the Astor Ballroom of the St. Regis Hotel, every notion she had about attending a benefit of this magnitude hid in shame. And she promised herself to never roll her eyes again when someone described an event as "breathtaking." Well, perhaps if they sounded like Marilyn Monroe when they said it, she might have to reconsider.

The scene before her was spectacular. Tens of thousands of sparkling white lights canopied the ceiling. Huge spindly trees wrapped in the same white lights branched across the room and met one another. Tables were draped in subdued silver cloths of polished cotton. The tailored chair covers matched the tablecloths but were anchored to the chairs with wide white satin ribbons wrapped around the backs and tied with generous bows. Riding the waves of conversations, the stringed music of the violins and harps sailed across the ballroom.

Thanks to Aretha, she didn't feel at all uncomfortable among the couture collections that surrounded her. Brady did attend, camera in hand, and she could tell by the appraising nod when he walked past her that he didn't, at first, recognize her. Aretha told her that he turned around, took a few steps toward her, then must have changed his mind because he stopped and headed in his original direction. Nina decided that if their paths did cross again that night, she'd ask him why he wasn't in New York with Janie scouting out places to live. Between bites of steamed asparagus stems, Aretha warned her that such a question was truly none of her business. "He doesn't owe you an explanation. And even if he gives you one, I don't know why you are torturing yourself. If he says there's no more Janie, are you really interested? And if you are, don't tell me. I don't want to lose all respect for you."

Nina ignored Aretha's dire predictions. "Let's go view the quilts before the silent auction ends," she said.

"I'll meet you there. I just saw someone I want to say hello to." Aretha dashed off before Nina had a chance to find out who the someone was.

The quilts were in the adjoining room. They covered every wall and just walking around the room was like stepping inside a giant kaleidoscope with a landscape of fabrics and textures and even dimensional objects. When Elise first gave her the tickets, Nina expected that the auction would feature quilts that memorialized family or friends lost to AIDS. But it was the money raised from the event that would go toward supporting the efforts of the NAMES Project and their ongoing work with the Memorial Quilt. The ones on display that night were sewn by local support groups throughout the Houston area. Nina recognized some of the traditional quilts, classic patchworks with patterns dizzyingly intricate. Lace, beads, even trinkets embellished some of the contemporary quilts.

Nina spotted a quilt whose funky design and colors she was certain Aretha and her little decorator-self would adore. It would be a perfect birthday present for her because Nina knew that it was a luxury she wouldn't buy for herself right now. Standing in front of the hot pink and lime green paisley print quilt, Nina was the first bidder and realized she had no idea how much she should bid. She looked around for people wearing "We Care" pins, which meant they were volunteers attending the benefit to help with the auction.

A few couples moved past her, and she spotted a lapel pin on the tuxedo of a man who stopped to bid on the giraffe quilt next to her. He was still writing on the bid sheet when she tapped on his shoulder. "Excuse me. I'm sorry to bother you, but I wanted to bid on this for a friend, and I saw your lapel pin—"

When he placed his pen down on the bid sheet to look up, there was the shock of mutual recognition as Greg Hernandez and Nina O'Malley stood face-to-face.

13

Brady, she expected to see. Greg Hernandez? Not so much.

And Greg Hernandez in a tuxedo? Not so shabby. In fact, she wanted to slap herself for the flicker of warmth she was certain flushed her face. Even if she did find him surprisingly attractive, she certainly did not want him to feel even a stitch of satisfaction to see it reflected in the blush on her cheeks.

They both tripped over their words like wires stretched across their mutual discomfort at finding themselves where they would not have wanted to be.

After swatting a few syllables in one another's direction, Nina managed a coherent sentence. "I didn't know you worked here," she said. *Another deserved slap for a ridiculous comment. Aretha, anytime you want to make an appearance and save me would be fine.* She shifted her weight ever-so-slightly to give her other foot a reprieve from the tingling that led to total toe numbness and would make a speedy escape improbable. "Volunteer, I meant I didn't know you were a volunteer." What she really wanted to say was that she was stunned to find him at an event supporting anything AIDS-related.

"Well, I didn't know I was one either until a week or so ago," Greg said. "It's given me something to do and kept me out of trouble." He smiled and added, "So far."

"There you are," the voice of relief tinged with frustration, sailed above the heads of the cluster of people. It originated from a woman who snaked her way through a cluster of sequined gowns against a backdrop of black tuxedos. Her cropped platinum hair seemed as no-nonsense as the simple black sheath she wore. Nina had heard about the death of his parents, so she knew whoever this was, she wasn't his mother. Her eyes flickered on Nina for only a moment, then she handed Greg a plastic cup and a bottle of water the size and shape of a coffee thermos. "Who'd want to go hiking with that?" She emphasized *that* and pointed to the container she'd given him. "Glass water bottles? Better off putting it in a can," she harrumphed.

Greg laughed. "You're the queen of practical. Thanks for the water." He set the cup and bottle down on the table next to them. "Did you need me for anything?"

"Crystal was following me. She had a question about taking orders from people who don't win the auction." She looked over her shoulders and back at Greg. "Guess she got sidetracked." Turning her attention to Nina, she said, "You're bidding on that one? Good choice," she said and walked off.

As she threaded her way back through the crowd, Greg watched her and shook his head, an amused smile on his face. "That was Martha. Her group made that quilt. She left so quickly, I didn't have time to introduce you."

"Oh, so you've been to this benefit before?" Nina said, trying not to lick her dry lips and wondering if her breath reeked of the grilled garlic-infused cilantro shrimp she'd sampled earlier.

Two women who walked over to look at the quilt squeezed past Nina, pushing her within inches of Greg. In high school, she dreamed of being this close to him. Close enough to punch him, which she knew would have hurt her more. Physically. She contemplated other ways of marring the face that so many girls in school wanted pressed against their own. After her brother died, she abandoned what she considered the smoke and mirrors of praying to an invisible God. But the one prayer she let escape her lips was that Greg Hernandez know pain. The gut-altering pain that she experienced.

Greg twisted what, at first Nina thought was a wedding band, but the ring was on his right hand instead of his left. "No, I haven't. My sister invited me, and Martha, well . . ." He stopped, drank some water, and looked into his cup as if expecting to find the rest of his sentence there. Greg set the cup on the table and when he looked at Nina, he said, "Anyway, I doubt you're interested in a rambling narrative about how I came about being here. What about you? Were you here last year?"

Nina wished he hadn't sounded so much like a polite customer service rep, trained to ask scripted questions. *Really? This is the second time you've seen one another in years. Why are you expecting more than feigned interest?* She considered an equally vague answer, but why? What were the odds their ships would dock at the same port? Might as well go for honest. "I wasn't here before either, and the only reason I'm here tonight is because I'm on assignment. Not that I don't think this is a worthy cause, but charity events, you know the who's who doing the what's what, aren't the stories I write." She moved to the side to avoid a possible collision into Greg, letting a couple holding hands and reeking of fresh love walk by. "I'd rather do more investigative reporting. But . . . my editor gave me the tickets. And, she's not someone I want to annoy by refusing. In fact, I wouldn't doubt she's the reincarnation of General

Patton, the female version. She's demanding and driven, and that's as diplomatically as I can describe her."

A carousel of expressions moved over Greg's face as she spoke. From expectant to thoughtful to confused to amused. She didn't remember being humorous. Perhaps the orchestra tuning up in the ballroom lent a dramatic backdrop to her tale of woe. Otherwise, what was that flicker of a smile?

"Oh, so you're a reporter. Local news station?" He poured himself more water.

"I'd rather be behind a camera than in front of one. No, I work for a local magazine called *Trends*. You might not have seen it yet if you just recently moved."

Greg almost choked trying to swallow his water. "Excuse me," he coughed out.

Nina opened her purse to find a tissue to hand him when she heard Aretha calling her. "Nina, look who I found." Her relief withered faster than a Southern girl in the Georgia sun when she looked up to see Elise trailing behind her friend. "Oh, great. Speak of the devil . . ." she said as she handed Greg the only thing she could dredge up, a napkin from Starbucks. "I'll tell her I'm interviewing you, which, of course, I planned to do next anyway, and maybe she'll march off in another direction."

He started coughing again.

If Greg had known that being a volunteer would provide him the front-row entertainment about to unfold before him, he would have signed on without his sister's persistence.

"If you're going to be there, you might as well have something to do and not wander around aimlessly," Elise had told him when she handed over his pin.

At first, he thought it was her ploy to assure that he'd show up. But walking in tonight, he realized that, by giving him a mission for the evening, she saved him from the awkwardness of feeling alone in a room full of people.

He expected to feel a bit awkward without Lily. He didn't expect that he would feel that way standing near the woman he least expected to see there. What made meeting her all the more uncomfortable was his realization that, even before he knew that he knew her, she'd captured his attention. Greg remembered thinking that only a woman as beautiful as she was self-assured would be able to pull off wearing a quirky, but stunning vintage dress to such an occasion. He would have never guessed that the girl he humiliated on the floor of his high school cafeteria would be the woman admired in the ball-room of a grand hotel.

It was reassuring that she was equally startled to see him. Of course, based on what he suspected was her perception of him—arrogant, spoiled, and unfeeling—her surprise didn't surprise him. The last time they'd seen one another was her appointment at the vet clinic with her dog, the squirmy dachs-hund that she'd named after some city. He didn't have a reason to discuss his daughter or his wife. Had he, she might have been less shocked.

When she started explaining her reason for being at the benefit, Greg thought her working for Elise would be too coin-cidental. Then, as she continued to talk, the notion became less unlikely. Describing her editor as demanding came close to Elise, but he almost couldn't stop himself from laughing aloud when she mentioned *Trends*. Then, as if on cue, his sister appeared. At first, he thought the comedy of errors would be amusing. But seeing the change in Nina's demeanor, the way she squared her shoulders and tugged on the pearl drop she wore, centering it in the hollow of her neck, he sensed a pending disaster. But the iceberg had moved in too close, and the ship was about to crash.

The petite woman his sister followed scanned him from head to toe, then turned her attention to Nina. "Elise and I bumped into each other at the pasta bar. And almost literally." She laughed.

Nina did not. With Elise a few steps away, Nina flipped a hand in his direction. "Aretha, this is Greg Hernandez. Aretha is my roommate. And this is—"

"There you are," said Elise.

Greg glanced at Nina and saw her open her mouth to answer, when Elise added, "Have you seen Peyton? I thought he'd be with you." Elise peered over her brother's shoulders as if she'd spot her husband hiding behind him. And before he could reply, his sister looked at Nina. "I'm sorry. I must seem so rude. Aretha told me I had to see your dress. It's lovely, just as she said."

Elise placed her hand on Greg's shoulder. "I didn't know you knew my brother."

⸎

The words *my brother* hurtled into Nina and if she didn't soon salvage the emotional wreckage, she would be crushed beyond recognition. She willed herself into composure, clasped her hands in front of her to still their trembling. Standing between Greg and Aretha, she heard the gasp of one and sensed the flinch of the other. Nina had looked at neither one of the two as her mouth and lips formed syllables into words and pushed them out to answer Elise.

Nina's face paled and Greg winced when she said, "I didn't either."

Elise looked from her to Greg and back again, the question on her face unanswered.

"Excuse me, please. There's something I must attend to," Nina said and walked away from her boss, her friend, and her betrayer.

14

Somewhere between moving her arm out of reach of Greg's grasp, Aretha calling her name, and the ladies' room, which was her intended destination, Nina slammed into Brady Lambert. Make that Brady Lambert's camera lens.

She pressed her hands to her throbbing forehead, squeezed her eyes to ease the stinging, and hoped whatever she exclaimed at the moment of the crash didn't require a censor.

"Whoa! Ma'am, are you okay? I didn't see you . . . you walked by so fast."

She felt herself wobble, and Brady placed his hands on her shoulders. "I'm fine. I'm fine. I just need to sit down . . . somewhere . . . ladies' room . . ." Something inside her welcomed the pain. It trumped the assault she felt her heart had just taken.

"Nina? Are we doing this camera collision again?" He sounded on the verge of annoyed, but Nina saw his expression soften when he looked at her. Brady cupped her head in his hands. "I'm so sorry. Here," he gently held her wrists, "let me see the damage."

If he could truly see the damage she felt, her body would be pumping fountains of blood. At least when he sees the tears in my eyes, he won't know they were already there. Nina slowly lifted her head as he moved her own hands away from her face. She hated and welcomed that his touch moved through her like a warm current. It had been a long time since he had held her so gently.

She sniffled and hoped her nose wouldn't be drippy as he brushed her bangs from her forehead, his fingertips whispers against her skin. Brady's eyes swept over her face, and she recognized that look of tenderness she knew he was capable of.

The orchestra broke into a medley of rock and roll tunes that sent couples around them scurrying to the dance floor. Pinched in the middle of the movement, he maneuvered them away from the swinging bodies to a bench along the ballroom wall. "The good news is you're not going to need to make an appointment with a plastic surgeon." He waited a beat, and when Nina managed a smile of sorts, he smiled, too. "But," he said, and softly feathered her bangs over her forehead, "you're going to have a bruise the size of a tennis ball. I'd suggest not wearing your hair back for a while." He looked around and waved one of the servers over.

A barely-out-of-his-teens waiter walked over, his black bow tie slightly askew, balancing a silver tray ravaged by the hungry. "May I help you?"

"Yes, please," said Brady. "It seems my camera lens and her lovely forehead met one another on the dance floor, and it wasn't a pretty sight. Would you bring us some ice before it swells into an egg?"

"Do you need a doctor? We have an emergency . . ." His concern was tinged with a smattering of polite eagerness.

Sensing his anticipation of a reprieve from strolling through the guests, Nina was tempted to say yes to avoid disappointing him. But even if she did need medical attention, she wasn't going to subject herself to it here. The sooner she left, the better. "No doctor, but I appreciate your concern." Nina lifted her head to speak to him and the throbbing slipped into her temples. "Ice will be fine," she whispered.

The young man walked off, and Nina opened her purse in hopes of finding another tissue.

"Searching for one of these?" Brady handed her a handkerchief. "And don't look so surprised that I have such an old-fashioned item. These belonged to my father."

"I didn't mean to look surprised," Nina said defensively. "Just trying to keep my eyelashes from sticking together." She didn't, though, ever consider Brady a sentimentalist. Perhaps this was the new, improved version as designed by Janie. A woman who probably never had raccoon eyes. "I appreciate your help, but you don't need to babysit me. I can wait for the ice man," she said, swiping the handkerchief under her eyes as she spoke. "I'm sure you have other things to do."

"Babysit you? Did you really just say that?" Brady shook his head. "I know I didn't end our relationship with dignity. In fact, I should have apologized a long time ago for being so—"

"Arrogant?" Nina eyed him. Brady appeared as surprised to hear her comment as she was to say it. Maybe being honest resulted from a bashed head and not a broken heart.

He nodded. "I was going to say 'pompous jerk,' so you cut me some slack on that one." He leaned against the wall, stared at the ceiling for a moment, then at the jitterbugging couples on the ballroom floor. "Sometimes, the grass is actually greener on the other side, but when you get there, you find out it's artificial turf. And you're wearing the wrong cleats."

In one of the full-length gilded mirrors in the ladies' room, Nina peered at the lump on her forehead. It looked like a messy papier-mâché relief of Rhode Island. Brady had barely finished comparing Janie to fake grass when the server walked over with a small zippered plastic bag of ice. When she stood to leave, Brady told her he was going to take more shots of The AIDS Memorial quilt on display, but he'd meet her at the same spot in a few minutes. He insisted on taking her home. "It's a rule. When you hit someone in the head, you're obligated to drive them home." He had grinned, and Nina couldn't help but do the same.

She emptied the ice in the sink and tossed the bag away. No point now in freezing her forehead and having the condensation trickle down her face. Her pale cheeks, bare eyes, and washed-out lips provided little evidence of the time she invested hours ago applying her makeup. She started to reapply her lipstick when her cell phone vibrated again in her purse. Talking to Brady earlier, she'd ignored the previous alerts. When she was ready to be found, like now, she'd let whoever might be looking for her know. Aretha had sent a text: "U OK? Where R U?????"

The multiple question marks loosely translated in Aretha-speak to, "I've been searching all over the place and can't find you and my patience is shot." Nina moved to the anteroom, found a bench to sit on, and started to return the message when the door slapped open and Aretha roared through.

"Finally!" Her friend's victorious tone echoed her hand pump. "You should be a magician . . . you've got that disappearing act mast—whoa, what happened to you?" Aretha grimaced as she pointed at Nina's forehead.

"Brady's camera and I had a bit of a collision." Nina touched the lump like it was a message written in Braille. Since it had stopped pulsating, it didn't feel as sensitive. But when she peered in the mirror, it didn't appear less angry.

"Was he trying to take a picture of you or something?" Aretha sat next to her, a shadow of suspicion on her face, and stared at Nina's forehead.

"Well, that would have been one heck of a close-up." Nina slipped her lipstick back into her clutch. "No," she said and paused to check her teeth, "in the heat of humiliation I wasn't paying attention to where I was going, and I walked right into his camera lens." When the door swept open again, Nina asked Aretha if Elise had followed her.

"I doubt it," she answered and waited until the young woman who entered walked past them. "I left your boss and her brother engaged in one of those 'who said what to whom and when' conversations. For what it's worth, he sounded intensely apologetic." She crossed her legs and bent over to adjust her sandals. "I know it's not my fault, but I'm the one who dragged Elise over there . . ."

"You're not the one who needs to apologize," Nina said. "I know I didn't flatter Elise when I talked about her. But did Greg have to humiliate me by being dishonest about himself? He knew Elise was already out of high school by the time I started. How was I supposed to make that connection?"

"Maybe I should back up before I say this," Aretha cautioned, "but 'didn't flatter'? Really? Could that be a more textbook example of understatement? After Elise walked away, he told me about your conversation. How was he supposed to handle that? Would it have been less humiliating to be at the magazine talking about Greg to Elise, not knowing they were siblings? There was no way this was going to turn out well."

"Everything always turns out well for Greg Hernandez. The man leads a charmed life," said Nina, not even trying to mask the contempt in her voice. "And once again, I'm the one left to look like a fool."

15

Y ou're letting Brady take you home?"

"Don't make it sound like I'm riding with a serial killer," Nina countered while letting Aretha gently powder her forehead. "Do you want to come with us?"

Her friend moved her head from side to side to examine the coverage. "No, he's a serial dater. Isn't a whop on the head enough?" Aretha snapped her powder compact closed. "And, no again. I'm staying. I saw this beautiful man who is in one of my design classes, and he's not only dreamy, he's single. We took a taxi here, I can take one home."

"You're sighing, and that's a definite warning sign. Don't let your heart make promises your head can't keep," Nina warned as she and Aretha stood to leave the ladies' room.

Aretha opened the door and let Nina exit. "Sweetie, coming from you, that's a gem."

Had Brady not been waiting outside, Nina might have responded. But there he stood, looking more appealing than she wanted him to.

"Oh, hello Brady," said Aretha. She pointed at his camera. "Didn't they ask you to check your weapon at the door?"

"Aretha . . . ," he said and smiled, "you look stunning." Brady glanced toward Nina, then reached out and clasped Aretha's hand. "I've missed your wit. How are you?"

For a minute, Aretha's expression reminded her of Manny's slight head tilt when Nina used her nice voice to tell him how annoying he could be.

"I'm quite content, thank you. So, where's . . . um," Aretha paused, "Janie, yes, that's it. Is she here with you?" She smiled like someone who'd just trumped in bridge.

Nina opened her clutch to avoid eye contact with either one of them. She felt a bit guilty for enjoying Aretha's deliberate attempt to make Brady squirm. But, in typical Brady fashion, the master of finesse, he replied, "How kind of you to ask about her. She's still in New York." He looked at Nina. "At least the last time I spoke to her that's where she was."

Aretha replied, "I see," in a way that suggested she didn't at all. "So, I know you're providing transportation for the wounded." She nodded toward Nina. "Best of luck in the Big Apple." When she hugged Nina, she whispered, "Remember, it's just a ride home. And don't forget to take Manny out when you get there."

After Brady and Nina made their way around the dance floor to the front of the ballroom, he asked her to wait by the entrance while he had the valet bring his car.

"Can you hold on a few minutes? I wanted to bid on a quilt, and got distracted. I won't be long." The orchestra stopped as Nina opened the door to the ballroom and, of all people, Elise was on the stage announcing only five minutes remained for silent auction bidding. Nina watched as tables emptied, and people streamed into the quilt room, their voices swarming around them. She debated if she had the energy to swim along with the crowd, but remembering how perfect that quilt would be for Aretha, she decided to plunge forward.

"Nina, can I talk to you?" She felt the tap on her shoulder before she heard Greg's voice. And as much as she wanted to, there was no way to avoid him. But she could evade him, even if he had already moved next to her. "Not now. I want to bid before the auction is over."

He stepped in front of her. "Please, this won't take long. I promise."

Not only did Nina not stop herself from rolling her eyes, she hoped her exaggerated display clearly conveyed her exasperation. They stepped to the side, away from the entrance to the room.

"Are you okay?" He stared at the lump on her forehead.

"Fine. I'm fine."

"Listen, I'm truly sorry—"

Nina held her hand up in front of his face. "Stop." She gripped her clutch with both hands. "Don't bother apologizing because, really, why should you now? You didn't all those years ago when you humiliated me. Why do you think it would matter to me now? At least, I know to not expect anything different from you."

Shoving his hands in his pockets, Greg stared at the floor. When he looked at Nina again, his face was taut. "I'm sure I deserve that. Tonight's not the time, but I can explain—"

"There's no explanation that can salvage the humiliation I felt all those years ago and what I felt tonight." Her head throbbed, but so did the buried resentment inside of her. After so much time being held hostage in her heart, the words she wanted to say finally freed themselves. "You're right. Tonight's not the time. But there may never be another time for me to say I prayed that pain would bury itself in you like it did in me. After all, what would someone with money and popularity and success ever need to suffer through?" She noticed heads turning in their direction, and lowered her voice. "I used to feel guilty about that prayer, but after tonight, maybe not."

Something shifted in Greg then, and Nina sensed she'd driven the stake into his heart just like she'd intended. She could see his pride turn to ashes just as surely as if she'd set the fire. A momentary recoil, and he said, in a voice so severe she almost didn't recognize it as his, "You can stop praying now. Your wish has already been granted. And because of it, if not for God, I might not be here tonight to make you so miserable." He checked his cell phone that had pinged several times while he spoke. "I hope your night is better." He nodded and walked away.

His response was a hurricane force wind instead of the breeze she expected. And, had she not already been leaning against the wall, it might have brought her to the ground. Nina watched him, cell phone pressed to his ear, stride toward the stage as Elise announced that the auction had ended.

Brady waved at the valet when Nina met him again. "How did the bidding go?" His hand resting on her shoulder, he moved her toward the exit.

"Bidding?" *The quilt. You left to bid on the quilt.* "I don't know . . . I . . . I missed it."

Outside, the night air pushed against them like a damp sponge. Brady led her to a pearl white Mercedes so polished it could have been lifted from a velvet case. The valet opened the door, and Nina eased onto the soft leather seat and welcomed the cool air coming from the vents.

Brady adjusted his seat belt and, as the car pulled away from the hotel, he said, "So, what happened that you weren't able to bid?"

Nina stared out the window, still sifting through her emotional conversation with Greg. "One of the volunteers stopped to talk to me, and I didn't make it back," she said. That was all he needed to know, and it was enough of the truth to not make her uncomfortable manufacturing a story. Besides, it was his stories she was most interested in hearing. "Tell me about New York. It has to be more exciting than discussing quilts."

He turned down the volume on the Adele CD and drummed his thumbs on the steering wheel. "Maybe not more exciting." Brady stopped at the red light and looked at Nina. "I'm not as certain about moving as I was when Elise asked me to go. Especially because of Daisy."

Daisy? New York? This must be my night for sabotages. She knew she couldn't let being stunned betray her or else Brady might stop talking. As she opened her purse to shut her cell phone off, she said, "Yes, of course," as if she'd yawned the words out.

"When Janie first told me about Daisy, and everything going on with her family, it made sense that she'd want to live close. Then, Daisy started wavering about the decision. She didn't know what to tell Elise she wanted to do about the New York job after all she'd done to get it for her . . . I turn up there, right?" Brady pointed to the street ahead.

Nina nodded and hoped her composure would last longer than the rest of the drive.

"Anyway, now Janie's playing armchair therapist and big sister to Daisy, and she's neglecting everything else she needs to do to prepare herself for this new position."

"You mean neglecting you?"

Brady slowed the car as he turned into her driveway, then shifted into park. "Janie's helped me realize something," he said and looked at Nina.

She wanted to repeat her eye-roll performance, but his serious expression actually surprised her. Once again, she relied on her airy tone. "And what is that?"

"I know what it feels like to not be important in someone's life anymore, especially when that person is someone you thought wouldn't disappoint you." He cleared his throat. "I wasn't at all kind to you, Nina, and I hope you can forgive me for being such an idiot."

So, this is betrayer and forgiveness night? Whatever hope she felt by his admission was reined in by suspicion. *What was his agenda here?* "Forgive, yes. Forget, I'm still working on."

He leaned toward her, and Nina forced herself to ignore wanting to move closer and wait for him to kiss her. The space between them no longer felt like a force field, but a magnet. But she couldn't allow herself to be pulled in. At least not tonight. Brady moved his finger slowly down Nina's bare arm, from her shoulder to her wrist, then wrapped his hand around hers. "Maybe you won't have to forget. Forget what it was like for us to be together, I mean."

"I haven't forgotten what that was like, Brady." Nina slid her hand out from under his and opened the car door. "What I meant was I'm working on forgetting the damage you left behind. I'm not Plan B when you and Janie hit a speed bump on your way to wherever it is your relationship is going."

"You don't believe in second chances?"

Nina thought for a moment. "Brady, I don't even believe in first chances. People shouldn't take chances loving one another. Love should be intentional."

16

Greg was grateful for the text message that provided a legitimate excuse for him to leave Nina's presence. Her bitterness spewed from a wound that had festered so deep and for so long, that it had to be pierced to have any chance of healing. But her scathing attack and hearing that, for years, she wanted nothing more than for him to experience pain, horrified him. Would she be one of those people so full of hatred that, when it left, the shell she'd built to contain it would crack, and she'd find herself empty? Was this what happened to people who never knew or understood forgiveness? Who never asked, "Who were we to choose unforgiveness when God forgives us over and over and over?"

After Lily's death, he struggled desperately, knowing what he needed to do, but not wanting to do it. He wanted to feel anger, to build a shrine to it, and know that it would be there every day. Like Lily used to be. The accident, which he mostly didn't call it, as a man doesn't drink by accident or drive by accident, robbed him of his wife. It wasn't going to rob him of resentment and hate. Greg clothed himself in righteous indignation. But, with each passing day, the feelings weighed him down more and more until their weight almost broke him in two. Then he came across a quote from Corrie ten Boom, a Christian woman who'd been a prisoner in a Nazi concentration camp, "Forgiveness is to set a prisoner free, and to realize the prisoner was you." And that's when he had fallen on his knees and asked God to forgive his unforgiveness. Greg knew that only God working through him could make him strong enough to forgive the man who devastated his life.

But Nina didn't know or didn't choose to know that there was another way. Greg guessed she'd dragged the heaviness around so long, the thought of being weightless terrified her. Without the history, maybe the confusion about Elise would have been less traumatic for Nina. She probably thought he'd relay their conversation verbatim and, once again, she'd be the humiliated kid in the middle of the floor. Except this time it would be a ballroom floor.

As he told her she could stop praying for him to know pain, he saw glimpses of confusion in her eyes, as she scanned his face searching for evidence of dishonesty. Greg wanted to turn the wall behind them into a scoreboard, draw a line down the center, and ask her what she could write on her side that could possibly win out over his losing a wife and his daughter, a mother. But he wasn't going to use the memory of Lily as the highest score. Walking off when he did had spared each of them regret in the future.

The text, from one of the emergency clinics he'd recently worked in, updated him on the status of one of the sick animals he'd seen there. He went outside to call the vet tech who'd contacted him and saw Nina leave the hotel with someone driving a late model Mercedes convertible. She was going to miss the auction, which meant she wouldn't find out that he'd placed the highest bid on the quilt she wanted.

"Look, Manny, the princess is descending from her royal tower to join us." The dachshund yelped and trotted back and forth between Nina and Aretha, then sat to watch Nina walk down the stairs.

"Twenty years ago, I might have just stuck my tongue out at you for that," said Nina, taking each step as if it were underwater.

Aretha grinned. "Twenty years ago, I might have followed that with running after your princess fanny." She pointed to the kitchen. "I made breakfast, but you missed the best part. Pancakes right off the griddle with strawberries and warm syrup. I saved a few slices of bacon, and you can pop the left-over cakes in the toaster or the microwave."

Nina sat on the bottom step and scratched Manny behind the ears as she listened to Aretha roll out the breakfast menu. "What time did you wake up to get all *Barefoot Contessa* on me? I couldn't have slept that late . . . did I?" Nina felt her wrist, no watch. She checked the pockets of her sleeping scrubs, no phone. "We need a clock."

"I've been saying that for months. It's after ten o'clock, so, yes, you did sleep that late. You left your cell phone down here, and your mother's been lighting it up like a Christmas tree with phone calls." Aretha yawned, and stretched out her arms and legs. "I woke up at the tender hour of eight o'clock. What time did you get to sleep?"

"You woke up at eight? I didn't go to sleep until after two, and you still weren't home. If you hadn't returned my text at almost one, I was about to put out a Missing Persons alert." She turned her phone off to avoid having to talk to her mother, zapped a cup of coffee in the microwave, and picked at the sliced strawberries she found in the refrigerator.

"Who knew Mr. Beautiful and I had so much to talk about? After we left the benefit, we drove around trying to find some place for breakfast. Ended up at Katz's Deli . . . had no idea how late it was until you sent that text." Aretha hugged her knees to her chest and smiled. "And why were you still awake? Having a long conversation with Brady?"

She decided to hold off telling her about talking to Greg before she left the benefit. Her emotional reserves were waning, and she had yet to deal with her mother. The Greg drama could wait, except for that last statement he made to her. The one about her prayer being answered already. It unsettled her, the way it did when she remarked one day that homeless people caused their own problems, and then found out Daisy had been one of those very people when her father left them.

Nina carried her coffee, a plate of bacon, and strawberries to the den, Manny following her waiting for crumbs to fall. "Sorry, buddy, you're out of luck today," she told him as she set everything on the coffee table. He resigned himself to curling around her feet. "For the record, my conversation with Brady ended not long after he turned into our driveway."

"Can't wait to hear this one."

Nina told Aretha the from-hotel-to-home story with Brady, hoping she sounded as lucid retelling it as she thought she was the night before. Since Aretha listened without an interruption, she must have achieved her goal.

"Have to admit, I wouldn't have thought you'd be able to stand up for yourself like you did. I suspect somewhere in that heart of yours there's a pitter-patter left for him."

Nina shrugged. "I suppose, but I wonder if I want a victory over Janie more than a relationship with Brady. Doesn't matter now. I don't have either one."

"Careful," warned Aretha. "You're backsliding into your comfortable victim role." She checked her cell phone and smiled. "Mr. Beautiful just sent me a text. He wants to take Manny and me for a walk, and lunch." She patted Manny on the head. "We have a date. Aren't you excited?"

Manny blinked a few times, then he assumed his sleeping position.

"He's not understanding this concept of dating, since it doesn't happen too often around here. And, in case I'm here when he shows up, does Mr. Beautiful have a real name?"

"Luke. Luke Samuelson. And when I return, you're going to tell me why you were on sleep deprivation. But now I'm going to look for that cinnamon V-neck sweater of yours that I love to wear."

"It's either in the laundry room or my closet. Better hope it's in the closet . . ." Nina said. She wasn't sure she wanted to tell Aretha she stayed awake researching writing positions available in New York, places to live there, and more background information for her political corruption story. Then again, watching Aretha bounce down the stairs waving the sweater like a victory flag, Nina wasn't sure Aretha would care.

Nina mentally reviewed the excuses she could give her mother for backing out of lunch, but her mother would know that's exactly what they were. And she'd label them all flimsy and tell Nina any daughter who invented excuses not to have lunch with her parents probably didn't deserve them. She'd already called Nina six times in three hours, so Nina's failure to return calls meant not only was she now up the proverbial river without a paddle, she just drilled a hole in her boat.

She counted to ten then forced herself to hit her parents' phone number. Less than three minutes later, it was all over. After Nina stumbled through the news she wouldn't be there, her mother responded with, "Good. I called so often this morning in an effort to inform you not to come here today because your father and I didn't feel up to company."

Was there any point in mentioning that someone's own daughter shouldn't be considered "company"? Except that in her parents' house, that's exactly how Nina felt. Apparently they did, too.

Nina checked the time on her phone. Unless she wanted to meet Mr. Luke the Beautiful in her wrinkled, hot pink, polka-dotted scrubs, she needed to find something more presentable to wear. A quick shower, a pair of jeans, and a black turtleneck later, Nina declared herself ready when the doorbell rang. She tapped on Aretha's door as she opened it. "He's here," she announced to an obviously undressed roommate who looked uncharacteristically frantic.

"I don't know what to wear." She sat on her bed and held up a pair of black pants, "These make me look like I'm ready for Halloween wearing them with that sweater. And these," she tossed a pair of jeans to the floor in disgust, "are too tight. . . ."

The doorbell rang again. Aretha hissed, "Don't just stand there. Go let him in before he thinks no one is home."

Nina looked in Aretha's closet, shoved hangers back and forth, parting waves of clothes until she reached for a pair of khaki pants. "Here, wear these. They're capri length on me, so they should be the right length for you. And let it be known that I'm nice to you even when you're not." She heard an "I'm sorry" as she closed the bedroom door.

She scooted Manny out of the way, and opened the front door, anxious to see the man who captured her friend's attention. Instead, she saw the one who once captured her own.

Brady Lambert stood on her doorstep behind a bouquet of far too many long-stemmed white tulips.

"I wanted to surprise you," Brady said as he handed Nina an armful of flowers. "And make sure you didn't still have a lump on your forehead."

Nina held on to the tulips like she was hauling delicate firewood. "Well, you've surprised me," she said, still slightly stunned. "Um, thank you for these . . ."

"May I come in or were you on your way out?"

Dressed in his typical starched, button-down shirt and knife-pleated jeans, Brady always had that "on his way to somewhere" look. Unlike Nina who tended to look like she wasn't sure where she was going. Like today.

"Of course. I wasn't going anywhere," she said, but then wished she hadn't admitted it because she just lost an out for his leaving. She juggled the bouquet and tried to hold Manny back from dashing out the door as Brady entered.

"You're not Luke." An equally surprised, but finally dressed, Aretha peered over the steps after Nina shut the door.

"Hello again, Aretha. And, no, I'm not." Brady smiled, but not unlike someone who just told the cat where the canary was hiding. "Just checking on Nina's injury."

Nina set the tulips on the counter and moved her bangs aside to show Brady the swelling had gone down. "No more egg. Just a little bruise."

She found the only vase-like accommodation for such an armful of flowers, a tall ice bucket. She filled it with water, tried to arrange the not-so-cooperative tulips, and hoped Aretha would save her from a task at which she was totally inept. Nina watched her friend descend the stairs, and she wasn't rushing to help. In fact, she leaned against the granite bar, arms folded, and surveyed Brady and his flowers.

"Great choice, Brady," Aretha said. "Nina, I think you may have to trim the stems." She looked back at Brady. "Don't worry, that won't lessen their meaning."

Nina rifled through rubber bands, a collection of twist ties, and pens in what was supposed to be the utensil drawer for the kitchen shears. "Meaning? What meaning?" She found the shears mixed in with ladles and spatulas. "Aha," she said and held them up like a trophy. No one else seemed to be impressed. Not even Manny who growled as if on a timer, every few minutes, at nothing or no one in particular.

Brady cleared his throat. Without a camera slung over his shoulder, he lost his casual, cool factor. He looked so uncomfortable, Nina almost felt sorry for him. Almost. "The florist told me they mean, um, forgiveness. I guess since Aretha hinted at it, it must be true."

She looked from Brady to Aretha. "How did you know this?"

Aretha walked over and took the shears from Nina. "Because studying design isn't limited to furniture. I wouldn't want to decorate a lawyer's office with lavender, which signals distrust." She snipped the stems of the tulips and dropped them into the ice bucket. "Not the most elegant of containers, but the rustic look offsets the tulips quite nicely."

"She can't help it. The decorator gene just has to flaunt itself," Nina explained to Brady as she placed the arrangement in the center of the kitchen table.

Aretha tossed the pile of stems in the trash. "Okay, I'm done here. Going back upstairs for the finishing touches." She patted Brady on his arm. "Best of luck in New York," she said.

He opened his mouth as if he intended to respond, but instead he smiled and nodded. "Thanks, Aretha. I appreciate that."

Since Brady had never arrived unannounced, Nina wasn't sure of the next step. Or if he had one in mind. She wanted to stay and meet Luke, but the thought of four people as awkward as strangers in a crowded elevator nixed that idea. But close quarters in Brady's little convertible, when he looked and smelled so appealing, and her defenses were weak from the same environment less than twenty-four hours before? Another idea she should nix. But she had to do or say something to counteract the weird vibes.

"Would you like something to drink . . . coffee . . ." she opened the refrigerator, "diet drink, water . . . not much else there."

"No, thanks. I can't stay long, but I thought, maybe, we could talk," he said, glancing up the stairs.

Talk as in without Aretha overhearing. Okay. You're on.

"Sure. I need to take Manny out for his post-breakfast stroll. I'll leave a note for Aretha, and then we can go." Nina scribbled a smirk-inducing note, "Manny and I out with Brady. Please don't hate me for dognapping Luke's excuse for a walk. Back soon," and they headed out.

"There's a dog park about a block down on the right. He likes hanging out there," said Nina. Manny trotted ahead on the sidewalk, ears flapping. "Funny you should stop by today. Usually I have dinner with my parents on Sundays. If I hadn't overslept, I would have really been surprised to find flowers on my doorstep."

"More surprised than you were to find me?"

"No, I suppose not. I don't remember you ever making unannounced visits . . ." Nina reined Manny in closer, and moved off the sidewalk when she saw a tricycle headed their way.

"Sadly, I don't think I did." He slowed his stride to match Nina's as Manny intermittently sniffed bushes and gardens along the way.

"You said you wanted to talk. About . . . ?"

"I heard you're going after that political corruption story. Impressive," he said, and he actually sounded as if he meant it. "You seemed out of your element at that society benefit."

Nina blinked a few times. She saw Brady, but her mother's voice just popped out of his mouth. "And that means, what exactly?"

"I meant that as a compliment. I think you have more to offer as a journalist than writing about the Houston movers and shakers and their charity galas. Daisy told Janie you drew the short straw on covering it because she wasn't there."

Apparently, he was researching last night as well, but his information source had to have been Janie, not Google. They reached the park, and Nina hooked Manny's leash to one of the stakes and let him roll and flop in the grass. She and Brady sat on a wrought iron bench facing a fountain that, depending on the breed, served as a watering hole, a swimming pool, or both.

"Was this what you wanted to discuss? My choice of assignments?" Nina brushed off her black sweater, which had become a haven for pollen, falling pine needles, and whatever other smut was in the air. Smoke drifted from across a wooden fence that bordered the park, and the unmistakable scent of barbeque must have reached her and Manny at the same time. They both turned toward the aroma, though Nina hoped she didn't sniff quite as noticeably as her dog did.

Brady crossed his leg over, resting the ankle of one leg on the knee of the other. He tugged a bit at the hem of his jeans. "I called Janie this morning, and I suggested she postpone the party she's been planning to celebrate the New York move."

"Postpone it until when?"

"Until I decide if that's really what I want to do."

17

Nina unhooked Manny's leash, freshened his water bowl, and read the note Aretha had left in place of hers. "Mr. B and I going out to eat . . ."

She and Brady hadn't been gone that long, so Luke must have arrived right after they left. Nina wished she could text Aretha to relate yet another bizarre Brady-encounter. He'd left as soon as they returned, walked straight to his car, and said he'd be in touch. All Nina could think was, "Why?" Calling off Janie's party? The man must have a death wish. Or at least no fear of finding himself a mangled mess in an ER. But the man who recently growled at her after she saturated his expensive sweater with coffee was now purring?

If today and yesterday were math problems, the addition was definitely off. She wasn't sure what was missing from the equation, but her gut suspected an unknown variable. Her gut also rumbled its need for food, but nothing in the refrigerator looked as appealing as the barbecue over the park fence had smelled. She found the menu for Happy All Cafe and decided a delivery order of Beef with Orange Peel and Chili Peppers would silence her stomach.

While she waited, Nina opened her laptop to check the news. Brady's obvious admiration for her story flattered her, but his comments about her being at the benefit were flashbacks to his tendency toward elitism in journalism. For Brady, what you wrote reflected who you were and where you were on the magazine staff food chain. By trashing the fund-raiser, he unwittingly threw down the gauntlet. Proving Brady wrong might be worth investing herself in a feature story that didn't have the power to expose the corruption of local governments. After she finished her news story, she could elevate a feel-good feature into something that garnered attention.

She jotted some notes to check on Monday, then looked up The AIDS Memorial Quilt site. Aretha and her overnight infatuation arrived at the same time as her food. Manny almost collapsed from his barking frenzy after the delivery man and another strange male invaded his territory. Nina could hardly hear Aretha introduce this tall, ebony version of Patrick Stewart. He exuded charm, but not the kind that made Nina feel like she'd just been dipped in a vat of oil. He stood in the kitchen as if he'd been there all his life and watched Manny with calm amusement.

After several minutes of Manny's performance for Luke, which included a snarling rendition, Aretha grabbed his leash. "Come on, mister, we're going to take this Oscar-winning mad dog routine to the street," she said. He stopped barking, but locked his eyes on Luke while she attached the leash to his harness. Aretha handed Luke a dog biscuit, "Here, put this in your pocket. And if you value that strong hand of yours, don't put it anywhere near his mouth for now."

By the time they returned, Luke was Manny's new best friend, one worthy of lap jumping and face licking.

"The man must be a dog whisperer. I've never seen Manny fall so fast for someone," Aretha remarked.

Nina smiled. Luke seemed to be an Aretha whisperer as well.

⚬⚬⚬

"If I can know I don't like somebody in less than two days, why is it impossible to know the reverse of that?" After dinner, Aretha stretched out on the sofa with her sketch book propped on her bent legs, moving her pencil back and forth between her palms as if she was rolling dough. "You think I'm crazy, don't you?"

"Yes, but I've always thought that." Nina looked up from her laptop where she sat at the kitchen table, half-hidden by the bucket of tulips. She bookmarked her page, then moved the flowers over so she could see Aretha. "You mean the Luke thing? For starters, you certainly weren't crazy about the beautiful part. That he is. If you tell me the two of you are running off to Vegas tomorrow, then you're definitely certifiable."

The pencil stopped. "Not tomorrow, of course not." It started again. "But I do like him. As in, if he doesn't call me this week, I'll be in mourning. And devastated. And maybe therapy." She started sketching again.

"Now that, my friend, is crazy. You met him less than two days ago. Have you even run a Google search on the man? Checked out one of those sexual predator sites? Due diligence. Do it."

Her pencil danced from one side of the pad to the other as she spoke. "Is that distrust because that journalistic blood of yours flows through the river of suspicion? If I told you he was an attorney or a doctor, you'd feel better?"

"Maybe, but being a doctor or lawyer doesn't save people from being skanky. His career choice isn't the issue."

"True, but would you even be the slightest bit interested in Brady if he worked as a mechanic or a plumber?"

Nina laughed. "Sister, I'd be more interested because I'm certain his income would be much better in those two careers. Why? Do you think I'm a job-snob?"

She shrugged. "Nah. You'd be more interested in Dr. Vet if you were, regardless of his sibling."

Nina pushed the flowers to the other end of the table. "Being a veterinarian doesn't exempt him from anything, and it's not his sibling who's an issue. Except that it's one more reason to distrust him. I know his history, and that's the reason I'm not interested."

Aretha looked up at Nina. "Kind of a shame, really. He is."

Nina lowered her Coke to the table. "He's what?"

"Attracted to you. I saw it at the benefit. His body language, the way his eyes lingered on your face—"

"Stop. Not only would he be wasting his time, just the thought of that makes me wish I could give my brain a bath," Nina said.

"Okay, we'll go with that for now."

Nina considered raising another objection, but she didn't want another Greg conversation. And she knew Aretha had a way of drawing things out of her. Admitting she might have had just the flicker of a feeling for him wasn't news she wanted Aretha to use as evidence.

Manny pattered back and forth from the sofa to the table motored by a whine that grew louder with each trip.

Aretha, still focused on the pad, said, "He's hungry."

Nina had already headed for the dog food. "I'm on it." She spooned the canned duck formula into his bowl, and Manny tap-danced below her while she mashed it up for him. "Look," she said as she set his bowl on his doggy placemat, "I'm not telling you it's ridiculous to want to spend more time with

Luke. I just don't want to see your picture on the television one night as a crime statistic." She washed her hands and sat down at the laptop again. "What does he do? And what are you so busy sketching over there?"

"He's a detective." She grinned as she turned the sketchpad to face Nina. The name *Luke*, styled in a fanciful calligraphy, stretched from one end of the page to another.

Nina groaned. "Great. He brings out your junior high tween-self."

18

Omitting the praise from Brady about her nose for news and his benefit bashing, Nina pitched the feature idea to Aretha. "I think writing human interest stories about the families in these support groups could earn me some promotion points, don't you?"

"That's your angle? Promotion points? Do you want to write these stories?" Aretha had retired her sketchpad for the night and folded towels fresh out of the dryer. The scent of Mountain Spring fabric softener competed with the lemon oil Nina was using to polish the table.

"Can't this be a case of the end justifies the means? I'm not all that excited about chummying up to these families, but if the end result is a ticket to New York, I could stand it."

"And you're not afraid that the stories will reflect your wafer-thin veneer of compassion? And you're comfortable using these people?"

Nina refolded the dust cloth and wiped the kitchen table again. "You're making me feel like a con artist. If their message gets out, will they care? Isn't that the Christian thing to do . . . you know . . . sacrifice for the greater good or glory or something like that?"

Aretha shook her head as if Nina had just said she'd eaten a bowl of jellybeans for breakfast. "A little advice. Don't go trying to be something you're not. Or, worse, be condescending because they operate on a level of faith."

"They'll be happy to have a forum to promote their cause. And I'll be happy to have a cause to promote myself. It's a win-win," Nina said.

Aretha moved a stack of dish towels into the kitchen drawer. "You better check your attitude at the door, that's all I'm saying."

Nina stayed awake long after Aretha had gone to bed. After Saturday night's identity confusion, Nina wasn't sure what the temperature of her boss's mood would be. She wanted to be ready for Elise in the morning, and that meant doing her homework that night.

What she discovered about The AIDS Memorial Quilt was more than she could digest in one late night-early morning research session. Knowing the weight (54 tons) and number of panels on the quilt (over 47,000) were almost trivial compared to its impact since 1985 when it was conceived. In 1987, a small group gathered in San Francisco to not only create a memorial for people who died of AIDS, but for that memorial to help everyone else understand the impact of the disease. A year later, the quilt had more than eight thousand panels. Eight years later, the quilt covered the entire National Mall in Washington, D.C. That would be the last display of the entire quilt because it became too heavy and too unwieldy to continue. Visitors to the quilt numbered more than eighteen million.

By 2008, the Memorial Quilt bore the names of more than ninety-one thousand men, women, and children who had died from AIDS. Since the inception of the Memorial Quilt, the tours raised more than four million dollars to heighten awareness of AIDS. The names on the quilt included babies who had died of AIDS from being breast-fed by their infected mothers, people who died from blood transfusions . . . the stories were endless.

Nina fell asleep scrolling through panel after panel after panel after panel.

———

Driving to work the next morning, Nina pulled through the first Starbucks on her route, ordered an extra shot in her latte, and hoped she wouldn't nod off at a red light. She'd stayed up until almost three o'clock researching the We Care benefit and The AIDS Memorial Quilt, determined to show Aretha that the only story waiting to be found was a "feel good" feature that showcased the sewing talents of a team of little old lady quilters and the charitable contributions of the Houston wealthy.

The benefit had the potential to garner that promotion she wanted. Nina figured that if she could track down some families, she could expand one story into almost as many as Elise would give her space to feature. How tough would it be to pretend to be emotionally invested in their lives for a week or so?

All she needed was a buy-in from Elise, and Nina knew she could summon enough enthusiasm for the story just thinking about the pay-off. By the time she had parked her car, Nina knew the angle she'd pitch to Elise. And by the time she walked through the front door of *Trends*, Nina had practiced it enough that she felt confident she'd impress her boss.

"Good morning, Michelle." Nina tossed her empty coffee cup away and headed for her desk.

"Not so fast. The delivery service dropped this off for you," said the receptionist and handed Nina a box large enough for a winter coat. "It's kind of heavy. You might want to just open it here. Unless it's something private . . ."

"Michelle, for anything private to be this heavy, it would take half the shelves in Victoria's Secret." Nina set her purse on the counter. "There's no return address. You sure it's not going to explode?"

"I didn't hear any ticking, plus it came through the service we use all the time." Michelle handed her a pair of scissors. "I mean, anything's possible, but it just doesn't strike me as a bomb-like package. Especially because," she turned the box around where a piece of the brown paper had been torn, "I recognize this paisley wrapping paper." She spoke barely above a whisper, "It's cotton and silk. Ex-pen-sive."

Nina, joining the whisper conspiracy, said, "And how do you know it's so ex-pen-sive?"

"Because Elise asked me to order gift wrap from this company online, and I saw it there. It's not the pattern she used, though."

"Interesting . . ." said Nina as she cut the brown paper away and revealed the teal and pink paisley patterns splashed against the white silk paper like peacocks. She and Michelle examined both sides of the box, but they didn't see a card. She carefully cut the wrapping paper away, and opened the box underneath. Taped to the tissue paper, its shades matching the paisley patterns wrapping, was a square white envelope.

Nina opened it, saw the initials at the top of the card, and quickly scanned the note. "You've got to be kidding."

"What? What does it say? Who's it from?"

She slipped it back into the envelope, which she knew would only increase Michelle's curiosity, but she didn't want the office involved.

If Nina hadn't opened the tissue paper when she did, Michelle was so impatient, that she might have done it for her.

Underneath the layers of tissue was the quilt she meant to bid on at the We Care benefit. The one she wanted to give Aretha for her birthday.

The monogram at the top of the note was the letter H between a G and an L. The note read, "Nina, I hope your friend cherishes this quilt. I know, due to circumstances that night, you were unable to place your bid. It would have been a shame for your friend to miss your thoughtfulness. Regards, Greg."

"Don't you want to take it out?" Michelle ran her hand over the fabric.

"I know what it looks like. Can you hold on to the wrapping paper? I'm going to take this to my car." Whether she ultimately intended to keep the quilt or not, the more people who saw it and heard about the special delivery, the more complicated the story would become.

"But . . . but . . . I'd love to see it." Michelle watched as Nina wiggled the top of the box back, looking from Nina back to the quilt as if she'd just been shown dessert and told she had to go to bed without it. "This is perplexing, Nina. Why are you in such a hurry to whisk this away? Are you okay?"

Nina heard Michelle's tone shift into mother-mode. "I'm fine. Just fine. I just don't want to make a production out of this." Seeing the receptionist slink behind her desk and quietly roll the wrapping paper, she felt guilty for her abrasiveness. "I didn't mean to sound so rude. I'll explain, but just not now."

"No, really. You don't owe me an explanation. It's not my business, and I shouldn't have intruded." She flashed Nina her receptionist smile, the one that came with the job. "I'll put this," she said and waved the roll of wrapping paper like a baton, "on your desk as soon as I'm finished."

"Thanks, Michelle. Really." She hesitated. "I'm sorry. It's not your fault." *If Greg Hernandez would just stay out of my life, I wouldn't have reasons to be angry.*

19

Greg set the kitchen timer as he did every morning and every evening to remind himself, and now Paloma, to give his daughter her medicine. One of the biggest threats to HIV-positive children was becoming resistant to the drug therapy, and one of the ways to become resistant was not following a schedule for the doses. Jazarah's meds needed to be administered at the same time every day, and it was crucial that she not miss a dose.

He also set his and Paloma's cell phone alarms as backup, or in case, for any reason, they might not be home at the dosage time. Lily had joked that Greg would make a deal with the Emergency Broadcasting System if necessary. When the routine started, it was Lily who scheduled the times so that, years later, when their daughter started school, she'd take her meds before and after the school day. Everything involved with caring for Jazarah, what to do with the laundry if she should cut herself, preparing a portable first aid kit, had been orchestrated by Lily. And now that he was responsible without her, Greg said a prayer of gratitude every day for what his wife did to insure their daughter would have everything she needed.

"Daddy, tiss me, tiss me!" Jazarah bounced up and down on her toes, her arms outstretched. Greg picked her up and twirled her around, both of them making sputtering airplane engine noises. At close range, he detected apple juice fueled his daughter's plane, and some of it was now spotting his lab coat.

"Big smacky kiss for Dad," he said, and she obliged by planting her cupid lips on his as he brought her in for a floor landing.

And, as he did every morning, he didn't leave without the pat down to make sure he had his cell phone in one lab coat pocket, his wallet in one pants pocket, keys in the other, and his worn copy of *My Utmost for His Highest,* a devotional book by Oswald Chambers that belonged to his father. Some days Greg didn't have time to read; in fact, many days it wasn't until he arrived home in the evening that he did. He just liked carrying it with him. Knowing it was there seemed to ground him.

After making sure for the fifth time that Paloma had the name and phone number of the clinic where he'd be that day, he left. He had taped a note to his steering wheel to remind himself to call Elise on the way. His first call went right to her voicemail, but she called back before he'd even finished leaving her a message.

"Just hanging up with Peyton when you beeped in. You're starting early today. Where to?"

"Outside of Houston. A clinic in Cypress. First time there, so I wanted to give myself some extra time."

"Smart move. Have some good books on your iPod? Between the distance and the traffic, you might get in one or two today. People tell you Cypress is outside of Houston, but it's going to feel like you hit the outskirts of Austin. So don't panic, unless you find yourself actually in Austin . . ."

"Guess I should have packed two lunches. I'll call Paloma and warn her not to hold supper, bath, or bedtime."

"Do you need me to do that for you?"

"No. Wait. Okay I got it. I got it." Greg said as if speaking to someone who doubted his sincerity.

"Excuse me?"

"Sorry, the GPS chick thought I wasn't changing lanes. Anyway, I don't need you to call the nanny, but I do have a favor to ask," Greg said as he focused on the exit signs that were like huge shiny green tabs on a wide concrete tablet.

"I'm almost to my office. Want me to call you back?"

"I'll talk fast because I need you to know this before you get there. And try not to ask too many questions. I'll explain when I have more time." He told her about the quilt delivery to Nina, but he didn't want Elise to mention it unless Nina did.

"And why did you feel compelled to purchase this and send it to her?"

Elise's voice put its mom-clothes on, but Greg understood that she didn't know about Nina losing out on the bidding process, which he then explained. "If she does bring up my name, which is highly unlikely after Saturday night, please don't say anything about Jazarah or Lily."

"Strange request. You don't want her to know you're a single father of an HIV-positive child from Ethiopia and your wife died in a car accident caused by a drunk driver? Any particular one or all of those?"

Listening to his sister roll out his life that way, it sounded like a script from a sappy daytime drama. *If only it had been. I could have rewritten the script.* "I'm not trying to keep any of that a secret. Don't be dishonest if she asks questions. Which I know you wouldn't be, which is precisely why I wanted to talk to you. I just have to work some things out, and I don't want her to make decisions based on pity."

"All of this from a misunderstanding at the benefit?"

"Unfortunately, no. It goes back a long way. But that's something I'll have to tell you later."

"How much later? Never mind. I just pulled into the garage. I'll text you as the day goes on. And Greg . . . I know you wouldn't ask all this if you didn't have good reason. I trust you."

"Thanks, Elise," he said, relieved that she would back him and that he spotted the exit for 290.

Now if he could just convince Nina to trust him.

⚬⚬⚬⚬

When Nina walked back into the office after moving the quilt to her car, Michelle was on the phone. She looked up when Nina passed, nodded, but her smile looked like one she'd worn the night before and forgot to take off. If she'd been Michelle, she would have picked up the phone and pretended to be on a call just to avoid a conversation. It occurred to Nina that perhaps the reason she didn't trust other people or their feelings was her assumption they might be acting out of the same motives she would. And since, most of the time, her feelings were such a cosmic mess, she barely trusted them herself.

Nina might have pondered that longer if not for two distractions. An email from Elise asking to see her, and a message from Greg Hernandez. Was her morning starting with sibling rivalry or was this a cooperative attack? She needed a strategy and decided her best course of action was to see Elise first. If she spoke to Greg first, and the conversation crashed and burned, which she expected, then Greg might have time to relay that to his sister before Nina saw her. Then again, she had to ask herself if they would actually behave this way or was she, once again, presuming how they would act based on what she would do?

She had fifteen minutes before her appointment with Elise, so she opened her iPad and typed her pitch about the AIDS Quilt feature and facts about it that she thought would heighten its appeal. Nina checked the archives of *Trends* for any features similar to the one she wanted to write. With the exception of an article over seven years ago about an eighty-panel display at Rice University, there was nothing that would make the feature a recycle. She'd need a photographer, but Elise would have to make the call on that. No telling where Brady might be, especially in the next few weeks. He didn't seem to know where he'd be in the next few days.

Nina checked the time, examined the front of her black and white color-blocked dress for coffee spots, and applied sheer gloss to her lips. She looked over at Daisy's desk, and her stomach still hit her emotional bottom floor with an elevator-like thud. After hearing Brady talk about her being in New York with Janie, Nina suspected that thud might be permanent.

Before she saw Elise, she needed to find Shannon. She'd emailed the intern a list of questions, and she wanted to discuss the possibility of Shannon joining her on some of the interviews and possibly going to some of the quilter's meetings on her own. Nina walked around the office, but Shannon wasn't at her desk. She left a "please see me" sticky note on the intern's computer monitor, and entered a reminder in her iPad calendar to ask Shannon for her cell number.

Nina walked to the elevators, pressed the button, and almost went into cardiac arrest when someone suddenly came up behind her, squeezed her shoulders, and said, "Where do you think you're going?"

One yelp later, she whipped around to find Brady standing behind her.

"If you weren't so tall, and if I didn't value my iPad so much, I'd whack you on the head so hard, you'd be looking up at me when I was finished."

Brady laughed. "I wanted to surprise you. Obviously, I succeeded."

"That was not surprise you heard. That was fright. What are you now, twelve? Don't you know better than to sneak up on someone?" She pressed the button again and hoped he thought the warmth that she was sure flushed her skin signaled irritation not infatuation.

"I wasn't stalking you," he said and grinned.

The grin that, if Nina had been butter, would've melted her onto the floor. She stared at the doors to avoid eye contact.

"I just walked in, needed to go upstairs, and saw you waiting . . . it seemed amusing when I thought of it."

"Whatever. I think an alien child is overtaking your body." The elevator doors yawned opened, and Nina stepped to the side to let Brady on first. No more blindsiding. "Why are you here anyway?"

"New dress? It fits you well."

Nina was relieved his eyes weren't hands. "Not new, and thank you. But you didn't answer my question about your reason for coming in today."

The door opened on Elise's floor and Brady exited with her. He pointed in the direction opposite from where she was going. "Human Resources. I have an appointment to discuss some matters there."

She didn't have time to ask for details, but she was beginning to realize the less she knew, the better. Brady seemed like a human boomerang lately. Every time she thought he'd be away for good, he returned.

"Good luck. I'm off to see the Dragon Lady."

She'd taken about four steps when Brady said, "Nina, wait."

Nina tapped her watch. "Can't be late. What's up and hurry?"

"How about dinner tonight?"

She thought about wanting to return that quilt to Greg. Or at least pay him for it. Nina considered the possibility of Brady being hungry for more than food, and the fact that she might welcome being on the menu. She mentally duct-taped the voice of impulsiveness and answered, "I don't think tonight will work."

Disappointment replaced the invitation in his eyes. "No problem. I'll call later. You can tell me about your visit," he said, pointed in the direction of Elise's office, and walked down the hall.

Why would he think I'd be sharing information about an appointment with Elise? Brady acted as if his relationship with Janie was a wrinkle in time, and he'd simply stepped over it and back to her.

Those strange variables in the math equation that was Brady continued to increase.

20

Before Nina had an opportunity to dazzle Elise with her feature pitch, Elise announced that she officially released her from the bondage of human-interest stories.

"Daisy will be returning next week, and she can write the benefit follow-up." Elise scribbled something in her desk planner, and added, "When I talked to her this morning, she mentioned that it's the twenty-fifth anniversary of The AIDS Memorial Quilt, which would make a great sidebar story." She leaned back in her chair, tapped her pen against her hand, and stared out the window. "Probably a story all its own."

Anxiety fluttered over Nina like a sheet, and if she didn't move quickly, it would smother the very reason she wanted to see Elise. She clenched her iPad to avoid wringing the sweat out of her hands. She wanted to know why Daisy gave up New York or gave up on it, but that didn't matter now. Nina sensed Elise's interest in this story and, if it was important to her, then it was important to Nina. "I have a better one," she blurted.

The pen stopped tapping, and Elise turned her chair to face Nina. "A better what?"

She flipped open her iPad. Seeing her notes settled her and sent the anxiety drifting to the floor. "A better idea for the benefit and AIDS Memorial Quilt. A feature series."

Elise leaned forward. "I thought you liked the hard-hitting, down-and-dirty news stories. This one could easily go to Daisy. I'm curious as to why you want it."

Nina knew the buy-in had to happen here, and it certainly couldn't be based on the means to the end pitch she gave Aretha. She had to convince Elise she had a stake in the story.

"Not everyone in Houston could attend the benefit, but we could bring the benefit to them. The story isn't the gala or even the Memorial Quilt itself because it's been around for a quarter of a century. The people are the story. The people behind all those quilts hanging on the walls that night. Every one of those quilts is a story, just like every panel of the Memorial Quilt represents someone. When we give AIDS a face, or in this case, *faces,* then contributing to or participating in the benefit isn't just about the quilts people can buy there. It's about the power of support and community giving people a way to work through their grief to create something of beauty that can honor those they love." Nina stopped because, though Elise nodded as she spoke and seemed focused, there would be no point in explaining more if she didn't approve.

"That's quite a passionate pitch. So, how would you make that happen?"

"My idea is to attend the support group meetings, follow a quilt from its inception to the final stitch. A different person in the group would be highlighted in each feature, with their permission, of course. The last feature would highlight The AIDS Memorial Quilt. We could go to D.C., and maybe some of the quilters could make the trip as well. In fact, with each story we could include the directions for making a panel and invite our readers to participate. They could form their own groups or just send the panels to us, and we could deliver them to Washington."

Elise walked over to the window of her office.

Nina waited. The quiet clanged in her head, but she knew if she didn't outwait Elise, she'd start babbling. She didn't want to beg for the story. Though she would if it came to that. She occupied herself counting the number of roses in the vase on Elise's desk, the number of pictures on the shelf to the right of her desk, and she was about to start counting the books when Elise broke the silence.

Still standing with her back to Nina, looking out the window, she said, "And you're sure you can do this?"

Inside herself, Nina jumped up and clapped. The outside Nina, firmly and clearly responded, "Yes, Elise. I can do this."

"Okay, then," said Elise as she returned to her desk. "Let's talk about the publication schedule, and we'll take it from there."

Almost two hours later, Nina didn't see any signs of Brady when she left Elise's office. She had a text message from Shannon asking if they could meet in the morning, and one from Aretha that she was meeting Luke for dinner. Three consecutive days? Did he not have enough detective work to keep himself busy? Maybe she should have accepted that invitation from Brady because it was about to turn into a drive-through fast food or pizza delivery night. She scrolled through her messages and saw a few numbers she didn't recognize that she'd have to check against her contact list that could be callbacks for her political story.

She opened her iPad and glanced at the pitch she had prepared for Elise. With the exception of the first sentence, nothing she said to Elise came from the original pitch she'd written. Looking at those words now, they seemed hollow, commercial. How did she manage to summon such passion for this feature? Wherever it came from, it rang true enough to Elise. And that was enough for Nina.

———✺———

It wasn't until Nina opened her car door that afternoon and saw the large box on her back seat that she remembered the day had started with the quilt delivery from Greg Hernandez.

Her original knee-jerk reaction plan—to find out where Greg lived, then march to his door with all the righteous indignation she could gather and her checkbook, demand that he either take it back or take a check in payment—required revisiting. Telling the brother of your editor that you refused to keep the very item you used as the centerpiece of your pitch was likely a prelude to her assigning you obituaries and weddings.

Still, she didn't feel comfortable giving Aretha a gift that she didn't buy, and it would be dishonest of her to not tell her it came from Greg. So, she needed to figure out a way to contact him without involving Elise because that would take uncomfortable to an entirely new level. She could explain why she wanted to reimburse him, and if he wouldn't tell her what he paid for it, there might be a way for her to contact the benefit organizers. *Really, Nina, what kind of journalist are you if you can't get someone's address or find out what that quilt sold for?*

Her rumbling stomach interrupted her. She'd been occupied with scenarios in her head and neglected the ones involving food. At the traffic light, she called Aretha thinking they might not mind if she joined them. Brazen, but how intimate does dinner have to be when they'd just started dating? When Aretha answered, she told Nina they wouldn't have minded at all except they were already on their way to Kemah.

"You're driving almost an hour across Houston to Galveston Bay for dinner?"

"It's not that far." She stopped to tell Luke who she was talking to. "We felt like eating seafood, and the weather's so nice, we thought when we got to Kemah, we'd spend some time on the Boardwalk."

"Okay, then. I'll go to Plan B."

"Sorry. If you get desperate, there's still a pizza in the freezer." *I'm becoming Plan B.* Nina heard the distraction in her voice. She imagined Aretha talking to her while she pointed out places to Luke along the way or that shrug and partial eye-roll while she mouthed, "Sorry . . . won't be long" to him. "That would be Plan W. I'll figure something out. See you later."

A few blocks away from home, she pulled over for gas, and considered calling Brady. But he told her when they were both outside Elise's office that he'd call her. Making the first move toward anything resembling a date could send the wrong message to Brady. A small voice within her tapped on the shoulder of her conscience and whispered, "But what if it's the right message?" She hushed it as she settled in her seat and closed the car door. "Guess we'll both have to live with no message," she said to the steering wheel and started the drive home.

At least she knew one male who'd be excited to see her. Nina just wished he didn't have four legs and a cold nose.

After gaining no satisfaction from a round of sniffing to determine if the large box Nina set on the coffee table was edible and paw slapping it to elicit a squeak, Manny ignored it and returned to his rawhide bone.

"Well, since Aretha abandoned us both, at least I can look at this without having to sneak around, right?" Manny didn't even bother to stop chewing. "You're going to have to be better company than that if we're going to be spending more time alone, mister."

She opened the box, carefully lifted the quilt, and spread it out on the sofa. Removed from the other quilts on display that night, its explosion of color and sophisticated, bold design were more evident. And made it all the more perfect a gift for her friend. On one corner, an attached, hand-stamped card read, on one side: Threads of HOPE, stitched by people of FAITH, for those we LOVE. On the other was a thank-you for purchasing the quilt and a telephone number. A label sewn on another corner simply had the words: Threads of Hope, Jeremiah 29:11.

Nina entered the number in her phone and set a reminder to herself to call it in the morning. If she asked the cost of making one like it, she'd have an idea of what to offer Greg. And then, pulling a Brady, she could show up unannounced and drop it off. If she called him, he'd probably tell her he didn't want the money.

She placed the quilt back in the box then shoved it under her bed where Aretha would be least likely to look. Or vacuum.

By nine o'clock, Brady hadn't called, texted, or attempted any other form of communication. Nina surprised herself by not being surprised. Not following through was behavior more typical of the Brady she knew.

Now that Elise had assigned her the feature, Nina dragged out her laptop to continue researching. Manny, seeing her stretched out on the sofa, jumped up and wiggled next to her, resting his head on her knee. She started with the history of The AIDS Memorial Quilt, which went back to 1985, when the idea of the quilt sprang from the way placards of those who died with AIDS were placed against the wall of the San Francisco Federal Building. The first quilt, created in June of

1987, was displayed on the National Mall in October of the same year.

Nina thought about that first small group that met in a San Francisco storefront, afraid the names of those they loved would be lost forever, and so they created a quilt as a way to document their lives. Twenty-five years later, groups like the ones whose quilts were auctioned at the benefit, met to carry on that mission, to memorialize those who died of AIDS. Except that, and sadly, over the years, the names of women and children were added. From 1985 until the year 2000, the number of AIDS-related deaths in a year increased by 429 percent. Little wonder, with those statistics, why the quilt weighed fifty-four tons today.

Hours later, Nina still hadn't arrived at the end of her research, and Aretha still hadn't arrived home.

21

Greg checked his cell phone again. Nothing from Elise. By late afternoon, when Greg still hadn't received any messages or phone calls, he wondered if the quilt had even been delivered.

He contacted the delivery service and was told the package had been signed for early that morning. Two patients later, he sent Elise a text. Maybe Nina wasn't at work, so there wasn't any reason for Elise to contact him. Four patients later, she sent a text in response: "Nina here. No mention. Call me on your way home."

No mention of the quilt? The Saturday night episode? Both? Maybe he attached more importance to both than did Nina. Bypassing the drama was a relief, but bypassing any mention of having received the quilt seemed, well, like bad manners. And he'd already dealt with his quota of the discourteous by the time the clinic closed. Like the couple whose Lab used the waiting room as his bathroom, then expected the desk staff to do potty patrol. And the little boy about his daughter's age who entertained himself rearranging the food and supplies merchandise on display while his father lifted his head from his e-reader every few minutes and said, "Stop that." He closed his car door, leaned his head against the steering wheel, and said a prayer of gratitude for his family. Compared to that gift from God, what did his receiving or not receiving a thank-you note matter?

Seeing the gridlock on Highway 290, Greg contemplated abandoning his car and walking the forty or so miles home. He should have brought along *Anna Karenina*, the 976-page novel Lily always wanted him to read. With this traffic, he'd stand a good chance of getting halfway through it. He still needed to call Elise, but he called home first. He talked to Paloma and affirmed that he wouldn't make it there until after Jazarah's bedtime. He could barely hear her for his daughter's chanting in the background. "Talk to Daddy. Talk to Daddy." Paloma excused herself, and Greg heard her calm, soft voice, "We must wait and be kind, and not speak when someone else is speaking."

When she returned, Greg expressed his appreciation for her making sure Jazarah wouldn't grow up to be what Elise labeled an "S.B.K.," spoiled brat kid.

"You are welcome. It is my opinion that the two of you together in public will attract attention even if both of you say nothing. Her behavior will be scrutinized more so than other children's. This, I know."

And that was another reason she made the perfect nanny for his daughter. Like Jazarah, she, too, was adopted from Africa, an HIV-positive preteen, into a blue-eyed, blonde-haired, and freckle-skinned family. The attention was sometimes cruel, but Paloma learned grace and, as she said, "to stand on God's promises."

"One message before you speak to your sweet daughter. A lady, Amelia, called to say she and her husband will be in Houston next month, and they would like to visit. Now, here is Jazarah."

Amelia and Dale were traveling here? Thinking of them brightened his otherwise gray day. A train of questions rumbled through his head, but his daughter's lyrical chatter ran them off the track. Greg inserted a few "Really?" and "That's great" responses as she recalled what sounded like her itinerary for the day. Then, in the middle of a discussion of flowers and peanut butter, she announced, "Bye, Daddy!" and the conversation ended. He smiled imagining that Paloma setting the table for dinner diverted her attention.

His conversation with his sister didn't require many more responses than those he'd just used with his daughter. On her way home herself, Elise said she only had time to hit the highlights. Essentially, Nina pitched a feature series around the AIDS quilt and the local benefit that excited Elise. Their time together was focused on those details, so his name or Saturday night never came up.

"I have to say, Nina's passion for this project was unexpected. I called her in to tell her she was off the human-interest story hook, but she didn't want to let it go," said Elise.

"Yes, that surprises me, too," Greg said, too late realizing he just played a card his sister didn't know he held. He could picture her narrowed eyes as her brain whirled around what he'd said.

"Why would it surprise you?" The emphasis in her question fell on *you.*

How was he going to extricate himself from this one without revealing his conversation with Nina that night at the benefit before Elise arrived on the scene? He didn't want to tell her Nina complained about having to write a feature story and cooperated only because his dragon lady sister of a boss wanted her to. Something must have changed for her between then and today, and the last thing he wanted to do was something that would, once again, sabotage Nina. But, he couldn't lie to her either. *Good thing traffic's moving three miles a minute or I'd be too distracted to think.*

"When we first started talking, I didn't even know she was on the *Trends* staff. She mentioned how much she enjoyed hard-hitting news stories," he shared with Elise.

But Greg continued to wonder, for most of his journey home, what caused such a radical change of heart in Nina.

When Nina left for work, a fully-dressed Aretha was snoring, curled up on the sofa, the dog wrapped around her bare feet. Nina had finally dragged herself upstairs not long after midnight, so Aretha didn't make it back until after that. She checked Aretha's work schedule that she always left on the refrigerator to make sure she'd be safe not waking her up. She was off, and she didn't have any classes, so Nina skipped making breakfast and eased herself out as quietly as possible.

Michelle hadn't arrived yet, so Nina left the blueberry scone she'd bought for her on her desk. She wrote, "to M, from N, and I'm still sorry."

Shannon was already hovering around Nina's desk. "Do you need some help?" She looked like she wasn't sure what to grab first.

Her coffee in one hand, her oatmeal in the other, her purse, her iPad case, and her messenger bag slung over her shoulders, Nina perpetually had that pack-mule look about her. "Believe it or not, everything balances, so if you take just one item, I might topple over." She looked at Shannon as she placed her breakfast on her desk. "Did you eat? Need to get coffee or anything before we talk?"

"No, I'm good. I ate at home and brought coffee," she pointed to the petite stainless steel Thermos on her desk.

Nina peeled off her bags. "Another good reason to have your cell number. Next time I can call you on the way in." She sat down, stirred her oatmeal, and told Shannon to pull up a chair. "Since you're good to go, let's get started."

For the next half hour, Nina outlined how the intern could help her. "I'm sending you copies of what I've already put together for my story on the political corruption. I need you to fact-check and proofread what I have so far. Then, you'll need to open a file on your laptop, just label it 'Quilts' for now. And here's the information I want you to research." She handed Shannon a list starting with the We Care benefit, the sponsors, the contributors, background on The AIDS Memorial Quilt, local support chapters. Nina stopped there. She recognized the eye-darting, first-rung on the panic ladder look on Shannon's face. "If you have questions, ask me. Seriously. We don't want to have a problem with sources or research that might have been easily solved, okay?"

"Yes. Absolutely." Shannon stood up, and Nina imagined she felt the anxiety fall off like scales. "I'll get right on it."

Nina watched her walk away, but instead of going to her desk, she headed for the door. "Are you leaving?" She couldn't have overwhelmed her already.

"Just long enough to go to Brew Who next door."

"The coffee shop? But didn't you say you brought it from home?"

"Oh, I'm not going for coffee. I left my Bible there. A few of us have a short Bible study one morning every week."

Well, this piece of news went right over my head. A Bible study? Seriously? "How did I miss that? You'd think for a place that reported news—"

Shannon looked like someone next in line to walk over hot coals. "We just started a few weeks ago. I mean, a few of us go to the same church. With the others, it was just word-of-mouth, you know . . . You're welcome to join us. Really. We never meant to exclude anyone . . ."

Nina flashbacked to a middle school moment, sitting cross-legged on the cold hard floor of the hallway on Valentine's Day, pretending to do homework she'd actually finished the night before. While girl groups giggled around her and exchanged hand-drawn cards, glittery red boxes of candy, and white fluffy stuffed bears whose hearts beat outside their bodies, Nina invested herself in the algebraic importance of helping x find y. Because none of the girls looked for Nina.

"Would you like to go with me?"

Shannon's question pulled Nina back to reality, but to one that didn't feel all that different than the one she'd just left. *But this wasn't one day of "will u b mine" messages. This was a lifetime of it. You don't even go to church. Or pray. Why would you want to go to a Bible study?*

"Thanks for the invitation. Maybe another morning, but tell me," Nina ate a spoonful of oatmeal. "Who else is there?"

Shannon started rattling off names, but it wasn't until Nina heard "Michelle, Elise . . ." that she had a coughing spasm from almost swallowing her coffee into her lungs.

———

Nina's fingers hit the telephone number for Threads of Hope, but her brain burbled at jet speed, ready to make a landing right into Aretha's ears. Even as she heard the phone ringing, the words "Bible study" stayed in her head like uninvited guests, the overnight variety.

She heard "Hello," on the other end. Finally, her mouth had something to do. Nina identified herself as a staff writer at *Trends*, forcing the belligerent child in her head to not blurt, "Who recently discovered she was ostracized from the Bible study." She informed the voice that she attended the We Care benefit, where she bid on one of their quilts—

"Which one?"

Nina told her it was the paisley-patterned quilt, which elicited a squeal. *How old are these people? This may be a more painful feature than I thought.*

"That's the one I helped sew. We really appreciate your support—"

This conversation may last longer than an all-day sucker. "I'm sorry what did you say your name was?"

She laughed. "You hadn't asked my name, but it's Crystal. My mother, Kelley, usually takes the calls, but she's out right now. Do you want her to call you back?"

Nina's tolerance groaned. "No, in fact, I think you can help me. I'd like to come to one of your meetings. The magazine would like to run a feature . . . but I can explain that when we see one another. When will you all be getting together again?"

"This Sunday at two o'clock. We meet at the Faith Church Fellowship Hall. Do you need directions? It's that little church—"

"I'm sure I'll be able to find it." *Otherwise, my GPS is worthless.* "Sunday at two, right?"

Crystal confirmed and when Nina hit "off" on her phone, she wondered how she was going to be able to pull this off.

22

It's not that funny." Nina went downstairs to the lobby atrium where she called Aretha after hanging up with Crystal. The more she talked, the more Aretha laughed.

"Do you hear yourself?"

"Yes, and I hear Manny barking. What's your point?" Nina paced in front of a metal sculpture that looked as if someone had thrown car parts in a blender, then dumped them on the ground.

"Manny and I are stretching our legs. You, on the other hand, aren't stretching something enough. Sister, you're making that group sound like terrorists. Afraid they're going to sneak in the office and whomp you with their Bibles?"

"Don't be ridiculous. I don't so much care that they're having a Bible study. Though it does reek of 'look how holy we are.' I couldn't care less if they gathered to study the fax machine instruction book. What bothers me—"

"What bothers you, way down deep, is that no one included you. What bothers me is, why do you care? You don't go to church, you don't read the Bible . . . It would be like my getting offended because I wasn't invited to join the Garden Club. What do I know about gardens? I know things grow in dirt, and some are trees and some are flowers and then there's everything else."

"What does that say about what they think of me . . . that they didn't even think of me? I'm a good person." She located a padded bench next to a fountain wall. Nina considered pulling off her shoes and soaking her feet in the water.

"I'm guessing they think you wouldn't be interested. Being good isn't an admission ticket. And if you did study the Bible, you'd know that's something to be grateful for."

"If I'd known Elise was there, I would have been interested."

"Nina, are you really thinking you could use Bible study to earn points with your editor? I guess people fake it, but I don't see how they do. That's not a risk I'd be willing to take. Eventually, you'd be as obvious as a cat at a dog fight."

"Here's the thing . . ."

"Wait. Let me get Manny. He thinks he's going to tear after Mr. Pete's Lab."

Nina examined her cuticles, not remembering the last time she and Aretha had a mani/pedi day. Maybe this Saturday. *What was taking so long?* She checked her watch. Time for her to get back to the office. She could finish talking to Aretha later. "Aretha, you there?" Nina tried again, louder, "A-re-tha . . ."

When she did hear her friend, her scream shot Nina up from the bench as if it had reached out of the phone and pulled her by the hair. Aretha shouted Manny's name, but Nina didn't hear him. "What's going on? Aretha? Where are you?" The pitch in her voice rose, and the words wrapped inside her so tightly she could barely breathe.

"Nina, Nina." Aretha sounded as if she'd just finished a marathon, but there was no mistaking the hysterical urgency.

Before she even heard the words that a car hit Manny, Nina had kicked off her shoes and sprinted up the stairs to Elise's office. With every step, she repeated, "Be there, be there, be there . . ." until her own breathing was as labored as her friend's. Nina had pushed on the phone speaker and when she started the stairs for Elise's floor, Aretha said, "Mr. Pete's helping. He's breathing, Nina. We'll take him to Dr. Alvarez—"

"No. Wait one minute. Just one minute."

She opened the stairwell door. Elise was standing outside her office on her cell phone. Nina saw what she felt mirrored in Elise's face.

"Nina? What happened?"

"Where's Greg? Please call Greg. Manny. Aretha called and said a car hit Manny." Nina didn't remember Elise's office being so cold. Her cell phone shook in her hands.

"I just hung up with him." Elise pressed call. "I'll call him back right now."

Greg must have answered because Nina watched Elise's lips move, but the words bounced like beads off a broken necklace.

"Is that your friend on the phone?"

Nina looked down at her hand and nodded.

"Hand me your cell phone, so I can tell her what to do." Elise said more words into the phone, then turned to her receptionist. "Would you cancel my lunch appointment? I'll be back as soon as possible." She handed Nina her phone, and closed her fingers around it. "Hold on to this."

"Greg?"

"He's going to meet us at the Animal Emergency Clinic. And I'm driving you there." She looked at Nina's feet. "You probably want to put your shoes back on. We're taking the elevator."

~∞~

Greg, Paloma, and Jazarah were on their way to lunch, singing, "Don't worry about a thing, cause every little thing gonna be all right" along with Bob Marley when Elise called. As soon as Greg heard the sound of his sister's voice on the phone, he pulled into the first parking lot he could find. He sensed it wouldn't be good news.

"Hey, a car hit Nina's dog. She's here at work, and the dog was with Aretha, her friend. I know you're off today, but can you help? She asked me to call you."

"Shh! A few minutes for Daddy, okay?" Greg lowered the volume, and he needed only to exchange one glance with Paloma for her to distract his daughter with her new book, *The Very Hungry Caterpillar*. "I'll call Dr. Cadoree at the emergency clinic. I've done some relief work for him, so they can meet me there. Does Nina know anything about the dog's condition?"

"Doubt it, and if she did, I don't think you'd get too much right now. She's holding her cell phone, so Aretha might be on the line."

"Find out. I need to talk to her as soon as I can. Time is crucial here."

Elise took Nina's phone and relayed information from one to the other. "Dachshund. Almost two. Neighborhood street, not going above 20. Breathing. Trying to move a bit. No blood in ears."

"Tell her to support his back, neck, and limbs and as gently as possible, wrap him in a blanket and head to the clinic. If someone can drive her, that's better, and please drive the speed limit. We don't want to have a dog hit by a car in the car with two humans who are hit by one."

Greg called the emergency clinic to tell them about Manny in case they arrived before he did. He didn't have time to take Jazarah and Paloma home, so they'd have to come with him. He figured Paloma, listening to the conversation, already understood the Elvis Presley Memorial Combo at Chuy's Restaurant wasn't going to happen. "Okay, Princess Jazarah, Daddy has to hurry to take care of somebody's little dog that just got hurt.

So, you and Paloma will have lunch, then pick up Daddy, and we'll all go somewhere for ice cream."

"Um," she looked back and forth between Greg and Paloma. "Choc-lit?"

Greg smiled. "Of course. Whatever flavor you want. Do you want to sing some more?"

She clapped and kicked her feet against the bottom of the car seat. "Yes! Yes!"

When they pulled up to the clinic entrance, Paloma replaced Greg behind the driver's seat. "Here's my credit card. Call me when you finish lunch, and I'll let you know how I'm running on time." He opened the door and leaned in to kiss Jazarah. "Love you. Be good."

When Aretha arrived ten minutes later, Greg was encouraged Manny made it to the hospital. Animals that did, especially small ones, had a good chance of survival. And, if the car that hit him wasn't going fast, possibly a better chance.

23

Alone with Elise, no distractions, with time to discuss her future at the magazine, to solve the mystery of Daisy, Brady, and Janie . . . but, instead, Nina stared out the window and wished the car could move as fast as her heart pounded. The thought of what Manny might look like when they arrived at the emergency clinic scared her almost as much as the thought that she might not make it there in time.

Elise's phone rang, and she quickly muted the Bluetooth and picked it up off her seat. Nina held her breath and waited. As soon as Elise said, "Great," she stopped clutching the arm rest and came up for air. A few one- or two-word replies, then Elise hung up. "That was Greg. He said Aretha just arrived with Manny. When we get there, which should be in a few minutes, he might be in surgery. He said the fact Manny made it to the clinic is a really good sign."

When Elise pulled up in front of the clinic, she handed Nina the box of facial tissues from the back seat. "Take this. Do you want me to stay, because I can?"

"I'll be okay. Aretha's here. Thank you so much for . . . for everything. Calling Greg, driving . . ."

"I'm glad I could help." Elise squeezed her hand. "It's hard when someone you care about is hurt. But, look, Greg is a good doctor. Actually, he's a great doctor, and he'll do everything he can. And I'll pray for all of you."

Nina flashbacked to that morning, and her irritation over Elise and the others at Bible study. And now, she appreciated that Elise prayed.

"That means a lot to me. Thank you." Nina closed the car door, and she walked into the clinic. Aretha was at the counter filling out papers on a clipboard, and as soon as she saw Nina, she dropped the pen and hugged her.

"I'm so sorry, Nina. So sorry. Please forgive me." She sobbed, and Nina held her and patted her back.

"It's not your fault. You adore Manny. I don't blame you." Nina let the tears course down her cheeks for the first time since she heard Aretha's strangled voice telling her what happened. "Where's Mr. Pete? I was so confused when you called. How did Manny get loose? What happened?"

Aretha explained how she attached his leash to his collar because he wasn't wearing his harness. When he saw the Lab, he wiggled himself right out of the collar. "We were already on the sidewalk, so he didn't have far to go to get to the street. So, I'm calling him, and he stops. When I got closer, he took off." She paused, her shoulders slumped. "I didn't see the car coming, but the driver had to know he hit Manny."

"What do you mean, 'had to know'?"

"He stopped for a minute, and he looked at me, so I know he saw me screaming. Then, he took off."

Nina waved her hand in front of Aretha. "Wait. Wait. Wait. He did what?"

"He left. But," she pulled her cell phone out of her pants pocket, "not before Mr. Pete got a picture of his license plate." She scrolled through her pictures. "And he sent it to me, and I sent it to Luke." She showed it to Nina. "And whoever this is, will be getting a visit, I hope real soon, from one not-so-happy detective."

Nina finished filling out the papers and handed the board back to the receptionist.

"Thank you," she looked at the top page, "Miss O'Malley. My name is Tessa. Dr. Hernandez will be out to talk to you as soon as he can. There's a little kitchen area down the hall," she said and pointed to a door on her left, "if you want something to drink, and there's a machine with snacks." She smiled and added, "Some of them are even healthy."

"Do you know how much longer he'll be?"

"No, I don't. But, since you're the only ones here right now, I can go back and check for you."

Nina sat next to Aretha who already had a little pile of crumpled used tissues in her lap. "I'm so glad Elise gave you these. I've been wiping my face and my nose on my T-shirt."

Nina looked at her herringbone cropped jacket and trousers, her black silk shell. "Manny's worth a dry cleaning bill, right? Not like he hasn't cost either one of us that before."

"Miss O'Malley," Tessa held a door open off the waiting room, "Dr. Hernandez said you can see Manny now."

Nina and Aretha walked into the treatment area where Greg and a young man in scrubs hovered over Manny.

Nina felt her heart pinch. "He's okay, right? I mean, he's so still . . ."

"We gave him something to tranquilize him," said Greg as he waved them closer to the table and moved aside so Nina could stand near Manny.

As if testing the temperature for one of Manny's baths, Nina reached out until her hand rested on Manny's soft, warm fur.

Greg told Nina. "You have a few options, though I'm sure you won't take the first one, which is if you'd like to go home, I can call you when the surgery's over and let you know how he did."

"Even if she wanted that to be an option, which I know she doesn't, neither of us has a car here," Aretha said. "Luke offered earlier to pick us up, but he won't be able to get here for at least another hour. Unless you want to call Brady."

Greg saw the answer on Nina's face as soon as Aretha said Brady's name. But before Nina could even respond, Aretha said, "You know, maybe you should call him. After all, he went with you to get Manny, and he did help you name him."

Had the two women been sitting at a dinner table, Greg thought Nina might have stretched out a leg and side-kicked her friend. This was one of those times he attempted to be invisible. The name did sound familiar to him and, if Nina knew him, most likely he worked at the magazine.

"No. He's not someone I need or want to call. I'm fine waiting for Luke." She turned to Greg. "What are the other options?"

"Well, the second one is like the first, except that instead of going home, you could go grab a coffee or something to eat, and we could call you when the surgery's over. But, since there's a car issue, looks like the third one is it. You can just hang out here."

"Then we'll take door number three. In the meantime, I'll call Luke and find out for sure when he can get here. Maybe he can bring us something to eat," Aretha said. "I'll go call him now." She bent down and whispered something to Manny, then kissed him on top of his head.

Nina stroked Manny behind his ears. "Elise told me this was your day off. I'm sure you weren't expecting a call from me . . ."

Greg checked the IV drip in Manny's paw and glanced at Nina out of the corner of his eye. *No, not expecting. But if we hadn't had a rough second start, I wouldn't have minded if you did.* "That would have been a surprise."

"I appreciate your taking time away from your family . . ." she said, adjusting the warming blanket around Manny. "I've never bothered to ask you if you have a family, beyond Elise, I mean. The last time we saw each other, I said some awful things to you."

He nodded. That was a truth they both knew couldn't be diminished.

"I shouldn't have been so mean, and I'm sorry for that. That you're here helping Manny, after the way I've treated you, is humbling. I owe you, I really do."

"Well, you can pay me back by taking me out to dinner one night. Just as a way of clearing things up between us, that's all. And beyond that, you'll just owe the emergency hospital," he said.

Tessa opened the door. "Dr. Cadoree is here."

"Great. That's the orthopedic doctor I called, so we're ready to start."

He saw that cloak of fear and love wrap itself around her when it was her turn to whisper in Manny's ear and kiss the top of his head.

Greg prayed, as she walked out, that he would not disappoint her again.

24

Luke arrived with food from Le Madeleine and the information on the person who hit Manny.

"Driver was a seventeen-year-old who was supposed to be in school, but he decided not going would be much more fun." Luke explained as they sat in the employee break room while he handed out the containers of spinach salads and croissants stuffed with chicken salad. "He was on his way to his girlfriend's house. He thought he might have missed the dog, but when he heard Aretha scream, he knew he didn't. In typical kid fashion, he got scared and left. And go figure. He went to school and checked in late."

"How could he think he missed Manny? He didn't feel the tire hit something?" Nina pushed every word out with commando force.

Luke shook his head. "I don't know. He probably doesn't want to think about it, especially now that we found him. So, now he's dealing with an Animal Cruelty Law and his parents."

"Nina and I want him to crawl on his hands and knees over small rocks for at least five miles, but I don't think Texas has that law. What happens to him?" Aretha stabbed the strawberries in her salad and transferred them to Luke's.

"Could get up to a year in jail and a $4,000 fine. It's his first offense, probably probation, community service, maybe even require him to have some psychological counseling," said Luke.

Nina drummed her fingers on the table and stared into space while she thought. "Can he work in an animal shelter as community service? That's what he needs to do, and he should have to pay for Manny's surgery."

"That, I'm not sure of. Not bad ideas though." Luke answered Nina, but he watched Aretha as she picked through her spinach salad.

"Not so crazy about bacon, either," she said and continued her hunt.

"I'll remember for next time," he said.

She patted his hand and smiled. "I'd rather a next time with strawberries and bacon, than no next time without it."

When they walked back into the reception area, they were greeted by a little girl wearing a bright purple T-shirt decorated with fuchsia butterflies that tucked into a sequined layered purple tutu.

"Hi. Do you like to dance? I have music," she said, her eyes as shiny as her sequins. She pressed the button on the CD player she carried and twirled several times along the row of chairs.

"We're too old to twirl," Aretha told her. "But you're a cutie pie. Why don't you dance, and we'll sit and watch?"

She abandoned twirling in favor of moves that matched the reggae music she listened to and lip-synced the lyrics.

Nina didn't see any other adults except for Tessa who wasn't watching the performance. She leaned over to Aretha and whispered, "The kid looks perfectly content, but I don't think she drove here alone."

Aretha spoke as softly and pointed, "I think her mom's walking in now."

The young woman who opened the door exuded calmness. Nina felt it ripple through the room as soon as she entered. Dressed in knife-pleated jeans and a white peasant blouse, she still managed to appear almost regal. "I found your book," she said and handed the little girl a book with a green-bodied, red-headed caterpillar inching across the cover. But before she let it go, she asked, "Now, what do you say when someone has done something nice for you?"

"We say, tank you, and . . . you say . . ." The child hugged her book and leaned toward the woman.

"You are welcome." Nina smiled as the little girl placed the book and the CD player in the empty chair next to where Aretha sat. "I'm going to Miss Tessa."

Aretha said to the child, "You are beautiful just like your mommy."

The little girl tilted her head and looked wide-eyed at Aretha. "You know my mommy?"

"Well, I don't know her yet. But when she comes back, I can meet her."

She shook her head from side-to-side, her expression, serious. "No, you can't." She opened the book, then looked at Aretha. "She not here."

Aretha attempted a quick recovery and pointed to the young woman speaking to Tessa. "Oh. I thought she was your mommy."

Nina tapped Aretha on the shoulder and murmured, "Maybe you should just stop there. Otherwise—"

"Miss O'Malley, Dr. Hernandez is on his way out to talk to you," Tessa said.

Nina started to put on the shoes she'd kicked off when Greg walked out into the reception area.

"Daddy!" The little girl closed the cover of her book and, with her tutu bouncing, skipped across the room to Greg.

Nina almost dropped the shoe she held as she watched Greg.

"How's my princess?" He lifted her, kissed her forehead, and lowered her to the floor. "Daddy's almost finished, okay?"

Aretha looked at Nina. "Well, who knew?"

Nina would have preferred sprawling out in the back of Luke's SUV for the ride home. Instead, she sat in the second seat and tried to use the middle armrest and cup holder as a pillow. "I'm just too tall to make this happen." She groaned in defeat, closed her eyes, and settled for the headrest.

Thanks to Greg, she'd be able to sleep tonight. Manny's fractured left leg, not his pelvis, was all that required surgery. When he told them, Aretha rubbed Manny's head and said, "No problem. He uses his right hand anyway." But Greg also said there might be nerve damage to the leg, but that would have to be a wait-and-see situation.

Nina didn't want to leave until Manny opened his eyes. When he did, the thread of fear inside her unraveled and fell out of every muscle it seemed to have taken residence in. She knew she'd never see Greg the same way now that his unselfish heart and capable hands saved her pet. She didn't tell him that, of course. Besides, she realized as she relaxed against the headrest, she forgot to ask for a number where she could contact him.

"I'm very confused with this Greg and child situation. Nina, are you awake?" Aretha stretched her arm over the front seat and tapped Nina's knee.

She answered without opening her eyes. "Am now."

"If that lovely woman isn't that child's mother, then who is?"

"You were there, too. Why didn't you ask him?" Nina wished Aretha had asked because she wondered the same thing. If he was in a relationship with that woman, then Nina needed to stop feeling gooey inside when he shook her hand or accidentally brushed past her. Even in her anger the night of the benefit, she realized how incredibly handsome he looked. And his being unaware of his own good fortune in the way his features ended up so well-placed on his face made him even more attractive.

"For the same reason you didn't. How would that have gone? 'Thanks Dr. Hernandez for saving our pet's life. Now, where did this child come from and how is that beautiful woman related to her?' Why wouldn't we think that was her mother? Two white people do not have a black child. Maybe there's an anomaly somewhere, but . . ."

Luke cleared his throat. "May I interrupt? Why do the two of you care so much about Dr. Hernandez's marital status?"

Aretha and Nina exchanged glances.

"That's a good question," said Nina and leaned back against the headrest, closed her eyes, and waited for Aretha to announce they were home.

<hr />

Greg called Elise and updated her on Manny's status as he, Paloma, and Jazarah were on their way to Marble Slab for ice cream. "Nina is meeting me at the hospital before she goes to the office tomorrow morning. While I'm checking her dog, at least she can spend some time with him."

"That was a nice thing you did, making yourself available."

"That's my job. Animal repair and maintenance," he said. "I'm just grateful he's going to make it because if he didn't, she'd be convinced for life that I'm the enemy."

"I don't even pretend to understand why she would think that about you. But, I suppose that's part of what you're going to explain to me later, right? Now, go have ice cream and enjoy yourself."

The next morning, Greg arrived at the hospital to find both Nina and Aretha in the waiting room. Nina looked rested, the puffy-eyed redness of yesterday replaced by clear, deep brown eyes. Her face softened by layers of curls that rested just below her cheekbones. She smiled when she saw him, an unexpected reaction that warmed him like his first cup of coffee on a cold morning.

"Good to see both of you more relaxed today," he said as he shook hands with Nina and Aretha. He was as glad to see Nina as she was to see him. *Not so fast, buddy. Maybe she's just happy because she'll be able to visit her dog now that you're here.* "Manny's a popular guy this morning," Greg said as he moved his stethoscope from his lab pocket to around his neck.

"I didn't remember until we were home that I left my car at the office. Fortunately, Aretha has time to drop me off, but she has to get to class, so I won't be able to stay long," Nina explained.

"No problem. A quick visit is probably best anyway. An ER for the four-legged is just as unpredictable as one for the two-legged," said Greg. "Manny's over here," he walked behind the reception area and opened the door marked "Visitor Room."

"He looks so small in there," said Nina, her voice as soft as the blankets on which Manny had been placed.

Manny's tail thumped as soon as he heard Nina's voice. His face looked like it had just bloomed out of a clear plastic cone edged in felt.

Nina bent down to stroke his nose. "Does he really need this? It seems so uncomfortable."

"Those Elizabethan collars—"

"Wait," Aretha halted Greg's explanation with a wave of her hand. "As in Queen Elizabeth? What's she doing in a veterinary hospital?"

"And that's why we refer to them as E-Collars . . . less explaining. But, you're right. It's named after all those high-collared ruffles women wore then. But, for pets, it's not fashion. Those collars prevent them from scratching, biting, or in Manny's case, trying to get to his IV line," said Greg.

"Well, guess that's better than finding a use for those corsets. Right, Manny?" said Aretha, bending down to pet him.

"Can I take a picture of him?" Nina reached in her purse and took out her cell phone.

"Let's not make this a magazine photo spread. I hate to rush you, sister, but we need to get going or else the traffic is going to strangle me," said Aretha, keys jangling in her hand.

"Pictures are fine," Greg told Nina. "And, if you want to stay a little longer, I can drop you off at the office on my way to work. There's something I need to give Elise anyway." He had no idea what that thing was, but he'd find something.

"That okay with you, Nina?" Aretha looked at her watch.

Nina looked at Greg. "It wouldn't be out of your way?"

He wasn't certain if she wanted it to be or not. "Isn't at all. Really."

Aretha stopped fidgeting with her keys. "Great, then I'm off."

A round of good-byes, and she scurried out, leaving a cavern between him and Nina. The kind of space that, with

Christa Allan

friends, would fill with conversation. Between two people who emotionally circled one another as if in a wrestling match, it echoed.

They fumbled chatting through the few photos Nina snapped with her cell phone, while Greg made notes on Manny's chart. He gave some instructions to the veterinary technician, then excused himself to return a text and a call he'd received earlier.

"By the time you finish, Manny will probably be ready for me to go anyway," she said.

He didn't recognize the telephone number that showed on his phone, but the text originated from the same place. They were both from Dr. Percy Maxwell, who owned two hospitals, one in Houston and one in Galveston. The doctor Greg worked for at the Cypress clinic referred him to Dr. Maxwell as he'd been searching for a full-time veterinarian to join his staff. While Greg appreciated the flexibility of a relief practice, it also meant working more weekends and the strong possibility of working holidays because that's when other doctors wanted vacation time. Knowing he could be at the same clinic every day, with a schedule that would be better for spending time with Jazarah, was appealing. Not being his own boss . . . that would be the challenge. But he trusted God would lead him down the path he needed to follow, and if it meant someone else walked ahead and cleared it, well, so be it.

Greg discovered both of them graduated within four years of one another from L.S.U.'s School of Veterinary Medicine, which, Dr. Maxwell, joked would make football season less contentious. They arranged to meet Sunday afternoon, so Percy would have more time to show him the clinic and answer questions without the interruptions of the staff and clients.

So, now Greg did have something to "drop off" to Elise, this new information. He smiled. One God-incident at a time was enough to take one more step forward.

25

Nina buckled her seat belt, relieved Greg drove something roomy, with open space between the front seats. Just being alone with him created enough tension that she expected static electricity to lift her hair off her head when he opened the door to his black Volvo SUV.

Nina surveyed the leather seats, the plush interior, the built-in entertainment systems in the back headrests. "Very nice for . . . " she paused for something more diplomatic to pop into her brain than, "for what it is."

He laughed as he started the engine. "It's okay. You can say it. It's nice for an SUV." He stopped before leaving the parking lot. "I can drive through Starbucks or something on the way in, if you'd like a coffee."

"Thanks, but Michelle probably has some made at the office by now, so I'll just get a cup there." Had she been talking to Aretha she would have added, "And I'm such a klutz, I'm sure I'd be wearing half my latte on my white angora sweater." She reached into her purse to turn her cell phone back on. "I appreciate the extra time with Manny. It was so strange walking into my house last night, not hearing him yelp or his nails clicking against the floor." Nina stopped. "Good grief, that sounds more melodramatic than I thought it would."

"Not at all. I understand."

When he glanced at her, Nina sensed that he truly did. "Speaking of high drama . . . I never did thank you for the quilt you sent to my office. Before all this happened with Manny, I intended to get in touch so I could reimburse you. I wanted to give it to Aretha for her birthday, so I don't think you should have to pay for my gift to her."

"You know, now that I've spent time around Aretha, I see why you thought of her when you saw it. She's quirky with attitude . . . and style." He took the exit off the freeway to Nina's office. He smiled. "But, I know a better way you can pay me back."

Nina's rapid blinking must have radiated the heat that just caused a reddish flush on his face. "Excuse me?"

"Whoa, talk about something not sounding like you thought it would. What I should have said was, instead of reimbursing me, why don't you send a check to We Care for whatever you would have bid? I'd probably have done that with the money you would have given me, anyway. This way, the benefit . . . benefits," he said and grinned.

"Okay, clever." That did make sense, especially since she considered he might not have told her what his final bid actually was. "You were right. Your idea is better. I'll mail them a check this week."

"But don't think I let you off the hook for that dinner. Just let me know when and where."

"I'm sure I owe you an entire banquet for what you're not charging me to take care of Manny. I don't expect you to lose money taking care of him."

He eased into a parking spot in the garage and looked at Nina. "I'm not, but I appreciate your saying that. For me, it's a chance to pay it forward. There have been times where people have reached out to help me, and those unexpected blessings made a huge difference in my life. God's making it possible right now for it to be my turn."

Nina's conscience squirmed at the mention of blessings and God. As yet, no one convinced her that a few lucky breaks meant God orchestrated them. Her brother dying, her bizarre relationship with her parents . . . were God's arms long enough to reach out to help with those? And, if they were, why hadn't He? *A conversation for another day or month or year, Nina.* "Then, I suppose I can start my own paying forward with dinner. I'll check my calendar, send you a few dates that work, and you can pick the day and the place."

"I should leave the place up to you. I don't do dinner out much, so I'm not all that familiar with where to go." Greg checked the time on his cell phone. "Guess it's time for you to start reporting. I'm glad this worked out . . . being able to talk."

Nina opened the door, but Greg still hadn't turned off the engine. "Aren't you going up, too? To see Elise?"

"Oh, I, you know, this is probably a busy time for her, and I didn't warn her I was coming. I'll call her. Not like I can't find her outside of her office."

He looked like a man who'd just been caught by his office mates doodling a woman's name in his planner. She decided to leave him with his dignity. "Of course. When I see her, I'll tell her you didn't want to disturb her." Nina eased out of the leather seat. "Thanks so much for the ride. Talk to you soon."

"No problem. Glad to help. And, um," he shifted to reverse, "you have a good day."

As he drove off, Nina was proud of herself for not asking him if he'd really needed to see his sister. She was pretty sure she knew the answer to that question. And it made her smile.

Checking her text messages as she exited the elevator, Nina might have worn Brady's coffee had he not called her name in time to avoid the collision.

"Nina, where have you been?" He sounded like a teacher who'd just nabbed kids lurking in the hall during class. Carrying what was atypical for Brady, a leather briefcase, he rather looked like he was on his way to school, too.

"I'm sorry. I didn't know it was your turn to watch me." She slipped her phone back into her purse and checked the front of her sweater to be sure she escaped splatters. "Why does almost every encounter between us have to involve coffee or cameras? Anyway, you're the one who fell off the planet since I last saw you headed to the HR office."

"About that . . . well, first, what's this Elise tells me about Manny? Why didn't you call me?"

Nina moved to the side, away from the elevator traffic. "Do we have to stand here? I'm hoping Michelle made coffee, I need to check in with Shannon . . ."

"I have some time, and I needed to talk to you anyway. But let's sit in the conference room where we'll have some privacy."

She didn't expect, when they finally sat at the boat-shaped table, the mahogany gleaming with polish, that it might be the last time she'd see Brady sitting there.

"Did you just tell me you're quitting, as in no longer working here?" Nina wiggled her high-back chair closer to the table. "You're leaving *Trends*?" She turned her coffee mug in her hands, and looked at Brady. "I'm confused."

"I know. For a while, I was too. The past few weeks, I learned an important lesson. Be careful what you ask for, because you might get it." One side of his mouth went up, like he just got his own joke. "I thought I wanted New York—"

"Wait," Nina said. "*You* wanted New York? I thought you wanted Janie, and *she* wanted New York for you." She leaned back, sipped her coffee, and waited.

He moved a hand across the grain in the table. "That's harsh," he said, but his tone wasn't accusing. "But you're right. And that's why I came back. It's hard to live someone else's dream. I thought once I was in Manhattan, I'd get caught up in it. But the tornado skipped right over me."

"So, what was your fascination with me when you returned?"

Brady cast his eyes down and when he looked up, he reminded her of a child on the verge of confession. "I owe you an apology for that. Not that I meant to use you. I thought, maybe, after I figured out what I didn't want, I needed to revisit my other decisions."

Nina swiveled in the chair. "Hmm . . . then you're telling me you wanted to make sure leaving me wasn't a mistake, too?" She eyed him over the rim of the cup as she finished her coffee. "I'm flattered," she said in a way that indicated she wasn't at all.

His mouth opened, but his thoughts never made their way out because he pressed his lips together. His cell phone scuttled across the table, the vibration sounding like humming metal. He checked the number. "That one can go to voicemail." He turned to Nina. "If you're really honest with yourself, you know the mistake would have been to stay together. Assuming that would have been possible at all." He grinned. "Though I know I'm so handsome, Brad Pitt won't be seen in my presence for fear of being overshadowed."

She knew he was right. She liked the idea of a relationship with Brady more than a relationship with Brady himself, and she didn't like feeling that she lost to Janie. *And since when did competition and a trophy enter into loving someone?* "You're right. About all of it. But, honestly, it's taken your not being around for me to arrive at that conclusion. Except for the Brad Pitt thing. I would have said Channing Tatum."

Brady looked relieved. "I didn't want to leave unless we'd straightened this out between us."

"Done. Now what?"

"I've always wanted to freelance, but I liked the security of being here. If New York did anything positive, it showed me it was time for me to go after my own dream. That's what I've been talking about to Elise and HR. I'm not leaving Houston. I'm going out on my own."

"Good for you. You're a talented photographer, and I'm proud of you for going after this. I hope Elise can throw some work your way . . . speaking of which, I was counting on you for my feature," Nina said. "Has Elise said anything to you about that? I'd hate to have to break in somebody new, especially since I've already been branded with your camera lens on my forehead."

"Funny. She did, and that's the other thing I needed to mention. Since I was still on the payroll when she approved the series, she's given me the go ahead to finish it out with you. You'll need to let me know your schedule and how this is going to roll out."

Nina checked her calendar. "There's a meeting this Sunday afternoon. I'll email you the information. Can you make it?"

Brady scrolled through his phone. "Booked it. Oh, and speaking of emails . . . you'll be getting one from Janie soon. Seems like there aren't e-UNinvites. Party cancelled this weekend. You're free Saturday night."

Nina opened her calendar. *I'm free every Saturday night.*

26

Nina meant to call her mother about Manny's accident, but dread and busyness kept her from it. Not that her mother would be all that interested in his misfortune, but Nina wasn't going to leave him to go to her parents' house for lunch on Sunday. Especially if it meant going somewhere she didn't want to go. Every dinner there was like going for an annual checkup. You knew it was going to be miserable, but you had to go through it to get past it. But this time, her mother would be caught off-guard by Nina's pre-emptive strike call, so she wouldn't have as many prepared sighs and guilt trip vouchers as usual.

"Nina, something must be wrong or else you wouldn't be calling me. Right?"

"Hello, mother. How are you?"

"Are you really calling to find out how I am . . . because you usually don't bother."

I don't bother because of this exact conversation. "I won't be there for dinner this Sunday. Manny, my dog, was hit by a car, and his leg's fractured. It's hard for him to get around, so he needs someone with him."

A long sigh. "So, you're choosing a dog over your parents?"

"No, mother. I'm choosing to stay home because Manny needs help right now. You and dad are welcome to come eat over here." Nina cringed hearing the words that escaped from her mouth. *What did I just say? Please don't agree. Please don't agree.*

Silence.

"Mother? Did you hear me?"

"Yes, but I am surprised that you invited us. You know your father is more comfortable watching his own television."

So, a father can choose a television over his daughter?

"Well, unless he can bring the television here, I guess we won't be seeing one another."

"You know, your brother's birthday is next month. He would have been thirty-two. Your father would want you here, you know."

"Of course he would." *But not you?* "It shouldn't be a problem. By then, Manny should be back on his own four feet." She felt her mother's eye-roll through the phone.

"We'll be expecting you then."

Most times after a conversation with her mother, Nina had enough pent-up frustration to heave plates against the wall like Frisbees. Today she could have gone through a place setting for twelve.

"You're kidding? You rode in the car with that man, and you didn't ask him about his daughter or that woman with her?" Aretha carried a bowl of still steaming popcorn to Luke on the sofa. She handed him the bowl and plopped next to him. "Baby, that's job security right there. You won't ever have to worry about Nina out-detective-ing you."

"'Detective-ing'? Did you just invent that word?" Luke laughed and grabbed a handful of popcorn.

"Between you looking at Aretha like she just invented a new language and the smell of that butter wafting from the kitchen, I might need Pepto-Bismol," said Nina. "And, as for my sloppy detective work, I'll have you know that there was no wedding ring on his left hand. There wasn't even a tan mark where one would have been. But, nothing we discussed transitioned into asking about his daughter."

"I know this much. If he was attached to that woman with his daughter, I doubt if he would have agreed to the two of you having dinner. He doesn't seem like the kind of man who would be unfaithful," Luke shared between bites.

"You're the hotshot detective. Why don't you and Nancy Drew come along?" Nina slipped her iPad into her portfolio, then reached in the refrigerator for a bottle of water.

"If we go with you, how will we ever be alone?" Aretha elbowed Luke who rewarded her with a kiss on her forehead.

"Exactly," said Nina. "Which is why, while I go meet the quilt people, you two are going to the clinic for visiting time with Manny. Greg said he'll release him Monday."

"We should get him a homecoming happy. A new squeaky rubber ball. He loves the ones that look like basketballs," Aretha said as she carried the empty popcorn bowl back into the kitchen.

"Let's leave now, so we'll have time to swing by a pet store after we visit. I have to get back for late shift. And if I don't wash my hands first, they'll be sliding all over the steering wheel from all that butter," said Luke.

"Isn't he adorable?" Aretha said as she watched him amble into the kitchen.

Nina smiled. "If I have to say so myself."

Probably because of her smarty-pants attitude about her GPS when she spoke to one of the quilters a few days ago, Nina drove right past her destination. Faith Church and the Fellowship Hall perched on a corner at the edge of a hodge-podge residential neighborhood. A stand of pine trees obscured the front of the white-bricked Fellowship Hall, so when she turned around, she had to trust that the GPS voice telling her she'd arrived at her destination was directionally smarter. It was. Nina didn't see Brady's car. She hoped he remembered.

At the door, she didn't know whether she should knock or just walk in, so she did a combination of the two. "Is this the Threads of Hope group?" she asked once inside. Had she surveyed the room for thirty seconds, the question would have been unnecessary.

Bolts of fabric draped several of the long tables on one side of the room. On the other side, four tables surrounded by chairs had been pushed together and held pieces of fabric, scissors, and rulers of all shapes and sizes.

A young woman with a shoulder-length waterfall of sand-shaded ringlets walked out of one of the side rooms. She set the bundle of clothes she carried on a chair. "You must be Nina. I talked to you on the phone," the young woman shook Nina's hand.

"Crystal. Yes, I remember. Nice to meet you." After their first conversation, Nina expected to meet someone barely out of her teens, but Crystal looked not much younger than she was.

"Come on in, I'll show you around and introduce you to everyone. They should all be here soon."

By the time Brady arrived, Nina had met Crystal's mother Kelley, the hospice nurse Becca, Pam, Lacey, and Jenny. "There are more people here sometimes, but since we just finished the quilts for the We Care benefit, we're just working on designs right now," Kelley explained.

Nina introduced Brady and, while he snapped pictures, she explained the feature series, her idea to spotlight the different people involved and bring attention to The AIDS Memorial Quilt and their group's contributions. "Of course, I'll need your permission, and I understand you might need to think about it first, so you don't need to give me a decision today."

"Actually, Crystal had told us about the feature part. We talked about it already, and we all want to help. If our stories can make a difference, we want to tell them," said Pam, who joined Becca as she cut squares from the stack of clothes Crystal plopped on the table. "There're two more people who usually come, but they're both going to be late. We hadn't talked to them yet, so if you'll still be here, you can ask them, too."

"Great," said Nina, adding more notes. "What are their names?"

"Martha is one. She's just running late today. The other one had an appointment, so we're not sure when he'll make it. His name is Dr. Hernandez, but we just call him Greg."

27

Greg left his meeting with Dr. Maxwell and called Elise. He wanted to tell her about the interview before he arrived at the quilting group. "I'm going back on one of the clinic days, and that will tell me a lot about the practice as well. But, I'm thinking this could be a blessing. It's close to the house, and the owner is someone I really think I can work with."

"I'll add it to the prayer list," she said. "Do you realize the older we get, the longer the list is?"

"And with that, I'm calling Paloma," he said. She and Jazarah were making cookies. He pictured the kitchen decorated with chips and icing and his daughter probably finger-painting with cookie dough. That was a mess he didn't mind missing right now.

It was later than usual when Greg arrived at the fellowship hall, so he was surprised to see so many cars still in the parking lot. He opened the door and saw a man taking pictures. And Nina. *Nina?*

She smiled when she saw him. "Don't worry, I looked like you do now when they told me you were actually a part of this group," she said. "I didn't know, of course, that night at the benefit that you actually designed the quilt I liked. You're a man of many talents, Dr. Hernandez."

And you're a woman who continues to surprise me. Which he might have actually said had he not been distracted by the scent of gardenias that lingered after she'd reached out and patted his shoulder. "See, I'm not just another pretty face, am I?" he said, but Nina didn't participate in his smiling. Greg saw the way her eyes searched his face, and he realized it wasn't a joke to her. It was exactly what she thought of him. Ever since high school.

She looked at him and, like someone who'd just decided to participate in the auction bidding, nodded. "My eyesight must have improved over the years. I see exactly what you mean," she said and mirrored his grin with her own. "Okay, time to exude your boyish charm for the camera. I want you to meet Brady."

Greg recognized him as soon as he introduced himself. The man driving the white convertible the night of the benefit. The convertible with Nina in the passenger seat.

"I photographed quilts the night of the benefit. Your group's quite talented," said Brady.

"Thanks," Greg replied, "I'm blessed to be surrounded by creative people. Who make cookies and keep me coming back."

The women at the table laughed. Brady walked over to Nina who was examining some quilts in progress. Greg watched Brady and Nina. Actually, he watched Brady watch Nina as she pointed to places around the room. Could he have missed some connection between the two? A connection more than a reporter and photographer? He waited as they spoke and looked for those suggestions of intimacy between a couple. Hands, eyes, laughter that lingered, or the space between them narrowing as if drawn together by their sheer magnetism. Greg witnessed none of those between the two, and the relief he experienced was its own signal.

Greg joined Brady and Nina. He reminded himself to focus on the conversation and not the tilt of her head when she asked a question or the curve of her waist as she held a square up to examine or how she used her thumb to twirl the pearl ring on her ring finger as she spoke.

The three of them walked around the room. Greg showed them patterns, sample squares, bolts of fabric, and pictures that had been taken of other quilts they'd sewn. "One of the goals we're working on is to make a panel for everyone in the group who's lost someone to AIDS. It's taking a while longer than we expected because we work on those when we can. But it gives the group time to save money for another goal. We hope to be able to personally deliver those squares to D.C."

"Impressive," said Brady. "You know, a friend of mine, someone I grew up with, died of AIDS five years ago. I don't know if they've ever thought of creating a panel for him."

Crystal's mother, Kelley, sitting nearby, turned to Brady. "Didn't mean to be eavesdropping, but there is a way for you to find if there's already a panel for your friend."

"Thanks, but if you mean going to a display, I don't have time—"

"No. No. You don't have to travel at all. Watch," Kelley said and asked Nina if she could use her iPad. "Even the Quilt is joining the 21st century. Look." She showed them the web app that people can use to browse the entire collection of panels and even read personal stories.

"What a great sidebar this will be for the first profile," Nina said.

"Guess I need a tech training session. I didn't realize you were so app-aware, Kelley," Greg said as he bookmarked the site on his cell phone.

"I'm not," Kelley said as she pointed to her daughter. "Crystal's the one who's always searching and researching." She tucked the ringlets that curtained her daughter's face behind as ears as Crystal steered her scissors around yellow and orange flowers on what was once a skirt.

"Because if I didn't," Crystal said as she moved the skirt into a basket of other shorn clothes, "you would still be using a cell phone the size of a shoe box."

"True," Kelley said and helped her daughter spread out a large chintz curtain.

Brady took a few more shots, then left after he and Nina scheduled a series of interview times. Greg scanned the list she showed him. "You didn't ask me," he said.

"You're right. Interviewing the person who helps design all these quilts would be another angle." Nina opened her calendar.

"Is that what I am? An angle?" Greg shook his head as if dismayed by the revelation. "Sorry, Miss O'Malley, but you have it all wrong."

Nina's eyes drilled into him. "I what?"

"I'm not your angle," he said. Greg knew he was about to learn more about Nina O'Malley than she would learn about him. "Jazarah, my daughter, is the angle. She's HIV-positive."

Sitting in Carraba's, the one restaurant that Nina could think of in a stunned state, she looked across the table at Greg as he listened to a voicemail about one of his patients. She wanted to tell him that she didn't mind at all that he had a pretty face. In fact, she wondered why this man, who walked into a room and women knew he was there, might be interested in her.

Or, Nina, maybe he's not. Being nice to someone doesn't equal a relationship.

When Nina heard his daughter's name, she felt like that spinning beach ball that appeared when a program on her laptop wasn't processing information. Greg not only had a daughter, she was Ethiopian and HIV-positive. Nina realized that everything she thought she knew about Greg was about to be redefined.

When her belated response to him was, "I'm confused," he told her he understood. And that's when he suggested dinner, so he could, as he said, "unconfuse" her.

The waitress, whose name badge read "Roxie," brought their meals, grilled salmon with tomato basil vinaigrette for him and tilapia with garlic for Nina. When Greg thanked her, she flashed him a lipsticked smile that could have melted pats of butter. "Need anything else?" She didn't even pretend to look at Nina.

"I'd appreciate a refill," said Nina and held up her iced tea glass.

Roxie barely turned in her direction. "Sure, I'll be right back." She picked up the glass like she was taking it in the kitchen to dust for fingerprints and strolled off.

Nina laughed when she walked away. "I think Roxie would like for you to be quite needy."

"Really? Why?" He handed Nina the bread basket.

"You're oblivious. It's endearing," said Nina. "So, tell me about your daughter. Who, by the way, oozes personality." A quality that definitely could have connected her genetically to Greg.

"She does, doesn't she? Makes me think that in ten or so years, I'm going to have to be quite a vigilant father." He smiled and, though he looked at Nina, it was as if a picture of his daughter was behind her. "We brought her home, underweight and underdeveloped, and depended on prayer and love. And, so far, it's working."

Nina ate a few bites of her tilapia contemplating how to send the train of their conversation down a different track so she could ask about his wife. Maybe the divorce was messy, maybe she cheated on him, or maybe she was home scraping his uneaten dinner down the waste disposal. The suggestion of that discombobulated her and sent her fork to her plate in a noisy landing.

Of course, Roxie appeared with her fresh glass of iced tea at that moment, and Nina could almost hear Roxie's brain telegraphing Greg, "Oh, you're such a kind man to participate in Take a Klutz to Dinner night." Roxie set Nina's glass on the table, then let her eyes linger on Greg for a while and announced she'd return later with a dessert menu. *Hoping I'll order something so calorie-evil, I'll need a different size dress to leave the restaurant.*

Nina, you're a journalist. If you can't ask the hard questions, Elise will assign you to Cub Scout banquets. First, she put her fork down, then she spotted Roxie serving a table of eight, she knew she couldn't wait or else she'd be detailing the ingredients of every dessert on the menu to Greg. She plunged in. "Did things not work out between you and your wife?"

Greg's reaction came in waves, starting with surprise, then confusion, then he sat back in his chair as if pushed there by the force of her question. He looked down at the table, but when his eyes met Nina's, she heard the sad understanding of his response, "When you live with something for a long time, you start to assume everyone knows." Greg placed his napkin on his now bare plate. "Lily died in an automobile accident right before Jazarah's second birthday."

She was about to say she was sorry when a memory rushed forward, pulled by the weight of his words. The night of the benefit, her angry retort, "I prayed pain would bury itself in you," and his reply that she no longer needed to utter that prayer. If shame had its own taste, it coated her mouth like mucous. The horror of her arrogance spilled out of her eyes and trembled in her hands. Her heart's voice couldn't be heard above the deafening roar of regret.

Before she could speak, Greg silenced everything in her that screamed at her own meanness. He reached across the table, his hand quieting hers. "Nina, you didn't know. You didn't know."

With her other hand she blotted her face with her napkin. "That's not an excuse for . . ."

"You're right, it's not. But I forgive you, I really do."

"Forgive me? How can you? I don't deserve forgiveness—"

"If we deserved it, it wouldn't be forgiveness. And I can do this because God does it for me. Sometimes on a daily basis."

28

Nina left the table to rid herself of "the black streams of tears" flowing down her face. Greg called Paloma and asked if it would be a problem if he was home later than he anticipated.

His nanny laughed. "Dr. Hernandez, you do not have a curfew, but I am glad you called. Jazarah saved you cookies, and she put them on the fireplace. 'Like Santa,' she said. So you must eat them . . . or something . . . so they will be gone when she awakes."

He promised he would and told her he'd be home within the next two hours.

"Are you still at the quilting meeting?" She sounded concerned that he might be.

"No, I'm having dinner with a friend, Nina O'Malley. Her dog, Manny, is the one I got the ER call about when we were on our way to lunch. If fact, she was in the waiting room the same time you and the little princess were. Tallish, short dark hair." He looked up to see Nina ease into her chair, then tuck her bangs behind her ear, only to have them slide back down. A familiar gesture, one he used to see in Lily whenever she felt self-conscious. Greg smiled at her, then realized he had no idea what Paloma had said. "I'm sorry, could you repeat that."

"Have a good time, Dr. Hernandez."

"I already am. Thanks." He ended the call, and Roxie appeared at his elbow asking about coffee and a dessert menu. They both ordered coffee and, to their waitress's disappointment, passed on dessert.

Roxie delivered the two coffees, telling Greg she'd "be delighted, for sure" to provide him refills, and swayed away.

"Is it painful? To talk about her, I mean. Lily must have been a remarkable woman to open her heart to adopt an HIV-positive child."

Greg leaned forward, hands clasped on the table, and smiled. "No, not now. After she died, people sometimes apologized if her name came up in conversation or, worse, didn't talk about her at all. As if she never existed."

His neighbors Dale and Amelia, whose son died of cancer at the age of twenty-eight, understood the importance of not smothering the memories of loved ones under blankets of silence. Greg knew it was that empathy that drew him to involvement in the We Care benefit and supporting The AIDS Memorial Quilt.

Every panel represented a family sharing and celebrating the life of someone they loved. Greg told Nina about Lily's passion for life, how when she loved, she gave it all away. Her drive to bring Jazarah home sometimes drove a wedge between them because when she decided to go after something, she was not going to be denied. Greg would argue, when the paperwork and the politics overwhelmed the process, that maybe they should wait or try to adopt in the states.

One night, she must have printed copies of the picture she'd taken in New York of the quilt panel of the five-month-old little girl who died of AIDS. When he woke up the next morning, they were taped all over the house. On his bathroom mirror, the refrigerator, doors, cabinets. Even the rearview mirror of his car. He'd walked back inside that day, wrapped his arms around her waist, and whispered, "You win. There's a baby waiting for us to pray her home."

They prepared themselves for having an HIV-positive child by talking to other families and reading whatever they could find that would help. They knew the virus could impair her immune system's ability to control viral infections, bacterial lung and ear infections. But they also knew she would have a normal life expectancy because modern drug therapies made the virus almost undetectable. A week after starting her antiretroviral therapy, her virological suppression was at 90 percent. Within a month, it was 99 percent.

"Ironic. Lily spent so much time and energy doing all she could to make sure Jazarah would live, and she was the one who died."

On her way to the office on Monday, Nina received two texts from Greg. One asked her to call him to discuss Manny going home. The other, saying how much he enjoyed their time together, asked if she had plans for Saturday. She smiled, remembering him walking her to her car after dinner. How no matter how old you are, there's that geeky awkwardness of saying good night to someone you're attracted to, which resulted in a clumsy kiss somewhere between her lips and her ear. For Nina, it was enough to let her know, she'd try again.

Dinner with Greg had trumped the anxiety of Daisy returning, so that walking to her desk, Nina was surprised by the familiar scent of rain, which meant she was back. Her earth-friendly accessories surrounding her as before, Daisy settled in as if she'd never left.

"Nina, I'm so excited to see you," said Daisy, springing from her chair, her shock of sprouting hair now gathered into a neat bun at the nape of her neck.

Setting her briefcase on the floor, Nina hugged Daisy, who seemed smaller and frailer than she remembered. "I'm glad you're here, but I don't know why you left in the first place," Nina said. "Now, let me look at you. Did you even eat while you were in New York?"

"I so owe you an apology. Maybe several. You deserve an explanation. Do you have time to talk now?"

"Let me find Shannon. She's been helping me, and doing a bang-up job at it, too. I'll be back."

After getting notes from her intern, who proved her savvy by delegating some of the work to another intern, Nina returned to her desk. "Did you want to talk here?"

"Here is fine." Daisy scooted her chair around the partition. "I'm going for the condensed version because, well, I'm exhausted. My flight was late yesterday, and I didn't get to bed until after midnight, so I might not be too coherent."

"We don't have to do this now—"

"No, I want to. I've wanted to since I left." She kicked off her sandals and sat, cross-legged on the chair, her cotton skirt pulled over her knees. "Here's what happened . . ."

Daisy's mother had moved to New York months before with a man who promised he'd marry her as soon as he started his job there. The job started, but the marriage didn't. "My mother called, hysterical, that she wants to move out, but she doesn't want to be homeless again. And then she pummels me with guilt about her being all alone, no one to help her . . . I talked to Elise because I thought there might be a way for me to get on staff in New York. I could get my mother situated, stay for a while, come back here . . . I told her I didn't want to step on your toes because I knew how much you wanted to be there."

Elise had called Daisy the day after Janie made her grand announcement to tell her there was a possible opening. But it was Elise's suggestion that Daisy not make a permanent decision until she arrived there, checked on her mother's situation, and spent time in the New York office.

"She told me she'd keep my job open here, so I didn't want to create high drama. Janie already had her production going on, but there just wasn't enough time for me to explain it all. And, if I ended up back here anyway—ta da!—then I would have put us both through that for no reason."

Daisy said that her mother lived in an apartment almost worse than the car they lived in for weeks. Janie offered to let them stay with her. "And that was the beginning of the end. My mother was making me crazy. Janie kept pressuring me to stay, mostly because I think she saw Brady slipping away. And, Nina, the New York office, is this place," she moved one outstretched arm in a circle, "on steroids."

Nina sat straighter in her chair like someone about to be rewarded. She'd thrive in that energy.

But it debilitated Daisy. "I told my mother that if she wanted to live with family, then she needed a Houston zip code. She balked at first. I'm not even sure why, because she wasn't all that devastated leaving," she gazed at the ceiling, "I think his name was Eric. Finally, I convinced her to come back with me. She's been here less than twenty-four hours, and she's already complaining. She's been homeless so much throughout her life that I think having what could be a real home feels strange to her."

After she and Daisy finished talking, Nina called Greg to make arrangements for picking up Manny. As she waited for him to answer, she surveyed the office. Nests of submarine gray partition walls separated the staff writers from the ad writers from the classifieds. Days closer to deadline, the nest swarmed with the energy of people moving from hive to hive, the impatient rings of telephones, the electrical current of voices that punctuated the stillness between.

Would she exchange this for the frenetic pace of the New York office? Without a doubt.

"This is Dr. Hernandez."

When he knew that she was on the other end of the line, his professional tone gave way to the one with which she had become familiar.

"Hey, Nina. How's your day going?"

"So far, so good," she answered. "Thanks for your text. I had fun, too. I'd love to get together Saturday."

"Great. We'll talk soon about that. In the meantime, can you meet me at the ER clinic around four this afternoon? We can release Manny then, and I can go over what he'll need. He's making great progress, and I'm sure he's ready to be home."

"Aretha and I have missed the little yapper. Tell him we'll see him in a few hours."

Nina then contacted Kelley and her daughter Crystal, and they arranged to meet the next morning over breakfast.

Daisy and Nina had lunch with Elise in her office to work out story assignments. Nina arrived before Daisy and was relieved Elise made no mention of her having been with her brother. While policies existed for office romances, she had no idea how to handle a relationship with a boss's sibling. *Getting ahead of yourself, Nina. One dinner isn't a relationship, but I wouldn't mind if more did make it so.*

Elise had arranged for a local deli to provide salads and a tray of fruit, with a side of chocolate gelato. "Figured we'd be tossing ideas around, might as well toss salads, right?" She looked at Daisy and Nina. "Guess that wasn't as funny as I'd hoped."

Nina expected to play polite tug-of-war over some of the assignments. But Daisy offered to take over the political corruption story without any protest, so Nina could focus on the feature.

"But I thought you didn't like writing those stories," Nina said.

"I'm learning to stretch. Besides, you might want to get back to politics after you dabble in the wild side of feature writing," Daisy said and handed Nina her salad bowl for a refill.

Elise closed her laptop. "Sometimes life works out so much better than we anticipated," she said and smiled in Nina's direction.

29

Kelley and Crystal waved Nina to their table where they already had coffee waiting.

"After all those years of using, Carlys surprised us by not dying of a drug overdose. Never would have thought it though. That girl checked in and out of rehab hospitals like they were resort hotels."

Crystal, her twin, handed her mother a biscuit. "Except that the resorts might have cost less."

Kelley squeezed her daughter's hand. "Might be right on that one. Anyway," she breathed in as if Nina had pressed a stethoscope to her chest, "last time out, she stayed clean for months. Then, we started to notice she was sleeping longer. 'Course we were suspicious, how could we not be? But when Crystal told us about her night sweats and her complaints of fever, we figured one monster of a cold was headed her way."

The monster wreaking havoc upon Carlys wasn't a cold. It was AIDS.

"The doctor told us she probably shared a dirty needle with someone who was infected. Of course, Carlys had no idea who that someone might be." Crystal rubbed her arms like the temperature dropped. "It's so weird to think a stranger killed my sister, and doesn't even know."

"Almost a year later, Carlys died. And she stayed clean. She was proud of herself for that. But . . ." Against a backdrop of dishes clattering, the thick smell of bacon, and the wait staff carrying trays like large brown halos, Kelley shared the pain that ripped through her every night. The wound that would never heal.

". . . people who knew Carlys, just figured it was drugs that killed her. I never told them otherwise. Couldn't make myself say my daughter died from AIDS." She looked at Nina. "What kind of mother lies about why her child died?"

When Nina returned to her office, she didn't remember eating breakfast at all.

"Do you realize that Kelley's daughter might have been saved by something that costs less than a dollar?" Nina handed Aretha the article she'd been reading on syringe exchange and needle share programs and their importance in reducing and preventing HIV. "These programs provided a way for drug users to be given free sterile syringes. That one difference could have saved her from being infected."

Aretha leaned against the pine tree and propped the tablet against her knees. "I'd like to read this. Make sure Mr. Manny doesn't try to escape."

"As if," said Nina. "He's basking in the outdoors, content to be home." She carried him outside, as per Greg's instructions, for what Aretha referred to as his daily "constitutional." After their first adventure into the front yard yesterday, Aretha told Manny he needed a few less amendments to his constitution.

The sun hadn't yet disappeared into a pocket of clouds when the three of them settled on a patch a grass, the two women sitting cross-legged in front of the dog, blocking the street. Even if he had a yearning to dash in that direction, there was no way he'd outrun them. So, Manny alternately lifted his head to catch a breeze, then rested it on top of his bandaged leg.

Nina scratched behind his ears, remembering Greg's litany of instructions when they checked Manny out of the clinic. He helped Aretha settle the dog in the car while Nina wrote a check for his treatment. Once outside, she'd thanked him for his help with Manny and with the charges. "I appreciate all you did for Manny, and I meant it when I said I didn't want this costing you more than it cost me," she told him

"Not at all. And even if it did, you . . . I mean Manny, was worth it."

Aretha was packing a dinner to take to Luke who worked late shift, and Nina had started writing her feature about Carlys when Greg called about dinner and a movie Saturday night. "Or it could be a movie and dinner, either way."

They were still talking when Aretha came back almost an hour later.

"Did you read it? What did you think?"

Elise and Peyton had stopped by Saturday on their way home from lunch to spend time with their niece, but Greg knew his sister. She didn't want to just hear his reaction to Nina's first article, she wanted to examine every pore on his face for a reaction.

Greg relocated a collection of stuffed bears from the couch to the coffee table so his sister and brother-in-law could have a place to sit. Sheets had been loosely tented on the furniture in one-half of the family room. A play kitchen, art easel, and a stack of books took up space in the other half.

"I haven't had a chance to read it yet because I've been a tent-building, water-coloring, tea-partying daddy most of the morning," Greg said as he picked two dolls and a broken cookie off the floor. "I may need to spend time at the gym to build stamina just to play with my daughter."

Peyton looked around the room. "Ever thought of putting up a train or a race track? Get one of those, and I'll join the play group."

While Peyton talked, Jazarah's little round singing could be heard coming from one of the flowered tents. "I hiding. I hiding. I hiding."

"I'll write them both on your Christmas list, Peyton," said Elise. "We'll entertain the princess. You go read that piece that Nina worked on for the past three weeks." Elise slipped out of her heels, and in a too-loud voice said, "Uncle Peyton, we have to find our little lost niece. Where could she be?"

A soft giggle floated into the room. Greg watched as his sophisticated sister and her husband crawled the short space to where Jazarah hid under a sheet draped over a chair. As Greg left the room, he heard Peyton exclaim, "There you are!" followed by the delighted squeals of his daughter.

In that moment, Greg realized God's reunion with Lily must have sounded much the same. And if what Greg experienced with his daughter was a mere shadow of what God experienced with His daughter, he knew Lily's joy was more spectacular than he could imagine.

Have fun, my sweet Lily. Fill the heavens with your laughter.

The features had started weeks ago when Nina opened her email to read one of Elise's "see me" directives. Nina closed her laptop and waited for her insides to stop practicing aerobics. At one time, the internal gut-bouncing meant she feared the dragon-lady's fire belching. Not now. Not today. The knot was her own.

"Nina, these interviews are powerful and poignant. The feedback we're receiving is incredible. Every story resonates because this disease may be pandemic, but it's personal. And you're not only telling stories, you're weaving in facts that people might not ever know or feel comfortable asking."

Elise's office door was already open when Nina arrived. As soon as she walked in, Nina eyed a stack of magazines on her desk.

"Have a seat." Elise's voice was the excited impatience of someone waiting for a show to start. "Water?"

When Nina turned down the offer of water, Elise picked up the magazine with her first article, the one featuring Kelley's daughter Carlys, from a stack on her desk. "The information here about federal funding of needle exchange programs, the number of infections from injection drugs, is getting people's attention."

The second interview, with Pam and Eli, already parents of three biological children, told their story of finding their adopted son Jacob begging on the streets. "If Eli had not been there with the medical team, Jacob and his sister would probably have died by now. We saved two children," Pam had said, "but since 1984, over 14 million children have been orphaned in Southern Africa because of AIDS." Elise said local organizations contacted her to thank her because they'd experienced an increased interest in volunteer teams after the article published.

Nina appreciated Elise's enthusiasm, but knew if she didn't say something soon, her courage would stomp out like an unwelcome visitor. Before Elise picked up another magazine, Nina blurted, "Elise, there's another story I want to discuss with you."

Elise's eyes switched to high beams. "Another series?" She grabbed her notebook.

Nina's body was firmly planted in the chair across from her boss, but her mind paced up and down the office. "Well, only if a series of dates would . . ." She inched forward. "I don't know why I'm trying to be clever, here. You know Greg and I have been seeing each other, and I think you and I have handled the boundaries well."

"If you consider pretending it's not happening to be handling it well then I agree with you," Elise said. "Wait, I meant that to be amusing. Peyton's always telling me I don't do amusing well. I need to listen to the man more."

Nina loosened her grip on the chair arms. "Okay, I'm glad you clarified that. I just figured there would be a time when one of us would have to bring it up. And, this is it."

Elise's expression was guarded, but Nina had prepared herself for the worst. So far, the discussion was miles ahead of what she expected. "Greg wants me to meet Jazarah this weekend, and I know this is a huge step for him. I care about him very much. The challenge is, I'd love to end the series with an interview with him. But, before I approached him, I wanted to talk to you. Not just because of Greg, but because of what it would mean for you as well."

Elise tapped her pen on her planner and stared out the window as she was prone to do when she wrestled with a decision. The pen slowed to a stop, and Nina saw a softer, less intense Elise. Even her eyes, usually like two dark drill bits ready to bore into someone, appeared relaxed. "Like you, I've been wondering when we'd have to cross the line from colleagues to, well, two women who care about the same man. Once we stepped over it, we'd have to be able to move back and forth, and yet not get our roles confused." She left her desk and closed the door to her office. She pulled a chair from the corner and moved it next to Nina's before she sat. "Of course, I've known you and Greg have spent time together. When he finally shared the high school and benefit night disasters, I was surprised and impressed that you both moved past that." She looked away for a moment, and then continued. "Elise, Greg's sister, who knows that she's not seen her brother this happy in a long time, has hesitated telling you this. But, Elise, your editor, knows she must."

Nina, had she been given a minute of privacy, would have checked under her chair to see if her stomach had gone there. Elise couldn't possibly be setting her up for something negative, could she? Nina wished now she'd taken her up on that offer of water earlier.

"We're pulling Janie out of New York. It's a disaster. The job is yours, if you want it."

30

Nina experienced, for the first time, that exquisite moment of dream becoming reality, when the word surreal becomes palpable, and you recognize that if this one thing is possible, then so is the second or third or anything after. She feared she might not be able to respond to Elise for the horn-blowing celebration marching through her head. "I'm happily stunned. Happily. Stunned." This time, her grip on the armrests was to prevent her from leaping out of the chair and clapping like a cheerleader.

"Of course, your discretion and confidentiality are expected at this point. And you don't need to make a decision now or even this week." Elise looked at her watch. "My cell phone, my telephone, my email will all be assaulted in the next hour after the editor talks to Janie. It's going to take a solid two weeks for movement, and I'm certain it's going to be a struggle. But it's not one you need to involve yourself in." She grabbed two water bottles out of the small refrigerator near her desk and, this time, Nina accepted one. "I want you to give this serious thought, write down any questions or concerns you have, and we'll talk next week."

Nina streamed out a chorus of, "Great. Good. Sure. Of course," as Elise spoke. She was about to thank her, when Elise said, "Oh, one more thing. And I'm going to cross that boundary, but I feel it's necessary. If and when you discuss this with Greg or tell him your decision is your call. By the time this is all finalized, should you move ahead, it might be at least three or four weeks. Getting close to Jazarah and then leaving is going to be tough. I'm not suggesting you don't meet her. Everyone should, she's an amazing kid. But, be aware that she's one of those kids who forms attachments quickly. Breaking them is tough."

"I understand. And, Elise, thank you for this chance."

"You're welcome. Just be sure it's still what you want. I have no doubt you can make it work. But remember, geography isn't a magical cure."

⊸⊶⊷⊶⊶

Stepping out of the elevator, Elise's offer bouncing around inside her, knowing she'd been given the choice to stay or to go, Nina's vision of the office was already one degree of separation away. But the empowerment she felt inside the *Trends* office didn't transfer so easily to her life outside of it. The closer her car brought her to home, the less detached she felt about her surroundings.

She wouldn't be relocating her life as she knew it and reconstructing it in Manhattan. Aretha, her home, her Girls' Night Out group would stay in Houston. Manny? What would she do about him, especially since she had no idea where she'd live? No backyards in a high-rise to run around in. By the time she unlocked her front door, she'd already started finding the flaws in her diamond.

When Manny didn't bark at the sound of her key in the lock, Nina dropped everything and ran to the kitchen to check his crate. Once she spotted the note taped to it, her heart made its way down, and out of her throat. Aretha said she and Luke took Manny for his follow-up visit because Greg wasn't going to be at the clinic Saturday.

About to be annoyed she missed a chance to see Greg, Nina's brain kicked into gear reminding her she was the reason Greg wasn't working Saturday. They were taking Jazarah to the Butterfly Museum. And, now, having thought about being with him this weekend, she couldn't *not* think about him. Six little mini-Snickers, a handful of jelly beans, and several spoons of Blue Bell straight from the carton later, she still couldn't stop thinking about him. When the sugar therapy failed, she changed into yoga pants that had never seen the inside of a yoga studio and a T-shirt.

She decided to start doing research for her interview with Martha. In 1983, Martha and Frank drove to Women's Hospital when their son-in-law Dan called to tell them their daughter Jill was in labor and about to deliver their first grandchild. They arrived to learn Jill hemorrhaged during delivery and required a transfusion of two pints of blood, but she was stabilized and eager for them to meet their grandson, Adam. Jill nursed Adam for six months. He grew into a chunky little crawler. By the time he was a year old, he'd already started taking stiff-legged steps from one side of the room to the other.

A few years later, Martha made one of the most difficult telephone calls of her life. She'd heard a news report that said tainted blood transfusions could cause something called acquired immune deficiency syndrome. Jill tested positive, but Dan was negative. Adam, because he was breast-fed, also tested positive. Frank and Martha's grandson died at the age of six. No tested or approved drugs for pediatric patients with

AIDS existed at that time. By 1987, Jill was able to start taking AZT, an antiretroviral medicine that the FDA had approved.

Nine years later, Frank and Martha buried their daughter next to her son.

Researching the progression of AIDS for the story, Nina made notes of the three different stages. The first two were characterized as HIV, and the third and final stage of infection is AIDS. As she clicked from one site to verifying information and listing symptoms, she felt like someone playing *Jeopardy*. She had the answers, but she couldn't figure out the question.

Nina started again, thinking perhaps she'd just missed something along the way. When the question finally came to her, she wished that it hadn't because once you know something, you can't not know it. Which is not the same as pretending you don't know, and it was that very difference that turned her inside-out.

Luke, carrying Manny in his crate, and Aretha were walking toward the front door when Nina met them. "Thanks for taking Manny. I've . . . there's something I have to do. Won't be long."

"Nina, what's wrong? Something, for sure. You won't even go through a drive-through without being dressed." She turned to Luke. "Maybe I should go with her . . ."

"No. I appreciate the thought, but no. I need to do this on my own, and I'll tell you later. Just trust me."

Nina pressed the doorbell, which wasn't a bell at all. It sounded like a cattle prod. She pressed it again. And again. And again. Her parents were probably sitting within two feet of one another, each one waiting for the other to open the door.

"Hold ya horses out there."

"Dad, it's Nina. Open the door, please."

"Why, Nina, what brought you—"

"Is mom home? I need to talk to you both." She edged past her dad into the house. "Mom. Where are you?"

Sheila walked out of the kitchen, drying her hands on a frayed dishtowel. Nina recognized concern on her face, one she found at a fire sale.

"It's not Sunday. And where would you be going dressed that way?"

"I think, mother, you might want to pay more attention to my emotional cues, not my yoga pants. Should it matter how I dress to go to my parents' house? Were you expecting company?"

Her father patted his shirt pocket to check if he had his cigarettes. He quit smoking ten years ago, but the habit stayed. Especially when he felt uncomfortable or anxious. "Honey, what's going on?"

"Let's sit at the table," said Nina. "I have something I want to show you."

They sat, neither one of them taking their eyes off of her.

"I'm going to ask you a question, and I want you to tell me the truth. The real truth. Not the truth with a spin on it. Or the one you want."

"Nina, you're being—"

"Actually, Dad, I'm being Nina. The one that's been show-ing up at your house on Sundays? She's the lie. It's time for all of us to stop lying to one another." The way their eyes darted back and forth between themselves and Nina, the perplexed expressions? Nina considered they may not know the truth themselves. But she was about to find out.

"What really killed Thomas?" Each word held its own weight and landed on the platform of Nina's conviction.

"I can't believe my own daughter . . ." her mother pushed her chair back from the table.

Nina would have tackled her if she tried to leave the conversation. "You're not running away from this. And you didn't answer my question."

"Honey, why should she? You already know the answer," said her father, pleading like a child.

"I know what you told me. But there's more that you're not." She opened her iPad, found her notes, and handed the tablet to her parents. "Recognize those?"

Her dad reached in his empty shirt pocket. Her mother pushed the tablet back to Nina. "Do you know how much that hurts your father and me? Why are you making us look at all this? You know Thomas got sick, pneumonia, and died."

"You're not going to let go of that are you? Guess you've said it for so long, you believe it yourself." Nina closed the iPad. "For the past two months, I've been writing a series for the twenty-fifth anniversary of The AIDS Memorial Quilt. I need to research HIV and AIDS because of the families I interviewed. And there they were. It's not a coincidence that these symptoms were Thomas's symptoms. Or that you wouldn't let me go to the hospital. Or that you buried him without waiting for his friends or even some of your own relatives. Thomas died from AIDS."

She watched her parents' faces pale and shift until they bore almost the same expression Kelley's did when she said, "What kind of mother lies about why her child died?"

"We wanted to protect you," said her father. "Things were different then. Your mother and I didn't really understand or know what AIDS was until the doctor explained it to us. Even then, we were in shock."

"What did you think you were protecting me from? For all you knew, I could have used his toothbrush or shaved my legs with one of his razors . . . How was that keeping me safe?"

"Thomas made sure that didn't happen, Nina," said her mother, the exasperation evident in her voice. "We wanted to protect you from other people who might say things to you. What do you think would have happened to you at school if people knew your brother died from AIDS? Especially all those years ago, before people with HIV lived for decades. Even today, some people think you get AIDS from hugging or swimming or sharing food. What do you think people said then?"

"I don't know. But Thomas was my only sibling, and I never had a chance to tell him good-bye." Nina didn't try to stop herself from crying. "Were you ever going to tell me?"

Her parents looked at each other. Her father clasped his hands on the table. "I don't think so. We didn't want it to change the way you saw your brother."

"Why because of the AIDS or that he was gay or both?"

Nina's father leaned back in his chair and stared at his daughter. For the first time in years, Nina witnessed the man inside the shell he'd become."If you don't believe us, I guess I would understand. But your brother wasn't gay. His first year in college, his friends made fun of him because he was a virgin. They all went out drinking one night, and the next morning he wasn't alone in his room. She called him three months later to tell him she'd tested positive for AIDS.

"Guess you can understand how easy it is to make assumptions about people with HIV and AIDS. Even with all your research and interviews, you thought your brother was gay. That's exactly what we were trying to protect you from . . . people like you."

31

Paloma, that bow is almost as large as my daughter's head. Are you sure about that? I don't know if I'll be able to keep the butterflies out of it."

She laughed so much that even he and Jazarah joined in. "She will be very chic. This is a gift from your sister, so I am certain she would never select anything to make your daughter look like a bumpkin."

Greg arrived at Nina's house, unbuckled Jazarah, lifted her out of her car seat, and onto the sidewalk. He smoothed her pink smocked sundress and adjusted her pink bow just slightly off-center as Paloma showed him. "Okay, hold daddy's hand and let's go meet Nina and Manny."

Hearing Manny bark, Jazarah pushed in a bit closer to Greg. Nina opened the door, and Greg realized he hadn't checked the affection protocol for child of single dad meeting . . . what was Nina? Surely not girlfriend and boyfriend. That might have worked ten years ago. Or longer. More than a friend, less than a fiancé? The complications were exhausting, which was why many single parents stayed home, popped popcorn, and rented DVDs. Just gave up dating until the kids hit high school or older.

Lately, though, with Nina in his life, Greg considered himself one of the fortunates. Since Nina continued to say yes, Greg assumed she enjoyed his company as well. He prayed she continued to want to be with him, but he trusted that God had a path. He just needed to keep putting one foot in front of the other.

For now, all he had to do was walk forward to Nina and feel the curve of her cheek in his hand as he kissed her on the forehead. His daughter, still held his hand, but leaned as far as she could without letting go to peek at Manny, resting in his crate.

Nina crouched down to eye-level with Jazarah, introduced herself as a friend of her daddy's, and offered her hand for a handshake. Which she promptly took and pulled Nina closer and hugged her neck. Greg felt as concerned as he did comforted. Though Greg told Paloma she had to stay until she was ninety, he knew the day would come when his daughter's nanny might want to have a life somewhere else with someone else. He tried not to think about it because the separation for all of them, but especially for Jazarah, would be brutal. Yet, his relationship with Nina, while he wanted it to be more, was still, what did Elise call it, marinating. "Sooner or later, you have to get cooking," she said.

When Greg and Jazarah moved closer, Manny thumped his tail, and stayed perfectly still while Jazarah's little hand wiggled through the sides to pet him. She smiled at her father. "I yike him," she announced.

"I yike him, too," said Nina.

"Thanks, Manny," Greg whispered as they started to leave. "Tell the puppy good-bye," he said to his daughter. She turned and smiled sweetly and waved at the dog. "Bye-Bye, Ne Na."

Nina smiled. "The kid's got my number already."

"Definitely not just a kid's place," Greg said, awed by the simulated tropical rainforest that was the Cockrell Butterfly Center. A fifty-foot waterfall fell from the top of the three-story glass building that housed a lush pathway lined with exotic plants and flowers from top to bottom. Butterflies were everywhere, hundreds of them . . . like finely drawn artwork dripping with color flying around and through and over and under foliage and people and sprays from the waterfall.

Nina asked Jazarah if she could remove her bow. Greg waited to see if there would be a standoff. "Your bow is so beautiful, a butterfly might think it was a flower and not be able to get out. And that would be sad." Nina summoned a woeful expression as she spoke, and the performance paid off. Off came the bow, which she held as they walked along the path, and waved away a few curious butterflies.

Three floors of butterflies was Jazarah's limit, especially when one landing on her hand sent her into ambulance siren mode. When Greg suggested lunch, she applauded. He told Nina, "Guess that means it's time to eat."

They walked to a nearby deli for sandwiches, Jazarah between them, holding her hands and swinging her over cracks in the sidewalk. Greg appreciated how relaxed Nina was with his daughter. Sometimes people without children tended to get crazed about things that didn't matter. Things that, once you became a parent, you realized were insignificant. Like it wasn't important to wake a sleeping child to put her jammies on. Sleeping in play clothes was not going to lower IQ points or permanently damage their self-esteem.

Jazarah invited Nina to help her color the maze on her placemat. Filling in the lines with her green crayon, Nina asked Greg questions about his relief work, and when he planned to start working full time at Dr. Maxwell's clinic. Greg answered, but Nina seemed distracted. Entirely too focused on staying inside the lines, and not focused enough on the conversation.

After his daughter lined up her chicken fingers with the "just right" squirt of catsup, Greg asked Nina if she wanted to join them next weekend at the Children's Museum.

Nina chewed, sipped her tea, cleared her throat, and fluffed her napkin. There weren't many other distractions available unless she aligned Jazarah's French Fries with her chicken strips.

Greg swirled a fry in his daughter's mountain of catsup and received a stern warning to not eat her food, "Mine," she warned him, shaking a fry in his direction. She eyed him for a few more bites, then rearranged her pickle slices.

"Nina, did you hear me, about the Children's Museum? Would you want to go? I thought we could ask Luke and Aretha to join us. For some reason, those places are just as much fun for adults who don't have legitimate play time anymore."

"I heard. I'm sorry," said Nina. "I'm not sure yet if I'll be able to do that . . ."

"No need to apologize. It's wrong of me to assume you might not have other plans," he said. Greg didn't consider that she might be seeing someone else. Someone whose idea of an event didn't include shopping in the make-believe grocery store and arguing over who ran the cash register.

She looked around like she'd dropped an answer on the floor somewhere. Clearly, she had something to tell him. "I didn't plan to talk about this here."

"Unless it's something unfit for my daughter's ears, it's going to be here. You can't look as if you just left a horror movie and expect me not to wonder what you saw there."

"Then please don't ask me any questions until I'm finished, okay?"

He nodded, and she began.

As Nina explained the offer she and Elise discussed, Greg felt like someone about to be pushed off a ledge. He couldn't stop it, and he had no idea if there would be anything to hold on to on the way down. He controlled his voice so as not to alarm his daughter, but he wasn't sure if he'd be able to maintain it for the entire conversation. "You're moving to New York? As in the next week or so? I . . . I had no idea that was even on the menu."

"Neither did I. I thought it was off the menu, then it came back on."

Now he colored with Jazarah, not bothering at all with lines and making ever animal purple. He listened to Nina detail the Janie, Brady, Daisy show that was now becoming a one-woman show, featuring his woman. Or at least the one he had hoped would be.

A herd of what looked like high school kids sat at the next table. Greg almost paid them to stay, so he didn't have to be the loudest voice in what was quite a small restaurant. "Is this position one you have to fill?"

She narrowed her eyes, and he knew that was a precursor to the defensive position, but he couldn't make himself stop. "So, you're absolutely choosing to go." The crayon tip snapped off as he spoke. After Jazarah's "Uh oh," he took the one she handed him. "Say what, Daddy?"

He'd forgotten the very manners he wanted her to learn. "Thank you, princess."

She smiled and continued giving all the people green faces. Greg wanted a distraction while Nina spoke, especially one that meant he didn't have to have eye contact. His animals became red.

"No one's forcing me. No one needs to. Managing editor of the New York office is something I've dreamed about for years. How could I pass up this opportunity?" She creased her napkin edges with her thumb as she spoke, so he knew he wasn't the only person feeling like a balloon about to explode. "Elise told me to take my time, but the reality is, I've been thinking about this for years. And don't ask me if I've prayed about it because I don't do prayer."

"Why?"

"Because Thomas died anyway. If praying isn't going to fix anything, what's the point?"

"I hafta potty," said Jazarah, who, between coloring, had arranged most of the food on her plate in straight lines without eating hardly any of it.

"Would you like to come with me?" Nina held out her hand.

"Peas," his daughter answered. "I be back, daddy." She flashed him a smile that pinched something in his chest that he knew must be reserved for daughters.

Greg called Paloma to ask her if she'd be able to keep J. a few hours. For better or for worse, this conversation with Nina had to happen tonight.

Nina was grateful Jazarah knew the words to Bob Marley's songs because she provided the entertainment on their way back to Greg's house. He'd already talked to her about dropping J. off and going somewhere else. She suggested the park near her house.

When they arrived at Greg's, Paloma walked outside to retrieve Jazarah. She and Greg discussed something about dinner and medicines, then he kissed his daughter good-bye. Nina had been checking her cell phone messages while they spoke, so the knock on the car window startled her.

"Kiss. Bye-Bye to Ne Na?"

"Of course," she said. *How did this kid wheedle her way in so quickly?*

Greg pulled out of the driveway and turned to Nina. "You see the problem already, don't you?"

She saw it, and she felt it. *Am I supposed to allow a three-year-old to determine my decisions? One who isn't even mine?* But she didn't know what to do about it. "I understand what you're saying, but I'm not sure what you want me to do. Jazarah is a precious child. How could I not adore her?"

"Exactly. You can adore her. But you can't adore her then leave her. She's been through that already. And, fortunately for her, she's too young to remember her birth mother being the first woman to do that."

Nina talked to the window and the blurs of billboards and shops and offices that stretched between their homes. "Greg, I'm not doing this *to* you. I'm doing this for myself."

At the red light, he reached across the seat and covered her hand with his. "I get it, Nina, I really do. But, and maybe this is selfish on my part, I thought we were working toward something here between the two of us. The three of us."

She wished her hand didn't like the way his felt. It made this conversation all the more difficult. "Well, I thought so too . . ."

Greg let go to take the exit off the freeway. "Then why are you leaving? Could you consider, maybe, that all the things that have happened in your life and mine have brought us to this point for a reason? That your wanting to be a part of something important that can affect the world doesn't have to happen in New York? God is showering you with so many blessings, and you're running around looking for an umbrella."

"Well, it can rain in New York too, right?"

In the driveway, Greg shifted into park, but he didn't turn the engine off.

"I thought we were walking to the park," Nina said.

Greg leaned back against the headrest, closed his eyes for a moment, and turned to her. "Here's the thing. I care about you, I enjoy being with you, and I thought we could spend more time together . . . figure out where this might take us. But, if you decide that you want to stay there, I'm not moving to New York to start a veterinary practice to see if we can make things work. Elise, Peyton, Paloma, and Jazarah. My family is here."

"Maybe it won't work out, and I'll just be right back where I was before at *Trends*. And then we could . . ." She pushed the button to let the window down. Even the muggy air outside helped balance the sharpness of what she felt sitting next to Greg.

Greg shook his head. "We could, what? Jazarah and I could wait for you. Just in case you decided to come back? We're the consolation prize?"

"That's not what I meant at all."

"It's not my place to ask you to stay or to tell you to go. And since you didn't feel the need to discuss it with me before today, maybe that's something I need to think about. This is your decision. I wish it was yours and God's. I don't want my daughter in the next few weeks to grow attached to you. I don't want her to have to suffer through your leaving. And, what I'm about to say is so painful, I don't even want to hear myself say it. But, since you've made this decision, I think it's best we just stop where we are."

32

Please don't make me tell him good-bye one more time." Nina closed her eyes and held up her hand so Aretha would stop handing Manny to her. "It's bad enough the two of you had to get him a car seat, and he took the ride to the airport with us."

The exhaust from the cars, the taxis, and buses burned Nina's nose. At least that's the excuse she gave Luke for why her face was red and puffy, from the constant sniffling. As Luke emptied the trunk of Nina's bags, Aretha went through the roll call of tickets, purse, keys, cell phone, cash . . . .

"Got it. Got it. Got it."

Aretha handed Manny to Luke and held out her arms. "I'm praying for you, even if you can't pray for yourself. I love you, and you need to be careful. Call as soon as your plane lands, okay?"

Nina hugged her and wished that when she let go, she could take some of Aretha with her. She kissed Manny, who tried to wiggle his way out of Luke's arms. She stood on her tiptoes, hugged Luke, and ordered him to take care of her friend. "She needs someone to watch her."

He smiled. "I know. That's my job, and I'm good at it."

"I can't do this. We have to go," said Aretha. She turned to Nina on her way back to the car, "You know, no decision has to be forever."

Nina nodded, afraid if she spoke it would be to tell them she changed her mind. Before Luke pulled away from the curb, Nina walked into the terminal. She couldn't bear to hear Manny's yelps or watch the car become smaller and smaller until it finally disappeared.

She detoured into the nearest bathroom, took a deep breath, checked for mascara runs, and lectured herself. *This is want you wanted, worked for, and dreamed about. This is your opportunity. You earned this.* The woman she saw in the mirror still didn't look convinced.

Nina found the gate for her flight. She checked in her baggage, went through security, and looked for a place to eat breakfast. When she finally sat, choosing a place with just a few customers, the past two weeks of her life filled every empty chair at the table and then some. Elise, everyone at the office, Daisy, Shannon, Luke, Aretha, . . .

The interview with Martha nearly wiped her out, but Elise told her it was her best one yet. Nina sent notes to all the Threads of Hope people thanking them for opening their lives to her so that others could have hope.

Aretha's quilt had been under her bed for so long, she'd almost forgotten about it. But she'd wrapped the box before she left, and Luke was going to give it to her today. Nina decided it would be her good-bye gift instead of her birthday one.

Every time her cell phone rang, she hoped the name Greg Hernandez would flash on the screen. But it didn't. The time she and Elise were together, neither one of them mentioned his name. A boundary neither one of them wanted to cross.

She'd had dinner on Thomas's birthday with her parents. They moved around the house as if they were strangers in an elevator, careful not to invade each other's personal space. Nina wished she'd bought a cake. They could have celebrated the years they all had with Thomas. After finding out about her brother, she just didn't know how they could mend all that had broken for them as a family. Maybe, being away would help with that. Give her perspective.

Nina shivered, and rubbed her arms with her hands. What possessed her to wear a sleeveless dress on the plane? The person next to her would probably set the air on Arctic chill. Aretha thought the deep kiwi cotton dress was classic and made a statement. Nina hoped she remembered to tell her that whatever statement Aretha thought she heard, it was all wrong.

The waitress brought her a menu and poured her a cup of coffee. "Here you go. That should warm you up," she said and made the last three words sound like one, warmyaup. A snapshot of Jazarah reminding Greg to say "thank you" flashed before her. She blinked, and it was gone. She thanked the waitress who said that she'd be back for her order. "No rush," she said.

Nina set her cell phone on the table hanging on a thread of hope that Greg would call. Or like Richard Gere in *An Officer and a Gentleman*, he'd whip through the airport in his white lab jacket, scoop her up like she's Debra Winger, and carry her out of the terminal. *Why? So you could blame him if the staying behind didn't work out?* Nina closed her eyes until the silly romantic image disappeared. She didn't need Greg to save her from herself.

She propped her legs on the chair across from her while she scanned the menu. The Belgian waffles with whipped cream and pecans were winning out over the Blueberry Blintzes, but the omelets held promise.

Nina felt a tap on her shoulder and, though an odd way of taking an order, she thought it was the waitress. "Oh, I haven't decided what I want yet. . ."

"We could tell," the man standing behind her said.

"Can I help you?" Nina said to the couple, who appeared to be in their seventies, as they made their way around the table. She made sure her purse was zipped and still on the chair next to her.

The woman wore an ash gray peplum jacket and a gored skirt that matched. *Definitely not a flight attendant.* The man next to her was dressed in a charcoal-shaded suit that had a faint gray pinstripe, and his silver tie was almost the same shade as his hair. "Actually," the woman said, her eyes almost as dark as Nina's coffee, "we were going to ask if we could help you. Weren't we, Daniel?"

Nina looked around for cameras. Maybe this was some weird reality television show. There were still a dozen or so empty tables in the restaurant, so this wasn't the last place to sit.

He nodded. "That's right. We just thought you looked like you could use some company and, well, it's just Roberta and me traveling by ourselves, too."

Nina moved her legs off the chair, already a bit depressed her solitariness was a lighthouse beacon over her head. Greg's yammering on about trust wound its way through her brain. Her conscience shrugged its shoulders and said, *Might as well do a test run here, Nina. You're about to start the great adventure of your life.* Nina pulled out a chair, "Sure, have a seat. My name's Nina. And you are Roberta and. . . ?"

"Happy to meet you, Nina. My name is Daniel," he said and stood behind his chair until Roberta was comfortably seated in her own before he sat next to her.

The man seemed almost senatorial, and Nina's reporter brain whirred into action. She didn't want to see a newspaper later to discover she'd had no clue that she shared a breakfast table with a distinguished politician and his bride. But none of the files her brain flipped through made any connection. Still, they seemed to have that patina of gentility that grew more beautiful with age, and she hoped her brain hadn't misplaced an important file.

The waitress walked over. "Well, look at you. Made friends already," she said and pulled her pen out her apron pocket. "Y'all know what you want?"

That's why I'm here. Alone. Having breakfast with two elderly strangers. Nina searched the menu one more time. "I'll have the waffles. No, make that the blintzes." She handed the menu over and regretted she didn't stick with the waffles. Roberta and Daniel ordered coffee.

"Sharing those blintzes?" The waitress, eyes narrowed, looked at the couple.

Daniel smiled. "Actually, we've already eaten breakfast."

"Okey-dokey. Whatever," she said as if she'd been defeated.

Why are they stalking breakfast cafes if they've already eaten? Nina thought her conscience might be too eager for new experiences. She'd have to be careful to not disclose too much information about herself.

Roberta asked where Nina was headed. "New York. New job. I'll be working as an editor for a magazine." So much for careful.

They both nodded. "That sounds quite exciting," said Roberta.

Nina almost told her why she was so excited. She ushered her enthusiasm away, and asked, "And you? Where are you two going?"

They looked at one another and turned the same shade of blush pink. "You're probably going to laugh, but we'll tell you anyway. Partly why we wanted some company. Nobody to share our good news with."

Nina's journalist ears perked up. "Good news? I could use some. Spill it."

Roberta leaned toward Nina and whispered, "We're going on our honeymoon." Daniel nodded and smiled. He couldn't seem to stop doing either one.

"Honeymoon? Really?" Nina sipped her coffee, grateful she didn't laugh as they'd expected. How could she when their faces glowed like soft lamp light?

The waitress returned with two cups of coffee and Nina's breakfast. "There ya go, honey. Belgium waffles with whipped cream and pecans."

"But I ordered the blintzes," said Nina. *Didn't I?*

She reached for Nina's plate. "I can take these back. Thought for sure you said waffles."

"No problem. These are great," Nina told her. "Really."

She mumbled as she walked away.

Nina separated the waffles and spread the whipped cream over each. "Oh, so you renewed your wedding vows?"

"No. We just made them," said Daniel. He reached out and put his arm around his bride. "Just this morning we did." Roberta rested her head on his shoulder when he hugged her, then gently patted his chest. "Now Daniel, we shouldn't make a scene in public." When he let go, Nina didn't miss the fact that he moved his hand so that it rested on her knee.

"So, you just got married this morning, and you're leaving to go where on your honeymoon?"

"We're going to Hawaii," Daniel said. "We think it's time we learned how to surf. Don't you?"

Nina hesitated. If Roberta laughed, so would she. But she didn't. "We registered for private lessons. At our age, we didn't want the young people in a group to worry about us having heart attacks the first time we tried to stand on our boards."

Aretha would love this couple. Nina was quite infatuated with them already. Nina's stomach wasn't so infatuated with butter and whipped cream as breakfast choices and grumbled its disapproval. She set her fork on her plate and checked her cell phone. *Just in case.* Still silent. And so were Roberta and Daniel. Nina looked up from her phone. "I'm sorry. That was rude of me."

"We all get distracted, especially when we're not sure what we're looking for," said Daniel. He clasped Roberta's hand, intertwining their fingers so that their polished wedding bands, his next to hers, seemed to connect one to the other. "For a long time, we both had . . ." he looked at his wife. "What's that called?"

"Shiny ball syndrome." She leaned toward Nina and whispered, "His grandson told us about that."

"Guess I forget it because I don't want to remember having it. We spent too many years of our lives chasing after jobs that glittered, shiny things, even people we thought sparkled. Everything loses its shine after a while. It's what we're left with after the newness wears off that matters."

Roberta laughed. "I think we're proof God has a sense of humor, you know? But we learned the hard way that when our time is over here, no person in his right mind says, 'Wish I would have spent one more day at the office.'"

Daniel and Roberta left for their flight to Maui, and Nina gathered herself for the walk to her gate. She thought about what they'd said . . . about no one ever regretting the time they spent with the people they love. Did being alone in the job she dreamed of trump being with those she cared about, in the job that allowed her to be there with them?

Nina thought about her life, the one she was leaving behind. How many times the unexpected had provided for her, how the very boy she detested in high school grew to be the man who made her a better person, how being given the opportunity to attend the benefit resulted in the feature stories that could change lives.

And who made all that happen, Nina? Who brought that together, stitch by stitch, threading pieces of lives together to create something extraordinary? Just because you don't see Me, that doesn't mean I'm not there. Would you want Thomas to have lived longer if it meant being in pain? Was that prayer for you or for him?

Your entire life, you wanted to belong, to be loved, to be a part of something that could make a difference . . . and you had it. Just where you were.

Those were the desires of your heart, Nina. New York is the desire of your ego.

What if she gave God another chance? What if she prayed for Greg to meet her at the airport? That would prove God heard her, how could she not have faith after that?

Nina waited until she heard the final call before she handed over her boarding pass. Another prayer unanswered. Another loss. Another reason to doubt.

33

Elise, this is the third consecutive year you've called the night of the benefit to ask about picking me up," Greg said as he checked his tuxedo pockets for his cuff links.

He heard Peyton through the speakerphone. "That's because she's stubborn. I told her—"

"Please don't shout. You'll upset the baby."

Greg laughed. "The baby isn't due for another two months."

"Babies hear sounds eighteen weeks into a pregnancy, and loud noises startle them. I've done my research. I don't want her traumatized before she's born," Elise said.

"She? When did you find that out?" He checked his pants pockets. Still no cufflinks.

"We didn't. I just alternate between using her and him. We still want to be surprised."

"Whatever makes you happy. In the meantime, I don't want one of your surprises to be us being there late. I'm looking for my cufflinks, and she's almost ready." The bedroom door opened, and Greg smiled. "In fact, she's ready now. We'll be there soon."

Jazarah pranced in and stood in front of the full-length mirror and twirled. Her sapphire dress sparkled almost as brightly as her eyes. "You are so pretty," she said to her reflection. "Right, Daddy?"

Greg lifted her, kissed her forehead, and whirled her around. "You are beautiful, my little princess." As her feet touched the floor, he noticed they were still bare. "You can't go to the ball without shoes."

Paloma entered after a faint knock at the bedroom door. "She escaped to your room before her shoes and her sash. A few more minutes, and she will be dressed." She held her hand out to Jazarah, "Come, princess. It's almost time for you to leave, but you need to finish getting dressed."

His daughter blew him a kiss, and she skipped out of his room, her dark curls bouncing.

Again the door opened. "I found a pair of lovely silver monogrammed cufflinks. They must be yours since you're the only man in the house who'd be wearing them."

"You are not only beautiful, but useful in emergencies," Greg said before he kissed Nina. "This never gets old," he whispered and kissed her again.

"We have to stop now or we'll never make it to the benefit," she whispered back, her voice warm and silky. "I promise we'll pick up where we left off when we return."

"I'm a lucky man," Greg said and held out his arms so Nina could put his cufflinks on.

"Lucky? No. Smart? Yes." Her eyes drank in this man whose wife she had become because he trusted God. And, in doing so, showed her how to trust Him as well. Almost two years ago, she'd stepped out of a plane determined to start the life she'd dreamed of for years. When God didn't answer her prayer for Greg to meet her at the airport in Houston, by the time she arrived at JFK, she'd decided she could live without both of them.

Nina was on the phone with Aretha waiting for her baggage when someone tapped her on the shoulder. *What is it today with this shoulder tapping?* She turned around and found herself face-to-face with Greg.

He took the cell phone from her. "Hi, Aretha. She'll call you back." He ended the call and handed her the phone. "Do you need help with your suitcases?"

"Help with my suitcases? Are you kidding me?" She swatted her bangs off her forehead and resisted the urge to bash him over his head with her purse. "What are you doing here, and how did you know I was talking to Aretha?"

"Is this your way of telling me you're happy to see me?" He reached for her hand. "Let's talk over here. Away from the crowd."

Nina remembered looking around the airport to convince herself she hadn't fallen through some worm hole and into another life. She recognized the faces of passengers who were on the same flight, and she spotted her luggage as the conveyor burped it out of the belly of the plane. So she had landed exactly where she'd intended. But she was no less confused than she was before. "Look, I don't know how or why you're here. All your talk about faith and trust and prayer. I prayed and waited and waited and waited for you to meet me at the airport—"

His hands cradled her face. "Well, here I am. At the airport."

And that was her first lesson in understanding that answered prayer may look different than she expected.

And she could not have expected, standing in the airport baggage claim that day, the blessings that awaited her in the life she and Greg shared today.

He straightened his bow tie and turned to Nina, "Well? Should I whirl around like our daughter so you can see how beautiful I am?"

She laughed. "I should have made you sign a 'non-compete clause.' It's not fair that you turn more heads walking into a room than I do."

He sighed. "It's a curse I live with daily," he said but couldn't maintain his serious expression. Greg tapped his watch. "You have less than ten minutes to be stunning and ready to roll. And you're still waltzing around in your robe."

"Go check on Jazarah. Oh, and please make sure she's not trying to feed Manny. Or that he's not curled up in her lap or—"

"Should I be taking notes?" He looked at her with that lop-sided smile she knew characterized his sarcasm.

"No, dear. I'm the freelance writer in the family, remember? All I have to do is slip on my dress."

He sat on the edge of their bed. "Then maybe I'll wait . . ."

"Get out of here or else you'll suffer the wrath of hormonal Elise when we arrive late." She kissed his forehead. As he walked out, she said, "And, anyway, I know you won't leave without me."

He'd told her that when he'd surprised her at the airport. Greg said that Elise and his memories provided the fuel he needed to go after his own dream. His sister had called him and asked him why he was still home. "You may not like what Nina is doing, but she's at least going after what she thinks she wants. That takes courage. You, on the other hand . . ." He ended the conversation without letting her finish. Pacing in the den, he passed photographs of his parents and of Lily. Three people he loved, taken from him, by people and situations over which he had no control. *Will you let Nina be number four? Can you live the rest of your life knowing you never let her know you loved her?* He called Elise to apologize. "Accepted," she said. "Now, get to the airport because I already booked your flight out."

Over vending machine canned drinks and cheese crackers near baggage claim, Greg placed two tickets on the table. "I won't leave without you. Unless you want me to. If New York is what you want, then I'll tear one up and be on my way. But I couldn't let you go without telling you that what I want is a life with you."

Her second lesson in understanding: sometimes the answer appeared before the question. New York wasn't just an answer to a dream, it was the stuffing that filled the void of recognition, importance, self-worth. *And then what?* She pictured Daniel's and Roberta's faces, their joy so transparent she could see their hearts. Was she afraid to be that happy?

Her fingertips grazed the ticket. She couldn't bring herself to look at Greg. "I don't deserve this. Or you. I don't even know why God would do something for me. I've ignored Him almost my entire life."

He placed his hand under her chin and lifted her face to his. "None of us deserve happiness. That's what makes it a gift. And loving us even when we've ignored Him? That's why He's God, and we're not."

Elise's pregnancy was not only a happy surprise for her, but also one for Nina who would be wearing the dress Elise had ordered for herself. A one-shouldered sheer black tulle, the dress was offset at the waist by an Art Deco enamel pin set with glass pearls and Swarovski crystal. She'd just slipped it on when Paloma's voice came from the other side of the closet door. "Sorry to disturb you, but someone wanted to see you."

Nina stepped out and, as always, experienced the exquisite joy of seeing their son. His arms and legs churned the air as Paloma handed him to her. Thomas greeted her with a chorus of "ma-ma-ma-ma" with intermittent sprays from the motor-boat imitation he learned from his big sister.

Careful to avoid the pin on her dress, Nina transferred him to her hip and covered his face with kisses. He rewarded her with throaty giggles and a few more sprays, kicking his legs against her as if in a horse race. "One of these days, I suppose you'll have hair," she said as she caressed the blonde stubble on his head. Thomas's eyes darted back and forth across Nina's face. His mouth made a tiny "o" as he reached out a plump little hand and grabbed one of her diamond earrings.

While Nina balanced him, Paloma carefully unwound his chubby fingers from around the loops Nina wore. "He's definitely his father's son. When he sees what he wants, he goes for it," said Nina. "Be sweet tonight." She kissed him on each cheek, then turned him over to Paloma.

"Let's read a story, Mr. Thomas," she said. They left the room, her son babbling as if every syllable told a story.

Nina learned another important lesson through their son. Though the death of her brother Thomas devastated the O'Malley family, the birth of her son brought a promise of healing. Her relationship with her parents was still fragile, but their grandson awakened a hope in them that had been long ago buried. She and Greg gave them tickets for the We Care benefit tonight, and they said they would attend. Aretha and Luke were picking them up to make sure because Nina did not want her parents to miss the surprise she'd planned. Threads of Hope quilted a panel in honor of Thomas, and they would be taking it with them to Washington next week.

"Nina? We're walking to the car . . ."

That was her husband's two-minute warning. Nina made one last check in the mirror. She ran her fingers through her still short layers of curls to fluff what Thomas had flattened, made sure she didn't have lipstick on her teeth, and covered herself with one final spritz of perfume. She was about to walk away when she heard a familiar voice.

You're beautiful, Nina. You always were.

She whispered, "Thank you" and went downstairs to meet Greg, Jazarah, and the future they were stitching together.

Discussion Questions
(Spoiler Alert!)

1. When we first meet Nina, her single focus is the New York promotion. Is her self-worth connected to her job? Why? Do you find that, today, many people are like Nina in that they are defined by the work/career/profession they have chosen? If so, why? If not, why not?

2. What is Nina's relationship with her parents, especially her mother? Is Nina judging her harshly, is Sheila a harsh judge, or both? What is it that mothers and daughters expect and want from one another? How is that different for sons, or is it?

3. For more than ten years, Nina carries the high school incident with Greg Hernandez and his friends. What happened to this grudge over time? Did it shape the woman she became? Why is Nina holding on to those negative feelings?

4. What does Nina see in Aretha and Daisy that led her to consider them friends? Why doesn't either one of them or both discuss the New York decision with her? Should they have? At what point are we willing to risk the relationship with friends by honestly sharing about situations in their lives?

5. What, if any, of the information about The AIDS Memorial Quilt is new to you? Does its size surprise you? If you were already in a city where some of the panels were being displayed, would you go to the exhibit? Why or why not?

6. Were you already aware of the number of children who die in Third World countries because of AIDS? Would you have adopted Jazarah? Why or why not? Does it

concern you that children like her are being assimilated into our schools and society at large?

7. The stories the families shared were all different. Were they what you expected?

8. Should Nina's parents have told her the truth about Thomas? Were their reasons for not telling her justifiable? What would you have done in the same situation, same time? Would bringing this forward to the twenty-first century make a difference in Nina's parents' decision? In yours?

9. Do you agree with Nina's decision not to stay in New York?

10. Greg ends their relationship when Nina tells him about going to New York. Do you think he is being unnecessarily overprotective of his daughter and her feelings?

INSTRUCTIONS FOR MAKING A QUILT PANEL

The NAMES Project Foundation:
The AIDS Memorial Quilt

Step by Step: How to Make a Panel For The Quilt

You don't have to be an artist or sewing expert to create a moving personal tribute remembering a life lost to AIDS, but you do have to make a panel in order to add a name to The Quilt. It's not as complicated as many people think, though. It doesn't matter if you use paint or fine needlework, iron-on transfers or handmade appliqués, or even spray paint on a sheet; any remembrance is appropriate. (This is, however, the only way to have a name added to The Quilt—by making a panel to remember your lost loved one.) You may choose to create a panel privately as a personal memorial or you may choose to follow the traditions of old-fashioned quilting bees by including friends, family, and co-workers. That choice, like virtually everything else involved in making a panel, is completely up to you.

Here, in a few easy steps, is how to create a panel for The Quilt:

1. Design the panel

Include the name of the person you are remembering. Feel free to include additional information such as the dates of birth and death, hometown, special talents, etc. We ask that you please limit each panel to one individual (obvious exceptions include siblings or spouses).

2. Choose your materials

Remember that The Quilt is folded and unfolded every time it is displayed, so durability is crucial. Since glue deteriorates with time, it is best to sew things to the panel. A medium-weight, non-stretch fabric such as a cotton duck or poplin works best.

Your design can be vertical or horizontal, but the finished, hemmed panel must be 3 feet by 6 feet (90 cm x 180 cm)—no more and no less! When you cut the fabric, leave an extra 2-3 inches on each side for a hem. If you can't hem it yourself, we'll do it for you. Batting for the panels is not necessary, but backing is recommended. Backing helps to keep panels clean when they are laid out on the ground. It also helps retain the shape of the fabric.

3. Create the panel

In constructing your panel, you might want to use some of the following techniques:

- Appliqué: Sew fabric, letters, and small mementos onto the background fabric. Do not rely on glue—it won't last.

- Paint: Brush on textile paint or colorfast dye, or use an indelible ink pen. Please don't use "puffy" paint; it's too sticky.

- Stencils: Trace your design onto the fabric with a pencil, lift the stencil, then use a brush to apply textile paint or use indelible markers.

- Collage: Make sure that whatever materials you add to the panel won't tear the fabric (avoid glass and sequins for this reason), and be sure to avoid very bulky objects.

- Photos: The best way to include photos or letters is to photocopy them onto iron-on transfers, iron them onto 100% cotton fabric and sew that fabric to the panel. You may also put the photo in clear plastic vinyl and sew it to the panel (off-center so it avoids the fold).

4. Write a letter

Please take the time to write a letter about the person you've remembered. The letter might include your relationship to him or her, how he or she would like to be remembered, and a favorite memory. If possible, please send us a photograph along with the letter for our archives.

5. Make a donation

If you are able, please make a donation to help pay for the cost of adding your panel to The Quilt. The NAMES Project Foundation depends on the support of panel makers to pre-serve the Quilt and keep it on display. Gifts of any amount are welcome and greatly appreciated.

6. Fill out the panel maker information form

This provides us with vital information about you and your panel.

7. Send in the panel

Once your panel is completed there are several ways you can submit it to The NAMES Project so that it becomes a part of The AIDS Memorial Quilt.

You can send your panel to The NAMES Project Foundation or you can opt to bring the panel to a Quilt display or to a local chapter.

Send it to us directly at The NAMES Project Foundation

ATTN: New Panels

The NAMES Project Foundation

204 14TH ST NW

ATLANTA, GA 30318-5304

404.688.5500

Be sure to send it by registered mail or with a carrier that will track your package. We recommend panels be shipped via Federal Express or UPS.

Bring the panel to a Quilt display

Please be sure to contact the local display host first for more information on how and when they are collecting new panels (many displays accept new panels only on the last day of the event, while others are prepared to accept new panels at any time during a display).

Bring a new panel to one of our chapters

Your panel will stay in the community for up to three months, being used for education and outreach, and then will be sent to the Foundation to be sewn into the Quilt.

Important

No matter how you decide to turn in a new panel, please be sure to print out the panel maker information form, fill it out, and include it with the panel. This information helps us to stay in touch with you and keep you up to date on both the panel and The Quilt.

How your panel becomes part of The Quilt

When a new panel arrives at our national headquarters in Atlanta, it is carefully logged and examined for durability. Some panels might require hemming to adjust for size; others may need reinforcement or minor repairs. Next, new panels are sorted—some grouped geographically by region, others by theme or appearance. When eight similar panels are collected, they are sewn together to form a twelve-foot square. This is the basic building block of The Quilt, and it is usually referred to as either a "12-by-12" or "Block."

Once sewn, each 12-by-12 is edged in canvas and given a unique number, its "Block Number," which makes tracking the block possible. All panel, panel maker, and numerical information is then stored in our Quilt databases. Once this happens, you are sent information including which block the panel you submitted has been made a part of, how to request the block for displays of The Quilt, and a current display schedule.

The entire process, from our receiving the panel to incorporating it into a 12-by-12 in The AIDS Memorial Quilt, typically takes between three and six months.

Questions?

"The only dumb question is the question you have but never ask!" Email questions to: panels@aidsquilt.org or call Roddy Williams, Panel Maker Relations, or Gert McMullin, Production Manager, at 404.688.5500.

For information on panel making workshops contact: Jada Harris at 404-688-5500 ext. 228 or email jharris@aidsquilt .org.

PANEL-MAKER PARTNER BUDDY SYSTEM

The NAMES Project Foundation is launching a new Panelmaker Partner buddy system that will pair volunteers with individuals wanting to make a panel for the Quilt. Creating a panel on your own might seem daunting but with the help of a partner the process is suddenly much more manageable. This is a way you can ensure that a friend or loved one lives on as part of this epic handmade memorial—the largest piece of community folk art in the world and one of our most powerful HIV prevention education tools. If you are interested, a member of The NAMES Project Staff will contact you for further information and to find out how you would like to share the process. (See www.aidsquilt.org/callmyname for a link to the form.)

CALL MY NAME PROJECT

Call My Name is a program designed to draw attention to a public health crisis by fostering the creation of new panels for

The AIDS Memorial Quilt made by African Americans in honor of their friends, family, and community members who have died of AIDS. With the introduction of The AIDS Memorial Quilt, The NAMES Project redefined the tradition of quilt making in response to contemporary circumstances. Call My Name uses this model and through hands-on, panel-making activity brings people and communities together to remember loved ones, grieve, find support and strength, and engage in dialogues for change. Call My Name also enhances The NAMES Project's ability to collect and display greater numbers of panels that reflect the epidemic's impact within the African American community. As a result, Quilt prevention, education and awareness programs have greater capacity to deliver even more cultural relevance and provide poignant personal connections for African American men, women, and children who see it. (See http://www.aidsquilt.org/callmyname.)

Want to learn more about author
Christa Allan and check out other great
fiction from Abingdon Press?

Sign up for our fiction newsletter at
www.AbingdonPress.com
to read interviews with your favorite authors, find tips
for starting a reading group, and stay posted on what
new titles are on the horizon. It's a place to connect
with other fiction readers or post a
comment about this book.

Be sure to visit Christa online!

www.christaallan.com

We hope you enjoyed *Threads of Hope* and that you will continue to read the Quilts of Love series of books from Abingdon Press. Here's an excerpt from the next book in the series, Angela Breidenbach's *A Healing Heart.*

1

"Why in the world did I agree to do this?"

Mara Keegan's vision blurred as she stared at the old photo she'd picked from the box for the first block on Cadence's memory quilt. David's arm curled tightly around her pregnant waist, his other balanced a precocious three-year-old Cadence, and one-year-old Toby grinned up into his mommy's eyes. Louie, the new family border collie/lab pup sat at their feet ready to catch Toby's graham cracker.

A smile stole across Mara's lips. Louie nabbed that cracker and Toby wailed, right after the shutter clicked. But the picture captured the split-second happy moment forever. The perfect family with so much promise. A promise broken off prematurely by a whimsical God.

Mara's smile faded. She glanced over toward her sleeping fourteen-year-old dog curled up on one of his favorite oversized mutt mats. He'd been with their family since the early days. His black muzzle sported more white around his nose now. Louie seemed like the bridge from past to present as she looked back at the first picture. When would she be ready to try love again? Did she even need it? She broke out in a sweat in spite of the cold wind blowing the last of December past her windows. Not until she could trust God again. How could it have all gone so wrong? The wind gust whooshed against her office door and rattled the inset glass.

A burning sensation started in the center of Mara's chest. She wrapped her ankles around the wooden stool legs and anchored her feet as she rubbed her midsection. This gift took more out of her than she thought. With less than five months to Cadence's graduation, she had to design and create a quilt full of memories. Memories Cadence needed as she left for college. Memories to wrap around her when she felt far from home and family. Memories Mara promised Cadence, and Mara never broke a promise.

Mara dug in her purse for a chewable antacid tablet. They'd become her favorite candy the last few months. Especially today, since the official documents for the new contract were lost when her computer network crashed after the big windstorm tore down power lines last night. No one had power for the last twelve hours on this side of Bozeman. This government contract could change the future of her business and the community. But her business mentor, Rich, jumped in to help. He'd kept the emails. By the time the computers blinked on this afternoon, she'd have his advised changes and be able to print out another set, postmark a hard copy, and fax the acceptance before the close of business back East. Okay, maybe she should eat a little better. She popped one in her mouth, scowled at the mini bottle, and threw it back in her purse.

The box of photos held too many memories. To choose the right ones for Cadence, Mara needed to sort through them one by one. "Why didn't I just buy Cadence a car, huh, Louie?" Something easy that didn't rip her heart out every minute of the planning. The dog opened his eyes and cocked an ear at her. The burn radiated out further. She pressed hard against her stomach to ease the pain. The antacid should help soon.

She should have eaten more than a skim latte for lunch. She needed an early start on all the photos for the t-shirt transfers. Once the photos finished printing out on transfer paper, she could leave them with Tina at the t-shirt shop overnight and pick up the photos pressed onto the poplin tomorrow. Nausea built until it reached the middle of Mara's chest and wallowed there, squeezing the little bits of heart she had left. It figured she'd have the beginnings of an ulcer. Her neck muscles tensed and sent a shooting pain into her jaw. She opened and closed her jaw joint and wiggled the bones of her chin, but the motion didn't soothe the tension.

How long could she go on living with the way things turned out? The stress from carrying the entire business load left her with this constant tension and now the heartburn. Mara rolled her head from shoulder to chest to opposite shoulder. David's snowmobiling accident left her in charge of twenty-five employees, business loans, and a dream built for two. But now there was one. Three years from the moment the snow buried him in the avalanche. Three years since David breathed his last. And she hadn't stopped to breathe since. She hated the week after Christmas since the accident. Sacrilegious or not, she hated it.

Mara shook her head to clear the pity party. So a little more lost sleep, what's new? The sooner she plowed into this promise, the sooner she'd get the sleep she needed. This present would be done on time if it was the last thing she did. Breaking the family tradition, a quilt for graduation, was not an option. It meant too much to Cadence. Maybe she should switch out the lavender candle for a citrus scent and wake up her brain. She looked up at it. Maybe later. Mara inhaled the calm fragrance.

Her head pounded. The caffeine seemed to create more jitters than normal. She pushed away the remaining drink. It'd gone cold anyway. She pulled the hair band out of her high ponytail to loosen the tension on her scalp. Mara massaged tender spots under the thick mane with one hand while she spread out several photo choices on the white workspace. Maybe she should consider cutting off several inches. The weight alone might cause these headaches. But David had always loved her hair. She hadn't cut it more than to shape it in longer than she could remember. Had she even done that this year? Always in an updo for business, no one saw the condition her hair was in. She swept up the ends of her hip-length burnished brown locks and grimaced at them. Maybe a little change would do her good. Yeah, right. When was that going to happen? She picked up the family photo again unable to let it go. Change wasn't always good.

Mara's heart twisted, radiating out searing pain. She slapped a hand out for balance and instead flipped the box of photos over as she tumbled off the work stool onto the cold floor. The wooden chair clanged to the rustic clay tiles with her legs tangled in the chair rungs. The box rained down life-moment scenes as if a movie reel unwound in front of her eyes. Her son, Toby, at T-ball, Marisa's Disney Princess birthday party, and Cadence with her younger siblings tackling their daddy. Was she having a heart attack?

Louie barked in surprise and jumped up from his massive plaid dog pillow.

Pictures fluttered and scattered across the floor.

Mara's hand held fast to her family forever frozen in a joyful pose—before God pulled his whimsical trick.

Louie barked again and bounded across the room, sliding on slick paper, to stick his nose into the back of Mara's neck. He lay down with his muzzle across her right shoulder buried in her long brown hair.

Mara blinked. What just happened? Oh, there. She focused on David. His strong face, his tanned muscular arms that held her close, and those sparkling brown eyes grinning with little crinkles she used to trace with her fingers. David, David, I miss you. She closed her eyes.

—————

Mara Keegan. Joel sighed as he tucked the file under his arm. Would she remember? Would she throw him out? As he rang the doorbell, Joel heard a dog barking inside. Then a pretty teen with unusual golden coloring flung the front door wide.

"Louie, knock it off!" She yelled toward the back of the house. "Sorry, he's kind of protective. Can I help you?"

"Hi, I'm Joel Ryan," he stuck out his hand. "Here to consult with Mara Keegan on the government contract. Is she here?"

"Sure. I'm Cadence, her daughter." She invited him in and shivered as she flicked the ornate door closed. "Cold out there, huh?"

"Well, it's sure not as warm as my last consulting visit in California." Joel smiled. "But I'm used to it. I'm from Colorado."

She had a slight Native American look, but her hair was a reddish brown and dark freckles dotted her golden cheeks. Her eyes were almost rust and rimmed with long black lashes. She wore very little makeup.

Joel wondered about her mother, the woman he had yet to meet in person. Only a phone call five years ago, but now he hoped Mara didn't remember him. He swallowed. That wasn't one of his finer moments. Better to get it out of the way if she did put two and two together. By God's grace, he was a different person now. Would Mara have the grace to forgive?

Louie barked several more times. "Louie, that's enough!" Cadence yelled again. "I don't know what's up with him. He quits as soon as the doorbell does, but he's usually here all up in your face and checking you out, too." She looked around for the dog. "Weird."

"Nice Christmas tree." Joel nodded at the decorated fake evergreen to be polite. It was a nicer tree than his miniature on the coffee table, all designer perfect. The red and green plaid ribbons looked like someone tied each one exactly the same. His tree barely had lights.

Cadence gave the tree a small glance. "Yeah, thanks."

He checked his triple time zone watch. His favorite tool never disappointed. Travel and daily contact with clients from Pacific to Mountain to Eastern kept him in a constant chase of the correct time. Clients in any part of the country could count on his prompt call or arrival. Plenty of time to meet the deadline, but there was no sense in delay. "May I meet with Mara?"

"Sure, follow me. She's back in her workroom." A hint of resentment floated in her tone. "Like always."

The TV screen held a frozen Wii game with several cartoon Wii avatars. "Mom" wore a purple shirt and long dark hair. He sidestepped the Wii balance board on the floor and followed.

"There's another entrance for that part of the house, if you want next time." Cadence traipsed off into a long hallway with her braid swinging.

———— ❧ ————

"Mom!" Cadence rounded the corner.

Mara lay on her left side, stiff and chilled. She opened her eyes at the alarm in her daughter's voice.

Cadence knelt at Mara's feet, gently picked up her mom's top ankle, and unthreaded the wooden stool from Mara's legs.

"I'm okay—" Mara tried to sit up but only made it to her elbow. She didn't have the strength to push up all the way past the sharp pain in her shoulder. The dizziness rushed back. Her whole body didn't feel all that great now either since hitting the floor. But her left shoulder really ached all the way on the inside, wow!

"Cadence, is everything all right?" A man stood in the doorway. He wore a dark blue ski parka over a business suit. Louie growled as the hair along his backbone stood on end. He leaped and stood over Mara. The man jumped back into the hall away from the big dog.

"No, Louie, no!" Cadence kept her voice steady, but firm. "Joel, he's not mean." She shot off without looking away from her mother. She moved around to Mara's back and pulled Louie aside by his collar. "Good boy, now go lay down."

Mara glanced at the stranger near the door. He looked ready to take over, but Louie held him at bay. Her old dog stood on guard, disregarding Cadence's command.

"Here, I'll help you up." With her arm around Mara's back, Cadence tried to lift her.

"I don't think I can stand yet." Mara leaned against the table leg. "Just give me a minute to catch my breath." She shivered at the cold seeping up from the tiles into her legs. The shiver started a new spasm of pain in her shoulder and ankle.

"Sheesh, Mom, what did you do? How'd you end up on the floor?" Cadence still knelt beside Mara and waited.

"I don't know." Mara gasped for air. "One minute I was picking out pictures for your quilt and the next I fell. Maybe I have the flu. I'm a little light-headed." She pressed her stomach and fought for control of the nausea. "I might have twisted my ankle, though. Man it hurts!" She wanted to reach for her left leg, but the pain in her shoulders held her back.

"Louie." Cadence pointed at the dog bed. "Go!" Louie crept backward an inch at a time fighting his instinct to protect. His long ears stayed flattened back on his gleaming black head and his eyes trained on Joel without a flinch.

Joel eyed Louie and stepped into the room. "May I suggest we get you checked out?"

Mara dragged in another breath. "Who are you?" Her lips trembled and her heart fluttered out of control.

"I'm Joel, your new consultant from Business Mentors, Inc. I'm replacing Rich." He put a file down on her worktable. "I really think we ought to get you to the ER." He moved closer toward Mara and knelt down at her level.

"I don't need—"

"Mom, you don't look good at all. I think he's right. You're like, white as your shirt."

But she could ask the doctor to check her heart. No, that's silly. At thirty-nine, she probably just had a bad case of the flu. Mara's arm throbbed with sharp jabs, her neck and jaw muscles clenched tight. She'd probably sprained her shoulder now, too.

Exhausted she bit out, "Fine, fine. I probably need an antibiotic or something." Another shiver shot through her. "I'm sure it's the flu. I have the chills and ache all over." Mara rubbed her left arm.

Joel moved in to Mara's side to help her stand. Together both Cadence and Joel lifted Mara from the floor.

"Ow, ow! I can't—" Mara felt herself swing up. Her head lolled back from the motion.

"I've got you. You can trust me." He glanced over at her daughter. "Cadence, would you grab a blanket for her and let's go." Joel tipped his head toward the door. "We'll take my car so you can help your mom if she needs it."

"I don't need—"

"Really?" Joel's blue eyes captured hers again. "Can you walk?"

A shooting pain screeched through her left side.

QUILTS
of LOVE

EVERY QUILT
HAS A STORY

There is a strong connection between storytelling and quilts. Like a favorite recollection, quilts are passed from one generation to the next as precious heirlooms. They bring communities together.

The Quilts of Love series focuses on women who have woven romance, adventure, and even a little intrigue into their own family histories. Featuring contemporary and historical romances as well as occasional light mystery, this series will draw you into uplifting, heartwarming, exciting stories of characters you won't soon forget.

Visit **QuiltsofLoveBooks.com** for more information.

For more information and for more
fiction titles, please visit
AbingdonPress.com/fiction.

BKM122220005 PACP01223825-01

"C. S. Lewis famously observed, 'If you read history you will find that the Christians who did most for the present world were those who thought most of the next.'" Our problem is not that we think too much about heaven but rather think too little of it. In *A Place Called Heaven*, my friend Robert Jeffress has done a masterful job of helping believers think biblically about that future home Jesus is preparing for every believer."

Dr. David Jeremiah, founder and president,
Turning Point Ministries

"When it comes to the bottom line for Christians, heaven is it. Our life on earth is but a brief wisp of vapor compared to the eternity of heaven, so it makes sense to learn as much as possible about our everlasting home. Dr. Jeffress does a stellar job of answering peoples' questions about this marvelous place beyond our tombstones, and I highly recommend *A Place Called Heaven* to every Christ-follower. I also recommend it to those who do not yet follow Christ, as it will give the skeptical reader solid, biblical answers to their toughest questions about the world beyond the grave!"

Joni Eareckson Tada, Joni and Friends
International Disability Center

"We're all curious about heaven, and thankfully this book uses biblical teaching to enable us to get a peek behind the curtain. Read it to be reminded that the best is yet to come!"

Dr. Erwin W. Lutzer, pastor emeritus,
The Moody Church, Chicago, Illinois

"Why is it that most of us know so little about heaven? If how we live here directly impacts how we live there—in eternity—shouldn't we know more about the consequences of this life and about the place God is preparing for His heirs? I'm so excited about this book you hold in your hands. Dr. Jeffress is a strong Christian voice in this day of chaos. And *A Place Called Heaven* is a clarion call for us all to look up and consider afresh how much God loves us and how profoundly our lives on earth matter. Jesus is preparing a place in heaven for you, a place that fits you perfectly. Imagine! May you devour these pages, as I did, and begin to live more purposefully with eternity in mind."

Susie Larson, talk radio host, national speaker, and author of *Your Powerful Prayers*

"Robert Jeffress gets right to the point—in fact, he gets to ten of the main points people need to know and believe if they expect to go to heaven. *A Place Called Heaven* is clear and biblical in its approach. This is a good read for all and a great tool to use in sharing the good news of the gospel with others."

Dr. Mark L. Bailey, president, Dallas Theological Seminary, Dallas, Texas

"A thousand years from today you will be alive . . . somewhere. No one is really ready to live life to the fullest until he or she is ready to die. Robert Jeffress opens biblical truth with the desired end that you can have the assurance you will live forever in . . . *A Place Called Heaven*."

Dr. O. S. Hawkins, president/CEO, GuideStone Financial Resources, Dallas, Texas

"Dr. Robert Jeffress not only continues to have one of the most remarkable preaching ministries in America but also makes it available through the publication of many of those messages. The present book on heaven is no exception. The vast majority seem to fear preaching on eternal destiny and are much more moved by the social agendas of the day. But *A Place Called Heaven* answers serious questions that the average believer desperately wants to know. Further, this tome will generate a desire on the part of those who read it to experience for themselves the glories of heaven. The chapter on what people will do in heaven is one of the most perceptive I have ever read."

Dr. Paige Patterson, president, Southwestern Baptist Theological Seminary, Ft. Worth, Texas

A PLACE CALLED
HEAVEN

10 Surprising Truths about Your
Eternal Home

DR. ROBERT
JEFFRESS

BakerBooks

a division of Baker Publishing Group
Grand Rapids, Michigan

© 2017 by Robert Jeffress

Published by Baker Books
a division of Baker Publishing Group
PO Box 6287, Grand Rapids, MI 49516-6287
www.bakerbooks.com

Paperback edition published 2018
ISBN 978-0-8010-9367-8

Printed in the United States of America

The Library of Congress has cataloged the original edition as follows:
Names: Jeffress, Robert, 1955– author.
Title: A place called heaven : 10 surprising truths about your eternal home / Dr. Robert Jeffress.
Description: Grand Rapids, MI : Baker Books, 2017. | Includes bibliographical references.
Identifiers: LCCN 2017009763 | ISBN 9780801018947 (cloth) | ISBN 9780801076961 (ITPE)
Subjects: LCSH: Heaven—Christianity—Miscellanea.
Classification: LCC BT846.3 .J44 2017 | DDC 236/.24—dc23
LC record available at https://lccn.loc.gov/2017009763

Unless otherwise indicated, Scripture quotations are from the New American Standard Bible®, Copyright © 1960, 1962, 1963, 1968, 1971, 1972, 1973, 1975, 1977, 1995 by The Lockman Foundation. Used by permission. (www.Lockman.org)

Scripture quotations labeled NIV are from the Holy Bible, New International Version®. NIV®. Copyright © 1973, 1978, 1984, 2011 by Biblica, Inc.™ Used by permission of Zondervan. All rights reserved worldwide. www.zondervan.com

Scripture quotations labeled NKJV are from the New King James Version®. Copyright © 1982 by Thomas Nelson, Inc. Used by permission. All rights reserved.

Scripture quotations labeled NLT are from the *Holy Bible*, New Living Translation, copyright © 1996, 2004, 2015 by Tyndale House Foundation. Used by permission of Tyndale House Publishers, Inc., Carol Stream, Illinois 60188. All rights reserved.

Scripture quotations labeled Phillips are from The New Testament in Modern English, revised edition—J. B. Phillips, translator. © J. B. Phillips 1958, 1960, 1972. Used by permission of Macmillan Publishing Co., Inc.

Scripture quotations labeled TLB are from The Living Bible, copyright © 1971. Used by permission of Tyndale House Publishers, Inc., Carol Stream, Illinois 60188. All rights reserved.

All italics in Scripture quotations are the author's emphasis.

Published in association with Yates & Yates, www.yates2.com.

In keeping with biblical principles of creation stewardship, Baker Publishing Group advocates the responsible use of our natural resources. As a member of the Green Press Initiative, our company uses recycled paper when possible. The text paper of this book is composed in part of post-consumer waste.

20 21 22 23 24   7 6

To Randy and Kathie King

Thank you for your vision
for our Pathway to Victory ministry
as we share with the world
the message of Jesus Christ—the only Way
to that "place called heaven."

Contents

Acknowledgments

No book is a solo effort. I'm deeply indebted to the following people who were tremendously helpful in creating and communicating this encouraging message about "a place called heaven."

Brian Vos, Mark Rice, Brianna DeWitt, Lindsey Spoolstra, and the entire team at Baker Books, who caught the vision for this book immediately.

Derrick G. Jeter, our creative director at Pathway to Victory, who was an invaluable help to me in the development of this book's message.

Sealy Yates, my literary agent and friend for more than twenty years, who always provides sound advice and "outside the lines" creativity.

Carrilyn Baker, my faithful associate for nearly two decades, who helped keep track of the numerous drafts of this book while juggling a multitude of other tasks at the same time—and always with excellence.

Ben Lovvorn, Nate Curtis, Patrick Heatherington, Vickie Sterling, and the entire Pathway to Victory team, who share the message of this book to millions of people throughout the world.

Amy Jeffress, my junior-high girlfriend and wife of forty years, who makes everything I am able to do possible.

1

What Difference Does a Future Heaven Make in My Life Today?

> Keep seeking the things above, where Christ is, seated at the right hand of God. Set your mind on the things above, not on the things that are on earth.
>
> Colossians 3:1–2

My ministry necessitates a lot of travel. Even now, as I'm beginning this book on heaven, I'm preparing for an international flight. Every time I journey to a distant destination, I make a mental checklist of things I need to accomplish before leaving and items I need to take with me on my trip. This is especially true if I know I'll be gone for an extended period of time.

Right now, I'm preparing for a trip to London. So the items on my to-do list are a bit more involved than if I were flying to New York for a day or two. For example, I need to contact the post office and the newspaper to have my deliveries stopped. I need to contact my credit card company and notify them of where I'll be so they don't think my card or identity has been stolen and freeze my account. I need to call the cell phone company to have my phone enabled for international service. I also need to check the exchange rate of dollars to pounds, see what the weather is going to be like so I can pack appropriately, and most important of all . . . make sure I have my ticket and passport. Without a ticket I can't board the plane; without a passport I can't enter the country.

Wise travelers go through a routine to prepare for leaving home—even if it's just for a weekend getaway. Yet very few people ever take time to prepare for the ultimate journey to a distant land everyone will take. My trip to London will only be for a couple of weeks, but the journey I'm referring to is a one-way trip that will last for eternity: it's the journey every Christian will embark upon to that "place called heaven."

Admittedly, many Christians do not consciously spend a lot of time thinking about heaven—perhaps you haven't either. That's understandable. The overwhelming responsibilities of living in this world eclipse much thought about living in the next world. Additionally, the fact that we know so little about our home in heaven makes it seem both remote and irrelevant to our existence.

Yet we all inwardly yearn for a better world—especially when we experience the unexpected bad report from the doctor, the betrayal of a friend, the breakup of an intimate relationship, or the death of a loved one. At those times we want to believe—we have to believe—that there is a better place in which to live. Gifted author Philip Yancey captures that reality when he writes:

> The Bible never belittles human disappointment . . . but it does add one key word: temporary. What we feel now, we will not always feel. Our disappointment is itself a sign, an aching, a hunger for something better. And faith is, in the end, a kind of homesickness—for a home we have never visited but have never once stopped longing for.[1]

This book is about that future home . . . heaven. Heaven is not some fanciful, imaginary destination created by well-intentioned individuals to keep you from being overwhelmed and crushed by the harsh realities of life. Jesus Christ—the One whom Christians are banking on for their eternal destiny—assures us that heaven is a real place:

> In My Father's house are many dwelling places; if it were not so, I would have told you; for I go to prepare a place for you. If I go and prepare a place for you, I will come again and receive you to Myself, that where I am, there you may be also. (John 14:2–3)

As we will see in the pages ahead, Jesus is in heaven right now overseeing the greatest construction project in history—our heavenly home. And if He goes to the trouble of creating such an elaborate home for us, we can be sure He will return to gather us up and escort us into that indescribable new destination He is preparing for us.

There are many reasons we should be thinking more about our future home in that "place called heaven," but the most obvious reason is this: our departure for our future home is both certain and relatively soon.

The Inevitability of Death

"The statistics on death are very impressive," one keen observer noted. "One out of every one dies."[2] And when death comes, it comes suddenly—and often unexpectedly.

"Man does not know his time," Solomon wrote. "Like fish caught in a treacherous net and birds trapped in a snare, so the sons of men are ensnared at an evil time when it suddenly falls on them" (Eccles. 9:12). The Old Testament patriarch Isaac didn't know the time of his passing. In the twilight of his life, he confessed, "I am old and I do not know the day of my death" (Gen. 27:2).

Soldiers on the battlefield face the prospect of death daily. So do cancer patients who have been told their case is terminal. But have you come to grips with the fact that you are going to die—and that this event could be just around the corner? If it's true that God has ordained every day of your life—including the day of your death—every second that passes moves you closer to the grave. That's a great reason to start thinking seriously about your eternal home.

Jesus once told a story of a farmer content with the abundance of his possessions. Tearing down his old barns to build bigger barns to store his grain, the foolish farmer said to himself: "You have many goods laid up for many years to come; take your ease, eat, drink and be merry" (Luke 12:19). But God had other plans: "You fool! This very night your soul is required of you" (v. 20). The word translated "required" refers to a loan that has come due. Our lives are simply on loan from God. He can "call in" the loan anytime He chooses!

Yet few of us—unless we're of advanced age or suffering with a terminal illness—actually live in light of death. We view death as a distant possibility. And heaven? Well, that's a subject for another time—or so we think.

But our departure from this life is certain. No one gets out of this world alive. "A person's days are determined," Job said. God "decreed the number of his months and . . . set limits he cannot exceed" (Job 14:5 NIV). Run all the miles you can and eat all the bran muffins you want; you're not going to live on earth one second longer than God has predetermined.

The realization that our time on earth is finite should certainly motivate us to use our time wisely. Moses prayed, "Teach us to number our days and recognize how few they are; help us to spend them as we should" (Ps. 90:12 TLB). Every time I read that verse I think about one of the godliest men I have ever known, Harold Warren. Years ago, Harold served as the chairman of the search committee that called me to become the pastor of First Baptist Church in Wichita Falls, Texas. In his office, Harold had a small blackboard filled with chalk marks. One day I asked him what those marks represented. "Each mark indicates how many days I have left until I reach my seventieth birthday," he said. "Every day I erase one to remind me how little time I have left and to encourage me to make the most of my remaining days." Harold lived a few years past his seventieth birthday. On the day after that milestone birthday, he began *adding* a mark, reminding himself that he was living on "borrowed time." Harold understood what it meant to "number our days."

Recognizing how limited our time on earth is should cause us to think about what awaits us in eternity. Christian author Joni Eareckson Tada, who became a quadriplegic in a diving accident in 1967, has thought a lot about heaven since that time: "Heaven may be as near as next year, or next week; so it makes good sense to spend some time here on earth thinking candid thoughts about that marvelous future reserved for us."[3]

In light of the certainty of heaven for Christians, Joni encourages believers to invest in relationships; to seek purity; to be honest; to give generously of time, talent, and treasure; and to share the gospel of Christ. Why? Because such choices carry eternal consequences and rewards, as we will see in future chapters.[4]

Perspectives from the Past

Joni Eareckson Tada isn't the only person who has thought about heaven. Writers, philosophers, and prophets throughout history have all given serious attention to what Shakespeare called "the undiscover'd country."[5] And most, if not all, have concluded that those who make the greatest impact on this life are those who think the most about the next life.

We've all heard the old cliché about being so heavenly minded that we're no earthly good. Some people use this idea to justify focusing their efforts and affections solely on this world—deluding themselves into thinking such a limited perspective is actually a virtue. Like the foolish farmer who acted as if he would live forever, these people fail to realize the brevity of this life and the length of eternity.

As C. S. Lewis observed, the problem with most Christians is not that they think about heaven *too much* but that they think about heaven *too little*.

> If you read history, you will find that the Christians who did most for the present world were precisely those who thought most of the next. The Apostles themselves, who set on foot the conversion of the Roman Empire, the great men who built up the Middle Ages, the English Evangelicals who abolished the Slave Trade, all left their mark on Earth, precisely because their minds were occupied with Heaven. It is since Christians have largely ceased to think of the other world that they have become so ineffective in this. Aim at Heaven and you will get Earth "thrown in": aim at Earth and you will get neither.[6]

Here is the great irony: the more we think about the next world, the more effective we become in this world. I've seen that principle illustrated in my life every time I've been in the process of transitioning to a new church. Whenever a new church has called me as its pastor, there has always been an intermediate time of about a month during which I'm wrapping up my work at my former church while at the same time thinking about my new church. Usually, those four weeks are the most productive of my entire tenure at the former church. Why? I know my time is limited, I'm motivated to leave my work in good shape, and I am free to make what I believe are the best decisions for the church—after all, they can't fire me since I'm already on the way out! What a liberating feeling.

The realization that we are headed to a new location called "heaven" should be great motivation for us to spend our limited time on earth productively. No need to be concerned about piling up a large amount of money—we'll leave it all behind when we depart. No reason to be fixated on what other people do to us or think about us—our calling to our new location is assured. Instead, grasping the reality of that "place called heaven" that awaits us should liberate us to invest our few remaining years on earth as wisely as possible.

As you review the lives of the men and women in the Old Testament who made the most profound impact on this world—such as Abel, Enoch, Noah, Abraham, Isaac, Jacob, and Sarah—you discover one common denominator: they were captivated by the hope of the next world.

> All these died in faith, without receiving the promises, but having seen them and having welcomed them from a distance, and having confessed that *they were strangers and exiles on the earth*. For those who say such things make it clear that *they are seeking a country of their own*. And indeed if they had been thinking of that country from which they went out, they would have had opportunity to return. But as it is, they desire a *better country*, that is, a *heavenly one*. Therefore God is not ashamed to be called their God; for *He has prepared a city for them*. (Heb. 11:13–16)

David also yearned for that "better country." In Psalm 42 he wrote:

> As the deer pants for the water brooks,
> So my soul pants for you, O God.
> My soul thirsts for God, for the living God;
> When shall I come and appear before God?
>   (Ps. 42:1–2)

In the New Testament, Paul struggled with two desires: to depart for heaven as soon as possible and to remain on earth to fulfill his ministry.

> Knowing that while we are at home in the body we are absent from the Lord . . . [I] prefer rather to be absent from the body and to be at home with the Lord. (2 Cor. 5:6, 8)

Paul realized that every minute spent alive on earth was a minute away from the home Jesus had prepared for him in heaven. That's an interesting perspective of life few people consider. I'm thinking about that reality as I write these words. Shortly after I return from London, I will have to spend three days in Detroit, Michigan, fulfilling a speaking commitment. Now, I have nothing against Detroit, but Detroit isn't my home. I'd rather spend those three days in my comfortable and familiar home, enjoying my family. I was made for Dallas, not Detroit. Paul was made for heaven, not earth. He didn't want to spend one more minute here than absolutely necessary.

Yet Paul realized it was necessary to spend *some* time here on earth to fulfill the mission God had entrusted to him of guiding other people to heaven. To the Philippian Christians, Paul confessed:

> For to me, to live is Christ and to die is gain. . . . But I am hard-pressed from both directions, having the desire to depart and be with Christ, for that is very much better; yet to remain on in the flesh is more necessary for your sake. (Phil. 1:21, 23–24)

It wasn't just Paul who was torn between his duty in this world and his desire for the next world. Other early Christians also sensed the pull toward "a country of their own." Last year I visited the ancient catacombs underneath the city of Rome, which are painted with heavenly scenes of beautiful landscapes, children playing, and feasting. The tombs of Christian martyrs buried there bear heavenly minded inscriptions:

- "In Christ, Alexander is not dead, but lives—his body is resting in the grave."
- "He went to live with Christ."
- "He was taken up into his eternal home."[7]

Third-century church father Cyprian encouraged his congregation to "greet the day which assigns each of us to his own home, which snatches us hence, and sets us free from the snares of the world, and restores us to paradise and the [heavenly] kingdom." He then asked, "Who that has been placed in foreign lands would not hasten to return to his own country?" The answer was obvious: no one, because "we regard paradise as our country."[8]

But having their eyes set on that far country didn't mean these early believers were oblivious to what was taking place around them. In AD 125, an Athenian philosopher named Aristides wrote to the Roman Emperor Hadrian about the activities of Christians. After recounting a long list of their righteous acts benefiting believers and nonbelievers alike, Aristides told the emperor: "If any righteous person of their number passes away from the world they rejoice and give thanks to God, and they follow his body, as if he were moving from one place to another."[9]

A Glimpse of Heaven

For the follower of Jesus Christ, death *is* "moving from one place to another"—like moving from the frozen tundra of the arctic circle to the sun-kissed beaches of Hawaii. Paul described a Christian's change of location at death: being "absent from the body" means being "at home with the Lord" (2 Cor. 5:8).

If heaven is our future forever home, why wouldn't we want to know all we could about it? Imagine your employer tells you that you are going to be permanently transferred to a city you have never visited before: San Diego, California. You've seen a few pictures of San Diego and remember you had a cousin who used to live there, but for the most part you know nothing about the city. Don't you imagine you would try to discover the options for housing, the best schools for your children, something about the cost of living, the climate, and a hundred other things about your new location? Only a fool would say, "I'm too busy with work and family responsibilities now to invest any effort in finding out about my future home." Theologian J. C. Ryle wrote that every Christian will one day experience a similar—but eternal—"transfer":

> You are leaving the land of your nativity, you are going to spend the rest of your life in a new hemisphere. It would be strange indeed if you did not desire information about your new abode. Now surely, if we hope to dwell forever in that "better country, even a heavenly one," we ought to seek all the knowledge we can get about it. Before we go to our eternal home we should try to become acquainted with it.[10]

However, as we begin to search the Scriptures for information about this "place called heaven," we soon discover that the Bible doesn't tell us everything we want to know about our future home. What the Bible reveals is true but it's not exhaustive. Instead, God has given us a pencil sketch or line drawing of our future home.

For example, the apostle Paul received a personal tour of heaven when he was "caught up to the third heaven . . . into Paradise" (2 Cor. 12:2, 4).[11] Yet, this man who wrote most of the New Testament never jotted down a pen stroke of what he heard or saw in heaven! Why? Because what he heard were "inexpressible words, which a man is not permitted to speak" (v. 4).

And though the apostle John was given the most extensive vision of the future any Christian has ever received—recorded in the Book of Revelation—there were some aspects that John was commanded to "seal up . . . and do not write them" (Rev. 10:4). So why doesn't God tell us everything there is to know about heaven?

First, God knows that our minds are incapable of fully comprehending the complete magnificence of heaven. For example, how could you ever adequately describe the beauty of a sunset to a blind person who has never seen anything? What words would you sign to a deaf person to capture the all-encompassing majesty of Beethoven's Fifth Symphony? Our minds are designed to comprehend the experiences of this world but are incapable of processing the realities of the next world.

Additionally, if we knew everything about heaven we would never be able to concentrate on our God-given responsibilities here on earth. I realize this sounds like a contradiction to my earlier claim that being more heavenly minded makes us more earthly good, but it's not. Let me explain.

Suppose a child sits down at the dinner table and his mother places in front of him a plate of lima beans, which he normally wouldn't mind eating. But then his mother places a bowl of vanilla ice cream smothered in chocolate syrup and whipped cream on the table. What do you think the child will want to eat? The same thing you'd want to eat—the sundae! However, if the boy sits there with his plate of lima beans and his mother *promises* him an ice cream sundae after he eats his vegetables, then he'll dive into his lima beans with gusto, knowing something better is yet to come!

If God told us *everything* about heaven, we'd find it difficult to focus on the very important assignments God has charged us with during our brief stay here on earth. That is why God has given us just enough information about heaven to whet our appetite for the "sundae" that is yet to come.

Echoes of Eternity

The fact that God gives us only a glimpse of heaven shouldn't discourage us from discovering everything we can about our future home. Life is about much more than the seventy or so years we spend here on earth. Don't misunderstand what I'm saying: your life here on earth is extremely important. The choices you make, the character you form, and the affections you develop now will impact your life on the other side of the grave, as we'll see in chapter 8. As the fictitious Roman general-turned-gladiator Maximus Decimus Meridius told his men, "What we do in life echoes in eternity."[12]

Nevertheless, our existence beyond death deserves our serious consideration. As the Roman philosopher Seneca put it, "This life is only a prelude to eternity."[13] C. S. Lewis wrote about this in the final book of his Narnia series, *The Last Battle*. The children are involved in a terrible train wreck and are immediately transported to Narnia. They fear they'll be sent back to earth, but Aslan assures them that they've finally come home.

> "There *was* a real railway accident," said Aslan softly. "Your father and mother and all of you are—as you used to call it in the Shadowlands—dead. The term is over: the holidays have begun. The dream is ended: this is the morning."
>
> And as He spoke, He no longer looked to them like a lion; but the things that began to happen after that were so great and beautiful that I cannot write them. And for us this is the end of all the stories, and we can most truly say that they all lived happily ever after. But for them it was only the beginning of the real story. All their life in this world and all their adventures in Narnia had only been the cover and the title page: now at last they were beginning Chapter One of the Great Story which no one on earth has read: which goes on forever: in which every chapter is better than the one before.[14]

Four Benefits of Being "Heavenly Minded"

Indeed, if our brief time on earth is only the "cover and title page" of our eternal existence, it only makes sense that we would want to know what comes after the title page. Beyond satisfying our natural curiosity about what awaits us beyond the grave, contemplating the next life can result in four tangible benefits in this life.

1. Focusing on Heaven Reminds Us of the Brevity of Our Earthly Life

Life is short. Eternity is long. To illustrate this reality, Randy Alcorn asks people to take a piece of white paper and place a dot in the center, then draw a line from the dot to the edge of the page. It would look something like this:

The dot represents our years on earth, while the line represents eternity. Right now all of us are living inside the dot. Yet very few Christians think beyond the dot to the line—to the eternity that awaits us. How foolish it is to live for the dot that is only a blip on the screen of our eternal existence.[15]

Yet the dot and the line *are* connected to one another. As brief as our existence in this life is, it's very much connected to our eternal existence. There is no break between the dot and the line. My friend Bruce Wilkinson says it brilliantly: "Everything you do today matters forever."[16]

One of my closest friends and I both lost our parents when we were in our late twenties and early thirties. That shared experience has caused us both to talk frequently about how brief our time on earth is. When we are at dinner with our wives and something in the conversation touches on that topic, our wives will roll their eyes and say, "Oh no, here we go again with the 'life is short' speech!"

However, as much as I miss my parents, I see their "early departure" (at least from my perspective) as a gift from God that continually reminds me of how brief my life is. Their deaths remind me that while I live *in* the dot, I should never live *for* the dot. I must live for the line with eternity in mind. And that is true for you as well.

The New Testament writer James said it this way: "You do not know what your life will be like tomorrow. You are just a vapor that appears for a little while and then vanishes away" (James 4:14). And the apostle Peter observed:

> All people are like grass,
>> and all their glory is like the flowers of the field;
> the grass withers and the flowers fall.
>> (1 Pet. 1:24 NIV)

As one preacher in the Deep South said, "Life is like grass: It is sown, it is grown, it is mown, it is blown, and then it is gow-ne!" David not only agreed with this observation but prayed God would continually remind him of how brief his earthly life really was. In a psalm that echoed Moses's petition for the Lord to "teach us to number our days" (Ps. 90:12), David asked:

> LORD, make me to know my end
> And what is the extent of my days;
> Let me know how transient I am.
> Behold, You have made my days as handbreadths,
> And my lifetime as nothing in Your sight;
> Surely every man at his best is a mere breath.
>> (39:4–5)

Focusing on the reality and truth of heaven as we are going to do in the pages ahead is one very practical way to continually remind ourselves how fleeting our time on earth really is.

2. *Focusing on Heaven Prepares Us for the Certainty of Judgment*

"Everybody Is Going to Heaven" may be a popular song but it's also a horrendous lie. God's Word reveals that every-body is *not* going to heaven. In fact, very few people are going to heaven if Jesus can be trusted on this subject. The Lord urged people to "enter through the narrow gate; for the gate is wide and the way is broad that leads to destruction, and there are many who enter through it. For the gate is small and the way is narrow that leads to life, and there are few who find it" (Matt. 7:13–14).

Tragically, the majority of humanity is on the wrong road that ultimately leads to the wrong destination. From the moment we're born into this world we are on that road (or "way") that is heading away from God. It's the "way" of rebellion against God. As the prophet Isaiah wrote,

> All of us like sheep have gone astray,
> Each of us has turned to his own way. (Isa. 53:6)

No one has to do anything to end up in hell when he or she dies. All a person needs to do is continue traveling in the same direction he or she has been traveling since birth.

By contrast, relatively few people find the road that leads to heaven. In fact, to find that "way" a person must do a spiritual U-turn—which is the meaning of the biblical term *repent*. Repent (*metanoea*) means "to change one's mind." A simple definition of repentance is "a change of mind that leads to a change of direction." Only when a person admits that he or she is on the wrong road can he or she discover the right road. Jesus was clear that He is the only "Way" that leads to eternal life: "I am the way, and the truth, and the life; no one comes to the Father but through Me" (John 14:6).

Notice Jesus said that at the end of the road to hell and the road to heaven is a "gate"—one gate opening to eternal damnation and the other gate opening to eternal salvation. In each case, the gate is called "judgment." The writer to the Hebrews declares a succinct but sobering truth: "It is appointed for men to die once and after this comes judgment" (Heb. 9:27).

There is simply no escaping the fact that each one of us—Christians and non-Christians alike—will face God's judgment when we arrive at the end of our lives on earth.

The "gate" or judgment for non-Christians is often called "the great white throne judgment" and results in eternal death. (We'll look at this judgment further in chapter 9.) The apostle John provides a sobering description of this judgment of all unbelievers in Revelation 20:

> Then I saw a great white throne and Him who sat upon it, from whose presence earth and heaven fled away, and no place was found for them. And I saw the dead, the great and the small, standing before the throne, and books were opened; and another book was opened, which is the book of life; and the dead were judged from the things which were written in the books, according to their deeds. And the sea gave up the dead which were in it, and death and Hades gave up the dead which were in them; and they were judged, every one of them according to their deeds. Then death and Hades were thrown into the lake of fire. . . . And if anyone's name was

not found written in the book of life, he was thrown into the lake of fire. (vv. 11–15)

Contrary to what many believe, Christians are *not* exempt from God's judgment. At the end of every Christian's life is also a "gate" or judgment—but it's a different judgment than the one non-Christians will face. This judgment or evaluation is often referred to as "the judgment seat of Christ." Paul emphatically declared:

> For we must all appear before the judgment seat of Christ, so that each one may be recompensed for his deeds in the body, according to what he has done, whether good or bad. (2 Cor. 5:10)

This is not a judgment of condemnation leading to hell, like the great white throne judgment. Instead, this is an evaluation leading to commendation by God and rewards that will greatly impact the kind of heaven we'll experience. (We'll explore this in detail in chapter 8.)

Reflecting upon the reality of heaven reminds us of the reality of God's judgment at the end of our lives and serves as an incentive to make certain that we'll experience the judgment that results in God's rewards rather than His condemnation.

3. Focusing on Heaven Motivates Us to Live Pure Lives

Most of the television interviews I do for cable news are taped in the late afternoon or are live in the evening. That means I must concentrate on keeping my clothes clean throughout the day. I tuck a napkin into my shirt collar at lunch to prevent stains on my tie. I immediately use a wet towel to wipe off any dirt on my suit jacket. And right before the camera rolls, someone runs a lint remover over my garment. All of this attention is necessary because the bright lights and high-definition television equipment are unforgiving and will reveal to millions of people any imperfections in my attire.

Similarly, there's a day coming when every Christian's "clothing" or actions will be placed under the glare of God's judgment and will reveal any imperfections. That "day" is the day of Christ's return in which "each man's work will become evident; for the day will show it" (1 Cor. 3:13). As we'll see in chapter 8, the purpose of this judgment is to determine not the believer's eternal destiny but his or her eternal rewards.

The Bible often uses clothing as a metaphor for our spiritual lives. It's helpful to understand that in biblical times people often wore two different types of tunics: an inner tunic (comparable to today's undergarments) that no one saw and an outer tunic that was visible to everyone.

Every Christian also wears two kinds of spiritual garments. Our "inner tunic" is our *judicial* righteousness—meaning our "right standing" with God—that God places on us when we trust in Christ as our Savior. Paul referred to our judicial righteousness when he prayed that on the day he finally met God he might "be found in Him, not having a righteousness of [his] own derived from the Law, but that which is through faith in Christ" (Phil. 3:9). Our "inner garment" of God's forgiveness is something we receive from Him. There is nothing we can do to improve it, soil it, or remove it.

But no one wants to walk around wearing only undergarments! That's why, to be properly dressed, we must put on our "outer tunic." This "outer tunic" represents a Christian's *ethical* righteousness, which is how we live after we become a Christian. While judicial righteousness refers to our "right standing" before God, ethical righteousness represents our "right acting" before God after we are saved.

The Bible compares a Christian's behavior after he or she is saved to these outer garments. Unlike the "one-size-fits-all" inner garment, there are a variety of external garments we can put on, ranging from stylish to hideous and clean to filthy. The apostle John encourages believers to be dressed in our best "clothes" when Christ returns. "It was given to [the church]," John wrote, "to clothe herself in fine linen, bright and clean; for the fine linen is the righteous acts of the saints" (Rev. 19:8).

You would never think of attending an elaborate, formal wedding in Bermuda shorts or a halter top. You would put on your finest tuxedo or dress for such a special occasion. However, even if you were wearing expensive clothes, no one would notice your finery if your garment had a humongous chocolate syrup stain on the front!

As Christians we should adorn our lives with the finest "garments" or good works we can—not to earn Christ's forgiveness but to receive His rewards when He returns and consummates the "marriage" between Himself and His church. We should be careful to keep our lives "clean" and not stain those righteous acts with sin.

Of course, that's easier said than done. We live in a sinful world in which pollution seeps from our culture like toxic waste bubbling up from a garbage heap. Being surrounded on every side with messages and images of immorality, rebellion, and lawlessness makes it hard to keep our character clean—to keep it from becoming saturated with the stench of sin. And it's getting more difficult as the days go by.

One of the best detergents for keeping our lives spotless is keeping our eyes focused on the promise of heaven. The writer to the Hebrews said that Moses, the son of royal privilege who was surrounded by the luxuries of Egypt, willingly endured "ill-treatment with the people of God" rather than enjoying "the passing pleasures of sin," because "he was looking to the reward" he would receive in heaven (Heb. 11:25–27).

Moses understood that the pleasures and the treasures of this world last only for a moment. In due time they will be consumed, along with all creation—just as Peter said.

> But the day of the Lord will come like a thief, in which the heavens will pass away with a roar and the elements will be destroyed with intense heat, and the earth and its works will be burned up. (2 Pet. 3:10, 12)

Peter then asked, "Since all these things are to be destroyed in this way, what sort of people ought you to be" (v. 11)? The answer is simple: we ought to be people of "holy conduct and godliness" (v. 11). Randy Alcorn illustrates why focusing on heaven can be a strong motivation for pursuing purity in this life:

> If my wedding date is on the calendar, and I'm thinking of the person I'm going to marry, I shouldn't be an easy target for seduction. Likewise, when I've meditated on Heaven, sin is terribly unappealing. It's when my mind drifts from Heaven that sin seems attractive. Thinking of Heaven leads

inevitably to pursuing holiness. Our high tolerance for sin testifies of our failure to prepare for Heaven.[17]

4. Focusing on Heaven Places Suffering in Perspective

One of the questions I'm asked most frequently as a pastor is "Why did God allow _____ (some horrific experience in their life) to happen?" God never completely answers the "why" question when it comes to suffering. However, He has given us the promise of heaven to put suffering in perspective. The apostle Paul—who was well acquainted with suffering—wrote confidently:

For momentary, light affliction is producing for us an eternal weight of glory far beyond all comparison, while we look not at the things which are seen, but at the things which are not seen; for the things which are seen are temporal, but the things which are not seen are eternal. (2 Cor. 4:17–18)

Even though Paul had been shipwrecked, imprisoned, and beaten within an inch of his life on five different occasions, he described those horrific experiences as "momentary" and "light." How could Paul say such a thing? Was the apostle suffering from amnesia? No; his suffering could only be considered "momentary" and "light" when compared to the "eternal weight" of the future God had planned for him.

For example, you may be experiencing a difficulty you think will never end. Yet when compared to the length of eternity it is only "momentary." How long is eternity? One writer imagines a bird that comes once every million years to sharpen its beak on the top of Mount Everest. By the time the bird has succeeded in wearing that mighty mountain down to nothing—eternity will not have even begun! The time of our suffering on earth is "momentary" when compared to the eternality of our home in heaven!

Our afflictions—however unbearable they may seem—are also "light" when compared to the "weight" of heaven. Think of it this way: would you describe a two-thousand-pound block of concrete as "light" or "heavy"? Compared to a feather, it certainly is heavy. But compared to a fully fueled 777 jetliner, that concrete block is light.

Similarly, the most horrendous difficulties you experience in this life are light when compared to the indescribable future God is preparing for you in that place called heaven. Teresa of Avila observed, "In light of heaven, the worst suffering on earth, a life full of the most atrocious tortures on earth, will be seen to be no more serious than one night in an inconvenient hotel."[18] Focusing on the hope of heaven doesn't eliminate suffering in this world but it does help us put our suffering in perspective.

Heaven is the promise that God will eventually make all things right and that He will one day fulfill our deepest longings. Although God's promise is yet future, it should make a tremendous difference in our lives today. As Alcorn explained, "If we grasp it, [heaven] will shift our center of gravity and radically change our perspective on life."[19] This is the hope of heaven—that *all* of creation will receive what it has long desired: freedom from the crushing oppression of sin.

> For the anxious longing of the creation *waits eagerly* for the revealing of the sons of God. For the creation was subjected to futility, not willingly, but because of Him who subjected it, in hope that the creation itself also will be set free from

its slavery to corruption into the freedom of the glory of the children of God. For we know that the whole creation groans and suffers the pains of childbirth together until now. And not only this, but also we ourselves, having the first fruits of the Spirit, even we ourselves groan within ourselves, *waiting eagerly* for our adoption as sons, the redemption of our body. For in hope we have been saved, but hope that is seen is not hope; for who hopes for what he already sees? But if we hope for what we do not see, with perseverance *we wait eagerly for it*. (Rom. 8:19–25)

How we wait for this "place called heaven"—whether with anticipation or anxiety, whether with focused or unfocused living—matters both now and in the future. For what we do on earth today reverberates in the halls of heaven forever.

2

Is Heaven a Real Place or Is It a State of Mind?

In My Father's house are many dwelling places; if it were not so, I would have told you; for I go to prepare a place for you.

John 14:2

One morning in early 1971, famed Beatle John Lennon sat down at his Steinway piano and composed what would become one of his greatest hits and an anthem of the age: "Imagine." In a tribute to one-world utopian ideals, Lennon asked us to imagine that neither heaven nor hell exists.

As one who dabbled in Hinduism but lived as a practical atheist, it wasn't difficult for John Lennon to imagine no heaven above us. From Hinduism, Lennon learned that god is everything and everything is god, and that heaven is everywhere and nowhere at the same time. Therefore, the only hope at death is breaking the cycle of reincarnation—the great "do over"—and becoming absorbed into the "oneness" of the universal mind.

From atheism, Lennon learned that God is nothing and no one is God, and that heaven is nowhere because it doesn't exist—above us is only sky. Perhaps this stark conclusion is what led Lennon to imagine there's no hell—below us is only earth. After all, imagining no hell is the only hope atheists have.

Of course none of Lennon's musings about heaven answer the question of whether heaven is real or is merely a mental projection—a state of mind—of those who need the idea of heaven as a crutch for the harsh realities of life. Imagining heaven isn't real doesn't make heaven *un*real any more than imagining you're a turnip makes you a vegetable. Truth is not the sum of our imagination. Just because skeptics imagine heaven doesn't exist doesn't make it so.

Of course atheists quickly point out that just because we *can* imagine heaven doesn't make it real either. True enough. But atheists have long assumed that Christians have merely *imagined* heaven's reality and have accused people of faith of living in a fantasyland—of looking forward to a heaven that isn't there. "If it can't be proven scientifically that heaven exists, then it must not exist," they argue.

But, as my friend David Jeremiah counters, "Heaven is no figment of the imagination; nor is it a feeling, a state of mind, or the invention of man. Heaven is a literal place prepared by Christ for a prepared people."[1] And that's the truth we are going to explore in this chapter: the reality of heaven.

Heaven Is Real

If we accept the most basic definition of heaven, that it is "the abode of the Deity [of God],"[2] then we can assume God is

A Place Called Heaven

the one true expert on the subject. Therefore, if we want to know whether heaven is real or simply a state of mind, we should turn to God's book, the Bible, to answer that question.

The most definitive answer to the question about the reality of heaven is found in John 14. But before we get there, understanding its background is important.

Four days had passed since Jesus's triumphal entry into Jerusalem. In the waning hours of His earthly life, Jesus sat down with His disciples for a final Passover meal. At some point during the meal, Jesus rose and wrapped a towel around His waist and began washing the disciples' feet. With this task complete, He announced: "one of you will betray me" (John 13:21 NLT). Then He said:

> Dear children, I will be with you only a little longer . . . but you can't come where I am going. So now I am giving you a new commandment: Love each other. Just as I have loved you, you should love each other. (vv. 33–34 NLT)

It was a troubling evening. Jesus was troubled because of what lay ahead of Him—the betrayal of Judas, the soul-wrenching prayer in the garden, the arrest, beatings, trials, and crucifixion. The disciples were troubled because they didn't know what the future held, especially in light of Jesus's increasingly frequent talk about His impending death.

The disciples' hearts pounded in their chests and questions throbbed in their minds: *Will Jesus's death signal the end of the movement we have been part of for the last three years? Will we ever see Him again? Will our leader's death result in our deaths as well?* None of it made sense; it was all very unsettling.

But Jesus reassured them with some of the most familiar words the Lord ever spoke. Though they couldn't immediately accompany Him on His journey back to His Father, in due time Jesus would return and take them to heaven—to the "Father's house."

> Do not let your heart be troubled; believe in God, believe also in Me. In My Father's house are many dwelling places; if it were not so, I would have told you; for I go to prepare a place for you. If I go and prepare a place for you, I will come again and receive you to Myself, that where I am, there you may be also. (John 14:1–3)

When Jesus told the disciples about the "Father's house," He didn't speak of a place that "exists" in the fantasyland of our minds. Jesus used language that describes a real location. "Place" (*topos*) is used three times in John 14:2–3. This Greek word serves as the root for our word *topography*—the act of detailing the actual, physical features of land on a map. When used in the New Testament, *topos* almost always indicates a locatable and inhabited space. In some contexts it refers to a city or region;[3] in others it refers to an individual residence—a house or a room, which is the case in John 14:2–3.

But it's more than just the word *topos* that tells us heaven is real. Jesus also said "In My Father's house are many *dwelling* places" (v. 2). The Greek word for "dwelling" is *mone* and can also be translated as "habitat," "lodging," or "domicile."[4] Each of these words describes something that is real and physical.

When Amy and I started our family and our two daughters came along, we had a nursery for them. But when they were old enough, each of the girls had her own room—a place for them to paint and decorate as they chose and to play in and study in (more play than study!). They each had a real, physical place in our home to call their own. That's what Jesus is preparing for each one of us—a physical place for us to live in for eternity. And it's a place so fabulous that it defies imagination.

If Jesus's use of "place" and "dwelling" isn't enough to prove the reality of heaven, He twice said, "I *go and prepare* a place for you" (vv. 2–3). The act of going and preparing speaks to something tangible, not intangible. Jesus's "going" refers to His death, resurrection, and ascension. After giving final instructions to His disciples, the Bible records:

[Jesus] was lifted up while [the disciples] were looking on, and a cloud received Him out of their sight. And as they were gazing intently into the sky while He was going, behold, two men in white clothing stood beside them. They also said, "Men of Galilee, why do you stand looking into the sky? This Jesus, who has been taken up from you into heaven, will come in just the same way as you have watched Him go into heaven." (Acts 1:9–11)

The ascension of Jesus occurred on the Mount of Olives, outside the walls of Jerusalem—a physical, geographical location where I've stood many times. So when Jesus ascended from this real place (the Mount of Olives), where did He go? It's nonsensical to say Jesus left the physical earth and ascended into some metaphysical state of mind. Jesus traveled from one geographical location (the Mount of Olives) to another geographical location (heaven). And it is in heaven that Jesus is preparing a place for us. When the time is right, Jesus promised, "I will come again and receive you to Myself, that where I am, there you may be also" (John 14:3).

Where Is This "Place Called Heaven"?

Throughout His earthly ministry, Jesus made it clear that the path to heaven was paved by belief in Him—in His death and resurrection. After all the time they had spent with Jesus, the disciples should have known that, which is why Jesus told them, "you know the way where I am going" (v. 4). But they didn't know. They didn't fully understand that the "Father's house" was heaven (the where) and that going there required faith in Christ (the Way). So Thomas asked, "Lord, we do not know where You are going, how do we know the way?" (v. 5). In other words, if we don't know the destination, we can't know the direction.

To help them recalibrate their spiritual GPS, Jesus said to His disciples, "I am the way, and the truth, and the life; no one comes to the Father but through Me" (v. 6). The only way to heaven is through faith in Christ.[5] But where exactly is heaven? Jesus doesn't tell us, but the Bible may offer us one clue.

Scripture seems to indicate that heaven is "up." How do we know that? While Satan is not usually a reliable source of information for much of anything, his words occasionally reflect truth. Remember that Satan was originally God's highest-ranking angel, named Lucifer. But, discontent with his rank as God's second in command, Lucifer decided to mount a rebellion against God's authority, attempting to grab the title of "Sovereign Ruler" for himself. Lucifer's war cry against God included the words:

41

> I will *ascend* to heaven;
> I will *raise* my throne *above the stars* of God.
>   (Isa. 14:13)

"Ascend," "raise," and "above the stars" all indicate that the direction of heaven is upward. As we've already seen in Acts 1:9–11, Jesus's departure from earth into heaven was upward into the sky. Luke—the author of Acts—wrote that Jesus was "lifted up" into the clouds (1:9), and that the disciples were watching Him, "gazing intently into the sky" (v. 10). When the two angels addressed the disciples, they asked: "Why do you stand looking into the sky?" And then the angels said: "This Jesus, who has been taken *up* from you into heaven, will come in just the same way as you have watched Him go into heaven," meaning that He will come *down* from heaven at His second coming (v. 11).

Both God's holy angels and Lucifer indicate that the location of heaven is upward. Also, consider Paul's description of Jesus as the One "who descended" in His humanity as also being the One "who ascended far above all the heavens" (Eph. 4:10). Above us is more than sky. Above us is God's dwelling place.

But when people wonder about the location of heaven, they are usually thinking about more than the direction it is in. They are really inquiring about the realm in which heaven exists. They want to know if heaven is part of our time-space universe—far, far away, perhaps, but still somewhere that can be located. Or does heaven exist in a completely different dimension, outside of and beyond time and space (like the "fifth dimension beyond that which is known to man" described in the classic TV series *The Twilight Zone*)?

To answer that question, we need to distinguish between the present heaven where God resides and the future heaven Jesus is constructing for us. The present heaven—sometimes called by theologians the "intermediate state"—is where Christians go immediately when they die to enjoy the presence of the Lord as Paul describes: "We are of good courage, I say, and prefer rather to be absent from the body and to be at home with the Lord" (2 Cor. 5:8).

The future heaven is where all believers will one day spend eternity, and this future heaven is still under construction. It is the "place" Jesus is preparing for us now—and its final location may surprise you, as we will see in the next section.

The idea of a present heaven and a future heaven is sometimes confusing. But think of it like this: couples who plan to retire sometimes buy a little plot of land next to a lake, or in the mountains, or along the seashore and begin to build a house on it. They may continue to live in their existing home or move to an apartment while their future retirement home is under construction. Their current address may be wonderful—plush and comfortable—but it's only temporary. The couple could truly be said to be in an "intermediate state" as they await the completion of their future home. In the same way, those who are in heaven today (the present heaven) are enjoying a wonderful existence in the presence of God while waiting for the completion of their final, forever home (the future heaven).

Since this truth about both a present heaven and future heaven is a surprise to many Christians, let's look more closely at the difference between the two.

The Present Heaven

Theologians often point out that the Bible refers to three heavens. The first heaven is earth's atmosphere. It contains the air we breathe and the space in which birds and jetliners fly. The second heaven is what we often refer to as "outer space," where we find the planets, stars, and billions of galaxies that populate this vast universe.

The third heaven represents the presence of God. This is where all Christians immediately go when they die. (We will discuss this in detail in chapter 4.) It is sometimes called Paradise—the place where Jesus assured the thief on the cross he would go the moment he died. At some point in his life, Paul was caught up into this third heaven, where he heard "inexpressible words" (2 Cor. 12:4). When most Christians speak of heaven this is the heaven they mean—the one that is "up." This is the "present heaven" I referred to in the last section.

The Future Heaven

But there is also a fourth heaven—a future "heaven" God is preparing for us right now. This is the place of our future and forever home—and it is a geographical location. This fourth heaven includes the "new heaven" and "new earth" and the "new Jerusalem" John described in Revelation 21–22 as coming down from the third heaven to the newly created earth. The fourth heaven will literally be "heaven on earth." This future heaven will be the place where all believers—Old Testament saints, New Testament saints, and all Christians from the time of Jesus's death and resurrection to date—will live for eternity.

44

At some future point the present heaven—where God, the angels, and all believers who have died are—will be combined with the future heaven—the new heaven, new earth, and New Jerusalem. This will not take place until after the rapture, the seven-year tribulation, the battle of Armageddon, the millennial kingdom, and the great white throne judgment—just as Scripture states.[6]

The apostle John recorded in his end-times vision that he "saw a new heaven and a new earth; for the first heaven and the first earth passed away. . . . And I saw the holy city, new Jerusalem, coming down out of heaven from God, made ready as a bride adorned for her husband" (Rev. 21:1–2).

What will this new heaven and new earth and New Jerusalem be like? Before answering that question we must first understand the nature of "newness."

What Does "New" Really Mean?

What did John mean when he wrote that he saw "a *new* heaven and a *new* earth; for the first heaven and the first earth passed away" (v. 1)? Does this mean God will replace the first and second heavens (earth's atmosphere and outer space) and the earth we know with a re-created (new) heaven and earth? This certainly seems to be the case, at least according to the apostle Peter:

> By His word the present heavens and earth are being reserved for fire, kept for the day of judgment and destruction of ungodly men. . . . But the day of the Lord will come like a thief, in which the heavens will pass away with a roar and the elements will be destroyed with intense heat, and the earth and its works will be burned up. Since all these things

45

are to be destroyed in this way, what sort of people ought you to be in holy conduct and godliness, looking for and hastening the coming of the day of God, because of which the heavens will be destroyed by burning, and the elements will melt with intense heat! But according to His promise we are looking for new heavens and a new earth, in which righteousness dwells. (2 Pet. 3:7, 10–13)[7]

John (in Rev. 21) and Peter (in 2 Pet. 3) both used the same Greek root word for "pass away"—*parerchomai*. But Peter further describes what it means for the earth and the solar systems, along with their most basic building blocks ("the elements"), to "pass away." They "will be destroyed with intense heat . . . burned up" (v. 10). And just in case he wasn't clear the first time, Peter repeats: "the heavens will be destroyed by burning, and the elements will melt with intense heat!" (v. 12). John most likely meant the same thing when he wrote in Revelation 21:1, "the first heaven and the first earth passed away."

Scripture is silent on exactly how God will burn up the universe, but theologians and scientists have speculated about the intensity of heat required to destroy the earth. Some believe a nuclear holocaust, along the lines of Nagasaki and Hiroshima, only unimaginably more powerful, could incinerate the universe. Nuclear explosions produce heat of tens of millions of degrees, which would certainly explain how "the elements will melt with intense heat."

Others believe a massive asteroid fifty or sixty miles wide hitting the earth could be the catalyst for the destruction of the planet—perhaps like John's description of one of the judgments at the end of the tribulation: "And huge hailstones, about one hundred pounds each, came down from heaven upon men" (Rev. 16:21).

But all of this is just guesswork, something fun for scientists to speculate about. The truth is we don't know how God will destroy the heavens and the earth. But since He spoke the universe into being with just a word, it would be no problem for Him to destroy it with just a word.

But why does God need to destroy the old heavens and old earth to create a new heaven and a new earth? God created the existing heavens and earth as recorded in Genesis 1 and pronounced them "good." But sin spoiled all of that. Like leaving a classic 1955 Corvette to rot in the elements until it becomes a rust bucket, sin so corrupted our physical environment that God wants to create a better, newer model—one in which perfect righteousness dwells.

In some of the wealthier areas in my city, Dallas, it's not uncommon for wealthy individuals to buy old homes and completely raze them and their foundations, leaving only dirt. These homes aren't rickety haunted houses. In fact, most of the time they are beautiful old structures with intricate woodwork, stained glass windows, and detailed craftsmanship. So why demolish a perfectly good (old) house? Because the owners want something bigger and newer.

God is going to do something similar with the old heavens and earth. And when this happens—after the great white throne judgment and before believers enter into the New Jerusalem—God will have fulfilled His promise in Isaiah 65:17: "For behold, I create new heavens and a new earth; And the former things will not be remembered or come to mind."

The "New Earth" Versus the Present Earth

Ultimately, we won't go up to heaven and leave this earth behind forever. Instead, God will bring the new heaven down to a newly created earth. In many ways this new earth will resemble our present earth—but it will also be vastly improved.

This new earth—like the old one—will be *physical* in nature (Rev. 21). Resurrected believers with new bodies—bodies like Jesus after His resurrection—require a physical home. Disembodied spirits might be able to live in some ethereal, spiritual dimension, but physical human beings need an earthy, physical dimension. And God will create such a place for us—a physical place for physically transformed bodies.

The new earth will be not only physical in nature but also *familiar*. Frankly, many Christians aren't that anxious about the prospect of going to heaven because they believe heaven will be completely different from anything they've experienced before. We tend to be creatures of habit—I certainly am—and it's hard to get excited about something that's unfamiliar to us. Heaven—the new earth—won't be like moving from your hometown to a city in a foreign country where you don't know the streets or neighborhoods.

As I used to hear my longtime pastor and predecessor Dr. W. A. Criswell say, "I wouldn't look forward to God sending me to live for eternity on some planet I know nothing about a hundred million miles away. I like almost everything about earth. The only things I don't like are the tears, the separation, and the heartache. But those will be gone forever in heaven."

Indeed they will! In John's experience, he heard a voice saying, "[God] will wipe away every tear from their eyes;

and there will no longer be any death; there will no longer be any mourning, or crying, or pain; the first things have passed away" (Rev. 21:4). The curse leveled against this present world (described in Gen. 3) will be lifted and all of redeemed humankind will enjoy the world as God originally created it. Those who live on the new earth will experience unbroken fellowship with God and one another in joyous, loving relationships untainted by sin.

One of the most dramatic changes in the new earth will be the absence of the oceans. When John saw his vision of the new heaven and new earth, he said there would be "no longer any sea" (Rev. 21:1). We know the capital city of the new earth, the New Jerusalem, will gush with fresh, life-giving water (22:1), but it's not exactly clear why the new earth will have no oceans. Some speculate that the absence of the seas in the new earth is to provide more inhabitable space for citizens of heaven, since the oceans make up three-fourths of our current planet's surface.[8] Others say that because the seas are made up of salt, which is a preservative, they are unnecessary because there will be no decay in the new earth.[9]

At times I wonder if I will miss the salty air on my face and the sand between my toes—the beach vacation I enjoy every year. But I'm confident that for whatever reason God has for not re-creating the oceans, my first day on the new earth will make all my combined vacations on the old earth seem like an extended stay in a poorly maintained budget motel!

It's not just the oceans that will be missing from the new world. The new heavens will have no sun or moon. John wrote: "And the city [the New Jerusalem] has no need of the sun or of the moon to shine on it" (21:23).

Heaven has no need of these light sources because Jesus, the Light of the World, will illuminate the New Jerusalem for eternity. The new heaven and new earth will exist in perpetual daytime—"there will be no night there" (Rev. 21:25; 22:5)—fulfilling Isaiah's prophecy:

> No longer will you have the sun for light by day,
> Nor for brightness will the moon give you light;
> But you will have the LORD for an everlasting light,
> And your God for your glory. (Isa. 60:19)

Because the glory of Christ will shine forth, heaven will be a place of absolute safety—which we will discuss further in the next section.

Not only will oceans and darkness be missing from the new earth but so will preachers like myself! Preachers have two primary responsibilities: to proclaim the gospel and to condemn sin. But since "the earth will be filled with the knowledge of the glory of the LORD" (Hab. 2:14) and "there will no longer be any curse" (Rev. 22:3), I'll be looking for new work. A universal love for and devotion to God will permeate the new earth, meaning that we will no longer feel the sting of sin experienced every day in this world. Rather, our lives will be filled with uninterrupted and unending joy.

The New Earth's Capital: New Jerusalem

When Jesus told His disciples He was returning to His Father's house to prepare a place for them, the place He had in mind was a city that will be the focal point of the new earth: the New Jerusalem. This was the same city Abraham had long desired to find: "For he was looking for the city which has foundations, whose architect and builder is God" (Heb. 11:10).

The New Jerusalem—the "city of My God" (Rev. 3:12)—is an actual, physical city being built by Jesus in the present third heaven: the abode of God. I often say that the New Jerusalem is the ultimate in prefab housing! It's being built in one location but will be transported to another location. After the re-creation of the new heavens and new earth, the New Jerusalem will descend out of the third heaven and rest upon the re-created earth:

> And I saw the holy city, new Jerusalem, coming down out of heaven from God, made ready as a bride adorned for her husband. . . . And [the angel] carried me away in the Spirit to a great and high mountain, and showed me the holy city, Jerusalem, coming down out of heaven from God. (21:2, 10)

Though the New Jerusalem is a real city—complete with buildings, streets, and residences occupied by people who are involved in bustling activities, cultural events, and worship—it will be unlike any city we've ever seen.

Its *size* is overwhelming. For many, the gargantuan size of the New Jerusalem is its most striking feature. In Revelation 21:16 John describes an angel with a golden rod who measures the city's cube-shaped width, length, and height and finds it to be a staggering fifteen hundred miles![10] This makes the city's surface area two million square miles. By comparison, New York City is a puny 305 square miles.[11] With an area that large, if we placed New Jerusalem in the middle of the United States its borders would stretch from Canada to Mexico and from the Appalachian Mountains to California.

The height of the city is also mind-boggling. If the average story in a skyscraper is twelve feet high, the New Jerusalem will have 660,000 stories. By comparison, the tallest building in the world, Burj Khalifa in Dubai, is a puny 2,717 feet high, with 163 stories. One World Trade Center, which replaced the twin towers in New York City, is a mere 1,776 feet high, with 104 stories. And if this wasn't enough, the thickness of the walls in the heavenly city is "seventy-two yards" (Rev. 21:17)—nearly three-quarters of the length of an American football field!

Such an overwhelming measurement has led many to believe that the dimensions of the New Jerusalem are symbolic, not literal. But there's no logical reason to take these figures figuratively. In fact, John went out of his way to say that these dimensions were given in "human measurements" (v. 17).

When you think about it, a large, magnificent city made of precious stones, large pearls, and pure gold is one befitting our magnificent Creator. God has been known to create some fairly large objects—think Mount Everest, the Pacific Ocean, or the Milky Way galaxy. But more than that, God is also a God of beauty—consider a sunset over an ocean, a sunrise over a mountain, the tiny feet of a newborn baby, or a bride walking down the aisle. If God would bestow such beauty upon our fallen world, can you imagine what splendor He will lavish on the heavenly city He is preparing for us to live in for all eternity?

Additionally, the New Jerusalem must be large enough to accommodate the redeemed of all ages. We don't know how many residents will actually live in the New Jerusalem—only God knows that—but theologian Ron Rhodes wrote:

One mathematician calculated that if the New Jerusalem is shaped like a cube, it would have enough room for 20 billion residents if each individual residence were a massive 75 acres. There would also be plenty of room left over for parks and streets and other features that you'd likely see in any major city.[12]

The city itself is constructed of "a great and high wall, with twelve gates"—three facing north, three facing south, three facing east, and three facing west (Rev. 21:12–13). Each gate bears one of the names of the tribes of Israel. And stationed at each gate is an angel. The walls, the gates, and the angels—though very real—symbolize eternal *protection* from Satan, demons, and unbelievers.

Gates in ancient cities were always closed at night to protect the citizens sleeping inside. That practice continues today. Gated communities keep their entrances closed at night. Even "the happiest place on earth"—Disneyland—locks its gates every evening after the guests leave. But in the New Jerusalem the gates never close. They don't need to because Satan and his followers can never attack God's people or His city; they are eternally quarantined in the lake of fire.

In the daytime (for there will be no night there) its gates will never be closed . . . and nothing unclean, and no one who practices abomination and lying, shall ever come into it, but only those whose names are written in the Lamb's book of life. (vv. 25, 27)

My brother, who is a police officer, will also have to find another job because there won't be an HPD—Heavenly Police

Department. Heaven won't have prisons, courthouses, or lawyers. There will be no need to close the gates of heaven or even the doors of our new homes to keep evildoers away from us. There will be no evildoers residing in the new heaven and the new earth who need to be arrested, defended, or imprisoned.

That means in the New Jerusalem we will never have to lock our doors or hide our valuables. We can leave our windows open and the keys in our cars because it will be a place of perfect peace and protection.

Its *permanence* is eternal. The New Jerusalem will also be constructed to last forever, which seems to be the significance of the "twelve foundation stones" (Rev. 21:14). Each one is inscribed with the names of the twelve apostles.[13] Military brats, pastors' kids, and missionary kids can especially appreciate this. No more moving from one place to another; no more changing schools or making new friends; no more feelings of being uprooted, of not belonging, or of being the outsider. Heaven will not only be home, it will *feel* like home. It's a place where we can plant eternal roots.

Its *splendor* is incredible. The heavenly city is not just a place of peace, protection, and permanence; it's also a place of unimaginable beauty—even more spectacular than Oz's imaginary Emerald City. The New Jerusalem will be Paradise regained.

Because God dwells there, His glory will cause the city to shimmer like the luster of a diamond under the noonday sun—like "crystal-clear jasper," as John put it (v. 11). In the midst of the city sits God's throne, from which pours forth a life-giving and life-sustaining river—"clear as crystal," John wrote (22:1).

Coors advertises that their beer is brewed with "pure Rocky Mountain spring water" (as a Baptist pastor I cannot verify if that is true!). But in comparison to the water that gushes from God's throne, drinking Rocky Mountain spring water will be like drinking sludge. The "river of the water of life" (Rev. 22:1) will satisfy and bless all who drink deeply from its depths. And our thirst—both physical and spiritual—will be quenched forever.

Planted along the banks of this river is "the tree of life" (v. 2). After their sin, Adam and Eve were banished from the Garden of Eden and barred from the tree—Paradise lost. But in the New Jerusalem, access to the tree is free and unfettered—Paradise restored. The tree perpetually bears a different kind of fruit each month to sustain the immortality of the city's citizens. And the leaves of the tree give everlasting health to all the residents of the new earth:

> On either side of the river was the tree of life, bearing twelve kinds of fruit, yielding its fruit every month; and the leaves of the tree were for the healing of the nations. (v. 2)[14]

I don't pretend to understand what all of this means, but one thing is certain: on the new earth there will be no doctors to wait for, no hospital food to gag on, and no insurance companies to wrangle with because there will be no sickness.

One last thing: unlike the Old Jerusalem, in which the Temple was the central feature, the New Jerusalem will have "no temple" (21:22). Rather, the presence of God and of Jesus will turn the whole city into a temple. And it is there—in that very real "place called heaven"—that we'll live and play and work and worship God forever.

Heaven Is beyond Imagination

Jesus has gone to prepare a place for you. A place more beautiful than any place you've ever seen; a place of peace and protection; a place that will literally be Paradise on earth. And the place Jesus is preparing, He is preparing with you in mind. "Your place in heaven will seem to be made for you and you alone," C. S. Lewis wrote, "because you were made for it—made for it stitch by stitch as a glove is made for a hand."[15]

The popular Christian contemporary song says, "I can only imagine." The truth is the home Jesus is preparing for you is beyond imagination.

3

Have Some People Already Visited Heaven?

It is appointed for men to die once and after this comes judgment.

Hebrews 9:27

"God is calling me."

Those were the last words of the great nineteenth-century American evangelist Dwight L. Moody. The famed preacher had dedicated his life to the preaching and teaching of the gospel. Like Billy Graham who followed him, Moody traveled the world sharing the good news of Christ's death and resurrection, sometimes in revivals where thousands heard him preach. And like Graham, Moody ministered to some of the most politically powerful men of his day. But on December 22, 1899, Moody died in his East Northfield, Massachusetts, home.

The fact that Moody died is not noteworthy—that fate awaits us all. What makes Moody's death interesting is that he may have gained a glimpse of heaven before his actual death. According to the story published in the *New York Times*, Moody said, "I see earth receding; Heaven is opening; God is calling me."[1] Based on those who've had "near-death experiences"—or NDEs as they are often called—and those who study them, Moody's description of seeing earth fading, as if he were outside of his body and traveling through space, and heaven looming before him, is a classic near-death experience.

Raymond Moody, the father of the NDE craze and the great-nephew of the famous evangelist, believes his uncle did have a near-death experience, a term he coined in his 1975 bestseller, *Life After Life*. His seminars on near-death experiences and the popularity of his book fostered a movement that today includes the International Association for Near-Death Studies (IANDS), which is a research foundation that began in 1981, the *Journal of Near-Death Studies* (JNDS), and a glut of consumer-driven books and movies about NDEs. But there is one important difference between the near-death experiences Raymond Moody describes and the experience his uncle had: D. L. Moody never came back after death to tell people what he had seen in heaven.

With so much attention on the afterlife and so many stories in the media, what are we to make of near-death experiences? What does the Bible say about NDEs? And what can those who claim to have had a near-death experience tell us about heaven—if anything?

What Are Near-Death Experiences?

Before we can evaluate the validity of near-death experiences, we must first understand what they are. A good place to begin is with a definition. IANDS defines a near-death experience as "a profound psychological event that may occur to a person close to death or, if not near death, in a situation of physical or emotional crisis. Because it includes transcendental and mystical elements, an NDE is a powerful event of consciousness." They are quick to add, however, "it is not a mental illness."[2]

NDErs, as those who have had a near-death experience call themselves, typically share a common experience, following a similar order of events. The usual experience and sequence includes the following:

- Having the sensation of floating upward and viewing the scene around one's "dead" body.
- Traveling through a tunnel, or a dark space, toward a light.
- Spending time in a beautiful, otherworldly realm.
- Meeting God, Jesus, and/or angels.
- Encountering deceased loved ones, relatives, and friends.
- Seeing the story of one's life passing in review, as if watching a movie.
- Having the sensation of overwhelming peace and love—though some have reported experiencing terrifying scenes of demons and distress.
- Approaching a barrier of some sort, signaling the point of no return.
- Being called back and reluctantly agreeing to return to one's body and life.

Such an experience can be transformative. "It offers the possibility of an escape from something that holds you back, and a transformation into something better," Gideon Lichfield, a reporter who has studied NDEs, wrote. "If the NDE happened during a tragedy, it provides a way to make sense of that tragedy and rebuild your life. If your life has been a struggle with illness or doubt, an NDE sets you in a different direction: you nearly died, so something has to change."[3]

You may have never had a near-death experience, but chances are you've come close to death at some point in your life. Some illness or close call has brought your mortality into sharper focus. And that brush with death can be life-altering.

One of my associates told me of an incident he had while canoeing with family and friends when his canoe became wedged against a truck-sized boulder in the middle of the river. In a split second water poured into the canoe and forced it sideways. Knowing the canoe would capsize, he grabbed his six-year-old daughter just before being thrown into the turbulent waters. He could do nothing for his ten-year-old son, who, despite wearing a life vest, went under.

Finding his footing, my friend placed his daughter on top of the boulder and began a frantic search for his son. Fortunately, the boy popped up a few yards downriver and was pulled into another canoe. That evening, back in camp, my friend couldn't sleep. He spent the night in tearful prayer, thanking God for saving his children's lives. All concerns about work, debts, and mortgages—the stuff of life—instantly disappeared. It was as near to death as he had ever come (and as near to losing his children as he ever hopes to come) and it radically changed his life.

Coming face-to-face with the prospect of death—whether your own or that of someone you love—can be jolting. Such an experience is a stark reminder of the brevity of life . . . and the length of eternity. So it makes sense that those who have "died" and experienced the sensation of leaving their body and traveling to a world of peace and love would never be the same after they "return" to life on this side of the grave.

However, just because someone has had a life-changing experience like an NDE doesn't mean his or her experience is real. But valid or not, no one can deny that near-death experiences are becoming increasingly popular.

Why Are Stories about Near-Death Experiences So Popular?

Books about near-death experiences regularly top the best-seller lists because they supposedly allow us to pull back the curtain and discover the answer to the greatest mystery of all: What awaits us on the other side of the grave? Is there really an existence beyond death? If so, is that existence the same for everyone? And can those who claim to have had an NDE tell us anything about the reality of heaven or hell?

Don Piper's 2004 book, *90 Minutes in Heaven: A True Story of Death and Life*, created a resurgence of interest in NDEs. His book was followed by Bill Wiese's terrifying account of hell, published in 2006: *23 Minutes in Hell: One Man's Story about What He Saw, Heard, and Felt in That Place of Torment*. Since then, there have been an onslaught of NDE books, including Nancy Botsford's *A Day in Hell: Death to Life to Hope* (2010), Eben Alexander's *Proof of Heaven: A Neurosurgeon's Journey into the Afterlife* (2012),

61

and Mary Neal's *To Heaven and Back: The True Story of a Doctor's Walk with God* (2012).

But none of these books has been more popular than Todd Burpo and Lynn Vincent's *Heaven Is for Real: A Little Boy's Astounding Story of His Trip to Heaven and Back* (2010). This megaselling book recounts the story of four-year-old Colton Burpo, who "died" during emergency surgery, came back to life, and told his family about his three-minute trip to heaven. While in heaven, Colton claims to have seen his sister, whom his mother miscarried (and about whom his parents had told him nothing), his great-grandfather (whom he had never met), John the Baptist, Jesus, God the Father (who has wings), and the Holy Spirit, who apparently is bluish in color and transparent. The book has sold over ten million copies and spent over two hundred weeks on the *New York Times* bestseller list.[4]

But not every book about near-death experiences has been so well received, and at least one of those books has been fabricated. *The Boy Who Came Back from Heaven: A True Story*, by Kevin and Alex Malarkey, tells the story of Alex, who "died" and went to heaven after an automobile accident in 2004. Alex suffered brain trauma and severe spinal and neck injuries, leaving him a quadriplegic.

Capitalizing on the popularity of NDE books, a leading Christian publisher put the book out in 2010. However, five years after the book's release, Alex wrote an open letter recanting the contents of the book, confessing that he had lied. He asked Christian booksellers to pull the books from shelves.

"Please forgive the brevity," his letter began, "but because of my limitations I have to keep this short. I did not die. I did not go to heaven. I said I went to heaven because I thought it would get me attention."[5] Days later, the publisher released a statement: "We are saddened to learn that Alex Malarkey, co-author of 'The Boy Who Came Back from Heaven' is now saying that he made up the story of dying and going to heaven. Given this information, we are taking the book out of print."[6]

The popularity of these NDE books goes beyond our natural curiosity about the unknown. Implanted deep inside each of us is a longing for this "place called heaven." While there is much to love about earth—its people and places—we instinctively know there must be something more, something better. King Solomon wrote that God has "set eternity in [our] heart" (Eccles. 3:11), meaning we possess a deep-seated desire and natural inquisitiveness about what awaits us on the other side of death.

But where are we to look for the answers about what really happens to us after we die? Read carefully the confession of Alex Malarkey:

> When I made the claims I did [in his book *The Boy Who Came Back from Heaven*], I had never read the Bible. People have profited from lies, and continue to. They should read the Bible, which is enough. The Bible is the only source of truth. Anything written by man cannot be infallible. It is only through repentance of your sins and a belief in Jesus as the Son of God, who died for your sins (even though he committed none of his own) . . . that you can be forgiven [and can] learn of heaven. . . . I want the whole world to know that the Bible is sufficient.[7]

God has provided us with a wealth of information about the future that awaits Christians and non-Christians after death. Although God hasn't told us everything we may *want* to know, He has revealed everything we *need* to know. As Malarkey confesses, "the Bible is sufficient."

The Bible is sufficient because the Bible is true. And when it comes to evaluating NDEs, we must test all claims against its teaching. To do so fulfills John's command to "not believe every spirit, but test the spirits to see whether they are from God" (1 John 4:1), and puts us in the category of the wise Bereans who examined the Scriptures carefully to see whether Paul's preaching was true (Acts 17:11).

So let's see what God's Word has to say—if anything—about near-death experiences.

Are Near-Death Experiences Biblical?

It's easy to quickly dismiss near-death experiences as nothing more than imaginations gone wild. After all, NDEs are uncommon, and the experiences almost always tend toward the sensational. So, how do we really judge whether someone's near-death experience is real? How do we know that chemical reactions in the brain, under stressful situations, aren't fooling NDErs into thinking that they've actually gone to heaven? Certain drugs have been known to alter brain chemistry and give the impression of an out-of-body experience. And since we know our enemy, Satan, is a liar and deceiver, could it be that some (or all) NDEs are demonic in nature?

On the other hand, near-death stories often bring comfort to those struggling with the reality of their own death or the loss of a loved one. Should we deny them the truth that there is hope beyond death? And besides, what are we to think of those who have come to faith in Christ after having a near-death experience? Shouldn't we celebrate their salvation? And what about Christians who have experienced NDEs and, as a result, started living more God-centered lives? Why would we want to say anything that would diminish their newfound enthusiasm?

A friend who served with me on our staff for many years had an experience during a traumatic illness in which he came to heaven's gate but God prevented him from entering. This experience was so real to him that after he recovered he made some dramatic decisions that impacted every aspect of his life. This is a man of deep faith with a seminary degree who is well versed in the Bible. Should I simply dismiss his experience because it sounds sensational?

Christian researcher J. Isamu Yamamoto, who has studied near-death experiences, cautions us to be careful not to dismiss NDEs out of hand but also not to unthinkingly accept them at face value:

> Since NDEs are of a subjective nature, determining their source is largely a speculative venture. With divine, demonic, and several natural factors all meriting consideration, a single, universal explanation for NDEs becomes quite risky.[8]

When it comes to near-death experiences we need to think biblically. This involves determining whether an NDE corroborates or contradicts Scripture, whether it glorifies God or self, and whether it motivates the experiencer to know more of God and His Word or to seek additional experiences. Specifically, we should keep seven principles in mind while evaluating the experiences of those who claim to have already visited heaven.

1. Near-Death Isn't Death

Nearly dead is not dead! As Miracle Max told Inigo Montoya in the movie *The Princess Bride*, "Your friend here is only *mostly* dead. There's a big difference between mostly dead and all dead. Mostly dead is slightly alive. With all dead, well . . . with all dead there's usually only one thing you can do. . . . Go through his clothes and look for loose change."[9]

The Bible is clear on this point: "Each person is destined to die *once* and after that comes judgment" (Heb. 9:27 NLT). I can hear the objections already: "What about the people in the Bible who died and were brought back to life, like Lazarus?" We'll consider their experiences in detail, but keep in mind that Lazarus, and others who underwent death twice, were rare exceptions and were brought back to life for unique reasons. Miracles occur—but they don't occur every day. If they did, they would be called "usuals." The point of Hebrews 9:27 is that, for the vast majority of humanity, God's plan is for them to die once and then face eternity.

Near-death experiences are just that: *near*-death, not *once-for-all-completely-dead* experiences. Therefore, the stories told by NDErs may tell us nothing more about life after death than someone who has traveled near my city of Dallas can tell us about such local landmarks as Thanksgiving Square, Klyde Warren Park, or Reunion Tower without ever actually being within the city limits. Both NDEs (near-Dallas experiences and near-death experiences) lack certitude. And in both cases reliable maps *are* available for those planning a journey to an unfamiliar destination. The only certain map for navigating eternity is the Bible. And that leads to a second important principle about evaluating NDEs.

2. The Bible Is Sufficient

Books like *Heaven Is for Real* and *To Heaven and Back* give the impression that the Bible is insufficient to tell us what we need to know about life after death. Though these books might bring comfort and hope to those who've lost loved ones, we should be very careful about turning away from the Word of God and toward some other source during times of grief and sadness. Remember what Alex Malarkey said: "The Bible is sufficient." And don't forget Paul's words of comfort to those who wondered what had happened to their loved ones who had died:

> But we do not want you to be uninformed, brethren, about those who are asleep, so that you will not grieve as do the rest who have no hope. For if we believe that Jesus died and rose again, even so God will bring with Him those who have fallen asleep in Jesus. For this we say to you by the word of the Lord, that we who are alive and remain until the coming of the Lord, will not precede those who have fallen asleep. For the Lord Himself will descend from heaven with a shout, with the voice of the archangel and with the trumpet of God, and the dead in Christ will rise first. Then we who are alive and remain will be caught up together with them in the clouds to meet the Lord in the air, and so we shall always be with the Lord. *Therefore comfort one another with these words.* (1 Thess. 4:13–18)

Paul is saying to the grieving Thessalonian Christians: "God does not want you to be ignorant of what has happened to your loved ones. Here is everything you need to know about what happens to a Christian after death."

Never in my ministry have I felt the need to turn to a book about near-death experiences to comfort the grieving, to bring hope to the hopeless, or to assure the doubtful. Hundreds and hundreds of times over the decades, I have looked into the faces of family members at a funeral service who had just experienced the sting of death and witnessed immediate relief as they heard the reassuring words of comfort from God's Word.

3. Adding to or Taking Away from the Bible Is Condemned

The Bible is eternal, inspired, and infallible. And because it is, God places inestimable value on His Word. For those who obey there are blessings; for those who disobey there are curses. The bookend of blessings and curses is easy to spot in the book of Revelation. The book opens with a blessing, "Blessed is he who reads and those who hear the words of the prophecy, and heed the things which are written in it" (Rev. 1:3), and ends with a curse:

> I testify to everyone who hears the words of the prophecy of this book: if anyone adds to them, God will add to him the plagues which are written in this book; and if anyone takes away from the words of the book of this prophecy, God will take away his part from the tree of life and from the holy city, which are written in this book. (22:18–19)

The book of Revelation is God's definitive answer to what awaits every person—Christian and non-Christian—after death. In this book, God tells us everything He wants us to know. Adding to, subtracting from, or twisting the truth written in the book of Revelation is serious business and results in severe punishment.

Everyone who writes about heaven (including yours truly) should take this warning seriously. Unfortunately, many of the books and stories about near-death experiences—trips to heaven and coming back to tell the tale—come uncomfortably close to violating the warning in Revelation 22. For example, is the Holy Spirit *really* bluish in color, and does God the Father, whom no one has ever seen, *really* have wings as little four-year-old Colton Burpo claimed?[10]

4. Question the Identity of Any "Being of Light"

Not all who've had a near-death experience encountered a being of light, but those who have claim that being was Jesus Christ. However, many of these reports also claim that "Jesus" told them things contrary to the Word of God, such as:

"Sin isn't a problem."

"There is no hell."

"All people are welcomed into heaven."

"Every religion is equally true."

But how can this be if "Jesus Christ is the same yesterday and today and forever" (Heb. 13:8)? All of those statements contradict everything Jesus taught while He was on earth. It's impossible that these NDErs met the real Jesus, since He would never contradict His own Word. The only conclusion we can draw is that if these people experienced a legitimate near-death experience, the being they encountered was an antichrist—a counterfeit Christ.

J. Isamu Yamamoto anticipates the objection to such a declaration when he asks, "How can we conclude that this being of light is an evil spirit when he exudes love and joy and peace, and when he encourages people to love others?" Good question—and Yamamoto provides a good answer:

> It is tough to speak against such an argument. It is much easier to speak against a horned demon with a pitchfork who commands people to hate, hurt, and rebel. Spiritual warfare, however, is a battleground where it is often difficult to identify the enemy. Frequently he disguises himself as a beloved friend. Deception has always been this way, and it has been a deadly weapon in his arsenal evident since he used it in the Garden of Eden. Indeed, Paul warned Timothy that "in later times some will abandon the faith and follow deceiving spirits and things taught by demons" (1 Tim. 4:1). Of course, the most evil deception is when the Devil appears to be God. Again, Paul's words ring true: "Satan himself masquerades as an angel of light" (2 Cor. 11:14).[11]

Satan's strategy is similar to that of terrorists who disguise themselves as civilian noncombatants, making it difficult for allied soldiers to distinguish friend from foe. If Satan or his demons can deceive someone through disguise—wearing the mask of Christ to cover the heart of antichrist—then the result is one less person bound for heaven.

To make matters worse, popular thinker Dinesh D'Souza observed, "We interpret our experiences through a cultural lens." In other words, we see what we want to see. "A Christian may see a radiant being and say it's Jesus," D'Souza argues, "while a Muslim might say it's Muhammad. Since no one knows what either Jesus or Muhammad looked like—and let's assume the radiant being isn't wearing a name tag—clearly the identification shows an element of cultural projection."[12] If this is true, then the veracity of those who claim to have had a near-death experience, traveled to heaven, and seen a being of light must be called into question. In heaven, the options as to the true identity of a being of light cannot be between Jesus and Muhammad. In heaven, there's only one option: Jesus.

5. Beware of the Occult

It is highly probable that those who have met a being of light during an NDE have met a demon impersonating Christ, leading to an experience with the occult and not an experience with God. It is a fact that near-death experiences often resemble out-of-body experiences reported by those who practice the occult. In both cases, people claim to have had otherworldly contacts and their worldview changed. They also claim to have developed psychic powers like clairvoyance (the ability to see something about the past, present, or future beyond natural means) and telepathy (the ability to receive or send thoughts from and to another person).

For example, Diane Corcoran, the president of the International Association for Near-Death Studies (IANDS), emphasized in her opening remarks to the 2014 annual conference in Newport Beach, California, that the long-term psychic effects of a near-death experience are just as important as the experience itself. As Gideon Lichfield, who covered the conference for *The Atlantic* magazine, wrote:

Many people, [Corcoran] said, don't realize for years that they've had an NDE, and piece it together only after they notice the effects. These include heightened sensitivity to light, sound, and certain chemicals; becoming more caring and generous, sometimes to a fault; having trouble with time-keeping and finances; feeling unconditional love for everyone, which can be taxing on relatives and friends; and having a strange influence on electrical equipment. At one conference of NDErs, Corcoran recounted, the hotel's computer system went down. "You put 400 experiencers in a hotel together, *something's* gonna happen," she said.[13]

Of course Ms. Corcoran didn't mean that someone accidentally kicked the plug from the wall. Rather, she is suggesting that the psychosomatic energy of the four hundred NDErs frazzled the hotel's computers. If this actually happened, the power behind such an occurrence is attributable to the kingdom of darkness rather than God's kingdom of light.

Occultism and any hint of occultism is a clear violation of Scripture—both in the Old Testament and the New Testament—and should be avoided like the spiritual plague that it is.[14]

6. Jesus's Death and Resurrection Should Be Central to Any Revelation from God

Some people argued that Saul (Paul) had an NDE when he fell to the ground and saw a blinding light at his conversion. Here's how Luke described Saul's experience:

As he was traveling, it happened that he was approaching Damascus, and suddenly a light from heaven flashed around

72

him; and he fell to the ground and heard a voice saying to him, "Saul, Saul, why are you persecuting Me?" And he said, "Who are You, Lord?" And He said, "I am Jesus whom you are persecuting, but get up and enter the city, and it will be told you what you must do." (Acts 9:3–6)

For NDErs, Saul's conversion mirrors a near-death experience: the vision of a bright light, encountering Jesus, the transformation of Saul's life, and the charge of insanity—just as NDErs are sometimes labeled. However, there are a number of problems with this conclusion.

First, Paul was very much alive and nowhere near death at his conversion. Second, the light was something unlike a typical NDE because it literally blinded Paul until he later recovered. Third, in telling King Agrippa of his experience, Paul never mentioned anything remotely resembling a near-death experience. Finally, unlike the Jesus of typical near-death experiences, the Jesus Paul encountered commissioned him to evangelize exclusively in His name—to bring people to repentance and to humble themselves under the lordship of Christ.[15]

It is this last point that is particularly important. While it's true that some who claim to have had a near-death experience have subsequently come to faith in Christ and kept the death and resurrection of Jesus at the center of their story, most NDErs keep the focus of their experience on *themselves* or on some nondescript heavenly being. This wasn't the case with Paul—from the moment he encountered Jesus on the road to Damascus until he drew his last breath, his focus was on Jesus Christ—the exclusive Son of God. Paul summed up his life's mission when he told the Corinthian believers: "I

73

determined to know nothing among you except Jesus Christ, and Him crucified" (1 Cor. 2:2). Any story of near death that excludes Jesus Christ and His exclusive message of salvation for those who trust Him is highly suspect.

7. *The Bible Doesn't Record Near-Death Experiences*

The real question when evaluating any near-death experience is, "Does the Bible record any NDEs?" Some say yes, citing the examples of Lazarus, Jesus, Stephen, Paul, and John. We'll examine the experience of each of these men, but before we do let me make one point perfectly clear: in the past God occasionally raised people from the dead (meaning they were actually dead!) to illustrate a spiritual truth. God stopped raising people from the dead sometime during the New Testament era because this miracle was no longer needed to affirm the veracity of the apostles' message. Once the New Testament was completed, the test of any self-proclaimed messenger from God was his adherence to the Bible, not his ability to raise people from the dead. And that same test applies today.

Nevertheless, here are some examples of God bringing the dead back to life before the completion of the New Testament:

- Elijah and the widow of Zarephath's son (1 Kings 17:17–24)
- Elisha and the Shunammite woman's son (2 Kings 4:18–37)
- Ezekiel and the valley of dry bones (Ezek. 37:1–14)
- Jesus and Jairus's daughter (Matt. 9:18–19, 23–26; Mark 5:22–24, 35–43; Luke 8:41–42, 49–56)

- Jesus and the widow of Nain's son (Luke 7:11–15)
- Peter and Tabitha (Acts 9:36–43)
- Paul and Eutychus (Acts 20:6–12)
- Unnamed saints (Heb. 11:35)

Yet none of these examples qualifies as a near-death experience because no individual reported what he or she saw on the other side of death—a basic requirement for an NDE.

Consider the dramatic story of Lazarus, whom Jesus brought back to life after he had been dead for four days (John 11:17, 39, 43–44). Nowhere in the biblical record did John give an account of what Lazarus saw, heard, or experienced in heaven.

Of course, Jesus is the ultimate example of Someone who returned from the dead. All four Gospels agree on this point: Jesus died, was buried, and after three days was raised from the dead. But while Jesus hung on the cross approaching death, He experienced none of the typical near-death experiences. He had no incoherent out-of-body experience, He didn't travel through a tunnel toward a light, and He certainly didn't have an overwhelming sense of peace.

Rather, Jesus was cognizant and rational, forgiving those who condemned Him to the cross, promising one of the criminals a home in Paradise, speaking to His mother and His disciple John, praying to the Father, and surrendering His spirit. After His resurrection from the dead (not the "nearly dead"), Jesus didn't reveal any information about His experience in heaven. Instead, He prepared His disciples for the mission that lay before them, "speaking of the things concerning the kingdom of God" (Acts 1:3).

The stoning of Stephen is perhaps the closest thing to a near-death experience recorded in the Bible.

> Now when [the Jewish officials, the Sanhedrin] heard [Stephen's speech condemning them], they were cut to the quick, and they began gnashing their teeth at him. But being full of the Holy Spirit, he gazed intently into heaven and saw the glory of God, and Jesus standing at the right hand of God; and he said, "Behold, I see the heavens opened up and the Son of Man standing at the right hand of God." (Acts 7:54–56)

Some of the elements of an NDE were present in Stephen's case: an encounter with Jesus, seeing God, and witnessing the gates of heaven opening wide. Nevertheless, there are key aspects in Stephen's situation that prevent it from being classified as a near-death experience.

First, Stephen's vision of heaven and Jesus takes place before his stoning began. If Stephen's experience was a true NDE, we'd expect the vision to come just before death, after being pummeled by the stones. Second, the Scripture is clear that Stephen received his vision of Jesus and heaven because he was "full of the Holy Spirit," meaning that the Spirit of God granted him the vision to peer into the heavenly realm. I rarely hear people who claim NDEs attribute those experiences to the Holy Spirit.

Third, Stephen's vision was not unlike the visions given to Isaiah, Ezekiel, and Daniel—none of whom were near death when they saw scenes of heavenly splendor. Fourth, when Stephen was close to the moment of his death, the writer's focus was not on Stephen's vision of Jesus and heaven but on his prayer of surrender and forgiveness.

They went on stoning Stephen as he called on the Lord and said, "Lord Jesus, receive my spirit!" Then falling on his knees, he cried out with a loud voice, "Lord, do not hold this sin against them!" Having said this, he fell asleep. (vv. 59–60)

Finally—Stephen actually died instead of "nearly died." I can't emphasize strongly enough that the Bible does not record people who died (or "nearly died"), took a brief tour of heaven, and then returned from wherever they were to write a bestselling book about their experiences.

"But didn't the apostle Paul admit to having such an experience?" some might wonder. It is true that the famed apostle was "caught up to the third heaven" (2 Cor. 12:2), which some people equate with a near-death experience. Yet two important factors disqualify this as an NDE.

First, there is no indication that Paul was close to death when the experience occurred. The apostle confessed he didn't know whether his trip to heaven was physical ("in the body") or metaphysical ("apart from the body"), but it's clear that Paul hadn't died or almost died.

Second, Paul did not reveal any details about his experience or vision of heaven. He was instructed not to speak of what he saw and heard. If Christianity's greatest theologian, who wrote nearly half of the New Testament, was prohibited from publishing a firsthand account of his trip to heaven, why would God authorize someone today to pen such a book? It's certainly a question worthy of consideration. If anyone was allowed to write about their experience in heaven after having nearly died, we'd assume it would be Paul.

What does all of this mean? Very simply, there are no biblical accounts of the kind of near-death experiences we hear so much about today. And while I would never say that God is incapable of granting—or unwilling to ever grant—someone that experience, the weight of Scripture seems to argue against NDEs.

Skeptics claim that near-death experiences are no more real than alien abductions, psychic powers, or poltergeists—fodder for charlatans looking to make a quick dollar off the gullible and foolish. To skeptics, NDErs are no better than snake-oil salespersons.

And while we need not be as cynical as the run-of-the-mill skeptic about NDEs, there is good evidence to question anyone claiming to have had a near-death experience and telling us that heaven is really real. We already know that, because Jesus has promised He is preparing a place for us in heaven.

Everything you need to know about that thrilling "place called heaven" is revealed in the Bible—and in the pages that follow you will discover many stirring and surprising truths from God's Word about your future home.

4

Do Christians Immediately Go to Heaven When They Die?

While we are at home in the body we are absent from the Lord . . . and prefer rather to be absent from the body and to be at home with the Lord.

2 Corinthians 5:6, 8

In the dead of a Minnesota winter, a couple decided to thaw out on a Florida beach. But personal responsibilities kept the wife home an extra day, so she planned to fly down the day after her husband. When the husband arrived in Key West and checked in to the hotel, he unpacked and then shot off a quick email to his wife before going to the beach. Unfortunately, in his rush to get out the door he transposed two letters in his wife's email address.

Meanwhile, a minister's wife in Chicago had just buried her husband of forty-five years. Entering her home after the funeral, exhausted and numb from losing him so suddenly, she decided to check her email in hopes of reading messages of condolence to soothe her shattered spirit. Overlooking the address of the sender, she screamed when she saw the first message . . . and then fainted. Rushing into the room, her daughter saw her mother on the floor and revived her. Then the daughter read the message:

Darling Wife:

I'm sure you're surprised to hear from me. I've just arrived and checked in, and I wanted to send you a quick note saying I can't wait until you get here. The staff has everything ready for you. I'm looking forward to seeing you tomorrow. And if everything goes as planned you should get here as quickly as I did.

PS: It sure is hot down here. I know you're gonna love it!

Theologian Reinhold Niebuhr once advised: "It is unwise for Christians to claim any knowledge of either the furniture of heaven or the temperature of hell."[1] And while there is some truth to Niebuhr's warning, I think we can safely assume that hell isn't anything like Key West!

We can also assume, based on what the Bible reveals about the new heaven and the new earth, that Key West—for all its beauty—doesn't hold a candle to the splendor of the future home God is preparing for us. But one thing is certain: every human being is going to either heaven or hell when they die.

In his book *Heaven*, Randy Alcorn observes that "world-wide, 3 people die every second, 180 every minute, and nearly 11,000 every hour. If the Bible is right about what happens to us after death, it means that more than 250,000 people every day go either to Heaven or Hell."[2] The mind staggers at those statistics—a quarter of a million spirits depart the earth, every single day, bound for one of two destinies. Numbers like this prove the accuracy of the old adage: "No one gets out of this world alive." But why is death inevitable—both for Christians and non-Christians?

Why the Living Must Die

Death is the result of the universal disease infecting us all: sin. Solomon declared that death is the "fate for all men" (Eccles. 9:3)—"for the righteous and for the wicked . . . for the clean and for the unclean . . . [for the] good man [and for] the sinner" (v. 2). The universality of death is illustrated at every funeral and in every cemetery throughout the world. J. Sidlow Baxter was correct when he wrote:

> A million graveyards proclaim with ceaseless voice that man is mortal and that the living are dying. What wreckage of the race has Death made! What is this revolving orb on which we live but the vast cemetery of mankind?[3]

Death is every person's fate because every man, woman, and child is guilty of sin against God. "For all have sinned and fall short of the glory of God," Paul declared in Romans 3:23. And sin—the thumbing of our noses at God's moral code—is punishable by death, just as Paul wrote later in his letter to the Romans: "For the wages of sin is death" (6:23).

From the very beginning of human history, death was the just punishment for sin. God warned Adam and Eve that if they rebelled against His clear command not to eat from the tree of the knowledge of good and evil, they would die. And die they did.

With the exceptions of Enoch and Elijah (and those believers alive at the rapture of the church), every person since Adam and Eve has died or will die. The fact that death awaits us all strikes fear into the hearts of many people. Job called death "the king of terrors" (Job 18:14). The psalmist confessed that his heart was in agony because "the terrors of death have fallen upon me" (Ps. 55:4). And the writer to the Hebrews likened death to a slave master, chaining humanity in fear (Heb. 2:15).

Death is the nightmare of all nightmares for those who face death without faith in Jesus Christ. The actor Jack Nicholson knows the terror of death. He wrestled with his own mortality while making *The Bucket List*—a movie about two terminally ill men who leave a cancer ward for a road trip to do the things they always wanted to do before "kicking the bucket." In an interview promoting the film, Nicholson said:

I use to live so freely. The mantra for my generation was "Be your own man!" I always said, "Hey, you can have whatever rules you want—I'm going to have mine. I'll accept the guilt. I'll pay the check. I'll do the time." I chose my own way. That was my philosophical position well into my 50s. As I've gotten older, I've had to adjust. . . . We all want to go on forever, don't we? We fear the unknown. Everybody goes to that wall, yet nobody knows what's on the other side. That's why we fear death.[4]

It's understandable for unbelievers to fear death—they don't know what awaits them on the other side of the grave. But even for believers, the prospects of death and dying can be unnerving. Joni Eareckson Tada wrote:

> I look at my own degenerating body and wonder how I will approach that final passage. Will it be short and sweet? Or long and agonizing? Will my husband be able to take care of me? Or will my quadriplegia better suit me for a nursing home? It's not so much I'm afraid of death as dying.[5]

Without a doubt, the thought of death can fill us with terror and dread. However, knowing our destination when we depart this life can dramatically diminish that understandable fear.

Where the Dead Go When They Die

One of my mentors in seminary, Howard Hendricks, always encouraged his students to keep the hope of heaven at the center of our preaching because it is in heaven where life is found. He would say, "We are not in the land of the living on our way to the land of the dying. Instead, we are in the land of the dying on our way to the land of the living." How true that is!

For a Christian, death is not a terminus *of* life; death is a transition *to* life—real life. However, for the unbeliever, death marks a transition to what the Bible calls "the second death" (Rev. 20:14)—an eternal existence separated from God.

I believe every person born is presented with a choice at some point in his or her life: to either accept or reject God's free gift of salvation through Jesus Christ. It is a choice that can only be made in this life. Once we've passed through death's door into the afterlife, our choice is eternally fixed.

An epitaph on a century-old tombstone in an Indiana cemetery serves as a stark reminder of the certainty of death for all of us:

> Pause, stranger, when you pass me by;
> As you are now, so once was I.
> As I am now, so you will be,
> So prepare for death and follow me.

An unknown visitor to the cemetery saw the tombstone and, after a few moments in contemplation, scrawled a reply:

> To follow you I'm not content,
> Until I know which way you went.[6]

Whether you will die is not up for debate. The crucial question is this: "*Where* are you going after you die?" That question can only be answered by another question: "Did you trust in Jesus Christ for the forgiveness of your sins?" Your eternal destiny rests on your answer to that question.

Two Possible Destinations

The Bible employs various terms to describe the future destination of those who die—sheol, hades, Abraham's bosom, and Paradise—but ultimately there are only two destinies: heaven or hell.

However, as we saw in chapter 2, there is a present heaven—the "third heaven" of 2 Corinthians 12:2 where God dwells—and a future heaven that is being constructed for us as described in Revelation 21:1–2. The present heaven is the "temporary heaven" while the future heaven is the "permanent heaven." (We'll look at hell in greater detail in chapter 9, but, like heaven, there is both a temporary and a permanent place of suffering for the unsaved.)

Where Do Christians Go When They Die?

It is a great hope and comfort to know that at death the spirit of every believer is immediately ushered into the presence of God—the third heaven. And we have Jesus's promise to rely on for that assurance. He declared to the thief on the cross who, moments earlier, had professed his faith in Christ: "Truly I say to you, *today* you shall be with Me in Paradise" (Luke 23:43).

When Stephen was being stoned, he anticipated being with Jesus at death. Stephen "called on the Lord and said, 'Lord Jesus, receive my spirit!'" (Acts 7:59). Paul's great desire was "to depart and be with Christ" (Phil. 1:23). The Greek word for "depart" (*analuo*) was used in reference to a ship being loosed from its moorings so it might sail away. The "mooring" that kept Paul tethered to his earthly life was his commitment to the gospel ministry. But his ultimate desire was to "sail away" to Christ.

However, the most complete explanation of what happens to a believer the moment he or she dies is found in 2 Corinthians 5:6–8:

Therefore, being always of good courage, and knowing that while we are at home in the body we are absent from the Lord—for we walk by faith, not by sight—we are of good courage, I say, and prefer rather to be absent from the body and to be at home with the Lord.

Without getting lost in the grammatical weeds of the original language, let me point out two important insights from the Greek. First, the phrases in verse 6, "we are at home in the body" and "we are absent from the Lord," are in the present tense, representing continuous action. We might paraphrase verse 6 like this: "Therefore, being always of good courage, and knowing that while we are *continuing* to live at home in the body we likewise are *continuing* to live absent from the Lord."

In other words, while our bodies are here on earth, we're not in the presence of Christ in heaven, any more than I am in my home with my wife, Amy, in Dallas while I am also in a lonely hotel room in New York. Guess where I would rather be?

Second, the phrases "to be absent from the body" and "to be at home with the Lord" indicate actions that are completed rather than continuing. We might paraphrase verse 8 like this: "we are of good courage, I say, and prefer rather to have completely departed from the body and to be *finally* at home with the Lord."

That is exactly how I feel when I've been away from home too long. I'm ready to be completely absent from New York (or wherever I happened to be) and to be finally at home with Amy.

When I'm away from home, I'm thinking about Amy and can't wait to get back to her. But once I'm home, I certainly don't long to be in that lonely hotel room in an unfamiliar city. That's the point Paul is making in 2 Corinthians 5:6, 8. To be present here (earth) is to be absent from there (heaven), but to be absent here is to be present there. Once we leave our earthly bodies behind—which are nothing more than the cocoon from which a butterfly emerges—our spirits are instantly transported to our heavenly home where Christ is, as we await the time we will receive our eternal bodies. More about that in the next section.

The Third Heaven: Our Real but Temporary Home

Until the new heaven and the new earth are completed, all Christians who die are immediately transported into the presence of God—the third heaven. The apostle Paul is clear that at the rapture all Christians will receive their new, glorified bodies in which they will live for eternity. "All Christians" includes those Christians who died prior to the rapture ("the dead in Christ," as Paul calls them), as well as those Christians who are alive at the rapture and never experience death:

> For the Lord Himself will descend from heaven with a shout, with the voice of the archangel and with the trumpet of God, and the dead in Christ will rise first. Then we who are alive and remain will be caught up together with them in the clouds to meet the Lord in the air, and so we shall always be with the Lord. Therefore comfort one another with these words. (1 Thess. 4:16–18)

Paul describes the instantaneous change that both the "dead in Christ" and those Christians alive at the rapture will experience:

Behold, I tell you a mystery; we will not all sleep, but we will all be changed, in a moment, in the twinkling of an eye, at the last trumpet; for the trumpet will sound, and the dead will be raised imperishable, and we will be changed. (1 Cor. 15:51–52)

Not every Christian will die (or "sleep," as Paul describes what happens to the Christian's physical body at death) but all Christians—both those who are alive at the time of the rapture and every believer who has died since the time of Christ—will receive a new incorruptible and imperishable body that is designed for eternity.

One interesting question people often ask is about the physical state of those Christians who die *before* the rapture. Are they simply disembodied spirits who are ushered into the presence of the Lord, or do they receive some kind of temporary bodies until they receive their permanent, new bodies at the rapture?

Some writers such as Randy Alcorn believe Christians will be given temporary bodies when they die before receiving their resurrected, glorified, and eternal bodies at the rapture. Alcorn writes:

Given the consistent physical descriptions of the present Heaven [a term referring to the third heaven, where God is] and those who dwell there, it seems possible—though this is certainly debatable—that between our earthly life and our bodily resurrection, God may grant us some physical form that will allow us to function as human beings while in that unnatural state "between bodies," awaiting our resurrection.[7]

God created us body, soul, and spirit, not just soul and spirit. There has never been a time when we existed without a physical body. Before our conception in our mother's womb we didn't exist at all. But at our conception, when God breathed life into us, He gave us a body.

Furthermore, we will also exist in bodily form rather than as disembodied spirits in the new heaven and the new earth. These "made for eternity" bodies will be given to us at the rapture of the church. Thus, the reasoning goes, if we have always existed in bodily form in the past and will also inhabit physical bodies in the future, why would we exist only in spirit form during the relatively brief span of time between our death and the rapture?

The Bible does not definitively answer the question of whether Christians receive a temporary body before the rapture, but as we will see in the next section, the story Jesus told in Luke 16 about the experience of Lazarus and the rich man provides a strong clue to that question's answer.

Where Did the Old Testament Saints Go When They Died?

If Christians since the time of Christ go immediately to heaven when they die, where did those believers who lived before Christ go when they died? This is a little more complicated and debatable than answering the question concerning Christians who die today.

First, we need to understand who qualified as an Old Testament believer, or "saint," as some people call them. An Old Testament saint was anyone—Jewish or Gentile—whom God declared "righteous." In my book *Not All Roads Lead to Heaven*, I explain in depth that all believers—whether they lived before Christ or after Christ—are saved the same way: by the death of Jesus Christ. For those who lived before Christ, His payment for their sin was "credited" to their account the moment they exercised faith in God's revelation. Abraham lived thousands of years before Christ, yet "he believed in the LORD; and He accounted it to him for righteousness" (Gen. 15:6 NKJV).

Second, it's important to understand two important biblical terms that refer to the place of the dead: the Hebrew word *sheol* and the Greek word *hades*. Both words mean roughly the same thing: "covered" or "hidden." According to some scholars *sheol* is divided into two compartments: Paradise (or "Abraham's bosom") where the righteous reside, and a place of torment called hades where the unrighteous reside. According to these scholars, the best illustration of this division between Abraham's bosom and the place of torment is found in Luke 16:19–26:

> Now there was a rich man, and he habitually dressed in purple and fine linen, joyously living in splendor every day. And a poor man named Lazarus was laid at his gate, covered with sores, and longing to be fed with the crumbs which were falling from the rich man's table; besides, even the dogs were coming and licking his sores. Now the poor man died and was carried away by the angels to Abraham's bosom; and the rich man also died and was buried. In Hades he lifted up his eyes, being in torment, and saw Abraham far away and Lazarus in his bosom. And he cried out and said, "Father Abraham, have mercy on me, and send Lazarus so that he may dip the tip of his finger in water and cool off my

tongue, for I am in agony in this flame." But Abraham said, "Child, remember that during your life you received your good things, and likewise Lazarus bad things; but now he is being comforted here, and you are in agony. And besides all this, between us and you there is a great chasm fixed, so that those who wish to come over from here to you will not be able, and that none may cross over from there to us."

Some people believe that given the amount of detail in this story—including the use of the name Lazarus (no other parable uses a proper name)—this is not a parable but the actual account of the deaths of two different men who experienced two different destinies. Whether this is a parable or not, Jesus uses this story to reveal some basic truths about the hereafter.

The most obvious principle in this story is all people do not experience the same destiny when they die. Some, like Lazarus, are ushered into a place of peace while others, like the rich man, immediately begin to experience horrific suffering. Notice that the division between comfort and agony centered on being in or being away from Abraham's presence or "bosom." For the Old Testament believer, being in the presence of the beloved father of the Jewish people was synonymous with being in the presence of God Himself. For so-called New Testament saints and sinners—those who either accepted or rejected God's grace in the crucifixion and resurrection of Christ—the afterlife centers on being in or apart from Jesus's presence.

As I said earlier, some biblical scholars believe that "Abraham's bosom" was one of two divisions of this holding place for the dead called sheol that was reserved for those believers who died before the resurrection of Jesus Christ—such as Lazarus in Jesus's story. After having been carried away by angels to Abraham's side, Lazarus found comfort, blessing, and intimate fellowship with the Old Testament patriarch.

But to me this description sounds very much like the present (third) heaven where God is rather than one-half of a "duplex" that houses believers and unbelievers. After all, Abraham's bosom was said to be "far away" from hades (the place of torment for unbelievers), not an adjoining compartment. Also, Jesus promised the repentant thief—who died before Jesus's resurrection—he would be with the Lord—not just Abraham—in Paradise (Luke 23:43).

Additionally, the weight of Scripture supports the interpretation that Abraham's bosom is heaven. For example, it is strongly implied that faithful Enoch was transported directly to heaven and not to a holding place in sheol or hades, when God "took him" (Gen. 5:24; Heb. 11:5). Furthermore, 2 Kings 2:1 and 2:11 clearly say Elijah was taken "by a whirlwind *to heaven*." Moreover, David believed God would not "abandon [his] soul to Sheol," but would give him "fullness of joy" in God's presence (Ps. 16:10–11).

David also prayed that after "all the days of [his life]," he would "dwell in the house of the LORD forever" (23:6). That can only refer to one place: heaven. Finally, David's son Solomon observed in Ecclesiastes 12:7: "The dust will return to the earth as it was, and the spirit will return to God who gave it." In other words, Old Testament believers' bodies would decay and return as dust to the earth, but their spirits would continue to live in the presence of God—also known as "Abraham's bosom."

Where Do Unbelievers Go When They Die?

As we've seen, Old Testament and New Testament believers immediately enter the presence of the Lord when they die. They are very much alive and aware that they are in a place we refer to as the "third heaven" as they await the new heaven and new earth, in which they will reside for eternity.

But what happens to unbelievers when they die? According to Jesus's story of the rich man and Lazarus, they are immediately dispatched to hades—a place of unbearable pain and agony. Hades is the immediate, but temporary, destination of non-Christians when they die. Let me explain what I mean by "temporary."

Just as Abraham's bosom or "the third heaven" is not the eternal destiny of believers, hades is not the final destiny of unbelievers. Instead, hades is a holding place for unbelievers as they await the resurrection of their bodies for the great white throne judgment, as described in Revelation 20:11–15:

Then I saw a great white throne and Him who sat upon it, from whose presence earth and heaven fled away, and no place was found for them. And I saw the dead, the great and the small, standing before the throne, and books were opened; and another book was opened, which is the book of life; and the dead were judged from the things which were written in the books, according to their deeds. And the sea gave up the dead which were in it, and death and Hades gave up the dead which were in them; and they were judged, every one of them according to their deeds. Then death and Hades were thrown into the lake of fire. This is the second death, the lake of fire. And if anyone's name was not found written in the book of life, he was thrown into the lake of fire.

The lake of fire (also referred to as *gehenna* in the Bible) is the eternal destination for all unbelievers, just as the new heaven and new earth is the eternal destination for all believers. Just as the third (or present) heaven is the temporary destination for believers as they await the new heaven and new earth, hades is the temporary destination for all unbelievers as they await the eternal lake of fire.

Neither the third heaven nor hades is any kind of neutral "waiting station" for the dead. Although hades is only a temporary location for unbelievers, it is a place of indescribable suffering. Just as believers begin to immediately and consciously experience the comfort of being in God's presence when they die, unbelievers begin to immediately experience the horrendous suffering of being separated from God at the moment of their death.

Notice how the rich man in Jesus's story begs for mercy and asks whether Lazarus might come from heaven and "dip the tip of his finger in water and cool off my tongue, for I am in agony in this flame" (Luke 16:24). The rich man's request is filled with irony. During life, he knew of Lazarus and his suffering. Unable to buy food, or even fend off the dogs that came to lick his sores, Lazarus sat at the rich man's gate every day, begging for a few crumbs of food from the rich man's table (vv. 20–21). Yet the rich man did not lift a finger to relieve Lazarus's misery.

However, after he died, the rich man couldn't buy relief for himself. He's reduced to begging for mercy from the one he mistreated in life. The rich man reaped in death what he had sown in life, just as Jacob Marley did in Charles Dickens's *A Christmas Carol*. Marley's ghost lamented to Scrooge, "I wear the chain I forged in life. . . . I made it link by link, and yard by yard; I girded it on my own free will, and of my own free will I wore it."[8] And so it is with all who measure life according to self and not according to the Savior. Jesus said, "by your standard of measure it will be measured to you in return" (Luke 6:38). And what was measured to the rich man was "agony"—*odynaomai*, meaning continual pain and grief.

But the rich man was mistaken in thinking that Lazarus could leave Abraham's side and become a minister of mercy in hades. Even if Abraham had wanted to dispatch Lazarus to minister to the rich man he would have been unable to. God established an impenetrable barrier between the righteous and unrighteous—"a great chasm fixed" (16:26)—preventing those in heaven to travel to hades and those in hades to travel to heaven, thereby eliminating any possibility of salvation after death.

In fact, "the Lord knows how . . . to keep the unrighteous under punishment for the day of judgment" (2 Pet. 2:9). "Keep" is in the present tense, indicating that the wicked are held captive continuously, as a guard keeps careful watch over a condemned prisoner on death row. Once unbelievers die and are held for final judgment, their fate is fixed.

However, the rich man was not completely heartless—even in hades. Not wanting his brothers who were still living to experience his suffering, he pleaded with Abraham to send Lazarus to his five brothers to warn them about what awaited them unless they repented. But again, Abraham refused. The brothers had the Scripture, which provided all the information they needed about salvation.

But the rich man refused to take no for an answer, and stated his brothers would only believe if they had a miraculous sign of someone coming back from the grave. Abraham countered, "If they do not listen to Moses and the Prophets, they will not be persuaded even if someone [like Lazarus] rises from the dead" (Luke 16:31). These words from Jesus proved to be prophetic, for even when Jesus returned from the dead the vast majority of people continued in their unbelief.

Heaven or Hell: A Forever Choice

Here's the basic truth Jesus's story of Lazarus and the rich man reveals about what happens when we die: either we *immediately* begin experiencing the eternal bliss of being in God's presence or we *immediately* begin experiencing the unending horror of being separated from God.

It's true that at some future time after death, Christians will change locations from the third heaven—the presence of the Lord—to the new heaven and the new earth. Likewise, unbelievers will also experience a change of address after the great white throne judgment, moving from the place of temporary suffering (hades) to the place of eternal torment (the lake of fire).

But both cases are nothing more than a change of location and are not a change in experience. The most fundamental truth Jesus reveals in this story is that the moment we die our eternal destiny is sealed—forever.

As you contemplate whether you are traveling on the road leading to heaven or hell, consider these sobering words from my friend Erwin Lutzer:

Five minutes after you die you will either have had your first glimpse of heaven with its euphoria and bliss or your first genuine experience of unrelenting horror and regret.

Either way, your future will be irrevocably fixed and eternally unchangeable.

In those first moments, you will be more alive than you ever have been. Vivid memories of your friends and your life on planet earth will be mingled with a daunting anticipation of eternity. You will have had your first direct glimpse of Christ or your first encounter with evil as you have never known it. And it will be too late to change your address.[9]

If you wait until the moment you die to choose your eternal destination, you will have waited one second too long.

5

What Will We Do in Heaven?

Well done, good and faithful servant; you have been faithful over a few things, I will make you ruler over many things. Enter into the joy of your lord.

Matthew 25:23 NKJV

At a dinner party, guests were discussing the possibilities of future rewards and punishments after death. Sam remained quiet, which was unusual for him since he was a born talker. Not wanting him to feel excluded from the conversation, his hostess turned and asked his views on heaven and hell. "I don't want to express an opinion," Sam said. "It's a policy for me to keep silent. You see, I have friends in both places."[1]

"Sam" was Samuel Clemens, better known as Mark Twain, and in truth he spoke often of both places. For example, in one speech, Twain joked:

The election makes me think of a story of a man who was dying. He had only two minutes to live, so he sent for a clergyman and asked him, "Where is the best place to go to?" He was undecided about it. So the minister told him that each place had its advantages—heaven for climate, and hell for society.[2]

Twain's tongue-in-cheek story illustrates a lie many have embraced about heaven: it will be a place of perpetual boredom, populated by boring people.

Three Popular Myths about God and Heaven

Science-fiction writer and atheist Isaac Asimov also embraced that belief, once remarking, "I don't believe in the afterlife, so I don't have to spend my whole life fearing hell, or fearing heaven even more. For whatever the tortures of hell, I think the boredom of heaven would be even worse."[3]

You and I might agree with that conclusion if we believed some of the common myths about God, heaven, and eternity.

Myth #1: God Is a Cosmic Killjoy

Mark Twain might joke that the advantage of heaven is the climate and the advantage of hell is the company, but heaven and hell are no laughing matter. Believe it or not, many people—like Isaac Asimov—have made decisions about their eternal destiny based on where they think the real neverending party is going to occur. These people view God as a perennial party pooper and Satan as the life of the party. Those who've come to that conclusion are convinced that heaven must be as dull as watching paint dry, while hell must be as exhilarating as driving in a NASCAR race. Yet both of those flawed conclusions are based on basic misunderstandings about both God and Satan.

Have you ever been stuck at a dinner party seated next to a hopelessly boring personality? Minutes seem like hours and you are convinced the evening will never end. Satan is that kind of companion. There really is nothing interesting about him. He has never created anything in his entire existence. Who would want to be stuck with him for eternity?

But there is nothing boring about God. He is exceedingly and eternally fascinating: just look at the present world He has created for us to live in. Heaven is the place where everything will be eternally good, beautiful, enjoyable, refreshing, fascinating, and exciting because heaven's Creator is all of those things.

Myth #2: Heaven Will Be Monotonous

Some people are convinced that no matter how exciting the activities of heaven may be, doing the same thing over and over for eternity will become monotonous. "Too much of a good thing isn't good, it's boring," is their motto.

But the problem isn't heaven—the problem is us. A friend of mine used to tell her children whenever they complained of being bored that "only boring people get bored." It wasn't that my friend's kids didn't have enough to do—they had a house full of video games, televisions, movies, board games, sports equipment, pets, and friends; they just got tired of doing the same things every day. It is ironic that any child (or adult for that matter) in America could play with thousands of dollars' worth of video equipment and be more bored with life than a child in Africa playing with two sticks and a stone.

The truth is we can't handle the monotony of life on earth—even if it comes packaged as fun and games—so we assume life in heaven is just as monotonous and boring. But monotony doesn't have to be boring, as G. K. Chesterton pointed out:

A child kicks his legs rhythmically through excess, not absence, of life. Because children have abounding vitality, because they are in spirit fierce and free, therefore they want things repeated and unchanged. They always say, "Do it again"; and the grown-up person does it again until he is nearly dead. For grown-up people are not strong enough to exult in monotony. But perhaps God is strong enough to exult in monotony. It is possible that God says every morning, "Do it again" to the sun; and every evening, "Do it again" to the moon. . . . It may be that He has the eternal appetite of infancy; for we have sinned and grown old, and our Father is younger than we.[4]

The activities of heaven will never get monotonous—even if we do them over and over—because we will no longer inhabit aging bodies that grow tired or live in a sin-infected world that makes life tedious. In that "placed called heaven" we will enjoy an "excess of life." We'll be like children saying to our heavenly Father, "Do it again!"

Myth #3: Heaven Will Be One Long Church Service

The idea that heaven is an eternal worship service is a persistent one. A number of years ago we had a guest preacher at our church who said, "If you have trouble sitting through a two-hour worship service here on earth, you will be miserable in heaven because all we are going to do for eternity is praise God." I groaned when I heard that because it made heaven sound like a giant yawn-fest—as evidenced by the very few "Amens" from the audience.

Now don't get me wrong. I'm a pastor who loves to sing God's praises with His people. However, although we were created by God for worship, we were also created to do *more* than worship.

While worshiping God will be a central activity in heaven, it will not be our only activity. Just as Christians today can offer praise to God while engaging in other tasks throughout the week, Christians in the new heaven and new earth will worship God during special, designated times as well as while involved in other activities.

Two Primary Responsibilities: Worship and Work

When God created Adam, He gave him two primary responsibilities: to work and to worship. Scripture says that "the LORD God planted a garden toward the east, in Eden; and there He placed the man whom He had formed," in order "to cultivate it and keep it" (Gen. 2:8, 15). That was the work Adam was to accomplish.

But Adam was also created to worship God. Genesis 3:8 implies that Adam and Eve had daily fellowship with the Lord—they walked with Him "in the cool of the day." When Christ establishes our eternal home on the new earth, it will be an Eden-like existence. And just as Adam had two primary responsibilities in Eden, we will have two primary responsibilities in the new heaven and new earth.

Exhilarating Worship Like You've Never Experienced

One of the most remarkable aspects of our worship in heaven will be seeing Jesus face-to-face. Our response to that experience will be unlike anything we've ever known on earth. Perhaps this insight might help you catch a glimpse about what our worship experience will be like in that "place called heaven."

We know the angelic host ceaselessly worships the Father and the Son with shouts of praise. According to John, the number of angels probably numbers in the hundreds of millions—"myriads of myriads, and thousands of thousands" (Rev. 5:11). The sound must be unlike anything heard on earth.

Just a few years ago, fans of the Seattle Seahawks football team set a world record as the loudest fans in the NFL. On December 2, 2013, during a third-down defensive stand against the New Orleans Saints, the Seahawks fans produced an ear-splitting 137.6 decibels. (The roar of a jet engine one hundred feet away produces 140 decibels.) The Seahawks fans' "praise" was so loud it triggered a minor earthquake![5]

A crowd of screaming football fanatics is no match for the "heavenly fans" that are right now praising God in the third heaven. Occasionally, I hear complaints from church members about the music in our services being "too loud." Well, the worship in heaven is not going to be some soft, contemplative, private experience. How do I know that? Look at Isaiah's description of the angelic worship of God taking place right now in heaven:

> And the foundations of the thresholds [of the temple] trembled at the voice of [the angels] who called out [in worship to God]. (Isa. 6:4)

One day we will add our voices to that ground-shaking heavenly chorus of angels, shouting "Hallelujah!"—praise be to our God.

> I looked, and behold, a great multitude which no one could count, from every nation and all tribes and peoples and tongues, standing before the throne and before the Lamb, clothed in white robes, and palm branches were in their hands; and they cry out with a loud voice, saying, "Salvation to our God who sits on the throne, and to the Lamb." (Rev. 7:9–10)

The number and the sound of the worshipers in heaven will be unlike our worship on earth. But there's more to our heavenly worship than size and volume. In heaven no one will merely mouth the words or go through the motions of worship; all will sing with hearts ablaze. Worship in heaven will be spontaneous, genuine, and exhilarating. "Praise will not be something we will be assigned or commanded to do; it will be natural," Joni Eareckson Tada wrote. "A supernatural effervescent response of the born-again creature, new and fit for heaven."[6]

If you've ever had that incredible experience in a worship service in which the expressions of your lips truly represented the adoration of your heart, you understand what Joni is describing. And rather than being a rare exception to the otherwise rote and programmed activity too many church-goers engage in most Sundays, the kind of worship that flows out of the deepest recesses of our hearts will happen every time we are in God's presence in the new heaven and new earth.

But in the new heaven and new earth, worship will not be limited to formal times of praising God. Randy Alcorn asked whether we will "always be engaged in worship."[7] The answer is yes and no, depending on your definition of worship. If you limit worship to praising God, praying, and preaching, then the answer is no. We will be involved in an array of other activities beyond formalized worship.

On the other hand, if you define worship as Paul did, then the answer is yes. Paul wrote, "Whether, then, you eat or drink or whatever you do, do all to the glory of God" (1 Cor. 10:31). In other words, we should worship God when we sit down for a meal, converse with our spouse or friend, play with our children or grandchildren, drive to work, or enjoy a vacation.

Worship is a continual awareness of, gratitude toward, and submission to God in everything we do. God is honored with my worship while I'm enjoying dinner with my daughters and thanking Him for them, sitting on a beach in Maui reflecting on His majestic power, or preparing for a difficult conversation and asking that I might reflect His point of view. We must quit thinking that we can only worship God while doing *nothing* else. Rather, we worship while doing *everything* else.

Invigorating Work That You Actually Enjoy

God is a worker. He did not create the world and then retire (though He did take one day off). He worked before sin entered the world and continues to work while sin remains in the world. Jesus declared, "My Father is working until now, and I Myself am working" (John 5:17). Since we are created in the image of God, it should be no surprise that we have been created to work as well. Contrary to what many believe, work is not a "curse" from God as a result of Adam and Eve's sin in the garden. Before the first couple ever took a bite of the forbidden fruit, God gave them the responsibility of work: "Then the LORD God took the man and put him into the garden of Eden to cultivate it and keep it" (Gen. 2:15).

Although Eden was perfect, it was not self-sustaining. God did His part in creating this slice of Paradise on earth, but He gave man the responsibility of cultivating it—tilling the soil and planting and harvesting crops. While it's true that Adam and Eve's work became much harder after their fall because of God's judgment, work has always been—and will always be—part of God's plan for each of us.

One of my best friends told me that when he was a teenager his dad would occasionally find him sitting on a sofa watching television. He said his father's response was always the same: "Get off that sofa and do something! What do you think you are—an international playboy?" Our heavenly Father did not create us to sit around and do nothing. That's why the whole concept of retirement today is flawed—it goes against God's basic plan for each one of us to do something productive with our lives. While we might cease working for the employer who provides us a paycheck, we are never to stop meaningful activity in order to sit around like international playboys.

Since our lives in the new heaven and the new earth are simply extensions of our lives now, we shouldn't be surprised that God plans for us to continue working in the new heaven and the new earth. Heaven will not be a place of eternal retirement where we do nothing but play golf or pluck a harp while living off a 401(k) plan that never runs dry.

"Wait a minute, working for eternity?" you ask. "That sounds more like hell than heaven!" The only reason we wince at the concept of working for eternity is because our labor has been burdened by the effects of sin's curse: bodies that grow tired, relationships that become strained, government regulations that are burdensome, and an environment that is uncooperative.

But in the new heaven and new earth all of those effects will evaporate because "there will no longer be any curse" (Rev. 22:3). In this world, work—no matter how much we enjoy it—can be exhausting. In the new world, work will be nothing but exhilarating.

Obviously, once the curse of sin is removed from the earth some jobs will automatically disappear. For example, there will be no need for doctors (disease will be eradicated), dentists (decay will be nonexistent), firefighters (destruction will be a thing of the past), or funeral directors (death will be eliminated). As I mentioned earlier, even my job as a preacher will probably be eliminated since there will be no sin to preach against and "the earth will be filled with the knowledge of the glory of the LORD" (Hab. 2:14).

This doesn't mean that people like myself will be unemployed and living on welfare. Perhaps for us what was merely a hobby on earth will become a vocation in heaven. Or maybe God will assign us a new task—one that we will be uniquely suited to perform. The majority of Christians should not be surprised that their work in the new heaven and new earth may very well be an extension and enhancement of their work now—minus the impediments that currently drain the joy out of that work.

From Cultivation to Creation

If life in the Garden of Eden serves as a template of what we can expect in heaven, then we can look forward to an eternity cultivating and creating. In the beginning, God created nature and called it good. But God intended His image-bearers to cultivate nature—to work it and create something very good.

For example, cherries are good, but cherry pie is very good; avocados are good, but guacamole is very good; tomatoes and spices are good, but salsa is very good. So when God created the man and placed him in the garden, He commissioned Adam to cultivate and keep what God had begun. But more than a cultivator, Adam was also to be a creator, which he demonstrated when he employed his imagination to name the animals.

The job descriptions of cultivator and creator are still in effect in today's world. The automobile, airplane, computer, and iPhone are examples of humankind's God-given creativity at work to make the world an even more enjoyable place in which to live.

We shouldn't be surprised that we will continue our creative work in the new heaven and new earth. Why wouldn't we bake cherry pies, eat salsa, write books, make movies, produce songs, teach classes, or do a thousand other things we do on earth?

If you want a clue about what your work might be in heaven, ask yourself the question my friend Bobb Biehl once posed to me: "If money and education were not a factor and you could do anything in the world with the guarantee you wouldn't fail, what would you do?" Why is that a relevant question? According to Philippians 2:13, "God . . . is at work within you, giving you the will and the power to achieve his purpose" (Phillips). God is the One who plants the "will" or desire in our hearts to accomplish His purpose for our lives. One of the best indicators of what we should be doing in this life and what we will be doing in the next life is based on desires God has placed in our hearts.

God doesn't waste gifts, experiences, or desires on us—they are all essential components of our unique purpose—not just in this life but in the life to come as well. Remember, our lives are each a continuum that begins on earth and extends beyond the grave. Who we are on earth is who we will be in heaven. We don't become someone else when we die—with different interests, gifts, skills, responsibilities, or callings. Therefore, we can assume that our work on the new earth will in some way resemble the work God has called us to perform on this present earth.

One Specific Job Description: Rule and Reign

Besides cultivating and creating, Adam and Eve were to rule and reign as God's coregents over creation—to be king and queen of earth.

> Then God said, "Let Us make man in Our image, according to Our likeness; and let them rule over the fish of the sea and over the birds of the sky and over the cattle and over all

the earth, and over every creeping thing that creeps on the earth." (Gen. 1:26; see v. 28)

But their conscious decision to rebel against God forced them to abdicate their reign over creation. In time, God sent a "second Adam"—Jesus Christ—and established a second Eve—the church—to one day rule over a new kingdom. And when Christ returns and establishes His thousand-year reign on earth (a period of time commonly referred to as the millennium), He will appoint His faithful followers (you and me) to rule with Him.

Christ's kingdom will not be run by professional politicians (do I hear an "Amen!"?) but by His followers. The criteria by which leaders in the new world order are selected will be completely different than in today's world. Cronyism and compromise will play no role in the selection of rulers. Instead, men and women will be elevated to leadership positions in the new world according to their faithfulness and service to God in the present world.

However, our reign will extend beyond the thousand-year rule of Christ during the millennium into the eternal state of the new heaven and new earth. The prophet Daniel had a vision of the coming Messiah—Jesus—and was told:

The saints of the Highest One will receive the kingdom and possess the kingdom forever, for all ages to come. . . . [And] the sovereignty, the dominion and the greatness of all the kingdoms under the whole heaven will be given to the people of the saints of the Highest One; His kingdom will be an everlasting kingdom, and all the dominions will serve and obey Him. (Dan. 7:18, 27)

When this happens, we will fulfill on the new earth the role God originally assigned to Adam and Even on the old earth—we "will reign forever and ever" (Rev. 22:5).

Ruling and reigning with Christ sounds intriguing. But who is qualified to reign? What exactly does reigning entail? And what is the extent of our reign?

Who Gets to Rule and Reign?

I've heard countless preachers opine that those who will rule with Christ in the next world will be His lowliest followers in this world, those who perform the most menial jobs imaginable. The only requirement for being assigned a leadership role in the next world, these preachers claim, is having the right character qualities in this world—character traits outlined by Jesus in the Beatitudes: humility, purity, peacefulness, and mercy.

I couldn't disagree more. While character certainly counts with God in both this world and the next, character is not the only prerequisite for leadership. Those who will rule and reign with Christ in the new world will be those who have the *desire* and the *ability* to rule. Frankly, there are wonderfully dedicated Christians who are absolutely terrified at the prospect of having to be in charge of anything. For them, having vast leadership responsibilities for eternity would be more like hell than heaven.

If that's true of you, relax. If you enjoy working with your hands more than directing other people, chances are that is what you will be doing in the new world as well. If you are more comfortable working one-on-one with other people rather than casting a vision for thousands, don't be surprised if God places you in a similar role in the new heaven. Usually, the only people who get excited about ruling and reigning with Christ for eternity are those who enjoy leadership roles in this world.

However, just having the desire and skills necessary for leadership does not automatically qualify you to rule with Christ in the new world. The single greatest determiner of leadership responsibilities in the next life will be faithfulness to God in this life. As we've discussed before, what you do on earth echoes in the halls of heaven.

Jesus powerfully illustrated that truth in His parable of the minas recorded in Luke 19. The story—which is equally applicable to our role in the millennial kingdom and the eternal state—begins with a nobleman traveling to a "distant country to receive a kingdom" (Luke 19:12). This is a reference to Jesus's death, resurrection, and ascension to heaven, where He now rules at the right hand of God the Father.[8] When Christ returns to earth, as the nobleman returned from his journey, He will establish His kingdom—first during the millennium and then for eternity.[9]

However, before departing on his journey, the nobleman gave to each of his ten servants a single mina—a Greek coin worth one hundred drachmas, or about three months' wages. The mina represents the totality of the time, treasure, and opportunities God has granted to all of us in this life. Each one of us is given only one life to live and invest for the Lord before He returns. And just as the nobleman, upon his return, required his servants to account for their use of the minas, so Christ will one day require each of us to account for the lives He has entrusted to us.

In Jesus's story the first servant reported a 1,000 percent return on investment, earning the nobleman's praise. "Well done, good slave," he said to the first servant, "because you have been faithful in a very little thing, you are to be in authority over ten cities" (Luke 19:17). The second servant reported a 500 percent return and was given authority over "five cities" (v. 19).

But a third servant wasn't nearly as industrious. Instead of investing the money wisely, he hid the mina, fearing recrimination from his master if he lost the money through a poor investment. Instead of rewarding this servant, the nobleman condemned him. "Why did you not put my money in the bank, and [then] I would have collected it with interest?" the nobleman asked (v. 23).

His master had given this third servant one mina and he returned exactly one mina to his master. His mistake was failing to leverage what had been entrusted to him. Remember, the mina represents all that God has entrusted to us during our brief stay on earth. Everything we have—our time, our money, our gifts, our opportunities—is simply on loan to us from God to use to expand His kingdom.

But here's the paradox. Although our existence on earth is a "little thing" (v. 17) compared to eternity, we have the opportunity to leverage the value of our lives on earth by investing it in the expansion of God's kingdom. Our ability and willingness to make such an investment will determine our responsibilities in the new kingdom Christ establishes when He returns.

Unfortunately, the third slave failed to wisely invest what had been entrusted to him during his master's brief absence and received the nobleman's condemnation instead of commendation. And what had been given to the third servant was taken away and given to the first servant, because "to everyone who has, more shall be given, but from the one who does not have, even what he does have shall be taken away" (Luke 19:26).

God has placed within our hands not only a precious treasure—our life—but also a great responsibility: to use our limited time and treasure in this life to further God's agenda rather than our own.

What Does Ruling and Reigning Look Like?

Ruling and reigning with Christ in His new kingdom involves at least two responsibilities: judging and governing. In 1 Corinthians 6:2, Paul wrote: "the saints will judge the world." The Greek word translated "judge" (*krino*) can refer to pronouncing a verdict against someone or it can be a synonym for governing. As corulers with Jesus Christ we will be responsible for both judging and governing in His new kingdom. Although there is no indication in Scripture that you and I will pronounce judgments against other human beings, we very well could be involved in the future judgment of certain angels.

In 1 Corinthians 6:3, Paul asked: "Do you not know that we will judge angels?" This is a curious question, since Psalm 8:4–5 says God made humans lower than angels. But in the eternal state, our positions are reversed—we'll be elevated higher than angels. Perhaps Paul was referring to the fallen angels who are awaiting judgment for their sin of cohabiting with women as described in Genesis 6. Or Paul may have used "judge" as a synonym for our responsibility of ruling over the angelic orders in the new heaven and new earth. We'll have to wait for heaven to find the answer to this question.

I believe that those who rule with Christ during the millennium and in the new heaven and new earth will be primarily involved in governing God's vast kingdom. It was an ancient practice for kings to appoint faithful citizens to serve as coregents over all or portions of the king's kingdom. At least three men in the Old Testament were appointed as prime minister over their respective nations: Joseph over Egypt (Gen. 41:38–44), Daniel over Babylon and the Medo-Persian Empire (Dan. 6:3), and Mordecai over Persia (Esther 8:1–2; 10:3). Although Scripture provides few details about what ruling in God's new kingdom will entail, we can be confident the experience will be exhilarating and eternally fulfilling since it is a reward for faithfulness to God in this life.

God assigned Adam and Eve to reign over the Lord's old creation. In the same way, those who are rewarded with leadership responsibilities will be assigned to reign over the Lord's new creation—the new heavens and the new earth. That leadership will include the governing of Christians who will work in Christ's glorious new kingdom. And though our primary residence will be the New Jerusalem, our work will take us beyond the new earth and into the far-flung galaxies of the new heavens—the stellar space, with its innumerable stars and planets.

Three Permanent Perks of Heaven

Don't think that heaven will be all work and no fun. Even though performing fulfilling work is one thing we will do in heaven, it is not the *only* thing we will do. Beyond worshiping

God and working for God, the Bible indicates at least three other activities that will occupy our time in the new heaven and the new earth.

Enjoying Other Believers

We were made to live in community—and that need for other people will not disappear in eternity. But in the new heaven and new earth, we'll experience the most intimate and fulfilling relationships imaginable. My friend David Jeremiah observes:

> Because we will be God's people made over, we will be perfectly compatible with one another and able, for the first time ever, to enjoy the intimate fellowship that we all long for in our hearts.[10]

Gone will be the suspicion, impure motives, and selfishness that taint even the best relationships we experience now. We will enjoy perfect fellowship not only with those we already know but also with those heroes of our faith we have only read about.

Just imagine how fascinating it will be to talk with Adam about what life was like in the Garden before sin entered the world. We will sit riveted to stories of

- Noah and his experience during the Great Flood,
- God's last-minute intervention in Abraham's offering of Isaac,
- the children of Israel escaping Pharaoh's chariots,
- David's victory over the giant Goliath, and

- the surprising discovery of Jesus's followers on that first Easter Sunday morning.

We will talk theology with Augustine, Jerome, Martin Luther, and John Calvin; science with Blaise Pascal, Isaac Newton, and George Washington Carver. We will discuss courage with William Wilberforce and Martin Luther King Jr., or what it was like to compose Christianity's most beloved hymn with John Newton. We will review books with G. K. Chesterton, J. R. R. Tolkien, and C. S. Lewis. And we will learn what it was like to preach before thousands from Dwight L. Moody and Billy Graham.

From our first day in heaven, and for every day thereafter, we will walk the streets of the new heaven and new earth with astonishment: "There goes Jeremiah! And over there is Eve. I can't believe it—there's Paul talking with the Wesley brothers—John and Charles. And over there is Esther . . . and Caleb . . . and John . . . and . . . Solomon . . . and . . ."

Better bring your autograph book with you—it's going to be quite an experience.

Learning More about God

As we saw earlier, the prophet Habakkuk promised that a day was coming when "the earth will be filled with the knowledge of the glory of the LORD" (Hab. 2:14). Perhaps Paul had this verse in mind when he wrote to the Corinthians: "Now I know in part, but then I will know fully just as I also have been fully known" (1 Cor. 13:12).

In the new heaven and new earth we will certainly understand more about God than we do now. But exactly how will that knowledge come? At the moment of our death and entrance into the presence of God, will the Lord instantaneously download into our minds a perfect and complete understanding of Himself? Maybe.

But think about your most valued relationships on earth— your mate, your children, your closest friends. No doubt you've discovered the joy of learning more about them through the years rather than experiencing an information dump all at once. Imagine how boring eternity would be if we knew everything there is to know about God and had nothing new to discover for eternity.

I can just hear some seasoned student of Scripture shouting, "But what about Jeremiah 31:34? 'They will not teach again, each man his neighbor and each man his brother, saying, "Know the LORD," for they will all know Me, from the least of them to the greatest of them.' Doesn't that verse imply an instantaneous and complete understanding of God?"

The kind of teaching Jeremiah says will no longer be needed in God's kingdom is an exhortation to enter into a relationship with God. That's what he meant by "know the LORD." Everyone in the new heaven and new earth will already have a relationship with God. But that doesn't mean everyone will immediately and instantaneously know everything there is to know about God.

For example, when I first met my wife, Amy, in Mrs. Denny's seventh-grade math class, I knew nothing about her except that she was the prettiest girl I had ever seen! But as we began passing notes back and forth (and always getting into trouble for doing so) I learned more about her. Over time, that friendship blossomed into romance, leading to an engagement and eventually forty years of marriage. And with every year that passes I continue to learn new things about her.

If I can continue to learn new things about a finite human being like Amy, how much more is there to learn about our infinite God? As one theologian put it:

> We will constantly be more amazed with God, more in love with God, and thus ever more relishing his presence and our relationship with him. Our experience of God will never reach its consummation. We will never finally arrive, as if upon reaching a peak we discover there is nothing beyond. Our experience of God will never become stale. It will deepen and develop, intensify and amplify, unfold and increase, broaden and balloon.[11]

Experiencing Real Rest

We've already seen that in eternity we will not be consigned to floating on a cloud plucking a harp. God has a very real assignment for each of us—work that will exhilarate us and free us from the earthly encumbrances that exhaust us. This doesn't mean, however, that we will not rest. When God created the world He rested on the seventh day—not because He was exhausted but in order to reflect on what He had accomplished. And He set aside days, weeks, and years for the nation of Israel to rest.

God understands that we live under the tyranny of the urgent, which induces stress. This is why Jesus said to the exhausted and wrung-out: "Come to Me, all who are weary and heavy-laden, and I will give you rest" (Matt. 11:28). That promise transcends this old earth and carries forward to the new earth. In Revelation 14:13, the apostle John was commanded to write these words: "Blessed are the dead who die in the Lord from now on . . . that they may rest from their labors, for their deeds follow with them."

The promise given to John refers to those believers who will be martyred for their faith during the great tribulation. They will finally experience relief from their labors. John did not mean that they will never have to work again or that they will enter into an eternal nap. The Greek word *kopos*, translated "labors," means that these believers, along with future believers, will be released from the tiresome burden of trying to live a godly life in a godless world.

But the kind of rest we will enjoy in the new heaven and the new earth goes far beyond the absence of hostility and persecution. The rest Jesus promised actually has nothing to do with imperfect bodies that tire quickly because of sin's curse. The rest Jesus is referring to will be the same kind of rest our heavenly Father experienced after six days of creating the universe.

It is a momentary respite from work that allows us to savor the satisfaction of a job well done.

It is a cessation from labor that allows us to reflect upon what we have accomplished and to say, "It is good . . . it is very good!"

It is a rest that reminds us that as important as our work will be—even in the new heaven and new earth—there will be other aspects of life to be enjoyed as well, not least of which include the perfect relationships with others and with God we have always longed for.

6

Do People in Heaven Know What Is Happening on Earth?

For behold, I create new heavens and a new earth;
And the former things will not be remembered or come to mind.

Isaiah 65:17

Imagine you're dead. You're standing at the entrance to heaven. Peter is there to greet you. He takes your name and checks your reservation. Everything is in order so he welcomes you into heaven with a smile. As he escorts you to your room, he hands you a package: a white robe, a golden crown, and a theater ticket.

The robe and crown aren't necessarily a surprise—you remember reading something, somewhere, about heavenly robes and crowns. But a ticket—that is unexpected. "What's the ticket for?" you ask. "Oh, that's for the movie," Peter answers. "Tonight we're having a double feature. The first stars your friend, the one who died with you in the car accident. It's a tragedy . . . really, 'horror film' is perhaps a better description, because your friend didn't make it here. He's in hell. However, the second movie is about your life. It stars you, with a supporting cast that includes your mate, your children, and dozens of friends and acquaintances. The climactic scene is your funeral. It's a real tearjerker. But I don't want to spoil it for you. I think you'll really enjoy the show!"

Before you have a chance to respond, Peter says, "Ah, here we are. Here's your key. Get some rest. And be sure to get to the theater early. It's going to be a sellout. All of heaven will be in attendance." With that, Peter smiles, turns in his sandals, and walks away.

I'm pretty sure there aren't tickets given out in heaven to movies depicting your life. Or movies starring those who enter hell. But many people do wonder whether residents of heaven can watch what is taking place on earth, or even peer into the darkness of hell. And if they do, could they be watching you right now?

Heaven's Witnesses

After guiding us on a tour through the hall of heroes in Hebrews 11, the author concludes:

> Therefore, since we have so great a cloud of witnesses surrounding us, let us also lay aside every encumbrance and the sin which so easily entangles us, and let us run with endurance the race that is set before us. (Heb. 12:1)

At first glance, this verse appears to imply that the current occupants of heaven are like spectators at a track meet, sitting in the stands watching the occupants of earth run the race of faith.

If we're honest, there's something a little creepy about the thought of a billion eyes watching your every move. To think that Solomon—the author of the manual on marital love that bears his name—might have a peephole into your bedroom might be a little disconcerting. Or what about your grandmother watching you as you . . . well, you get the idea!

But is that what Hebrews 12:1 teaches? Although the word "witnesses" does imply spectators, the verse doesn't really teach that all of heaven's population is sitting around watching us while munching on popcorn and slurping Coke. In the context, the "cloud of witnesses" refers only to those Old Testament saints mentioned in Hebrews 11. The point the writer is making is that in light of the example of those who persevered in their faith, we should also keep moving forward in obeying God regardless of the obstacles we face.

Nevertheless, there is some indication that those in heaven are aware of what takes place outside of heaven. For example, Christ must be aware of the obedience and disobedience of Christians on earth, since He condemned and commended the seven churches in Revelation 2–3. Furthermore, the apostle Paul realized that a heavenly audience was witnessing his actions on earth since he described his life as "a spectacle to the world, both to angels and to men" (1 Cor. 4:9). We can assume from this verse that angels are also aware of the activities of people on earth.

But Scripture provides us with other examples of those in heaven who seem to know what is happening on earth.

Abraham and the Rich Man

We have already dealt with Jesus's story in Luke 16 of Lazarus and the rich man in chapter 4. But there is one more observation we need to make from this story. Once the rich man arrived in hades—the temporary residence of the unsaved dead—he was immediately aware of his own agony and Lazarus's joy in heaven. This is important because some theologians and Christian traditions (like Seventh-Day Adventists) teach that consciousness ceases to exist at death—an idea sometimes called "soul sleep."[1]

The rich man addressed Abraham, and Abraham answered the rich man—indicating that both were fully conscious. Both men thought, spoke, heard, saw, felt, remembered, and recognized each other. And both men knew what was happening in each other's world. The rich man knew of Lazarus's pleasure, while Abraham knew of the rich man's anguish.

It appears the occupants of hades are aware of what is taking place in heaven, and the occupants of heaven are aware of what is taking place in hades. But do people in heaven know what is taking place on earth?

The Tribulation Martyrs and the Judgment on Earth

During that terrible future time of God's judgment on the earth known as the tribulation—the seven years between the rapture of the church and the second coming of Christ— many will come to faith in Jesus. However, just as Christians in the Middle East today are being slaughtered for their faith, future "tribulation saints" will also be required to pay the ultimate price for following Christ. When John had his heavenly vision, he saw these martyred believers gathered around God's throne, crying out for justice against those who had murdered them.

> When the Lamb broke the fifth seal, I saw underneath the altar the souls of those who had been slain because of the word of God, and because of the testimony which they had maintained; and they cried out with a loud voice, saying, "How long, O Lord, holy and true, will You refrain from judging and avenging our blood on those who dwell on the earth?" (Rev. 6:9–10)

These slain Christ-followers in heaven were acutely aware of what was happening—or not happening—on the earth. Their persecutors on earth were continuing their assault against God's people without restraint. Their cry was, "God, how long are you going to allow these enemies of Christ to continue? It's time to step in and do something!" Obviously, their frustration over God's (seeming) inaction was only possible because of their awareness of what was taking place on earth.

Later in John's vision, at the end of the tribulation and before the climactic battle of Armageddon, all the saints of heaven rose up with a great roar of approval over God's judgment on earth. These saints shouted:

> Hallelujah! Salvation and glory and power belong to our God; because His judgments are true and righteous; for He has judged the great harlot [Babylon] who was corrupting the earth with her immorality, and He has avenged the blood of His bond-servants on her. (19:1–2)

Again, the praise of believers in heaven for God's judgment against His enemies on the earth will only be possible

125

if indeed the residents of heaven are aware of what is happening on earth.

Heaven's Saints and the Salvation of the Unsaved

Jesus loved to tell stories. Three of His most famous are in Luke 15: the parables of the lost sheep, the lost coin, and the lost son. All three of these stories share the same purpose: to contrast the attitude of the self-righteous Pharisees, who hated sinners, with the attitude of the truly righteous God, who *loves* sinners. Jesus's point in all three parables was the same: when you lose something of value—a sheep, a coin, a child—you don't curse the lost object. Instead, you search for it and celebrate when you've found it.

God has the same attitude toward people who are living apart from Him. God doesn't hate those who are "lost." He loves them and is overjoyed when He is reunited with them. But Jesus said that God is not the only One who is ecstatic when a sinner is reunited with God:

> I tell you . . . there will be more joy *in heaven* over one sinner who repents than over ninety-nine righteous persons who need no repentance. . . . [And] there is joy *in the presence of the angels* of God over one sinner who repents. (Luke 15:7, 10)

Jesus didn't say angels rejoiced over repentant lost sinners—though they probably do. Jesus said rejoicing took place "in heaven . . . in the *presence* of the angels," indicating that Christians in heaven are celebrating the salvation of sinners on earth. Think about this: besides God, who in heaven would appreciate the salvation of a non-Christian

126

(especially if that non-Christian happened to be a friend or family member) more than those who had already experienced redemption?

If citizens of heaven rejoice at the salvation of sinners, then they not only know what is taking place on earth in a general sense but they are aware of the specific choices individuals are making on earth—whether they have accepted or rejected Christ's offer of salvation.

Hell's Captives

Since it appears that believers in heaven are aware of the faith commitments of those on earth, will those same heavenly believers lament the damnation of others? And if so, how could anyone ever be happy in heaven, knowing that people they cared about on earth are being tormented forever in hell?

These are intriguing questions. But before I address them there are some truths about hell we need to understand.

The Necessity of Hell

Hell was not part of God's original creation—it wasn't necessary. When God created the universe He called it "good." In fact, it was "very good." But when Satan rebelled and enlisted the first couple in his coup against the Almighty, hell became a necessity. Author Warren Wiersbe explains why:

> Hell is a witness to the righteous character of God. He must judge sin. Hell is also a witness to man's responsibility, the fact that he is not a robot or a helpless victim, but a creature able to make choices. God does not "send people

to hell"; they send themselves by rejecting the Savior. . . . Hell is also a witness to the awfulness of sin. If we once saw sin as God sees it, we would understand why a place such as hell exists.[2]

Satan's purpose in the world is both sinister and simple: use every means available to undermine and destroy God's plan for His universe. And because every human being since the fall of the first couple has been infected with the sin virus, Satan has millions of willing accomplices to aid him in his efforts.

When people ask the question, "Why does God allow evil in the world?" they need look no further than the mirror! Human beings, not God, are responsible for the terrible conditions of our planet.

Why do our cities suffer with prostitution, gang warfare, and drug abuse?

Why do our corporations and governments struggle with lying, cover-ups, and corruption?

Why are families being destroyed by divorce, adultery, and pornography?

Why do churches split over issues such as worship style, pastoral personalities, and the pressure to be culturally relevant?

These are just some of the devastating consequences of rebelling against our Creator. But this rebellion will not last forever. One day the universe will be restored to its original state. Evil will no longer triumph—or even exist. But for that to happen, those who have refused God's love will have to be quarantined from believers in the afterlife. If unbelievers were not isolated in hell from the rest of creation, then evil would once again infect God's creation and destroy the new heaven and the new earth.

What Do We Mean by "Hell"?

As we saw in chapter 4, the Greek word *hades* refers to the temporary location of the unsaved dead. The New Testament uses two other Greek words to describe the destination of the unsaved we commonly refer to as "hell."

The apostle Peter used the word *tartaros* when he said, "God did not spare angels when they sinned, but cast them into hell [*tartaros*] and committed them to pits of darkness, reserved for judgment" (2 Pet. 2:4). Just as hades is a temporary destination for unsaved people, *tartaros* is a temporary prison for a certain group of wicked angels.

Most demons (angels who chose to follow Satan in his original rebellion against God) are free to roam the earth, engaging in destructive activities whenever they find opportunity. But the imprisoned demons in *tartaros* are not free to roam because they committed a particularly heinous sin against God. Many believe this sin was their cohabitation with women on earth as described in Genesis 6—a sin that caused God to immediately dispatch them to this holding place of *tartaros* until their final judgment:

> And angels who did not keep their own domain, but abandoned their proper abode, [God] has kept in eternal bonds under darkness for the judgment of the great day. (Jude 6)

129

That "great day" of judgment will be when God throws Satan and all his fallen angels into "the lake of fire and brimstone" (Rev. 20:10). The Greek word *gehenna*, which is also translated as "hell" in English Bibles, refers to this place of eternal torment for Satan and his demons, the Antichrist and false prophet, and all unbelievers. The name is derived from the Hebrew *gen hinnom*—"the valley of Hinnom" or "the valley of Ben Hinnom."[3] Eventually, the name was shortened to *ge-hinnom* and the Greek translation became *gehenna*.

The valley of Hinnom is located immediately southwest of Jerusalem. During Jeremiah's day, the valley was the place where Jews offered human sacrifices, including burning children alive to the false god Molech.[4] Jeremiah called the place "the valley of the Slaughter" (Jer. 7:30–33).

By the time of Christ, the valley had become Jerusalem's city dump and a burial ground for criminals. Because of the valley's sordid history with child sacrifices, Jews in the first century associated *gehenna* with the place of eternal damnation and punishment for the wicked. According to Jesus, *gehenna* was the place of "outer darkness; [the] place [of] weeping and gnashing of teeth . . . where their worm does not die, and the fire is not quenched" (Matt. 8:12; Mark 9:48). This is the eternal destination of everyone who refuses to trust in Jesus Christ for the forgiveness of sins.

What Is Hell Like?

In *The Screwtape Letters*, C. S. Lewis puts into the mouth of hell's chief demon these words: "Indeed the safest road to hell is the gradual one—the gentle slope, soft underfoot, without sudden turnings, without milestones, without signposts."[5] No doubt that is true. Jesus said the way to hell is broad and its gate is wide (Matt. 7:13). It's easy to get into hell but impossible to leave it. What does the Bible reveal about this very real destination for those who die without Christ?

As we piece together what the Bible says about hades (the immediate but temporary destination of the unsaved) and *gehenna* (the eternal destination of the unsaved, also known as "the lake of fire" or "hell"), we can discover some important information about this terrible place. For simplicity, from this point on we will use the general term "hell" to describe both the temporary and eternal destination of the unsaved.

Hell Is a Physical Location

Like heaven, hell has an address. In the story of the rich man and Lazarus, hell is described as being "far away" (Luke 16:23), consisting of flames (v. 24), and being separated from heaven by "a great chasm fixed" (v. 26). These phrases describe an actual location, not a state of mind. And John described hell as "the lake of fire" (Rev. 19:20; 20:10, 14–15). At the end of the final judgment, before the unveiling of the new heaven and new earth, John observed, "death and Hades were thrown into the lake of fire" (20:14). Only a physical place (hades) can be thrown into another physical place (the lake of fire).

Jesus's words in Matthew 25:32–46 about the separation of the sheep and goats strongly argue for the fact that hell is a geographical location. At the end of the seven years of tribulation Jesus will separate believers (sheep) from unbelievers (goats). He said the goats will "go away into eternal punishment" (hell), while the sheep will go "into eternal life" (heaven) (v. 46). It is simply illogical for Jesus to say that believers go to an actual location (heaven) while unbelievers are dispatched to an unpleasant state of mind (hell). Elsewhere in Matthew 25 Jesus leaves no doubt about the reality of hell when He describes unbelievers as being "accursed" and cast "into the eternal fire which has been prepared for the devil and his angels" (v. 41).

Though hell and its flames are real, the fires of hell will not consume the bodies or spirits of those thrown into them. Rather, these unbelievers will suffer physical and spiritual anguish for all eternity. Like burning your hand on a hot stove without scorching your flesh, those in hell will experience the sensation without the scars.

HELL IS A PLACE OF ETERNAL, PHYSICAL TORMENT

The Bible teaches that the bodies of everyone who has ever lived—Christians and non-Christians alike—will experience a "resurrection." Christians will receive a new body that will allow them to enjoy the indescribable pleasures of the new heaven and new earth. Unbelievers will receive a body that will allow them to experience the real and eternal suffering of hell.

If you have difficulty believing that God would give non-Christians a "new" body for the sole purpose of experiencing everlasting suffering, read carefully Jesus's words in John 5:

> Do not marvel at this; for an hour is coming, in which all who are in the tombs will hear [the Son of God's] voice, and will come forth; those who did the good deeds to a resurrection

of life, those who committed the evil deeds to a resurrection of judgment. (vv. 28–29)

John "saw" this future resurrection of the unsaved in his vision recorded in Revelation 20:11–15:

Then I saw a great white throne and Him who sat upon it, from whose presence earth and heaven fled away, and no place was found for them. And I saw the dead, the great and the small, standing before the throne, and books were opened; and another book was opened, which is the book of life; and the dead were judged from the things which were written in the books, according to their deeds. And the sea gave up the dead which were in it, and death and Hades gave up the dead which were in them; and they were judged, every one of them according to their deeds. Then death and Hades were thrown into the lake of fire. This is the second death, the lake of fire. And if anyone's name was not found written in the book of life, he was thrown into the lake of fire.

Some theologians have attempted to rescue God from the charge of cruel and unusual punishment by advancing the doctrine of annihilation. This belief theorizes that unbelievers are destroyed—or annihilated—instead of physically punished for eternity. One of the arguments proponents of annihilationism use is the fact that Jesus and Paul speak of the "destruction" of those who go to hell.[6] But the Greek word translated "destruction" (*olethros*) doesn't mean annihilation. It means "sudden ruin." It refers to separation from God and the loss of everything that makes life worth living.

As a pastor I frequently witness such destruction. For example, when a man destroys his family through adultery and divorce, or when an alcoholic destroys his reputation and dignity through addiction, the suffering they experience is not momentary but continues as long as they live.

The doctrine of annihilation also contradicts the clear teaching of Revelation 19:20 and 20:10. After the climactic battle of Armageddon and return of Jesus Christ to the earth, the Antichrist and the false prophet are thrown into the eternal "lake of fire" (Rev. 19:20). After a thousand years, Satan and his minions are also cast into this same lake of fire:

> The devil who deceived them was thrown into the lake of fire and brimstone, where the beast [the Antichrist] and the false prophet are also; and they will be tormented day and night forever and ever. (20:10)

Notice the phrase "where the beast and the false prophet *are*." If the Antichrist and the false prophet—both human beings—had been destroyed the moment they were cast into the lake of fire, John would have written: "where the beast and the false prophet *were*." But after one thousand years, these two are still alive and suffering in this place where "they will be tormented day and night forever and ever."

The phrase "forever and ever" is important because it reiterates Jesus's claim that hell is a place of "eternal [physical] punishment" (Matt. 25:46). It's also important because it is the exact same phrase used by John to describe our endless worship of God, the endless life of God, and the endless kingdom of God.[7] My predecessor at First Baptist Church Dallas, Dr. W. A. Criswell, used to observe that if you reduce by one minute the time unbelievers have in hell then you must logically subtract the same amount of time believers will have in heaven, since the phrase "forever and ever" is used to describe the experience of believers and unbelievers alike.

Hell Is a Place of Indescribable Loneliness

Many people joke that they'd rather go to hell than go to heaven because hell will be "party central." But there will be no parties in hell. No one will socialize in hell because no one will be able to see anyone or anything. Jesus described hell as a place of "outer darkness" (Matt. 8:12). It's a place without the light of Christ because everyone in hell will be "away from the presence of the Lord" (2 Thess. 1:9).

A friend of mine likes to explore caves. Many caves, like Carlsbad Caverns in New Mexico, are lit to accentuate stalagmites, stalactites, and other unusual rock formations. But on one of my friend's tours in a cave in Colorado, there was no light—except the light of flashlights or headlamps. Crawling on his belly over the muddy floor of the cave and squeezing himself through small holes, my friend was having the time of his life. However, when the guide told everyone to turn off their lights, the blackness of the cave enveloped him. He described the darkness as claustrophobic. Not only could he not see his hand in front of his face but he wasn't even sure whether his eyes were open or closed. He lost all sense of direction. And if it wasn't for his feet firmly planted on the floor of the cave, he couldn't have told you which way was up or down. There wasn't a speck of light anywhere. And though he knew people were around him—his wife, the guide, and other tourists—he had never felt so cut off from humanity in all his life. It was, he said, a darkness and isolation that cannot be explained or comprehended—only experienced.

That is something of what hell must be like for those who enter there—an abyss of utter darkness and loneliness.

HELL IS A PLACE OF NO RETURN

Hell is a forever destination. This was the point of the parable of Lazarus and the rich man. Abraham told the rich man, who was suffering temporary agony, that "a great chasm fixed" separated heaven from hades, "so that those who wish to come over from here [heaven] to you will not be able, and that none may cross over from there [hades] to us" (Luke 16:26). Once we die our eternal destinies are just that—eternal.

Novelist James Joyce, in *A Portrait of the Artist as a Young Man*, captures a hint of the hopelessness and despair all in hell must know. After describing for his congregation the suffering that takes place in hell, a preacher said:

Consider finally that the torment of this infernal prison is increased by the company of the damned themselves. . . . In hell all laws are overturned—there is no thought of family or country, of ties, of relationships. The damned howl and scream at one another, their torture and rage intensified by the presence of beings tortured and raging like themselves. All sense of humanity is forgotten. The yells of the suffering sinners fill the remotest corners of the vast abyss. The mouths of the damned are full of blasphemies against God and of hatred for their fellow sufferers and of curses against those souls which were their accomplices in sin. . . . They turn upon those accomplices and upbraid them and curse them. But they are helpless and hopeless: it is too late now for repentance.[8]

No one escapes the confines of hell. Hell is a forever destination. If you wait until you enter the gates of hell to repent, you will have waited too long.

Hell Will Be the Destiny of the Majority of Humanity

Many people believe there ought to be a hell for truly evil people—the Adolph Hitlers, Joseph Stalins, Pol Pots, Charles Mansons, and Osama bin Ladens of the world. But those same people find it inconceivable that many good people who've simply not trusted in Jesus for forgiveness would also be sentenced to a place of eternal torment. What about all those who've never heard the name of Jesus? Or those who have sincerely embraced other religions and are living moral, upright lives? Would God really consign them to such a horrendous place?

As I discuss in my book *Not All Roads Lead to Heaven*, Jesus taught that only a small percentage of the earth's population will ever discover the true path to eternal life. In Matthew 7:13–14, Jesus said:

> Enter through the narrow gate; for the gate is wide and the way is broad that leads to destruction, and there are *many* who enter through it. For the gate is small and the way is narrow that leads to life, and there are *few* who find it.

As difficult as it may be to accept, the "many" on the wide road are not just mass murderers, child rapists, and terrorists. Sincere, religious people who make good neighbors and love their children are also on the "highway to hell." Even people who claim they have performed religious works in the name

137

of Jesus will be cast into hell by Jesus on the judgment day, as Jesus Himself revealed:

> Not everyone who says to Me, "Lord, Lord," will enter the kingdom of heaven, but he who does the will of My Father who is in heaven will enter. Many will say to Me on that day [of judgment], "Lord, Lord, did we not prophesy in Your name, and in Your name cast out demons, and in Your name perform many miracles?" And then I will declare to them, "I never knew you; depart from Me, you who practice lawlessness." (Matt. 7:21–23)

We struggle with Jesus's claim that the majority of people will be in hell because of our *low estimation of God*. We assume that God should be as tolerant of sin as we are. After all, we regularly overlook sin in others and ourselves, so why can't God? However, our tolerance of sin is not evidence of our godliness but of our godlessness.

Listen to God's scathing indictment of the Israelites—and all of us—in Psalm 50:21: "You thought that I was just like you." God isn't anything like us. His "eyes are too pure to approve evil" and He will not "look on wickedness with favor" (Hab. 1:13). And for that reason, He must and will punish sin. Every sinner has an opportunity to receive Christ's offer of forgiveness. To do so means heaven. And every sinner has an opportunity to reject Christ's offer of forgiveness. To do so means hell.

We also struggle with Jesus's words in Matthew 7 because we have *too high an estimation of ourselves*. Our own inflated sense of goodness and justice causes us to set ourselves up as the measure of all goodness and justice. And by that measure, especially compared with the Hitlers or bin Ladens of the world, we measure up quite nicely . . . or so we think.

But God utilizes a different standard of moral measurement than ours. For example, the difference between the North Pole and the South Pole is negligible compared to the distance between the North Pole and the furthest star in the universe. In the same way, the moral difference between Adolph Hitler and us is substantial, but it's minimal compared to the difference between a perfect God and an imperfect humanity.

God's standard is perfect holiness. None of us meets that standard. And because we don't, Paul wrote: "For all have sinned and fall short of the glory of God" (Rom. 3:23). Unbelievers will spend eternity in hell, not because they're not good but because they're not *good enough*. In this, Christian philosopher Peter Kreeft was correct: "Hell is not populated mainly by passionate rebels but by nice, bland, indifferent, respectable people who simply never gave a damn [about Jesus Christ]."[9]

Will the Joy of Heaven Be Diminished by What Happens on Earth and in Hell?

It seems clear that believers in heaven know what is taking place on earth—at least in some sense. And they know what is taking place in hell according to the story of Lazarus and the rich man. So a natural question is how can we be happy in heaven while watching those we care about on earth suffering from devastating illnesses, broken relationships, or destructive addictions?

139

And how could we ever enjoy one pleasure of the new heaven and new earth knowing that some of those friends and family members we love the most will be suffering in hell? To put a finer point on it: Could you really enjoy all that God has prepared for you—no matter how spectacular—knowing that one of your children is being tormented day and night forever and ever?

This is a difficult question to answer because we lack the wisdom and insight to fully understand the mind of God. However, here are three possible answers to the question of how we can reconcile our joy in heaven with our knowledge of the suffering of our loved ones on earth and in hell.

Will God Purge Our Memories?

One Christian thinker frames the theory this way: "God may erase memories for a wayward son from the mind of his mother so that she may enjoy the full bliss of heaven unaware that she even had the son who is now damned."[10] This idea comes from Isaiah 65:17:

> For behold, I create new heavens and a new earth;
> And *the former things will not be remembered or
> come to mind.*

However, this can't mean that we'll forget *everything* about our former lives on earth. Many of the relationships we formed here will continue there—including our relationship with Christ. For example, Scripture says Jesus retains His scars (John 20:24–29). Seeing them will be a constant reminder that our sin compelled Him to endure the cross.

140

And the reminder of our sin that necessitated His death will compel us to enthusiastically worship Him for eternity.

The context of Isaiah 65:17 is verse 16. Speaking to the nation of Israel, the Lord said, "the former troubles are forgotten . . . they are hidden from My sight!" It is God who does the "forgetting," not us. This doesn't mean our omniscient God can't recall Israel's past transgressions. Rather, God *chooses* not to hold Israel's sin against her. When I forgive someone that doesn't mean I do a "memory wipe" of the wrong he or she committed against me. Even if I wanted to forget the offense, it would be biologically impossible to do so, since every experience we have is chemically and electrically embedded in our brain. Instead, forgiveness means letting go of my right to hurt another person for hurting me.

Nothing in Scripture indicates that God is going to erase our memories of those we know and love who may be suffering on earth or in hell.

Christians Will Be Preoccupied with the Joys of Heaven

We are all aware of the multitude of starving children, disease-ridden acquaintances and loved ones, and persecuted Christians in the world around us. Yet the knowledge of these suffering individuals does not prevent us from enjoying a good meal, a day at the beach, or time with our family. Some would claim that our ability to enjoy these blessings, in spite of others' suffering, is a testimony to our selfishness. "In heaven, we will be like Jesus, who wept over the fate of the lost," they argue.

While it is true that Jesus cried over the eternal destiny of the residents of Jerusalem while He was on earth, there is no indication that Jesus will do any crying in heaven. The writer of Hebrews notes that Jesus willingly "endured the cross" so that He could experience "the joy set before Him" when He "sat down at the right hand of the throne of God" (Heb. 12:2).

Additionally, Scripture teaches that complete joy will be the primary emotion of those in heaven:

> You will make known to me the path of life;
> In Your presence is *fullness of joy*;
> In Your right hand there are pleasures forever.
>   (Ps. 16:11)

In heaven we *will* be just like Jesus, who experiences the "fullness of joy" in spite of all that is happening on earth and in hell.

We Will Understand the Plan and Justice of God

In his book *The Eighth Day*, Thornton Wilder compares our lives to a tapestry. Viewed from the right side—the side facing out—we see an intricate work of art made from thousands of multicolored threads woven together to form a beautiful picture. But if we look at the backside of the tapestry, we see a jumble of threads of varying lengths crisscrossing one another. Nothing seems to make sense. Some threads are knotted, others are short, and still others are long.

The point Wilder is making is simple: God has a design for our lives. Some lives are twisted, knotted, or cut short. Other lives are of impressive length and color. Why? Not because one thread is more important than another thread, but because God's tapestry requires it.

Only from the perspective of heaven will we be able to see the right side of God's plan for our lives and understand how He is working all things "together for good" (Rom. 8:28). The tangled mess of broken relationships, catastrophic accidents, and sudden deaths that make no sense to those of us trapped in time and space on earth will be viewed completely differently from the perspective of heaven—even as we witness those tragedies being experienced by those we care about most.

But what about those we love who will be condemned to eternal torment in hell? It's important to note that God *doesn't* send people to hell; they freely *choose* to go to hell by rejecting God's gift of salvation through Jesus's death and resurrection. "God's wrath . . . is something which men choose for themselves," theologian J. I. Packer wrote. "Before hell is an experience inflicted by God, it is a state for which man himself opts, by retreating from the light which God shines in his heart to lead him to Himself."[11]

As difficult as this truth is to accept on this side of heaven—especially when talking about loved ones—the people in hell are there because they deserve it. But on the other side of heaven, we'll see God's justice in punishing those who refused to accept Christ's sacrifice as perfect, holy, and just. The apostle Paul claims that when we see Jesus Christ "dealing out retribution to those who do not know God and to those who do not obey the gospel of our Lord Jesus" (2 Thess. 1:8), none of us will accuse Jesus of injustice. Instead, Jesus Christ the Judge will "be marveled at among all who have believed" (v. 10).

Although this truth is hard to fathom, Packer offers some helpful words:

Remember, in heaven our minds, hearts, motives, and feelings will be sanctified, so that we are fully conformed to the character and outlook of Jesus our Lord. . . . In heaven, glorifying God and thanking him for everything will always absorb us. All our love for and joy in others who are with us in heaven will spring from their doing the same, and love and pity of hell's occupants will not enter our hearts. Their hell will not veto our heaven.[12]

And we can add with certainty that our awareness of anything happening on earth or in hell is incapable of diminishing the fullness of our joy in that place called heaven.

7

Will We Know One Another in Heaven?

Dear friends, we are already God's children, but he has not yet shown us what we will be like when Christ appears. But we do know that we will be like him, for we will see him as he really is.

1 John 3:2 NLT

Growing old isn't for the faint of heart—especially for those with a faint heart. With age come ailments and aches . . . and a few extra pounds. As humor columnist Erma Bombeck grew older she said something along the lines of, "I'm not telling you what I weigh, but when I measure my girth and then step on the scales, I oughta be a ninety-foot redwood."[1]

For many of us the battle of the bulge was a minor skirmish in our twenties. But it became total war in our forties and fifties. And if it wasn't the bulge, it was something else—wrinkles or sags or bags.

Have you ever gotten out of the shower and stared at yourself in a full-length mirror? For those of us of a certain age, it's unnerving. You ought to try it sometime; it'll jolt you awake—like an electric shock. One overriding thought will fill your mind: *I have everything I used to have. It's just a few inches lower than where it used to be.* Let's not kid ourselves: our bodies aren't the bodies we had in high school or when we first married.

Although you know it's *you* standing in front of the mirror, you almost don't recognize yourself. And if you're going to a reunion you wonder whether anyone else will recognize you. It's a good thing they place senior yearbook pictures on nametags at high school reunions, or you wouldn't have a clue whom you were talking to!

Unfortunately, most people don't age gracefully. Hearing loss, fading eyesight, and creaking joints accompany our advancing years. Getting older reminds me of what Jesus said to Peter:

> I tell you the truth, when you were young, you were able to do as you liked; you dressed yourself and went wherever you wanted to go. But when you are old, you will stretch out your hands, and others will dress you and take you where you don't want to go. (John 21:18 NLT)

If and when we get to the stage described by Jesus we'll hardly recognize ourselves anymore, nor will those who knew us in the vibrancy of our youth.

When it comes to the next life, we are naturally curious

as to who we will be in heaven. Will we be ourselves? And if so, which self—the young, energetic go-getter or the old, lethargic individual with hardly enough get up to go? Will we recognize friends and family, and will they recognize us—and which version of "us" will they know?

These are intriguing questions. However, before we answer them it is important to understand some important truths about the resurrection of the dead.

Will Everyone Receive a Resurrection Body?

At funerals, I sometimes hear people say things like, "This isn't the real Mary. This is only her shell. The real Mary—her spirit—is in heaven." Or, "This is the last time we'll ever see Roger in this body." It's natural to say things like this because we know that our earthly bodies are temporal and our spirits are eternal.

However, those realities have led many Christians to the wrong conclusion that there is a dichotomy between our bodies (what some believe are only the appearance of who we are) and our spirits (what they believe are the reality of who we are). They believe that since we leave our earthly bodies behind at death, we will exist in heaven as disembodied spirits.

Nothing could be further from the truth. In the new heaven and new earth we will not exist as sanctified versions of Casper the Friendly Ghost. Instead, just as we possess physical bodies in this world, we will also exist and relate to one another in physical bodies in the next world. How do I know that? Consider how God designed us and what His plans are for us.

God's Design: Body and Spirit

Throughout this book we've seen that heaven is primarily the re-creation of the original Eden—the earth as God originally designed it. If that is true, then it seems reasonable to assume that the residents of the new earth will exist in the same form as the original occupants of Eden. When we turn to Genesis 2 we find a very interesting statement about God's creation of the first couple:

> Then the LORD God formed man of dust from the ground, and breathed into his nostrils the breath of life; and man became a living being. (Gen. 2:7)

When God created Adam—and later Eve—He fashioned them as physical beings (dust) into whom He placed His Spirit (the breath of life), making each person a "living being." Notice that a person needs both a body and a spirit to be considered a "living being." Without a physical body he or she would not be a "being," and without a spirit he or she would not be "living." God created Adam—and every person since—as body and spirit.

Of course, there is a time coming when every human being will have his or her spirit separated from his or her physical body. The word *death* comes from the Greek word *thanatos*, which means "to separate." Death is the separation of our spirit from our physical bodies. As we saw in chapter 4, at that moment of separation the spirit of a Christian goes immediately into the presence of Jesus Christ, while the spirit of a non-Christian goes immediately to hades, the temporary place of torment.

But how long will that separation of body and spirit last?

As we also saw in chapter 4, some theologians speculate that at death, both Christians and non-Christians will receive some kind of temporary bodies while awaiting their eternal bodies. After all, they argue, God originally created us as body and spirit, and in eternity we will be body and spirit. Why would we think that in the intermediate state we would be disembodied spirits?

Others believe, since there is no direct evidence in the Bible that Christians and non-Christians who die will receive bodies before the final resurrection, we should assume that during the time between our deaths and the receiving of our new bodies we will exist as spirits only.

God's Plan: Two Resurrections

But here is one thing we know for sure: in the future, every Christian and non-Christian will receive a new physical body that is designed to experience the eternal pleasures of heaven or torments of hell. The Scripture repeatedly talks about the resurrection of both the righteous and unrighteous. For example, the patriarch Job believed he would see God with his own physical eyes when he declared:

> Even after my skin is destroyed,
> Yet from my flesh I shall see God. (Job 19:26)

The prophet Daniel believed that both the wicked and the righteous would be resurrected to receive their just rewards:

> Many of those who sleep in the dust of the ground will awake,
> these [believers] to everlasting life, but the others [unbelievers]
> to disgrace and everlasting contempt. (Dan. 12:2)

When will these resurrections of our bodies take place?

The First Resurrection

The Bible uses the term *first resurrection* to describe the time when all believers will receive their brand-new bodies for eternity. The apostle John wrote, "Blessed and holy is the one who has a part in the first resurrection; over these the second death has no power" (Rev. 20:6).

It is important to understand that the first resurrection does not occur at a single point in time. Instead, different groups of Christians will receive their new bodies at different times in the future. Paul explained: "For as in Adam all die, so also in Christ all will be made alive. But *each in his own order*" (1 Cor. 15:22–23).

The Greek word translated "order" is *tagma*, and refers to a military procession, with each corps falling in at its appointed time. At death every Christian's spirit is immediately ushered into the presence of God, but we do not receive our new bodies until our assigned time or "order." The chart on page 151 illustrates the various times different groups of Christians will receive the new bodies they will inhabit for eternity.

The Second Resurrection

While believers will participate in the first resurrection, every unbeliever since Adam will be part of what we might call the *second resurrection*. Unlike the first resurrection, the second resurrection will occur at a single point in time—prior to the judgment of all unbelievers at an event commonly known as the great white throne judgment:

What Happens to a Person after Death[2]

	At Death	Bodily Resurrection	Judgment	Eternal Destination
Old Testament Believer	Paradise/ Abraham's Bosom	Resurrection at Christ's Second Coming	Judgment on Earth for Rewards	Heaven
	The Grave			
Christian	Christ's Presence	Resurrection at the Rapture	Judgment Seat of Christ in Heaven for Rewards	Heaven
	The Grave			
Millennial Believer	Christ's Presence	Resurrection at the End of the Millennium	Judgment on Earth for Rewards	Heaven
	The Grave			
Tribulation Believer	Christ's Presence	Resurrection at Christ's Second Coming	Judgment on Earth for Rewards	Heaven
	The Grave			
Unbeliever	Sheol/Hades Torment	Resurrection at the End of the Millennium	Judgment at the Great White Throne for Sins	Hell/Gehenna/ Lake of Fire
	The Grave			

151

And the sea gave up the dead which were in it, and death
and Hades [the temporary residing place of all the unsaved
dead] gave up the dead which were in them; and they were
judged, every one of them according to their deeds. Then
death and Hades were thrown into the lake of fire. This is
the second death, the lake of fire. (Rev. 20:13–14)

Just as Christians will receive physical bodies in which they
can enjoy the eternal benefits of the new heaven and new
earth, unbelievers will be resurrected and receive physical
bodies in which to endure the eternal torment of the lake
of fire.

How Is a Physical Resurrection Possible?

First Corinthians 15 is the most complete explanation
of the resurrection in the Bible. The apostle Paul answers
many questions we naturally have about the resurrection
and the nature of our new bodies. For example, anticipating
objections to a physical resurrection, the apostle Paul writes:
"Someone will say, 'How are the dead raised?'" (1 Cor. 15:35).

Perhaps you have wondered the same thing. I want to be
sensitive here, but I'm often asked about those whose bodies have been destroyed in an accident or a tragedy, such as
the victims of September 11, 2001. How can their disinte-
grated bodies be resurrected? Or consider the passengers
in an airliner that explodes over the ocean. The bodies of
dismembered passengers are submerged in the water only
to be eaten by sea creatures.

When Roger Williams, the founder of Rhode Island, died,
he was buried at the foot of an apple tree. When his body was
disinterred years later, the roots of the tree had penetrated

his casket, grown through the top of his skull, and branched out down his arms and legs. The tree had literally consumed Williams's body, deriving nourishment from his corpse. So how is Roger Williams's body ever going to be resurrected?

Or consider what happens to the person who at death donates a part of his or her body to a worthy recipient. How can that person ever reclaim his or her vital organs if an eye went to Ethel and a kidney was donated to Sydney? This puts Paul's question in 1 Corinthians 15:35 in a new light, doesn't it? How could a decomposed body—scattered at sea, eaten by fish, consumed by an apple tree, or dissected for its organs—ever be put back together and returned to the original owner? Theologian John Calvin answered the question this way: "Since God has all the elements at his disposal, no difficulty can prevent him from commanding the earth, the fire, and the water to give up what they seem to have destroyed."[3]

The Analogy: Planting and Harvesting

Paul answered his own question about the possibility of a resurrection by using an analogy familiar to his audience: the planting and harvesting of a crop.

> That which you sow does not come to life unless it dies; and that which you sow, you do not sow the body which is to be, but a bare grain, perhaps of wheat or of something else. But God gives it a body just as He wished, and to each of the seeds a body of its own. (vv. 36–38)

Before a watermelon seed ever produces a watermelon it must first be placed in the ground, where it dies. When a farmer goes into the field to gather the harvest, he or she doesn't gather watermelon seeds but something much better—watermelons! The harvest is always superior to what was planted.

So it is with the resurrection. When we die, our human bodies are like "seeds" that are planted in the ground. The death of our human bodies—regardless of how it occurs—is not a hindrance to a future resurrection but a prerequisite for a greater "harvest." Why?

Notice Paul's words: "That which you sow does not come to life unless it dies" (1 Cor. 15:36). The apostle goes on to explain that our old bodies must die because they are not designed for eternity. "Flesh and blood cannot inherit the kingdom of God," Paul said, "nor does the perishable inherit the imperishable" (v. 50). While your body is perfectly designed for planet Earth, it is not suited for Mars, Pluto, or heaven. That is why we should not view death as "the end" of something great but as "the beginning" of something greater.

The body we receive at "harvest time"—the resurrection—is vastly superior to the body that is planted in the ground. Think of it this way: imagine it's a scorching summer day—100 degrees in the shade. You've been outside working in the yard. To cool down, you come into the house and open the refrigerator for something refreshing. Which would you rather sink your teeth into—a slice of ice-cold watermelon or an ice-cold watermelon seed?

Similarly, when our bodies are resurrected from the grave, it will not be our old bodies that are raised. The resurrection is not a reconstruction but a re-creation of our bodies. Those who have been blown apart, or cremated, or donated their organs to others won't be rebuilt versions of their dead selves any more than a watermelon is a rebuilt version of a watermelon seed. Rather, they are something new and vastly superior—the watermelon itself.

Superior but Similar

Although the "harvest" is *superior* to the "seed," the harvest is also *similar* to the seed. You don't plant a watermelon seed and harvest a kumquat! A watermelon seed produces a watermelon. Similarly, your new body that is raised at "harvest" time will not be something completely unlike your body that was buried at death. You don't die and become someone else in the resurrection. There will be some similarities between our earthly bodies and our heavenly bodies.

The perfect example of this is Jesus's resurrection body. And since Scripture promises that the bodies of resurrected believers will be like His (1 John 3:2), we should look closely at Jesus's resurrection body if we want to discover what our bodies will be like in the new heaven and the new earth.

Was Jesus's Resurrection Spiritual or Physical?

Of course, what follows in this section assumes that Christ's body was actually raised from the dead. Some members of the Corinthian church questioned whether anyone could physically come back from the dead. They had no problem believing that the spirit of Christ lived on—His moral example, His wise teaching, and His loving attitude—but were unsure that *He* lived again body and soul. But Paul consistently proclaimed the physical death and resurrection of Christ as the foundation stone of the gospel:

I delivered to you as of first importance what I also received, that Christ died for our sins according to the Scriptures, and that He was buried, and that He was raised on the third day according to the Scriptures. (1 Cor. 15:3–4)

Paul went on to argue that if this was *untrue*—if Christ hadn't died and wasn't raised from the dead—then the consequences were too terrible to contemplate.[4] Preaching would be worthless—hollow words of no consequence. Faith would be futile—we might as well believe in fairies and pixie dust. Christians would be charlatans—no better than cultists or used-car salespersons who lie. Sin would be unforgiven—you're on your own before the judgment of God. Death would result in damnation, not salvation. Christians would be pathetic—fools and knaves to have believed such nonsense. Practically speaking, if Christ's body still lies in a Jerusalem tomb we might as well give up on Christ and sleep in on Sunday mornings.

"But now Christ has been raised from the dead," Paul declared (v. 20). And what proof did Paul offer? Christ in His resurrection body "appeared to Cephas [Peter], then to the twelve. After that He appeared to more than five hundred brethren at one time . . . then He appeared to James, then to all the apostles; and last of all . . . He appeared to me also" (vv. 5–8). In fact, Scripture lists seventeen different appearances of the resurrected Jesus in bodily form.

On the day of His resurrection, Jesus appeared five times:

1. To Mary Magdalene (Mark 16:9–11; John 20:11–17)
2. To the other women (Matt. 28:8–10)
3. To Peter (Luke 24:34; 1 Cor. 15:5)

4. To the disciples on the road to Emmaus
   (Mark 16:12–13; Luke 24:13–35)
5. To the ten disciples, without Thomas
   (Mark 16:14; Luke 24:36–43; John 20:19–23)[5]

Over the next thirty-nine days, Jesus presented Himself to His disciples six times:

1. To the eleven disciples a week later, with Thomas (John 20:26–29)
2. To seven disciples by the Sea of Galilee (John 21:1–14)
3. To more than five hundred believers (1 Cor. 15:6)
4. To James, Jesus's brother (1 Cor. 15:7)
5. To the eleven disciples in Galilee (Matt. 28:16–20)
6. To the eleven disciples at the ascension in Jerusalem
   (Mark 16:19–20; Luke 24:50–53; Acts 1:3–9)

And before the final book of the Bible was written, Jesus appeared an additional six times:

1. To Stephen at his martyrdom (Acts 7:55–56)
2. To Saul at his conversion on the road to Damascus
   (Acts 9:3–7)
3. To Paul in Arabia (Gal. 1:12)
4. To Paul in the Jerusalem temple (Acts 22:17–21)
5. To Paul in prison at Caesarea (Acts 23:11)
6. To the apostle John on the island of Patmos
   (Rev. 1:12–20)

But Jesus did more than just show up and say, "*Shalom*, y'all." He conversed with His disciples on all seventeen occasions. He ate with His disciples on at least three occasions: after the encounter on the Emmaus road, during the visit with the ten (without Thomas), and at breakfast by the seashore. And on two occasions His disciples touched His body: the women who came to the tomb to anoint Him, and Mary Magdalene. Other times Jesus invited people to touch Him, including the disciples on the Emmaus road and Thomas. Jesus's physical appearance—especially His scars—was enough to convince Thomas that Jesus had been resurrected and was truly the Son of God. "Thomas answered and said to [Jesus], 'My Lord and my God!'" (John 20:28).

The disciples didn't interact with just Jesus's disembodied spirit after the resurrection but with Jesus Himself in bodily form.

What Was Jesus's Resurrection Body Like?

When Jesus received His new (postresurrection) body, it was both different from and similar to His old (preresurrection) body. Jesus's new body was superior to His earthly body as demonstrated by His ability to materialize at will—even through locked doors. This happened at least twice during the forty days Jesus walked around in His new body. The first time occurred on resurrection day. The disciples were shut up behind closed doors, fearing the Jews might find and crucify them, when, unexpectedly, "Jesus came and stood in their midst and said to them, 'Peace be with you'" (v. 19). The second time occurred a week later, when Jesus appeared to Thomas, who was "inside . . . the doors having been shut" (v. 26).

Because Jesus could appear at will, He could also disappear at will. The best example of this comes from the dinner in Emmaus after His resurrection. After explaining from the Old Testament Scriptures why the Messiah must suffer and die, Jesus sat down to share a meal with two disciples. "When He had reclined at the table with them," Luke wrote, "He took the bread and blessed it, and breaking it, He began giving it to them. Then their eyes were opened and they recognized Him; and He vanished from their sight" (Luke 24:30–31).

But there were also similarities between His new and old body—enough so that when He appeared to His followers in His new body they eventually recognized Him. I say "eventually" because there were instances in which the disciples did not immediately recognize the Lord—for understandable reasons. Some were so full of sorrow they couldn't see clearly (John 20:11–15). One appearance happened while it was still dark (20:1, 14–15). On another occasion the distance between Jesus and His disciples was great enough to obscure recognizable features (21:4). Some were disbelieving (20:24–25), while those behind closed doors were startled when He suddenly appeared (Luke 24:36–37). Finally, others were spiritually dull (vv. 25–26). Yet in all these cases the confusion was merely temporary.

Eventually, the similarities between Jesus's natural body and His new body caused His followers to recognize Him. Maybe the similarity was something as trivial as the way He tore apart a piece of bread. After speaking with the disciples on the Emmaus road, Jesus ate dinner with them—just like a man. But Luke records that "He was recognized by them in the breaking of the bread" (v. 35). Perhaps Jesus held the bread in His right hand as He tore it with His other hand because the Lord was left-handed in His natural body. If Jesus were left-handed in His natural body there would be no reason for Him to be right-handed in His resurrection body. His physical features, postresurrection, were similar to His preresurrection features—the nail holes in His hands and feet prove that.

What Will Our Resurrection Bodies Be Like?

Why this detailed examination of Jesus's resurrection body? Scripture promises that our resurrection bodies will be like Jesus's:

> Beloved, now we are children of God, and it has not appeared as yet what we will be. We know that when He appears, *we will be like Him*, because we will see Him just as He is. (1 John 3:2)

In Colossians 1:18 Paul referred to Jesus's resurrection as "the firstborn from the dead." The word translated "firstborn" comes from the Greek word from which we get our English word *prototype*. Whenever a manufacturer builds a new automobile or airplane, they first build a prototype. Every other car and plane is then patterned after that first one. In the same way, Jesus's resurrection body was an example of what our bodies are going to be like.

So in what specific ways will our new resurrection bodies be in "conformity with the body of His glory," as Paul promised in Philippians 3:21?

Our Bodies Will Be Physical

After making the case for the resurrection of Christ and the resurrection of believers in 1 Corinthians 15:1–19, Paul addressed the question of what kind of resurrection bodies we'll receive in verses 39–50. The simple answer is that we'll have different bodies than the ones we now inhabit—as different as the bodies of animals, stars, and plants are from each other. Paul explained:

> All flesh is not the same flesh, but there is one flesh of men, and another flesh of beasts, and another flesh of birds, and another of fish. There are also heavenly bodies and earthly bodies, but the glory of the heavenly is one, and the glory of the earthly is another. There is one glory of the sun, and another glory of the moon, and another glory of the stars; for star differs from star in glory. (1 Cor. 15:39–41)

Paul's point is this: the body of a fish is not the body of a bird; the body of a bird is not the body of a beast; the body of a beast is not the body of a human (a truth that obviously is contrary to the basic premise of evolution). A star is not a planet and a moon is not a star. Each one follows its own kind, just as God intended at the beginning of the creation.

Similarly, our heavenly bodies will differ from our earthly bodies. Why should we find it difficult to believe that there is one kind of body created for inhabiting earth and another kind of body for inhabiting heaven? But to ensure that we wouldn't misunderstand, Paul detailed the difference between our earthly and heavenly bodies:

> So also is the resurrection of the dead. It is sown a perishable body, it is raised an imperishable body; it is sown in dishonor, it is raised in glory; it is sown in weakness, it is raised in power; it is sown a natural body, it is raised a spiritual body. If there is a natural body, there is also a spiritual body. (vv. 42–44)

The Greek word for "body" used here is *soma*. In every instance in the New Testament, *soma* refers to a physical body. So, when Paul used *soma* in verse 44, in reference to the "natural body" and "spiritual body," he made clear that our resurrection bodies would be just as physical as our natural bodies are physical.

But just because our heavenly bodies will be physical doesn't mean they will be physical in the same way our earthly bodies are. For example:

- Our earthly bodies decay; our heavenly bodies will endure.
- Our earthly bodies are infected with sin; our heavenly bodies will be free of sin.
- Our earthly bodies are weak; our heavenly bodies will be powerful.
- Our earthly bodies are for the old earth; our heavenly bodies are for the new earth.

The differences between our earthly bodies and our heavenly bodies often lead people to ask whether we will eat and drink or wear clothes in heaven. And what age will we be? As with all questions about our resurrection bodies, we must look to the resurrection body of Jesus for answers since He is the pattern—the *protokos*—of our resurrection bodies.

We've already seen, on at least three specific occasions, that the resurrected Jesus shared a meal with His disciples. But even before Jesus's death and resurrection He promised His disciples they would gather at His banquet table and feast with Him during the millennial kingdom. "Just as My

Father has granted Me a kingdom, I grant you that you may eat and drink at My table in My kingdom" (Luke 22:29–30). Obviously this event during the millennium occurs after Jesus's and the disciples' resurrections, when they are living in their new bodies. This promise indicates that we, too, will share meals with Jesus and the disciples in our new bodies.

We'll also wear clothes in heaven. Some object to this idea because Adam and Eve, before the fall, didn't wear clothes. Although life on the new earth will be Eden-like, it won't be like the popular survival show *Naked and Afraid*, in which a man and woman attempt to survive in the wild for twenty-one days without clothes.

When John saw the resurrected Christ on Patmos, Jesus was "clothed in a robe reaching to the feet, and girded across His chest with a golden sash" (Rev. 1:13). And when Christ spoke to the church at Sardis, He told them: "He who overcomes will thus be clothed in white garments" (3:5), which John confirmed with his own eyes (7:9).

When the bride of Christ—the church—is presented to Jesus at His second coming, we will be clothed in "fine linen, bright and clean" (19:8). And when Jesus, the conquering King, comes to finalize His war with evil, it is said He will be "clothed with a robe dipped in blood" (v. 13).

We will also retain our sexual identity in our new bodies. Some have wrongly concluded that we'll be androgynous in heaven—genderless—because Paul claimed, "there is neither . . . male nor female . . . in Christ Jesus" (Gal. 3:28). But Paul wasn't referring to the sexual nature of our bodies in the next life. He was referring to our equality in Christ—in this life. The fact that some people did not recognize the resurrected Lord immediately (like the two on the road to

Emmaus) strongly argues that Jesus looked like any other man instead of some "otherworldly" sexless alien.

Our bodies will probably be resurrected at an ideal, youthful, and mature age. Though we can't be sure, many theologians believe we'll be in our thirties. Thirty is considered the peak of perfection, both mentally and physically. (I think I remember that!) It was the age when Old Testament priests began their ministry in the temple and when Christ began His public ministry. So, for those of us a little bit older, go back and look at old pictures and imagine your eternal self when you were thirty. And for those younger than thirty, including children . . . well, you have something to look forward to!

Our Bodies Will Be Perfect

We will have real, physical bodies. But, as we've seen, they will be different than the bodies we inhabit today— they will be free from sin and therefore free from disease, decay, and death. Remember, in heaven, "the first things [the things of the earth] have passed away" (Rev. 21:4). Cancer, heart attacks, and strokes will all be a thing of the past. So will blindness, deafness, and paralysis, as well as gray hair, wrinkles, and widening girths. Missing limbs will be restored. From the top of our heads to the bottom of our feet, we'll be perfect in every way.

"Can you imagine the hope this gives someone spinal cord–injured like me?" my friend Joni Eareckson Tada asked. "Or someone who is cerebral palsied, brain-injured, or who has multiple sclerosis? Imagine the hope this gives someone who is manic depressive. No other religion, no other philosophy promises new bodies, hearts, and minds. Only in the Gospel of Christ do hurting people find such incredible hope."[6]

We can assume that our resurrection bodies will be attractive and retain the same physical traits of our individual bodies today.[7] In other words, not every man will have the physique of a bodybuilder and the looks of a movie star. Nor will women have the shape of a fashion model and the face of an angel. Your face will be your face. Your body will be your body—tall, short, thin, or plump. But all will be healthy and appealing. We won't have to worry about body image, comparing ourselves with others. Plastic surgeons will not be needed in heaven. Nor will cosmetics—sorry all you Mary Kay–ers. As one writer claims, "We won't have to *try* to look beautiful—we *will* be beautiful."[8]

Our Bodies Will Be Personal

Your body, your memories, your gifts and talents, your passions, and your spirit are what make you *you*. In the resurrection, all of these will be perfected and glorified, "in the twinkling of an eye" (1 Cor. 15:52). But you won't become someone else or something else (like an angel). You will become the *you* God intended you to be.

When John wrote that we "will be like [Jesus]" (1 John 3:2), the apostle didn't mean that we will become mini-Christs, like Dr. Evil's "Mini-Me" in the Austin Powers movies. We will become like Christ in character and with a similar heavenly DNA, but we'll retain our distinctive personalities. In heaven, I'll be Robert Jeffress—only perfected. And if you're a believer, you'll be Sandy Smith or Bob Brown or [insert your name]—only perfected.

Think of it like this: you probably have a computer and use certain software for word processing or developing spreadsheets. When an upgrade becomes available, you don't get a whole new program; you get a better version of the same program—only with new and better features. Likewise, with our resurrection we'll have upgrades, including new features (though without the glitches or programming errors), but we'll still be who we are.

This was Jesus's point when He appeared to the disciples after the resurrection and said, "It is I Myself" (Luke 24:39). Who He was before His death and resurrection is who He is after His death and resurrection. Randy Alcorn made a strong case for continuity when he wrote:

> If we weren't ourselves in the afterlife then we couldn't be held accountable for what we did in this life. The Judgment would be meaningless. If Barbara is no longer Barbara, she can't be rewarded or held accountable for anything Barbara did. She'd have to say, "But that wasn't me." The doctrines of judgment and eternal rewards depend on people's retaining their distinct identities from this life to the next.[9]

Part of our distinctive identity is that we'll keep our own individual names in heaven. God promised the righteous citizens of Israel that their individual names would endure throughout eternity:

> "For just as the new heavens and the new earth
> Which I make will endure before Me," declares the
>   LORD,
> "So your offspring and your name will endure."
>   (Isa. 66:22)

166

And Jesus called those currently in heaven by their earthly names. "I say to you that many will come from east and west, and recline at the table with Abraham, Isaac and Jacob in the kingdom of heaven" (Matt. 8:11).

But some will also be given additional names in heaven. Speaking to the church at Pergamum, the resurrected Christ said, "To him who overcomes . . . I will give him a white stone, and a new name written on the stone which no one knows but he who receives it" (Rev. 2:17). These new names don't invalidate our old names, nor do they erase our personality. In fact, these new names reflect the true personality and responsibility of those who receive them. For example, Jacob, which means "heel-catcher" or "supplanter," was also Israel—"one who strives with God." Simon, which means "God has heard," was also Peter—"the rock." And Saul, which means "prayed for," was also Paul—"small" or "humble."

We've looked at a lot of details concerning our resurrection bodies. But what does it all mean? Simply this: when we get to heaven we'll recognize each other as the unique individuals we are. We'll even recognize saints whom we've never seen before. Peter, James, and John recognized Moses and Elijah when they appeared with Jesus at His transfiguration (Matt. 17:4).

The relationships we have formed on earth will continue in heaven. But they will continue without strife or enmity. In heaven, all things are made new. "Our eternal reunion with Christian loved ones and friends will be ceaselessly glorious," theologian Ron Rhodes wrote.

Keep in mind that we will no longer have sin natures. There will be no fights among loved ones. There won't be any resentment or envy or jealousy. There won't be any one-upmanship or rivalries. There won't be any cross words or misunderstanding or selfishness. Our relationships in heaven will truly be wonderful and utterly satisfying.[10]

Now that is something truly to look forward to in that "place called heaven."

8

Will Heaven Be the Same for Everyone?

Behold, I am coming quickly, and My reward is with Me, to render to every man according to what he has done.

Revelation 22:12

Jim Marshall was a defensive lineman on the Minnesota Vikings' famed "Purple People Eaters" in the 1960s and '70s. Though a Super Bowl champion, Marshall is best known for the mistake he made on October 24, 1964. In a game against the San Francisco 49ers Marshall saw a fumble, picked up the football, and began running the length of the field. Vikings players on the sidelines followed Marshall and began yelling . . . for him to run the other way! Marshall didn't realize he was running toward his own end zone. In spite of that mistake, Marshall played so well that the Vikings ended up winning the game 27–22.

But history has a way of recording the worst. Few people

remember Marshall's outstanding performance in the game, only his major mistake. In fact, to this day Jim Marshall is remembered by the nickname he earned that day: "Wrong Way" Marshall.

Making it to the end zone is the goal of football. But making it to the *right* end zone is the key to winning. A similar truth applies to heaven. Making it to heaven is the goal, but making it there to hear Jesus say, "Well done, good and faithful servant" is the key to ultimate victory.

While all true Christians will cross the spiritual end zone, many will enter only after spending some time running the wrong way. Some believers will be celebrated for how they played the game of life. But others who were ultimately on the winning side will still be evaluated as having done little to contribute to the success of the team.

It's a hard but inescapable truth: heaven will not be the same for every Christian. When "we . . . all stand before the judgment seat of God" (Rom. 14:10), some will receive great rewards and others will not.

A Divine Summons

Every person from the time of Adam to the present will have to appear before the divine Judge who "[will] judge the living and the dead" (2 Tim. 4:1). No one escapes God's judgment. As the writer of Hebrews declared, "it is appointed for men to die once and after this comes judgment" (Heb. 9:27). Notice the writer doesn't limit the generic term "men" (meaning "human beings") to only certain individuals or groups. Everyone will face God's scrutiny of his or her life.

However, there is not one single judgment for all humankind.

170

Instead, unbelievers will stand before Christ at what is called the great white throne judgment. This judgment is for all unbelievers since the time of Adam and will occur at the end of the millennial kingdom, resulting in condemnation—being cast into the lake of fire (Rev. 20:11–15). Believers will appear before a very different judgment, "the judgment seat of Christ" (2 Cor. 5:10), resulting in commendation for those the Lord deems to have served Him faithfully in their brief existence on earth.

An Appearance before the Judge

A few years ago, members from our church toured the ancient city of Corinth, where Paul spent eighteen months preaching the gospel. Many Corinthians came to faith in Christ through the apostle's preaching. However, others were incensed by Paul's message and dragged him before the Roman governor of the province:

> But while Gallio was proconsul of Achaia, the Jews with one accord rose up against Paul and brought him before the judgment seat, saying, "This man persuades men to worship God contrary to the law." But when Paul was about to open his mouth, Gallio said to the Jews, "If it were a matter of wrong or of vicious crime, O Jews, it would be reasonable for me to put up with you; but if there are questions about words and names and your own law, look after it yourselves; I am unwilling to be a judge of these matters." And he drove them away from the judgment seat. (Acts 18:12–16)

The phrase translated "judgment seat" is the Greek word *bema*. It refers to a raised platform on which a ruler or judge

171

sat to pronounce decrees or verdicts, similar to the raised bench judges sit at in modern courthouses.

As our group stood on the spot where Paul faced his judge, I wondered what it must have been like to be in Paul's sandals—standing before a man who held his fate in his hands. How did the apostle maintain his cool demeanor when facing his possible death? I think it's because Paul understood that Gallio's judgment—whatever it was—wasn't the final judgment on his life. One day Paul would stand before another judgment seat from which the Judge of the universe would evaluate Paul's faithfulness to Christ.

What makes the *bema* seat judgment different than the great white throne judgment is that everyone who stands before the judgment seat of Christ will be saved. No one will appear at this judgment who hasn't already been declared "not guilty" by God. The theological term for this declaration is *justification*. "Therefore, having been justified by faith," Paul wrote, "we have peace with God through our Lord Jesus Christ" (Rom. 5:1).

Think of justification this way: imagine you use your debit card to make a purchase, but in so doing you overdraw your account. The bank notifies you of the overdraft and applies a penalty for covering the purchase. If you will deposit the amount of the overdraft and penalty, the bank will forgive the debt and won't levy an additional penalty. The only problem is that you are bankrupt and have no funds to deposit. You are in a deficit position with the bank. However, a friend finds out about your dilemma and makes a deposit to your account to cover the overdraft and penalty.

In a sense, that is what Christ offers to do for us. All of us are "overdrawn" in our "righteousness" account before

God. And every time we sin we only increase our indebtedness to God. If we die spiritually bankrupt—unable to pay our debt—we face the penalty of eternal separation from God.

But when we trust in Christ for our salvation God credits our "righteousness" account with the perfection of His Son, erasing our debt and eliminating any future penalty. That means Christians never have to worry about a future judgment for the sins already paid for by Christ. Paul assures us that "there is now no condemnation for those who are in Christ Jesus" (Rom. 8:1).

However, justification does not exempt us from God's evaluation of our lives after we are forgiven for our sins. Paul declares:

> We must *all* appear before the judgment seat of Christ, so that each one may be recompensed for his deeds in the body, according to what he has done, whether good or bad. (2 Cor. 5:10)

Notice Paul said, "We must *all* appear." I've checked the Greek text and "all" means "all!" Every believer will appear before Christ's bench—there are no exceptions, exclusions, or exemptions. Each of us will appear before the Lord for an evaluation to receive whatever reward is appropriate. *Remember, the judgment seat of Christ is for the* commendation *of believers while the great white throne judgment is for the* condemnation *of unbelievers.* This is why Paul told the Corinthians to make it their "ambition, whether at home [in the body] or absent [from the body], to be pleasing to Him" (2 Cor. 5:9).

When Will Our Judgment Take Place?

When will this evaluation take place? Most probably it will occur right after the rapture of the church, when living Christians are immediately transported into the presence of the Lord and dead believers are resurrected to eternal life. While no single verse indicates that the *bema* seat judgment occurs immediately after the rapture, a number of factors point to this conclusion.

First, the twenty-four elders mentioned in Revelation 4:10 (who represent all believers) are portrayed in heaven as having already received their rewards (crowns) at the beginning of the tribulation. Additionally, when the church (the "bride of Christ") returns to earth with Jesus at the second coming—seven years after the rapture—the bride is said to be clothed in "fine linen, bright and clean," which represents "the righteous acts of the saints" (Rev. 19:8). Both of these facts imply that the evaluation of Christians' lives has already occurred.

Do Our Works Really Matter?

Many Christians are confused about the importance of obedience to God in this life. "My good works are worthless to God," they mistakenly claim. While it's true we are saved by God's grace apart from our works, God rewards us as Christians based on our works. While our works are worthless in securing us a *place* in heaven, they are integral in determining our *experience* in heaven.

Paul drew a distinction between works *before* salvation and works *after* salvation. This is what he said about our works before salvation: "For by grace you have been saved through faith; and that not of yourselves, it is the gift of God; *not as a result of works*, so that no one may boast" (Eph. 2:8–9).

And this is what Paul said about works after salvation: "For we are His workmanship, created in Christ Jesus *for good works*, which God prepared beforehand so that we would walk in them" (v. 10).

Before we became a Christian, our works were only sufficient to condemn us before God. But once we have become a Christian, our works should be sufficient to commend us to God. As we've already seen, we will all appear before the judgment seat of Christ and be evaluated on our works, "whether good or bad" (2 Cor. 5:10). The Greek word translated "bad" (*phaulos*) literally means "worthless."

If you think Google, Facebook, and Amazon collect a mountain of information on search histories, likes, and purchases, their data collection is a molehill compared to God's collection system. He knows every word spoken, every thought contemplated, every action taken, and every motive held. And one day He will bring it all to light. According to Scripture, the Lord will evaluate our actions, thoughts, and words; our use of talents, gifts, and time; as well as our treatment of others, hospitality to strangers, responses to mistreatment, efforts to win others to Christ, and attitude toward money.[1]

Nothing will be hidden from the Lord's scrutiny. Thinking about that future day of God's evaluation reminds me of a very thorough physical exam I once had (the operative word being "once"). Part of the examination entailed determining my body fat. The doctor's assistant instructed me to remove my clothes and get into a basket to be submerged into what is appropriately called "the fat tank." As I held my breath underwater, the doctor calculated my percentage of body fat.

But that wasn't the worst part. I was then forced to stand completely naked in front of my doctor while he used some sort of torture device to pinch different parts of my body to calculate body fat utilizing a different method. In that moment, I regretted every chocolate chip cookie I had ever eaten, every morning I had rolled over and hit my snooze alarm instead of hitting the treadmill, and every midnight trip to the freezer for another scoop of ice cream. Standing there without a stitch of clothing on, being pinched, poked, and prodded, while my doctor frowned, scowled, and grinned, caused me to think one thought: *He knows everything!*

At the end of this ordeal my doctor called me into his office. After a few pleasantries, he opened the file containing the results of my examination. First, he complimented me on my exercise program, the results of the stress test, and the bowl of Bran Flakes I ate every morning for breakfast. Then the corners of his mouth turned downward, and he got serious. "Now, let's talk about your body fat." *That's always a pleasant subject for conversation*, I thought. "You need to melt a few points off of that. And your cholesterol needs to be lowered, so quit eating that bowl of ice cream every night." While my doctor commended me for the good things I was doing, he also offered a critique of the not-so-good habits that were endangering my health. My exam wasn't the most enjoyable experience of my life but it wasn't the worst experience either.

Similarly, when we stand before the Lord's judgment seat every aspect of our lives will be laid bare before God. As Jesus warned, "For nothing is hidden that will not become evident, nor anything secret that will not be known and come to light" (Luke 8:17). God's frank evaluation of the totality of our brief time on earth will result in rewards or the forfeiture of rewards—but not in eternal condemnation.

What Actually Happens at the Judgment Seat of Christ?

Paul utilized three analogies to explain what will happen at the judgment seat of Christ. Paul's first illustration is that of a trust agreement with God:

> But you, why do you judge your brother? Or you again, why do you regard your brother with contempt? . . . So then each one of us shall give an account of himself to God. (Rom. 14:10, 12)

The idea of "giving an account" is built on the analogy of a trustee—one who is responsible and legally bound to administer something that belongs to another. At some future time, the trustee must give an account of how he or she managed that trust. For example, financial advisors serve as trustees of their clients' money. The money that these advisors invest doesn't belong to them—they are simply managers who oversee and hopefully multiply the owners' funds.

Similarly, all that we have is a trust from God: our lives, talents, skills, gifts, and opportunities. We don't own anything—we are simply managers who are responsible to use those assets to further God's interests. At the *bema* judgment we need to be prepared to answer the Lord's question, "What have you done with what I have entrusted to you?"

The trustee analogy highlights a basic but essential truth about how God will evaluate us at the judgment seat of Christ: God will not judge every Christian in the same way. For example, God will not judge me by the same standard by which He evaluates Billy Graham. God gave Dr. Graham a different gift than He has given to me. I don't have to worry that one day God will hold me accountable for opportunities that were never mine. A trustee is only responsible for that which has been entrusted to him or her.

Paul also utilizes the analogy of constructing a house as an illustration of the judgment Christians will face.

> According to the grace of God which was given to me, like a wise master builder I laid a foundation, and another is building on it. But each man must be careful how he builds on it. For no man can lay a foundation other than the one which is laid, which is Jesus Christ. (1 Cor. 3:10–11)

Every one of us is in the process of building our own "house" or life. The foundation of a Christian's life is his or her faith in Christ Jesus. However, once that foundation is laid we must determine what kind of life we construct, based on the building materials we choose. On the foundation of faith, believers can either build a life of "gold, silver, [and] precious stones" or we can choose "wood, hay, [and] straw" (v. 12).

When we stand before Christ, our lives—our houses—will be tested by fire: "each man's work will become evident; for the day will show it because it is to be revealed with fire, and the fire itself will test the quality of each man's work" (v. 13). The idea here is that the primary basis of God's evaluation of our lives will be how eternally significant our lives prove to be.

The only way to withstand the searing heat of Jesus's judgment is to construct our lives with durable materials. Building a life in pursuit of profits, power, or pleasures is like building a house made of straw. But unlike the children's story of the three little pigs, Jesus doesn't huff and puff to blow the house down—He simply sets a match to it! Every aspect of our lives judged to be temporal rather than eternal will be consumed in the inferno of His holiness, leaving behind only a pile of ashes.

However, building a life dedicated to glorifying God (gold), introducing others to the Savior (silver), and demonstrating a love for God and others (precious stones) is like constructing a building of steel and marble—it will be unscorched by the heat of Jesus's evaluation.[2] What endures will be rewarded. "If any man's work which he has built on it remains, he will receive a reward," Paul told the Corinthians (1 Cor. 3:14). A person's actions that end up being consumed will be lost forever—though the individual will be saved: "If any man's work is burned up, he will suffer loss; but he himself will be saved, yet so as through fire" (v. 15).

This analogy emphasizes that our lives will be judged based on durability—the choices we make in constructing our lives. But the *whats* of life aren't the only criteria by which Christ will evaluate our lives. He will also judge the *whys* of our choices.

Therefore do not go on passing judgment before the time, but wait until the Lord comes who will both bring to light the things hidden in the darkness and disclose *the motives of men's hearts*; and then each man's praise will come to him from God. (1 Cor. 4:5)

For example, if I give money to God out of obedience, He counts it as gold. But if I give hoping that others will notice how generous I am, He counts it as straw. Motives matter—whether I'm sharing the gospel with someone, going on a mission trip, or demonstrating hospitality to a stranger. "All the ways of a man are clean in his own sight," Solomon wrote. "But the LORD weighs the motives" (Prov. 16:2).

Some might wonder if investing your life wisely in order to earn future rewards is a wrong motive itself. Not at all! Consider the example of Abraham. Why was he willing to obey God by uprooting his family and leaving his friends for some unknown and unfamiliar destination? The writer of Hebrews says Abraham "was looking for the city which has foundations, whose architect and builder is God" (Heb. 11:10). The only city God has ever or will ever design and build is the New Jerusalem that is yet to be revealed. In other words, Abraham's obedience to God in this life was in anticipation of a reward from God in the next life.

Or think about Moses's experience. The future leader of God's people voluntarily surrendered the perks of living in Pharaoh's household and instead chose "to endure ill-treatment with the people of God than to enjoy the passing pleasures of sin" (v. 25). Why did Moses make that heroic choice? Simply out of dedication to God?

No, the writer of Hebrews reveals that Moses's decision was based on an objective calculation. Moses was "considering the reproach of Christ greater riches than the treasures of Egypt; for he was looking to the reward" (v. 26). The word translated "considering" means "calculating." In other words, Moses did the math and determined that the short-term pleasures of this life were negligible compared to the eternal rewards of the next life that result from obeying God.

Make no mistake about it, both Moses's and Abraham's motivation for obedience was a future reward. And that is the essence of faith—believing that in the future God will reward us if we build our lives around serving Him and His Kingdom. As the writer of Hebrews declares:

> And without faith it is impossible to please Him, for he who comes to God must believe that He is and that He is a *rewarder* of those who seek Him. (Heb. 11:6)

Some may question their motives, but these two men understood what my friend Erwin Lutzer has said: "Rewards are always dependent on faithfulness."[3] In other words, Abraham's and Moses's faithfulness in looking for the city of God and the heavenly reward revealed that their motives were holy, because ultimately their motives were to see Christ.

Paul's third analogy of the judgment is that of a track meet. Addressing the Corinthians once again, Paul wrote:

> Do you not know that those who run in a race all run, but only one receives the prize? Run in such a way that you may win. Everyone who competes in the games exercises self-control in all things. They then do it to receive a perishable wreath, but we an imperishable. Therefore I run in such a way, as not without aim; I box in such a way, as not beating the air; but I discipline my body and make it my slave, so that, after I have preached to others, I myself will not be disqualified. (1 Cor. 9:24–27)

The Isthmian Games were held every two years in Corinth and included footraces and boxing matches. The winner of these contests was awarded a crown. But unlike the gold medals handed out to Olympic champions today, the winner's wreath at the Isthmia was made of parsley, wild celery, or pine boughs. It eventually wilted and dried. Paul's point was to encourage the Corinthians (and us) to run the race of life in such a way as to win an "imperishable" crown—a heavenly reward that will never decay or die.

Track meets have simple rules. First, the race begins when the official fires the starting gun. We begin our race of faith the moment we place our eternal trust in Christ, not before. Second, runners must stay on the track or be disqualified. Christians have a unique "course" God has designed for us, and that course has no shortcuts. Finally, runners must avoid distractions and keep their eyes on the finishing tape.

Australian runner John Landy was in a heated contest with Roger Bannister as to who could be the first to break the four-minute-mile barrier. Bannister did it on May 6, 1954. A few months later, Landy and Bannister met at the British and Empire Commonwealth Games. Landy set a blistering pace and was winning the race. However, as he came around the last turn, Landy looked over his left shoulder to find Bannister. But just as Landy peered over his left shoulder, Bannister passed him on his right-hand side, winning the race and beating his record-breaking time for the mile.

It's all too easy for any of us to become distracted from life's finishing line. Giving too much attention to that which has little eternal value—television, the news, Facebook, Twitter, video games—can cause us to lose sight of "the race that is set before us" (Heb. 12:1). None of these activities is wrong in and of itself, but these diversions can cause us to forfeit the prize God awards to those who finish the race well.

What Future Rewards Will Mean to Us

Many Christians will be happy just to make it to heaven—that'll be enough reward for them . . . or so they think. But our rewards—or lack of them—will profoundly impact what kind of heaven we will experience. "Everyone in heaven will be *fully* blessed," theologian Norm Geisler said, "but not everyone will be *equally* blessed. Every believer's cup will be full and running over, but not everyone's cup will be the same size."[4]

This is not only biblical; it is just. If Christ rewarded us all equally in heaven, regardless of our behavior on earth, He would be an unjust Judge. But He's not. Think of it like this: a mother of two teenage boys is in the kitchen baking cakes. She tells them that if they will clean up their rooms she will bake each of them their favorite cake. Later, when she goes upstairs, she sees that one son has hung up his clothes, picked up his underwear and placed them in his dresser, and vacuumed the carpet.

However, the other son is sitting among a pile of dirty T-shirts, smelly socks, and pizza boxes playing video games. Both enjoy having their own room and both will enjoy a wonderful home-cooked meal, but only one will enjoy his favorite dessert.

The same is true for us. Although our works play no part in obtaining salvation, they play an integral role in obtaining rewards in heaven. Jesus said, "My reward is with Me, to render to every man *according to what he has done*" (Rev. 22:12).

Similarly, Paul echoed the importance of works when he explained that at the judgment seat of Christ, every Christian will be rewarded "for his deeds in the body, *according to what he has done*" (2 Cor. 5:10).

What the Winners Win

Imagine you spent years training to run in the Boston Marathon and, after pouring every ounce of life you had into the race, you crossed the finish line first. How would you feel if the race officials said, "This year we decided to change the rules. Instead of awarding those who finished in first, second, and third place, we are going to simply give everyone a participation trophy. We thought that would be more fair." Fair? It is unfair not to recognize and reward those who make the necessary sacrifices to win a contest.

The same truth applies to rewards in heaven. Those who run the race well, who administer their trust faithfully, and who build their lives with gold, silver, and precious stones—all with the right motives—will receive what the Bible calls "crowns." Scripture speaks of at least five different crowns we might receive at the judgment seat of Christ.

First, the "imperishable" crown (1 Cor. 9:25) is for those who live a disciplined, Spirit-controlled life. Like the fruit of the Spirit that never grows stale, moldy, or rotten, so is the reward for all those who live fruitful and productive lives.

Second, the "crown of exultation" (1 Thess. 2:19–20) is reserved for those who engage in evangelism and discipleship. In the context of 1 Thessalonians, the reward is the joy of knowing that many of the residents of heaven will be there because you and I played a role in their salvation.

As the late William Barclay wrote, "Our greatest glory lies in those whom he has set or helped on the path to Christ."[5]

Third, the "crown of righteousness" (2 Tim. 4:8) is bestowed on those who live obediently in anticipation of the Lord's return. It's not exactly clear what the reward is, but it evidently is a reward based on living obediently while on earth.

Fourth, the "crown of life" (James 1:12; Rev. 2:10) is awarded to those who love the Lord enough to faithfully endure the trials of this life without losing faith or denying Christ—especially enduring to the point of death.

Finally, the "crown of glory" (1 Pet. 5:4) is reserved for those who faithfully and sacrificially serve Christ's church, especially pastors who faithfully teach God's Word and shepherd the congregation God has called them to oversee.

What the "Crowns" Really Mean

"Jesus did not call us to wear a crown in this life," Billy Graham wrote. "He called us to bear a cross and live for Him in the face of ridicule. When we get to Heaven, though, we will put our crosses down and put on the crowns He gives."[6] Nevertheless, some people argue that whatever rewards believers receive in heaven will ultimately be meaningless because we will surrender those rewards to God, as evidenced by the twenty-four elders in Revelation 4:10 (who represent the church in heaven), who "cast their crowns before the throne" in worship to God.

But such a questionable interpretation negates the teaching of the rest of the New Testament that our obedience to God in this life has real consequences in the next life. Instead,

John's vision of this future scene in heaven is a reminder that everything we receive—including our salvation and even our rewards—is ultimately attributable to God's grace, for which we will eternally praise our Creator.

However, that realization does not mean that everyone's experience in heaven will be the same. So what will these "crowns" actually mean to us in heaven? Some believe these rewards are literal crowns we will wear throughout eternity. Others, like myself, believe that although they may be physical crowns (that very well may be cast before the throne of God), they also represent tangible and eternal benefits given to those who have been rewarded by Christ at His judgment seat. These benefits include:

- *Special privileges.* Have you ever been to the "Happiest Place on Earth"? I'm referring of course to Disneyland or Disney World. Amy and I traveled there many times when our girls were young. For a single price you can enter the Magic Kingdom and enjoy the attractions. But for those willing to pay a little more, Disney provides additional benefits: entrance to all the parks, nicer accommodations, and a chance to have breakfast with Mickey and Minnie—or the princesses. In the same way, the Bible teaches that some Christians will enjoy special benefits in heaven: a special welcome by God like a gold medal–winning athlete receiving a ticker-tape parade (2 Pet. 1:11), special access to the tree of life (Rev. 2:7), and even special treatment by Christ Himself (Luke 12:37).

- *Special positions.* We looked at this in some detail in chapter 5, but it bears repeating: those who are faithful on earth will be rewarded with additional responsibilities in heaven. In the parable of the talents, Jesus commended those who were "faithful with a few things" and rewarded them with the promise to put them "in charge of many things; enter into the joy of your master" (Matt. 25:21).

- *Special praise.* Most of us can recall the joy of hearing a parent say to us, "I'm proud of you." And no one forgets when a boss says, "You're doing a great job. You're an asset to our company." I remember being at the victory party when it was announced that Donald Trump had won the presidency. After his brief speech to his supporters, he walked down to shake hands. When he saw me, he strolled over and said, "Robert, thank you for all you did to make tonight possible. Without you this would not have happened." I will never forget those words! But no praise we receive in this life—even from the most powerful people in the world—will compare to the praise some will receive from Christ in the next life: "Well done, good and faithful servant!" (Matt. 25:21 NIV). That is a reward for which every true believer is striving. Yet it's reserved only for those who are obedient to Christ in this life.

What the Losers Lose at the Judgment Seat of Christ

Some believers will stand before the Lord full of confidence, while others will stand before the Lord full of shame. This is why John warned:

Little children, abide in Him, so that when He appears, we may have confidence and not shrink away from Him in shame at His coming. (1 John 2:28)

Those who will blush, hang their heads, and kick the dirt while standing before the judgment seat of Christ will lose what could have been received, which is why John also warned:

Watch yourselves, that you do not lose what we have accomplished, but that you may receive a full reward. (2 John 8)

Not everyone will experience the same degree of joy and satisfaction in heaven. Those who have built their lives around themselves instead of Christ will experience real, measurable loss. "If any man's work is burned up, *he will suffer loss*," Paul wrote (1 Cor. 3:15). And though his salvation is secure—"he himself will be saved, yet so as through fire"—the loss of heavenly rewards will result in genuine regret.

"But pastor, how can anyone be happy in heaven if they regret lost rewards?" Rejoicing and regret are not mutually exclusive. For example, suppose my insurance agent told me that my house was underinsured by $100,000 and that I should adjust my policy immediately. But instead, I put it off. One night, I awaken to discover my house is engulfed in flames. Groping through the smoke, I throw a chair through a window, and my wife and I barely escape death.

As we stand on the front lawn watching our house being destroyed, what are our emotions? Certainly I'm overjoyed that we escaped the flames and our lives were spared. But that joy is tempered by regret that I didn't make the right financial decision and invest in more insurance.

Many Christians will experience that same mixture of joy and regret at the judgment seat of Christ. While they will be eternally grateful for their escape from the lake of fire, there will also be regret as they watch their lives "go up in smoke" when God judges their works as worthless. And, yes, there will be a sense of loss as they realize the rewards they have forfeited because they invested their lives in the temporal rather than in the eternal.

I can hear some of you saying, "But I thought there would be no sadness in heaven. Doesn't God promise to 'wipe away every tear from our eyes?'" Well, yes and no. It is true that God will "wipe away every tear from their eyes" and that there is no "crying" in the eternal state of the new earth (Rev. 21:4). However, this promise comes *after* the judgment seat of Christ. It makes perfect sense that when we each stand before the Lord's *bema* seat there will be some aspects of our lives burned up in the fire of His holiness. And that loss will cause temporary tears. However, once the Lord has finished His evaluation, whatever tears may have been shed will be gone forever—but the consequences of losing our rewards will endure for eternity.

My former seminary professor and president of Dallas Theological Seminary, the late John Walvoord, encourages us to think about the judgment seat of Christ like a commencement ceremony:

> Some students graduate with honors or high honors, and others receive rewards for distinctive achievements. However, the overwhelming emotion of all the graduates is the joy of receiving the diploma after years of sacrifice and study; every graduate receives a diploma and thus experiences joy and fulfillment. On the one hand, the seriousness of the judgment seat of Christ should be considered; on the other hand, all believers can rejoice in the marvelous grace of God that will enable them all to be in heaven even though they are imperfect in this life.[7]

In heaven, there will be real regret for many. But there will be real rejoicing for all. To *underdo* the sadness of losing rewards is to make faithfulness to God in this life irrelevant. However, to *overdo* the sadness of losing rewards is to turn heaven into hell. The goal is to run the race God has set before us, to handle our trust with care, and to build our lives with actions and motives that have eternal value.

In his wonderful book *Your Eternal Reward*, Erwin Lutzer recounts the story of an Indian beggar who crossed paths with a rich rajah riding in a beautiful chariot. The beggar stood by the side of the road, holding out a bowl of rice, hoping for a handout. To his surprise, the rajah stopped and demanded, "Give me some of your rice!" The beggar was angry at the thought that a wealthy man would demand rice from a poor man. But the beggar gave the rajah one grain of rice. "I want more," the rajah demanded. So the beggar gave him another grain. "More rice." By now, the beggar was seething with resentment, but he handed the rajah one more grain of rice.

After the rajah departed, the beggar looked into his bowl of rice. And what he saw astonished him. There, in his bowl, was a grain of gold the size of a grain of rice. He looked more carefully and found two more grains of gold. For every grain of rice he had given, he had received a grain of gold in return.

Lutzer then draws this application: "If we clutch our bowl of rice, we shall lose our reward. If we are faithful and give God each grain, He gives us gold in return. And the gold God gives will survive the fire."[8]

Rice for gold is a pretty savvy trade—but not nearly as lucrative as exchanging temporary pleasures in this life for eternal rewards in that "place called heaven."

9

Who Will Be in Heaven?

I am the way, and the truth, and the life; no one comes to the Father but through Me.

John 14:6

Maps can be useful in navigating through unfamiliar territory. Unfortunately, I had to learn the value of maps the hard way, some years ago. A pastor friend had invited me to Canada to speak at his church's annual Valentine's banquet. I departed Dallas early one morning and, after a plane change in Minneapolis, landed in Winnipeg, Manitoba, around four o'clock that afternoon with plenty of time to spare.

After retrieving my luggage, I stood out front waiting for my host to arrive . . . and waiting . . . and waiting. After about thirty minutes, I strolled back inside the terminal to call the pastor's home. When I looked down at the invitation letter he had mailed a few weeks earlier to retrieve his phone number, I noticed that the city and province on his letterhead did not correspond with my present location. Because I had preached for the pastor at his church in Winnipeg ten years earlier, I had assumed he was still at the same church. Big mistake!

I took the letter with me to the airline counter and explained that I had apparently traveled to the wrong city. According to the pastor's letter, I needed to be in Vancouver, British Columbia. Not knowing anything about Canada, I innocently asked, "Is there a bus I can catch to Vancouver? I need to be there in thirty minutes." All the agents behind the counter started laughing and saying in unison, "You've got to be kidding! Vancouver is 1,500 miles west of here!"

Fortunately, a plane was getting ready to depart for Vancouver in the next few minutes. Even though it was a three-hour flight, the two-hour time change between Vancouver and Winnipeg would work in my favor and I could arrive at the church just in time to speak. I ran to the departure gate as fast as possible, and as I was about to walk down the jetway, the gate agent handed me a map of Canada (apparently the story of my mistake had already traveled from the ticket counter to the departure gate). "Here, read this; it might help you the next time you travel to Canada!" she said, and chuckled.

Accidentally traveling to a wrong location can be embarrassing. But there is one time in your life you don't want to end up at the wrong destination—and that's the day of your death. Many will be surprised at the people who will be in heaven. People we may think should be in heaven won't be there, while many people we don't think should be in heaven will be. The worst surprise of all will be for those people who assumed they would be welcomed into God's presence but will instead be turned away from heaven's gate.

The Bible clearly says that only those who have trusted in Christ for the forgiveness of their sins will reside in the new heaven and the new earth. When people argue against the exclusivity of Christ for salvation by saying, "No one but God can decide who will be in heaven," they miss a crucial truth: God has *already* decided the standard by which people will be admitted into His presence. When we declare that faith in Christ offers the only path to heaven, we are not creating our own criterion but simply repeating the requirement God established.

When I suggest that those who are in heaven will surprise us, I'm not at all implying that we will be shocked to see Hindus, Buddhists, and Muslims standing alongside Christians. As I explain in my book *Not All Roads Lead to Heaven*, the popular belief that all religions in the world lead to God negates the most basic teaching of Jesus, who declared, "I am the way, and the truth, and the life; no one comes to the Father but through Me" (John 14:6). The God who never changes is not going to suddenly surprise us by saying at the last minute, "I've changed My mind about this 'faith in Jesus' requirement. Everyone's welcome—come on in!"

What I am saying is that since only God is able to "judge the thoughts and intentions of the heart" (Heb. 4:12), He alone knows who has sincerely placed his or her faith in Christ for the forgiveness of sins. You may be truly surprised by others who are—or are not—in heaven. But, hopefully, you won't be surprised about your *own* eternal fate. If you wait until you have passed from this life into the next life to see whether you are welcomed into God's presence, you will have waited too long.

Unfortunately, many people will be shocked on the judgment day to discover that they will be turned away from heaven's entrance. Jesus described that reality with what I believe are some of the most disturbing words in the entire Bible:

> Not everyone who says to Me, "Lord, Lord," will enter the kingdom of heaven, but he who does the will of My Father who is in heaven will enter. Many will say to Me on that day, "Lord, Lord, did we not prophesy in Your name, and in Your name cast our demons, and in Your name perform many miracles?" And then I will declare to them, "I never knew you; depart from Me, you who practice lawlessness." (Matt. 7:21–23)

Notice it is not just a few people who will be disappointed to discover that they were wrong about their relationship to God. Jesus said "many" who thought they would be welcomed into heaven will instead be dispatched into hell. Why? Simple: they were on the wrong road that led to the wrong destination. Jesus said earlier in Matthew 7 that there were two very different roads or "ways" that led to two very different destinations:

> Enter through the narrow gate; for the gate is wide and the way is broad that leads to destruction, and there are many who enter through it. For the gate is small and the way is narrow that leads to life, and there are few who find it. (vv. 13–14)

How can you make sure you don't make the same tragic mistake? Suppose you live in Oklahoma and want to travel north to Winnipeg, Manitoba, in Canada (on purpose!). You pull your car onto the highway and sincerely believe you are on the right road heading to your intended destination. But several hours into your trip you notice highway signs reading, "Dallas, 100 Miles; Houston, 300 miles." Later on you see a billboard: "Enjoy a night's rest at the Holiday Inn, Laredo, Texas."

Hopefully, those signs would be enough to convince you that you are on the wrong road, heading to the wrong destination. In spite of your sincere belief that you are traveling north, you are, in reality, going south.

The Signposts Leading to Heaven

No one accidentally ends up in heaven or hell without warning. Instead, there are definite "signposts" along the way, alerting us as to whether or not we are on the right path leading to the right destination. The journey to heaven (or hell) begins in this life. If we are truly on the road that leads to heaven, there are four signposts we must acknowledge along the way.

Signpost #1: We Have a Sin Problem

Many people refuse to go beyond this point. They would rather turn around and head another direction than face the unsettling truth of Romans 3:10–12:

> There is none righteous, not even one;
> There is none who understands,

> There is none who seeks for God;
> All have turned aside, together they have become
>   useless;
> There is none who does good,
> There is not even one.

To be "righteous" means to be in a right standing with God. And how many people are naturally in a right relationship with God? Zilch, zero, nada—or as Paul said, "None . . . not even one." We are all sinners. Admittedly, we can always point to those who are worse than we are, such as murderers and child pornographers. We may not be as bad as we *can* be, but we are just as *bad off* as we can be. All of us have sinned, creating an eternal gulf between God and ourselves.

The sin virus we inherited from Adam infects every action, every motive, and every thought. In our honest moments we know that's true. Have you ever been minding your own business—maybe even sitting in church—when some horrible thought comes into your mind? *Where did* that *come from?* you wonder. It's a symptom of the sickness we have all contracted.

Yet even though we experience the symptoms of sin every day, some people still want to claim they are innocent—that the label "sinner" doesn't apply to them. These people are like the little boy who protests to his mother that he has been nowhere near the cookie jar—with crumbs dangling from his chin.

Similarly, we can claim our innocence as vociferously as we want. The problem is that the "cookie crumbs" of sin are all over us, pointing to our guilt. As the apostle John declared:

> If we say that we have no sin, we are deceiving ourselves and
> the truth is not in us [because] if we say that we have not
> sinned, we make [God] a liar. (1 John 1:8, 10)

Whether we acknowledge it or not, the fact remains: we are
all sinners. And the result of sin is death. "The wages of sin is
death," Paul wrote in Romans 6:23. As we saw in chapter 7,
the Greek word translated "death" is *thanatos*, which means
"separation." Just as physical death is the separation of our
body from our spirit, spiritual death is the separation of our
spirit from God. Physical death is temporary, but spiritual
death is eternal. Death is God's righteous judgment on sin.
And this leads us to the second signpost.

Signpost #2: God Is Sinless

Since God is the Creator of heaven, He gets to create the
rules—not unlike what I used to tell my teenaged girls: "My
house, my rules." And the standing rule of heaven is holiness. God's standard demands absolute perfection. No less
than six times does God command us, "Be holy because I
am holy" (1 Pet. 1:16 NLT).[1]

But we're not holy. And this compounds the problem of
sin because it separates us from God. So, how can a sin-
infected person ever relate to a sinless God? "Well, God can
just overlook our imperfection, can't He?" many ask. "After
all, shouldn't God be as tolerant of our sin as we are of other
people's sins?" Unfortunately (or fortunately), God is not
like we are. The word *holy* literally means "separate." God
is "separate" or "different" from humanity. The prophet
Habakkuk wrote:

Your eyes are too pure to approve evil,
And You can not look on wickedness with favor.
(Hab. 1:13)

When you couple the reality of this second signpost about God's holiness with the truth of the first signpost about our sinfulness—it's enough to make us very discouraged, very quickly. For example, imagine on your trip from Oklahoma to Winnipeg you see a sign that says, "Winnipeg, 1,300 miles." It's a long trip, but with perseverance you can make it—until you notice your gas gauge indicates only a quarter of a tank left. No problem. You pull into a gas station . . . only to discover you have no cash or credit cards with you. There is a serious deficit between what you have and what you need to get to Winnipeg. At this point you seriously consider doing a U-turn because there is no answer to your dilemma.

The Bible says that to make it to heaven our spiritual "tank" needs to be filled with perfection. The only problem is that none of us has enough goodness to make it all the way to heaven. We may have more than others, but even a tank that is seven-eighths full won't get us there. God demands that our spiritual gas tanks be full and running over if we are going to make it into His presence. So what's the solution? Look at the third signpost.

Signpost #3: Jesus Is the Only Solution to Our Sin Problem

Think back to your imaginary trip to Winnipeg. What if, somewhere in the middle of Kansas, you run out of gas? However, out of nowhere a huge gasoline tanker appears and stops on the road beside you. The driver asks, "What's the problem? Flat tire? Busted radiator?" No, you explain, you just ran out of gas—literally. He grins, points to his rig, and says, "Boy, is this your lucky day! I have more gas in this tanker than you could ever need in your little old car. May I fill your tank for you?"

When Jesus Christ died on the cross for our sins, two amazing transactions took place. First, Jesus—the perfect Son of God who had never sinned—voluntarily accepted the punishment from God we deserve for our sins. Because God is holy, He cannot simply overlook or decide not to punish our sins. Nahum 1:3 declares, "The LORD will by no means leave the guilty unpunished." Someone *has* to pay for our sin—and Jesus volunteered to do just that.

But the second transaction on the cross was even more amazing. God credited us with the righteousness—or perfection—of Jesus. Even though we don't have enough goodness to make it to heaven on our own, Jesus has more than enough and is willing to give us all we need to make up for our deficit. The apostle Paul described these two transactions—Christ getting credited for our sin and us getting credited for Christ's righteousness:

> He [God] made Him [Christ] who knew no sin to be sin on our behalf, so that we might become the righteousness of God in Him. (2 Cor. 5:21)

Jesus is the only Person qualified to bear the punishment for our sins and offer us complete perfection because He's uniquely different from any other person who has ever walked on this planet. He alone is the Son of God. The signpost declaring Jesus to be our sin-substitute is the one that causes many people to stop, stumble, and begin searching for an alternate road to heaven.

In my years of ministry, I have met many sincere, well-meaning, and faithful followers of other religions, including Buddhists, Hindus, Muslims, Jehovah's Witnesses, and Mormons. All of them believed Jesus was a good man, a holy man, a wise man pointing the way to either enlightenment or heaven. But none of them believed His claims to divinity and exclusivity as the *only* means of salvation and way to heaven.[2] C. S. Lewis called such a denial foolish:

> I am trying here to prevent anyone saying the really foolish thing that people often say about Him: "I'm ready to accept Jesus as a great moral teacher, but I don't accept His claim to be God." That is the one thing we must not say. A man who was merely a man and said the sort of things Jesus said would not be a great moral teacher. He would either be a lunatic—on a level with the man who says he is a poached egg—or else he would be the Devil of Hell. You must make your choice. Either this man was, and is, the Son of God: or else a madman or something worse. You can shut Him up for a fool, you can spit on Him and kill Him as a demon; or you can fall at His feet and call Him Lord and God. But let us not come with any patronizing nonsense about His being a great human teacher. He has not left that open to us. He did not intend to.[3]

We must either embrace Jesus's claim that He is God's Son or reject it. There is no intellectually honest alternative, given Jesus's claim that He is the only solution to bridge the gap between our sinfulness and God's holiness: "I am the way, and the truth, and the life; *no one comes to the Father but through Me*" (John 14:6).[4]

Because of the two transactions that took place on the cross—Christ receiving the punishment we deserve and our receiving the righteousness we don't deserve—God offers us entrance into heaven. Paul explained it this way:

> Therefore, having been justified by faith, we have peace with God through our Lord Jesus Christ. (Rom. 5:1)

"*Justification*," as my friend Chuck Swindoll defines it, "is God's act of mercy in which He declares believing sinners righteous while they are still in their sinning state."[5] Justification doesn't *make* us righteous, as if we would never sin again. Rather, justification *declares* us righteous, like a judge issuing a pardon to a guilty criminal. Because Jesus took our sins upon Himself and paid for them upon the cross, God forgives us and proclaims us pardoned.

However, God's forgiveness is not a blanket pardon from the penalty of sin for everybody. Instead, justification—God's declaration of "not guilty"—requires faith, just as Paul said: "having been justified by faith." This leads to the final signpost on the road to heaven.

Signpost #4: We Must Choose to Accept Christ's Offer of Forgiveness

If you have made it this far on the narrow road that leads to heaven, you are closer than the vast majority of people who have ever lived. When most people encounter messages declaring them to be guilty before God and deserving of His punishment, they make a U-turn and go the opposite direction. Others who are willing to admit their mistakes still can't come to grips with the idea that Jesus Christ is the only solution to our need for God's forgiveness and start looking for a different path.

However, amazingly, there are some who agree that they are sinners deserving punishment, that God is holy and demanding of complete perfection, and that Jesus is the only solution to their need for God's forgiveness. Yet their response is just to stop where they are and not travel the few steps further to embrace the truth that we must choose to accept Christ's offer of forgiveness.

Think back for a moment to the driver of the gas truck who offers to fill your empty tank so you can make it to your destination: you have a need (gas) and he has the provision for your need (lots of gas). Intellectually agreeing with both of those realities doesn't put one drop of gasoline into your empty tank. You must unscrew the cap on your empty gas tank and receive the gift of the fuel you desperately need.

Similarly, there has to be a point in time when by faith we acknowledge our need for God's forgiveness and accept His offer to allow Christ to pay for our sins and fill us with His perfection. God doesn't force anyone to receive His offer of forgiveness. Only those who choose to receive His gift will be granted entry into heaven.

> But as many as received Him, to them he gave the right to become children of God, even to those who believe in His name. (John 1:12)

This might be a good time to pause and ask where *you* are on the road to heaven. Perhaps you are ready and willing to open your heart to receive God's offer of forgiveness into your life so that you can be sure that one day God will welcome you into His presence. If so, I invite you to take a moment and pray this prayer to God. It's not a magic formula but rather a way to open your heart and receive God's offer of forgiveness.

> *Dear God,*
>
> *Thank You for loving me. I realize that I have failed You in many ways, and I'm truly sorry for the sin in my life. But I believe that You loved me so much that You sent Your Son Jesus to die on the cross for me. I believe that Jesus took the punishment from You that I deserve for my sins. So right now I'm trusting in what Jesus did for me—not my own good works—to save me from my sins. Thank You for forgiving me and helping me to spend the rest of my life serving You. In Jesus's name I pray. Amen.*

If that prayer represents the desire of your heart, you can be assured that you are on the road that leads to heaven. As the apostle John wrote, "These things I have written to you who believe in the name of the Son of God, so that you may know that you have eternal life" (1 John 5:13).

The Inhabitants of Heaven

Jesus was clear that there are only two possible eternal destinations that await us when we die: heaven or hell. He said, "These [the unrighteous] will go away into eternal punishment, but the righteous into eternal life" (Matt. 25:46).

Those who receive God's pardon for their sin by trusting in Jesus Christ are assured of "eternal life" because they are "righteous"—in a right standing with God. Everyone else is guaranteed "eternal punishment" because of his or her refusal to receive God's gracious gift.

What about those who've never had an opportunity to receive Christ's offer of forgiveness? Are they condemned to hell for rejecting an offer they've never heard or were incapable of embracing? Though I deal with this subject extensively in my book *Not All Roads Lead to Heaven*, it might be helpful to briefly discuss the answers to these questions by looking at three groups of people that seem incapable of trusting in Christ for salvation.

The "Heathen" Who Have Never Heard

Christians who hold to the exclusivity of Christ for salvation are often asked about the "heathen" in remote places who haven't heard about Jesus. "How can God send them to hell for rejecting a gospel they've never heard?" they protest. But you don't have to travel to Africa to find people who have never heard about Jesus. Many within our own borders have never heard about Christ, especially as our country becomes increasingly secular. But the question remains: If God is just, how can He condemn people to hell who have not had the opportunity to trust in Christ for salvation?

Paul answers this question in the opening chapters of his letter to the Romans. The apostle affirms that everyone is guilty before God: "For all have sinned and fall short of the glory of God" (Rom. 3:23). In Romans 1–3 Paul declares that those who "fall short" include faithful Jews who observe God's law, moralists who follow their own law, and Gentiles who have never heard about God's law.

In Paul's day, Gentiles were the equivalent of today's "heathen." Gentiles were non-Jews who did not have the benefit of reading the Old Testament or hearing the preaching of the prophets, since they had no relationship with Judaism.

So how could God justly condemn them if they had no opportunity to even know about the one, true God? The answer is that God has provided everyone on the planet enough information to know about God by simply looking at creation:

> For since the creation of the world His invisible attributes, His eternal power and divine nature, have been clearly seen, being understood through what has been made, so that they are without excuse. (Rom. 1:20)

Theologians use the term "natural revelation" to describe information about God that is available to everyone, regardless of whether they have ever read a Bible or heard a sermon. For example, while campaigning in Egypt, the great military leader Napoleon Bonaparte walked the decks of one of his ships anchored in the Mediterranean. One evening he overheard some of his officers mocking the idea of God's existence. The general paused and interrupted. Making a sweeping motion toward the stars, Bonaparte said, "Gentlemen, you must first get rid of these!"

Everyone can look at the world around them and know there is Someone greater than themselves who must have created the universe in which we live. As David exclaimed:

The heavens are telling of the glory of God;
And their expanse is declaring the work of His
hands.
Day to day pours forth speech,
And night to night reveals knowledge. (Ps. 19:1–2)

Is a belief in the existence of God enough to assure someone entry into this place called heaven? Absolutely not. As we've seen repeatedly in this book, the New Testament declares that *no one* can be saved apart from exercising faith in Jesus Christ. So you might wonder, "What use is 'natural revelation' if it doesn't give people the specific information about Jesus Christ they need to trust Him for the forgiveness of sins?" The late theologian Charles Ryrie explained that natural revelation is not sufficient to save a person, but it is sufficient—if rejected—to condemn a person.[6]

If the unbeliever who has never heard of Jesus rejects the "natural revelation" that God has provided about Himself through creation, Paul says that unbeliever is "without excuse" (Rom. 1:20). That unbeliever is not only condemned by his or her own sin but also by his or her refusal to accept the information about the one true God that nature reveals.

However, if that unbeliever embraces the truth about God that creation reveals, God will make sure he or she receives the information about Jesus Christ necessary for salvation. Remember, God wants to save as many people as possible, not as few people as possible. The apostle Paul affirms that God "desires all men to be saved and to come to the knowledge of the truth" (1 Tim. 2:4).

Obviously, not all people *will* be saved. The majority of humanity will reject God's offer of forgiveness. But the deepest longing of our heavenly Father is that everyone would respond to His gracious invitation of salvation. However, to be saved one must "come to the knowledge of the truth." And Paul defines that truth in the next two verses of 1 Timothy 2: "For there is one God, and one mediator also between God and men, the man Christ Jesus, who gave Himself as a ransom for all, the testimony given at the proper time" (vv. 5–6).

Doesn't it make sense that if God desires everyone to be saved and that the only way to be saved is by embracing the truth that Jesus Christ died for our sins, then God will ensure that anyone who wants to know God will receive that information about Christ?

A person's response to the natural revelation about God available through creation is a reliable gauge of whether that person truly wants to know God. If the heathen in Africa—or the heathen living next door to you—rejects that knowledge of the true God, then why would he or she respond positively to any more information about Jesus Christ and God's offer of salvation? However, if that person embraces the little information about God he or she receives through creation, we can rest assured that God will provide "the knowledge of the truth" needed for salvation.

The New Testament is filled with illustrations of those who received additional revelation—the special revelation about Jesus Christ necessary for salvation—based on their faith to whatever revelation they had already received. For example, the Roman centurion Cornelius was "a devout man and one who feared God" (Acts 10:2). Cornelius knew nothing about Jesus, but he sincerely wanted to know God. So what did God do? He miraculously orchestrated for the apostle Peter to come to Cornelius's home to share the gospel of Christ. As a result, Cornelius and all of his family were saved and baptized (vv. 44–48).

The same thing happened to an Ethiopian government official who had traveled to Jerusalem to worship the God of Israel. While on his way back to his homeland, the Ethiopian had an encounter with Philip, who had been dispatched by an angel. The Ethiopian was reading from the scroll of Isaiah about the coming Messiah but didn't comprehend what he was reading. So, "Philip opened his mouth, and beginning from this Scripture he preached Jesus to him" (8:35). And the Ethiopian responded, "I believe that Jesus Christ is the Son of God" (v. 37) and was baptized.

I can't tell you the number of times I have received an email or letter from someone saying, "I was flipping through the channels on television and just *happened* across your program, heard about Jesus, and trusted in Him for my salvation." The longer I live the less I believe in mere coincidences. When God sees a man, woman, boy, or girl who truly wants to know Him, He will make sure that person receives the information about Jesus necessary for salvation.

Whenever you are asked about those who have never heard about Jesus Christ, remember this simple truth: no one will ever be condemned to hell for rejecting a gospel they never heard. Instead, those in hell will be there for rejecting the information God has already provided about Himself.

Old Testament Saints Who Lived before Christ

How can we be certain that Adam, Eve, Noah, Sarah, Abraham, Moses, David, Solomon, Rahab, or any of the other Old Testament people we call "saints" are really in heaven? After all, these people lived before Christ's sacrifice on the cross, and God's Word is clear: "There is salvation in no one else; for there is no other name under heaven that has been given among men by which we must be saved" (Acts 4:12). So how can Christ in whom they had never trusted save those who lived before His time?

There is not enough space here to look at each person individually, so let's look at one representative for all those who lived in Old Testament times: Abraham. The average Jew thought of Abraham in the same way the average American thinks of George Washington: he was the "father of the nation"—figuratively and literally! In Genesis 12, God promised to make Abraham the father of the great nation of Israel. Abraham believed God's promise, uprooted his family, and headed toward the land of promise.

Abraham's life was marked by obedience to God: leaving the security of his homeland to head to the Promised Land, allowing his nephew, Lot, to get the best of him in a real estate transaction, and offering to sacrifice his beloved son Isaac to God. If anyone was a candidate for salvation by good works, it was Abraham.

Yet the apostle Paul declared it was Abraham's faith—not his works—that granted him right standing with God:

> If Abraham was justified by works, he has something to boast about, but not before God. For what does the Scripture say? "Abraham believed God, and it was credited to him as righteousness." (Rom. 4:2–3)

Paul's quotation comes from an incident in Abraham's life recorded in Genesis 15, which is key to understanding the apostle's explanation of the source of Abraham's salvation. Abraham had just rescued his nephew Lot from powerful kings in the East. Believing they would retaliate, Abraham feared his family name might come to an end. But then the Lord spoke to Abraham:

> Do not fear, Abram,
> I am a shield to you;
> Your reward shall be very great. (Gen. 15:1)

It looked to Abraham that the promise of Genesis 12—to become the father of a great nation—was about to evaporate. So Abraham wanted to know how the Lord planned to keep His promise: "O Lord GOD, what will You give me, since I am childless?" (v. 2).

But the Lord wasn't about to renege on the unconditional promise He had made with Abraham. God took him outside and told him to look up and "count the stars" (v. 5). Then God repeated His promise: "So shall your descendants be" (v. 5).

What was Abraham's response? The Bible records that Abraham "believed in the LORD; and He *reckoned* it to him as righteousness" (v. 6). This is the verse Paul quoted two thousand years later in Romans 4:3 to prove that Abraham's salvation was through faith and not through works.

The Hebrew word translated "reckoned" (*chashab*) is an accounting term that means "credited." Think of the faith transaction this way: imagine you go into a store to purchase a new sofa for your living room. The sofa costs $1,000 and you pay with your credit card. Amazingly, by simply allowing the salesperson to swipe that piece of plastic you are allowed to walk out of the store with a valuable piece of furniture. Why would the salesperson allow you to immediately begin experiencing the joy of a new sofa in exchange for a worthless piece of plastic? Although the card itself has no intrinsic value, it represents a promissory note—a promise to pay. Later, when the bill arrives in the mail, it must be paid.

In the same way, when Abraham and others in the Old Testament exercised faith in God, their faith represented a future "promise to pay." Abraham and the other Old Testament believers were immediately "credited" with salvation. And when the bill came due, the only Person capable of satisfying their sin debt paid it. When Jesus cried out on the cross "It is finished" (John 19:30), the word He used was *tetelestai*, a Greek accounting term meaning "paid in full."

Regardless of when a person lives in history, there is only one way anyone can be saved from eternal death—through the payment Jesus Christ made on the cross to satisfy our sin debt. Those who lived before Christ were saved "on credit"—a right standing with God was immediately "reckoned" to their account until Christ could pay their debt on the cross.

Children and the Childlike Who Cannot Believe

As a pastor, one of my most painful duties is ministering to a family that has lost a child, especially if that child was a newborn or infant. One question consumes the thoughts of every family member: "Is my little one in heaven?" Parents and grandparents of deceased teenaged or adult children who are mentally incapacitated to the point of being "childlike" ask this same question: "Are they in heaven?"

211

I wish I could point to one passage of Scripture proclaiming a resounding yes, but I can't. However, we do have the confident claim by one of God's choicest servants, some interesting observations from Jesus's teaching, and the rationale of theology to assure us that children and the childlike do go to heaven when they die.

Just as Abraham serves as an illustration of the faith of all Old Testament saints, so David serves as a representative of all parents who have lost a child before he or she could express faith. David's tragic story began one evening with a rooftop walk. The mighty king of Israel spotted a beautiful woman named Bathsheba bathing in the moonlight. David sent for her and the rest, as they say, is history.

When Bathsheba discovered she was pregnant, David attempted to cover up the fact that he was the father. He recalled Bathsheba's husband, Uriah, from the front lines and tried to convince him to spend the night in his own bed with his wife. Surely, everyone would then surmise that Uriah was the father of his wife's baby. When Uriah refused to indulge in this pleasure out of deference to his fellow soldiers who were still in the field fighting for their country, David arranged to have Uriah murdered, making his death appear to be a battlefield casualty.

Later, the prophet Nathan confronted David over his twin sins of adultery and murder. Instead of continuing the cover-up of his sins, David confessed his transgressions and received God's forgiveness. Nevertheless, God's forgiveness did not erase the temporary—and very painful—consequences of David's actions: a divided kingdom, a disloyal son, and the death of Bathsheba's child.

Immediately after his birth, David and Bathsheba's child became ill and lingered on the edge of death for seven days. During that week, David neither ate nor slept but fasted and prayed for his son's recovery. After the child died, David quickly recovered from his grief and began to eat.

His servants were perplexed. Tradition held that fasting and weeping took place *after* death, not before. Now that the child had died, how could the king go on as if nothing had happened? David's answer was simple and direct—and full of faith. Knowing God would not bring his son back to life, David said: "I will go to him, but he will not return to me" (2 Sam. 12:23).

As long as the child lived, David believed his petitions might move the Lord to heal his son. But once the child died, David knew no amount of fasting and praying would bring his son back. The king could pick himself up and look forward because he believed his son was with God in Paradise. If David believed his son had gone to hell or simply to the grave, he could not have honestly declared that he would see his son again. Instead, the king would have had every reason to continue mourning even more intensely. David's dramatic change in demeanor after his son's death was rooted in the belief that his child had gone to heaven.

Admittedly, David's claim doesn't prove definitively that children and the childlike go to heaven when they die. But if we couple David's claim with some of Jesus's teachings about children, I believe we can make a strong claim that children who die before they are capable of exercising faith in Christ are welcomed into heaven.

For example, in Matthew 18:1–4 Jesus uses a child to illustrate the spiritual quality of humility necessary to receive God's gift of forgiveness:

At that time the disciples came to Jesus and said, "Who then is greatest in the kingdom of heaven?" And He called a child to Himself and set him before them, and said, "Truly I say to you, unless you are converted and become like children, you will not enter the kingdom of heaven. Whoever then humbles himself as this child, he is the greatest in the kingdom of heaven."

Jesus could have selected any child to illustrate the spiritual lesson of humility, but if He had selected one destined for hell then the analogy wouldn't have made sense. The child Jesus selected represented all children—just as Abraham represented Old Testament saints and David's son represented deceased children. By His actions and words, Jesus indicated that all children (and those who are mentally childlike) are destined for heaven.

Beyond the belief of David and the teaching of Jesus, consider the testimony of Scripture. Nowhere in the Bible are children condemned to damnation. Of all the biblical descriptions of hell, infants or little children are never mentioned as residing there. Nor are infants and children described as standing before the great white throne judgment of Revelation 20, which is the precursor to eternal punishment in the lake of fire. I believe this is another piece of evidence that argues strongly for the presence of children in heaven.

Finally, we need to recognize that the Bible distinguishes between inherited sin and the sin of unbelief. As we've seen, humanity—including children—has inherited Adam's guilt and corruption. The fact that everyone—including babies and children—dies is proof that we have all contracted the sickness of sin. Nevertheless, God distinguishes between inherited sin and deliberate sin. He declared that people are responsible for their own sins, not the sins of others:

> The person who sins will die. The son will not bear the punishment for the father's iniquity, nor will the father bear the punishment for the son's iniquity; the righteousness of the righteous will be upon himself, and the wickedness of the wicked will be upon himself. (Ezek. 18:20)

We find a great illustration of the distinction between the guilt of adults and children in Deuteronomy 1. Because of their failure to believe in God's power to give them the Promised Land, God pronounced a sentence of death on the Israelites. They would wander in the wilderness until that unbelieving generation passed away. However, the Lord exempted one group of Israelites from His condemnation. The Lord said:

> Moreover, your little ones who you said would become a prey, and your sons, who this day have no knowledge of good or evil, shall enter there, and I will give it to them and they shall possess it. (Deut. 1:39)

God did not hold the children accountable for the sin of unbelief because they "had no knowledge of good or evil." In the Bible, the sin of unbelief is not simply failing to believe God; it is the deliberate choice not to believe what God has said. Unbelief is the willful rejection of God's revelation—a choice children and the childlike are incapable of making.

Again, none of these arguments is enough in and of itself to say definitively that children and the childlike automatically go to heaven. However, when we consider all of the evidence Scripture provides, I believe we can say that our loving God welcomes children into heaven. As Abraham declared, "Shall not the Judge of all the earth deal justly?" (Gen. 18:25). We can depend upon God to deal justly—and graciously—with those who are incapable of exercising faith in Christ.[7]

Who will be in heaven? It is significant that, outside of those who lived before Christ and children (and the child-like) who are incapable of trusting in Christ, there is no instance in the New Testament of anyone being welcomed into God's presence apart from a personal faith in the Lord Jesus Christ. To attempt to reduce the population of hell by ignoring that requirement and allowing other individuals or groups into heaven is something none of us has the authority to do—especially if we take seriously Jesus's claim that "no one comes to the Father but through [Him]" (John 14:6).

10

How Can I Prepare
for My Journey to Heaven?

Be careful how you walk, not as unwise men but as wise,
making the most of your time, because the days are evil.

Ephesians 5:15–16

When I began this book many months ago, I was preparing to
take an international trip to London. I told you about the list
of things I needed to do to prepare for a journey to a distant,
unfamiliar country—comparing my trip to that journey every
Christian will take one day to that "place called heaven."

My trip ended up being uneventful—except for one mistake: I forgot to pack extra socks. By the third day of the trip
I broke down and bought several pair at a nearby department
store. I knew it was time to do so when my original pair
was standing—instead of lying—at the foot of my bed! My
oversight was inconvenient (and perhaps uncomfortable for

my family members standing downwind from me the first few days), but there was no lasting damage from my lack of preparation.

However, failing to make adequate preparation for our inevitable departure from this life to the next life can have devastating and unending consequences. That is why I want to provide you with a "checklist" of six practical action steps you can take right now to prepare for your journey to heaven.

1. Make Sure You Have a Valid Passport

Making arrangements for your trip to heaven begins with making sure you have the proper "passport" that will allow you into the presence of God. I learned about the importance of passports a number of years ago. When I was a youth minister at the church I now pastor we took our student choir to the Soviet Union. It was during the Cold War and the atmosphere was so oppressive that we couldn't wait to get out of there. Our flight was scheduled to depart at midnight. I watched as our students went through passport control one by one, with obvious expressions of relief on their faces as they passed from bondage to freedom. As the leader, I waited until everyone else was on the other side to pass through myself. I reached inside my coat pocket for my passport—and it was missing.

Panicked, I frantically searched everywhere for the missing document with no success. I explained to the Soviet agent my predicament and that I had to pass through because I was the leader of the group. Trust me, he could not have cared less! No passport, no exit. My wife of exactly one year was standing on the other side crying, imagining her new husband imprisoned in a Russian gulag for the next twenty years!

After watching me sweat for a few minutes, a "friend" of mine appeared waving my passport, which he had taken as a joke. I can assure you that after forty years my wife still doesn't think it's funny. I will never forget the relief I felt as I finally settled in my seat on the plane and winged my way to freedom.

The absolute panic I felt that night more than three decades ago pales in comparison to the terror that will grip the hearts of those who will be denied entrance into heaven because they lack the proper "passport." As they stand at heaven's entrance expecting to be welcomed into God's presence, they will instead hear these words: "I never knew you; depart from Me" (Matt. 7:23).

The people who will be turned away from heaven's gate will not only be atheists and devil worshipers. They will include religious people who consider themselves Christ-followers because of the many good works they performed in the name of Jesus. In fact, they will use their righteous acts as an argument for why they should be allowed into God's presence:

> Many will say to me on that day, "Lord, Lord, did we not prophesy in Your name, and in Your name cast out demons, and in Your name perform many miracles?" (v. 22)

But God will be as unmoved by their pleas as the Soviet guard was by mine. No passport, no entry into heaven.

The only "document" that allows us entry into God's presence for eternity is one that is stamped "Forgiven," and it is given to us the moment we trust in Jesus Christ for our salvation. The theological term for forgiven is *justified*, which means, "to be declared righteous." Our justification before God is not based on our works but on His grace and is received by faith:

> Therefore, having been justified by faith, we have peace with God through our Lord Jesus Christ. (Rom. 5:1)

As we saw in chapter 9, faith in Christ is not just *one* way to heaven—it is the *only* way to heaven.

I realize that to claim Christ as the exclusive way to heaven isn't popular in a world that worships inclusiveness. Many, like billionaire Warren Buffet, believe they can earn their way—or buy their way—into heaven. In 2006, Buffet—the second richest man in the world—announced he was donating 85 percent of his $44 billion fortune to five charitable foundations. "There is more than one way to get to heaven," Buffet declared, "but this is a great way."[1] I commend Buffet on his generosity, but if he persists in believing he can donate his way to salvation, he's in for a rude awakening someday.

How sure are you that at the moment of your death God will welcome you into His presence? Years ago the now-defunct Northwest Airlines offered a promotional gimmick called "The Mystery Fare." For $59 you could purchase a round-trip ticket for a one-day excursion to any city in the continental United States. There was only one catch: you didn't find out where you were heading until you arrived at the airport on the day of the flight. The gimmick worked . . . for a while. Northwest had thousands of customers willing to invest a few bucks and a couple of days to take a chance that they'd end up somewhere exciting, like New York City, Chicago, or Las Vegas.

However, not all customers were happy once they learned of their destinations. One man, who was hoping for a trip to New Orleans, ended up with a ticket to an out-of-the-way city. He walked through the airport terminal bargaining with other "mystery fare" flyers, trying to trade his ticket for another city.

Mystery fares might be a fun chance to take for a one-day adventure, but there is one day in your life you never want to be holding a "mystery fare" ticket: the day of your death. To face eternity without knowing whether you are heading to heaven or hell is a risk no sane person would take. If you wait until the moment you die to discover whether your eternal destination is heaven, you will have waited one second too long. God doesn't want your eternal destiny to be a mystery. That is why the apostle John wrote:

> God has given us eternal life, and this life is in His Son. He who has the Son has life; he who does not have the Son of God does not have life. These things I have written to you *who believe in the name of the Son of God, so that you may know that you have eternal life.* (1 John 5:11–13)

If you do not "know that you have eternal life," why not pause right now and confess to God your need for His forgiveness and express your dependence on Christ's death on the cross for you to save you from the eternal consequences of your sins? When you do that, you can be sure that you have made the most basic preparation necessary for your journey to heaven.

But while that decision is foundational, it is not the only thing you should do to prepare for your journey.

2. Live with a "Destination Mindset"

Trying to live in two places at the same time can be difficult, but it is what every Christian has been called to do—temporarily. Since we don't know when we will suddenly be called away to that "place called heaven," we have to learn how to fulfill our responsibilities in this world while preparing for the next world. Although we are still residents of earth, our "true country" is heaven, as Paul reminded the Philippians: "We are citizens of heaven, where the Lord Jesus Christ lives. And we are eagerly waiting for him to return as our Savior" (Phil. 3:20 NLT). Yet God has charged each of us with responsibilities in this world that involve our work, our families, and especially our ministry for Him as "ambassadors for Christ" (2 Cor. 5:20).

God has called each of us to live with a "here/there" mindset. While living and working here on earth, we are busily preparing for our lives "there" in heaven. Admittedly, it's challenging to live in one location while preparing to live in another place, but it can also be motivating.

I remember when Amy and I were called to the pastorate of my first church in Eastland, Texas, more than thirty years ago. I was serving as a youth minister (at the church I now pastor) but had dreamed of the time I would shepherd my own church. I will never forget that weekend in June 1985 when Amy and I traveled to that small West Texas congregation to "preach in view of a call." After my trial sermon, they ushered us into a small room and fed us pie while the congregation deliberated, debated, and voted. I will never forget the exhilaration I felt when we learned they had voted to call me as their pastor. We could barely sleep that night in our little motel room as we contemplated the adventure before us.

However, the next morning reality set in. We had to drive back to Dallas and spend the next month wrapping up our ministry there. For that month I tried to concentrate on doing the best job I could in Dallas, but my heart was already at my new church ninety miles away. The bulk of my time during that month was devoted to my current responsibilities in Dallas, but some of my energy was devoted to preparing for my new ministry in my new location. Yet I noticed something strange. During that final month in Dallas I had more motivation to work hard than I had experienced during the last seven years—mainly because I knew my time was limited and I wanted to leave things in good shape! Focusing on "there" (my new home in Eastland) profoundly impacted my life "here" (in Dallas).

In the same way, as Christians we have God-given assignments to complete during our brief stay on earth, even though we will soon be departing for our eternal home. Yet while we temporarily reside in this world, we are to guard against becoming entangled in it. Instead, we are to live as "strangers and exiles on the earth" (Heb. 11:13), as we "set [our minds] on the things above" (Col. 3:2).

The great Puritan preacher Jonathan Edwards lived his life with an eternal rather than temporal perspective. Since childhood, Edwards was taught "to think of his own dying, or to live as though he had only an hour left before his death or 'before I should hear the last trump.'"[2] Heaven was so real to Edwards that he wrote:

To go to heaven, fully to enjoy God, is infinitely better than the most pleasant accommodations here. . . . Therefore, it becomes us to spend this life only as a journey toward heaven . . . to which we should subordinate all other concerns of life. Why should we labor for or set our hearts on anything else, but that which is our proper end and true happiness?[3]

Because Edwards chose to live with eternity in mind, when he was nineteen years old he set forth seventy resolutions that guided his life as he prepared for heaven. Here are a few of them:

- "Resolved, to endeavor to obtain for myself as much happiness, in the other world, as I possibly can."
- "Resolved, that I will live so as I shall wish I had done when I come to die."
- "Resolved, to endeavor to my utmost to act as I can think I should do if I had already seen the happiness of heaven and the torments of hell."
- "Resolved, never to do anything I should be afraid of doing if it were the last hour of my life."[4]

As we mentioned in chapter 1, the more seriously we take heaven, the more seriously we'll take earth. Life is short—you don't know when it will be your last day. To be a "heavenly minded" Christian means to live every day as if it were the last day before God calls you home—because someday it will be!

3. Refuse to Allow Death to Paralyze You with Fear

As the departure date for my trip to London approached a few months ago, I experienced a number of emotions: anticipation over visiting a city I had read about, excitement over spending quality time with my family, and urgency to complete my to-do list before I left. But one emotion I never felt was fear. Why should I be afraid of a trip I had planned for and looked forward to for months?

The same principle applies to our journey to heaven. Admittedly, some people—even Christians—are fearful of death. Winston Churchill, who faced death on many occasions during his storied career, feared death's icy grip. He quipped, "Any man who says he is not afraid of death is a liar."[5] One reason Christians are fearful of death is that they are unaware of what awaits them on the other side of it (which is one of the primary reasons I wrote this book). But there are two reasons that Christians do not need to fear death.

First, if you are a Christian you can be assured that you will not depart this earth one second before God's appointed time. That was certainly Paul's conviction. While preaching to the Jews in the synagogue in Antioch, the apostle retraced the history of God's dealing with Israel to prove that the resurrected Jesus was the Messiah. When Paul got to the history of King David, he said, "David, *after* he had served the purpose of God in his own generation, fell asleep, and was laid among his fathers and underwent decay" (Acts 13:36). David didn't die *until* he had served God's purpose during his time on earth. The same is true for us.

"But what about those who die prematurely, such as a teenager in a car accident or a young mother who leaves her small children behind?" you ask. From God's perspective no one dies "prematurely." The psalmist declared, "My times are in Your hand" (Ps. 31:15). God determines our days and numbers our years.

225

Peter said that Jesus's death occurred according to "the predetermined plan and foreknowledge of God" (Acts 2:23). Just as the day of Jesus's death was determined by God, so is yours. In Ephesians 1:11, Paul wrote that all things in our lives—including death—have been "predestined according to His purpose who works all things after the counsel of His will." No death catches God off guard. He has everything under control. Those who die in faith—whether they are nine or ninety—lived exactly the number of years God prescribed for them. As one person notes, "Every person is immortal until his work on earth is done."

But there is an even more foundational reason Christians don't need to fear death: death is a necessary transition from this world to the next world. Let's stay with our "passport" analogy a moment longer. Once the immigration official has stamped your passport, do you "fear" passing through that little gate that allows you entry into a new country? Of course not—in fact, it's quite an exciting experience, especially if you're leaving the tyranny of the Soviet Union for the freedom of America.

For a Christian, death is nothing more than a transition from an inferior country to a superior one. In fact, without experiencing death we could never travel to that "place called heaven." Paul explains why in 1 Corinthians 15:50:

> Now I say this, brethren, that flesh and blood cannot inherit the kingdom of God; nor does the perishable inherit the imperishable.

Suppose you were traveling from this world to Mars. While your body is perfectly suited for the earth's atmosphere, it is totally unsuitable for the "red planet" (or any other planet). Similarly, our present body of "flesh and blood" is specifically designed for life in this world but could never function in the next world. That is why there must be a time when we are separated from our earthly body. As I've noted before, the word *death* comes from the Greek word *thanatos*, or "separation." Death is a necessary separation from our earthly body so we can put on our new body.

Here's another way of thinking about death. Imagine you were invited to a presidential inauguration ball like Amy and I once attended. Men, on the morning of the event would you object to exchanging your pajamas for a Brioni suit? Ladies, would you resist taking off your bathrobe and putting on a Chanel dress? I don't think so! God has invited every Christian to a magnificent location for which we must be properly dressed, and He has provided the appropriate "wardrobe." Death is nothing more than exchanging inferior clothing for superior clothing.

Randy Alcorn, in his book *Heaven*, employs yet another metaphor to describe death: a surprise party.[6] Suppose a friend invites you to a party where you will know some people but not many. The food is adequate but nothing extraordinary. You enjoy meeting some new people and visiting with the few familiar people you know. Suddenly your friend announces it's time to leave. Although you're not quite ready to leave, you acquiesce because he's your ride home.

When your friend drops you off at your house, you place your key in the lock and turn the knob. Just as you open the door the lights suddenly come on. "Surprise!" Your family and your closest friends are there. They've brought gifts and have covered your table with your favorite delicacies. The first party was simply a ruse to get you out of the house so that the second party could be organized. Had you stayed at the first party, you would have missed the real party—the one at your home.

Life on earth is like the first party—pleasant enough. But at death you open the doors to your true home and discover that the real party is taking place there.

I wish I could tell you that every Christian I know who learned he or she was terminally ill faced their death with great anticipation and no fear. But that wouldn't be honest. Through the years, some believers I have talked with who were facing the end of their life expressed regret about "leaving the party too soon" even though they had great faith about their future home in heaven. They were sad over what they might be missing on earth.

However, the real party is already underway in heaven! Any sadness Christians feel over leaving this earth will be more than compensated for with the hilarity of heaven. I believe this is what Jesus had in mind when He promised, "Blessed [literally, "Happy"] are you who weep now, for you shall laugh" (Luke 6:21).

4. Make the Most of Your Time on Earth

Though Moses beat today's average life span by forty or fifty years—dying at 120—his admonition about the value and brevity of life is worth heeding:

Seventy years are given us! And some may even live to eighty. But even the best of these years are often empty and filled with pain; soon they disappear, and we are gone. . . . Teach us to number our days and recognize how few they are; help us to spend them as we should. (Ps. 90:10, 12 TLB)

I'll never forget the first time I heard someone speak on these verses. I was a freshman in college at Baylor University sitting in an orientation chapel, pining for my girlfriend (now my wife) who was one hundred miles away at the University of Texas. It would be two weeks until I saw her, and Moses's observation about the brevity of time seemed profoundly untrue. Time moved like molasses back then! Yet, the older I get the more I understand what Moses was saying. As one wag put it, "Life is like a roll of toilet paper—the closer you get to the end, the more quickly it goes."

The apostle Paul picked up and expanded on Moses's idea of numbering our days and learning to live wisely:

Be careful how you walk, not as unwise men but as wise, making the most of your time, because the days are evil. (Eph. 5:15–16)

"Walking" in the Bible is a metaphor for living. And whatever consumes your time determines "how you walk"—the way you live. For example, try this simple exercise: make a list of your top three priorities in life. Then, over the next few days, track how much of your time you actually spend on these three priorities. Are you "walking"—spending your time—on those things you deem most important in your life? As one person has said, "Life is like a dollar. You can spend it any way you want, but you can only spend it once."

Paul admonished us to live wisely by "making the most of [our] time" (v. 16). Literally, that phrase means to "buy up" the time. In other words, invest in life and take hold of it—seize the day, *carpe diem*. Philosopher Henry David Thoreau feared that when his death-day came he would "discover that [he] had not lived." He wrote, "I did not wish to live what was not life. . . . I wanted to live deep and suck out all the marrow of life . . . to put to rout all that was not life, to cut a broad swath and shave close."[7] Simply put: don't waste time—life is too short and precious for that.

Spending hours watching television, playing video games, or scrolling through Facebook and Twitter would have been unthinkable to Thoreau and Paul. For both men, life was too valuable a commodity to waste. Thoreau believed he could "buy up" life by secluding himself in the woods, "to live deliberately, to front only the essential facts of life, and see if I could not learn what it had to teach."[8]

Paul had a different motivation for "making the most of [the] time." He saw "the days [as] evil" (v. 16). Make no mistake: Satan will do whatever it takes to prevent you from living a purposeful and God-honoring life. Satan will entice you to squander your time (and therefore your life) on worthless pursuits rather than your God-given priorities in life. I think the paraphrase by J. B. Phillips best captures what Paul had in mind about making the most of your brief time on earth:

> Live life, then, with a due sense of responsibility, not as men who do not know the meaning and purpose of life but as those who do. Make the best use of your time, despite all the difficulties of these days. Don't be vague but firmly grasp what you know to be the will of God. (Eph. 5:15–17)

5. Minimize Your "Predeparture" Regrets

Have you ever been at the departure gate at an airport about to board a plane when you think *I should have remembered to stop the newspaper*, or *I wish I had remembered to pack a warmer coat*? Such "predeparture" regrets are real, but they are also trivial compared to the deep regrets many people feel as they prepare to leave this world for the next one. In my position as a pastor, few things are more heartbreaking than to sit at the deathbed of someone consumed with regrets, hearing them weep over the things they wished they had said—or not said—to their loved ones or over the things they wished they had done or not done in life.

Nothing will steal your joy faster or devour your days more completely than regrets. Poet John Greenleaf Whittier captured this mournful emotion with these lines:

> For all sad words of tongue or pen,
> The saddest are these: "It might have been."[9]

Working in a palliative care center, author Bronnie Ware heard many deathbed confessions, and was able to create a list of the top five regrets of the dying:

1. "I wish I'd had the courage to live a life true to myself, not the life others expected of me."
2. "I wish I hadn't worked so hard."
3. "I wish I'd had the courage to express my feelings."
4. "I wish I had stayed in touch with my family."
5. "I wish I had let myself be happier."[10]

Regrets are like cancer. They eat away at your soul, consume your peace of mind, and are no way to spend your days preparing for heaven. My father was a successful man by any standard. He was a follower of Christ, held an important position in the airline industry, enjoyed an upper-middle-class income, traveled the world, was respected by colleagues and friends, and was loved by his family.

Yet during the months preceding his death from pancreatic cancer, I listened to him lament over the "what ifs" and "if onlys" of his life: trips he wished he had taken, career opportunities he didn't maximize, words he should never have spoken, and relationships he didn't fully appreciate. He even regretted not wearing new suits he had purchased for fear of "wearing them out."

My dad's final months on this earth were not altogether happy ones. Through his experience I learned that regrets have the power to extinguish the joy of an otherwise happy life. I also learned that in the end, someone else is either going to sell or give away your clothes—just as we did with my dad's suits—so you might as well wear them today.

As you prepare for your journey to that "place called heaven," one of the best resolutions you can make is to rid your life of any unnecessary regrets. One way to do this is to honestly evaluate your life. Take a sheet of paper and divide it into five columns: God, family, friends, career, and finances (it might look something like the chart below). Under each column write three goals you'd like to achieve in each of these life areas before you die.

God	Family	Friends	Career	Finances

If it helps, think back to Jonathan Edwards's list and write your goals as resolutions. For example:

- Resolved: I will glorify God so I might hear Him say, "Well done, good and faithful servant."
- Resolved: I will appreciate, enjoy, and value the mate God has given me.
- Resolved: I will endeavor to point my children to Christ, to earn their respect, and to celebrate their uniqueness.
- Resolved: I will treasure my friendships by praying for and spending time with those who enrich my life.
- Resolved: I will choose a lifework that utilizes my giftedness and passions, and will strive to provide a stable financial foundation for my family both now and in the future.
- Resolved: I will make sure that my finances are in order and my family is provided for when I die.
- Resolved: I will ask forgiveness from anyone I have wronged so that when I'm gone they will always remember I tried to make things right.

As you honestly evaluate your life, maybe you feel badly about mistakes you've made, opportunities you've squandered, or people you've hurt. The truth is that it is impossible to erase the past. Life has no rewind button. But with God's help you can make some changes in your life right now that will reshape your tomorrow and your eternity. If you don't believe that, consider the story of one Swedish philanthropist.

Alfred Nobel was a nineteenth-century chemist who made his reputation and fortune by stabilizing nitroglycerine. By adding a specific compound to the highly volatile liquid, Nobel was able to turn it into a paste, which he called "dynamite." Intended for commercial construction—blasting mines, drilling tunnels, and building canals—dynamite was quickly adapted by governments into an instrument of war.

During his lifetime, Nobel was best known as the inventor of dynamite—and for the death and destruction it caused. In fact, when his brother Ludvig died in 1888, French newspapers confused Ludvig for Alfred and reported, "The merchant of death is dead." This mistake meant that Alfred Nobel had the opportunity to read his own obituary in the newspaper.

Realizing that when he died he would only be remembered for enabling the killing of untold millions of people, Nobel decided right then to make a significant change in his life. He determined to dedicate the remainder of his life to scientific, artistic, and peaceful endeavors that celebrated humanity. He set aside a sizable sum of his vast wealth and established the Nobel prizes we're familiar with today.

Few of us will achieve the fame and fortune of Alfred Nobel, but all of us can redirect our time, our money, and our energy to things that will allow us to live and die without regrets.

6. Take Care of the Practical Matters before You Depart

One last item to check off before departing on your heavenly journey: make sure those you leave behind will be adequately cared for. That's what the prophet Isaiah told King Hezekiah: "Thus says the LORD, 'Set your house in order, for you shall die'" (2 Kings 20:1). Good advice.

234

A friend of mine attended a seminar about the need to make adequate financial preparations for families in the event of the death of a husband or wife. My friend returned from the conference convicted that he needed to have a frank talk with his wife about what she should do if he preceded her in death. "Honey, I think you should plan to stay in the house since the mortgage is almost paid," he said. She agreed. "And if you choose to remarry, that's fine with me. In fact, I would have no problem with your new husband and you occupying our bedroom." Again, no disagreement from his wife.

"And also, I would want him to feel free to use my golf clubs if he was as passionate about the game as I am," he added. "Oh, no! That would never work!" my friend's wife said. "Why not?" her husband wondered. "Because you're right-handed and he's left-handed!"

Funny story. But what isn't humorous is a scenario I've seen played out far too many times: a spouse dies without ever discussing financial affairs, the location of his or her will or life insurance policies (if either exist), security passwords, funeral desires, or any other vital information with the surviving spouse or children. The result is that the family is completely in the dark about critical issues, leading them to waste energy and time that should be directed toward grieving and recovery.

I've said it before in this book and I'll say it again: death is inevitable. You are going to die and leave your family behind. As popular speaker Tony Campolo notes, one day your family and friends will cart your casket to the cemetery, drop you in a hole, throw dirt on you, and go back to the church and eat potato salad. But what will your family do after the potato salad?

235

One thing you could do is follow the example of Jim Hindle, a Certified Financial Planner. A few years before his death, Jim wrote an article on how to leave your financial house in good order. Jim based his advice on 1 Timothy 5:8: "If anyone does not provide for his own, and especially for those of his household, he has denied the faith and is worse than an unbeliever."

Besides having a will, Jim advised, families should create a notebook, listing assets and liabilities, checking and savings accounts, stocks, bonds, CDs, IRAs, pensions, real estate, life insurance policies, and annuities. The notebook should also include obituary information as well as contact information for an attorney, accountant, banker, and stockbroker.

A few days after Jim's death, still reeling with the new reality of his passing, his wife, Audrey, went to see her attorney— Jim's notebook in hand. "After looking at the book," she writes, "he shook his head and said, 'This is incredible.'" She concludes:

> Jim demonstrated love, godly character, and integrity by leaving a part of himself in his book. I have never felt abandoned or insecure. My husband took good care of us in his life, and is still taking care of us in his death.[11]

Do that for your family. You won't regret it . . . and neither will they.

The early death of both of my parents had a profound effect on my life. Both were strong believers who taught me not only how to live as a Christian but also how to die as a Christian. But their premature deaths (at least from my perspective) steeled my resolve to live without regrets and to die without regrets.

If I were to compose my own epitaph to be engraved on my headstone, I couldn't come up with anything better than the one engraved on Abraham's headstone: "[He] died in a ripe old age, an old man and satisfied with life; and he was gathered to his people" (Gen. 25:8). Abraham came to the end of his life without a long list of "if onlys" or "what ifs." He was satisfied—contented—with his past. By faith in God's grace he knew his past mistakes had been forgiven. He was satisfied, knowing that he had passed along his faith in God to his children and grandchildren. And he was at peace with the future—prepared for his journey to heaven where he would be "gathered to his people."

Are you ready for your journey to heaven? If you are a Christian, you need not fear the journey—especially when you consider the destination. One of the most moving illustrations of the journey and destination that await every Christian was penned many years ago by John Todd. Born in Rutland, Vermont, in the autumn of 1800, John moved with his family to the tiny hamlet of Killingsworth. A few years later, young John was orphaned when his mother and father died. His siblings were parceled out to family members—and a kindhearted aunt agreed to take in six-year-old John.

John lived with his aunt for fifteen years, then in his early twenties he left to study for the ministry. As the years passed and John reached midlife, his aunt fell ill. Realizing death was close, she wrote to her nephew. She was frightened about the prospect of dying. Moved with compassion, John responded, recounting the night when he, a frightened little boy, was welcomed into the warm and loving home of his aunt:

It is now thirty-five years since I, a little boy of six, was left quite alone in the world. You sent me word you would give me a home and be a kind mother to me. I have never forgotten the day when I made the long journey of ten miles to your house in North Killingsworth. I can still recall my disappointment when, instead of coming for me yourself, you sent your colored man, Caesar, to fetch me. I well remember my tears and my anxiety as, perched high on your horse and clinging tight to Caesar, I rode off to my new home. Night fell before we finished the journey, and as it grew dark I became lonely and afraid.

"Do you think she'll go to bed before I get there?" I asked Caesar anxiously. "O no," he said reassuringly. "She'll sure stay up FOR YOU. When we get out of these here woods you'll see her candle shining in the window." Presently we did ride out in the clearing and there, sure enough, was your candle. I remember you were waiting at the door, that you put your arms close about me and that you lifted me—a tired and bewildered little boy—down from that horse. You had a big fire burning on the hearth, a hot supper waiting for me on the stove. After supper, you took me to my new room, you heard me say my prayers and then you sat beside me until I fell asleep.

You probably realize why I am recalling all this to your memory. Someday soon, God will send for you, to take you to a new home. Don't fear the summons—the strange journey—or the dark messenger of death. God can be trusted to do as much for you as you were kind enough to do for me so many years ago. At the end of the road you will find love and a welcome waiting, and you will be safe in God's care.[12]

A Final Thought

Heaven is the destination that awaits all those who love the Lord Jesus Christ. And it is more glorious than mere words can begin to describe. Not long ago I attended a stage production of the classic musical *The Sound of Music*. The Rogers and Hammerstein score is timeless and the actors were superb. But when the curtain rose for the opening act, I had to keep myself from laughing out loud.

There was the young nun Maria singing and frolicking in front of a painted scrim depicting the Austrian Alps. A few months earlier I had been in the Alps visiting the actual locations where the movie was filmed. The disparity between those real majestic mountains and the artistic rendering on a piece of fabric was laughable.

I've thought about that disparity over the last six months as I have written this book. The words on these pages—or even the pages of Scripture itself—are only a pencil sketch of that very real location Jesus is preparing for you right now.

It's a place more magnificent than you could ever imagine.

It's a place where every heartache will be erased and every dream will be fulfilled.

It's a place reserved for those who have received God's forgiveness through faith in Christ.

It's a place called heaven.

Notes

Chapter 1 What Difference Does a Future Heaven Make in My Life Today?

1. Philip Yancey, *Disappointment with God: Three Questions No One Asks Aloud* (Grand Rapids: Zondervan, 1988), 276.

2. Author unknown, as quoted in Robert Jeffress, *How Can I Know: Answers to Life's 7 Most Important Questions* (Brentwood, TN: Worthy Publishers, 2012), 137.

3. Joni Eareckson Tada, *Heaven: Your Real Home* (Grand Rapids: Zondervan, 1995), 15.

4. Ibid., 110.

5. William Shakespeare, *Hamlet*, 3.1.79, in *William Shakespeare: The Complete Works* (New York: Dorset Press, 1988), 688.

6. C. S. Lewis, *Mere Christianity* (San Francisco: HarperSanFrancisco, 2001), 134.

7. Spiros Zodhiates, *What You Should Know about Life After Death* (Chattanooga, TN: AMG, 2002), 49.

8. Cyprian, "Treatise VII: On the Mortality," 26, in *The Ante-Nicene Fathers*, vol. 5, ed. Alexander Roberts and James Donaldson (New York: Charles Scribner's Sons, 1903), 475.

9. Aristides, "The Apology of Aristides on Behalf of the Christians," 15, trans. J. Rendel Harris, *Texts and Studies: Contributions to Biblical and Patristic Literature*, vol. 1, no. 1, ed. J. Armitage Robinson (London: Cambridge at the University Press, 1893), 49.

10. John Charles Ryle, *Shall We Know One Another and Other Papers* (Moscow, ID: Charles Nolan Publishers, 2001), 5–6.

11. The third heaven referred to by Paul in 2 Corinthians 12:2 is the place of God's presence—"Paradise" (12:4; see Deut. 26:15; Ps. 14:2; Matt. 6:9–10; 18:18; 28:2). The first heaven is the earth's atmosphere (Gen. 1:20, 26, 28; 8:2; Deut. 28:12; Job 35:5; Ps. 147:8; Matt. 8:20; 13:32; 16:2–3). The second heaven is the stellar universe, the place of stars and planets (Gen. 1:14–15, 17; 15:5; Deut. 4:19; 17:3; 28:62; Acts 2:19–20; Heb. 11:12).

12. "Hell Unleashed," *Gladiator*, directed by Ridley Scott (2000; Universal City, CA: Universal Studies, 2004), DVD.

13. Lucius Annaeus Seneca, "Consolations Against Death from the Providence and Necessity of It," in *Seneca's Morals by Way of Abstract*, trans. Roger L'Estrange (London: Sherwood, Neely and Jones, 1818), 237.

14. C. S. Lewis, *The Last Battle*, in *The Complete Chronicles of Narnia* (New York: HarperCollins, 1998), 524 (emphasis in original).

15. See Randy Alcorn, *Heaven* (Carol Stream, IL: Tyndale, 2004), 436.

16. Bruce Wilkinson and David Kopp, *A Life God Rewards: Why Everything You Do Today Matters Forever* (Colorado Springs: Multnomah, 2002), 16.

17. Alcorn, *Heaven*, 471.

18. Teresa of Avila, as quoted in Lee Strobel, *The Case for Faith: A Journalist Investigates the Toughest Objections to Christianity* (Grand Rapids: Zondervan, 2000), 65.

19. Alcorn, *Heaven*, 460.

Chapter 2 Is Heaven a Real Place or Is It a State of Mind?

1. David Jeremiah, *Answers to Your Questions about Heaven* (Carol Stream, IL: Tyndale, 2013), 3.

2. "Heaven," *The Merriam-Webster Dictionary* (Springfield: Merriam-Webster, 2005).

3. See Luke 10:1 and John 11:48.

4. The Vulgate—the Latin version of the Bible—translates the noun *mone*, "dwelling," as *mansiones*. The King James or Authorized Version transliterates this into "mansions." However, the point of Jesus's teaching in John 14:2 is not that believers will live in their own individual mansions but that we will live in God's mansion and be given keys to our own individual rooms. The idea comes from the marriage custom of Jesus's day. The bridegroom would retrieve his bride from her home and bring her back to his father's house, where an apartment was built for the new couple.

5. On Jesus being the only means of reaching heaven, please see my book *Not All Roads Lead to Heaven: Sharing an Exclusive Jesus in an Inclusive World* (Grand Rapids: Baker, 2016).

6. If you are unfamiliar with end-time events, please see my book *Perfect Ending: Why Your Eternal Future Matters Today* (Brentwood, TN: Worthy, 2014).

7. Other biblical passages that speak of the passing of the present heavens and earth include Psalm 102:25–26, Isaiah 51:6, and Matthew 24:35.

8. See Ron Rhodes, *The Wonder of Heaven: A Biblical Tour of Our Eternal Home* (Eugene, OR: Harvest House, 2009), 135.

9. See Jeremiah, *Answers to Your Questions about Heaven*, 115.

10. We believe the New Jerusalem is cube-shaped (as opposed to, for example, pyramid-shaped) because the Holy of Holies, God's dwelling place in Solomon's temple, was cube-shaped (1 Kings 6:20).

11. Sam Roberts, "It's Still a Big City, Just Not Quite So Big," *New York Times*, May 22, 2008, http://www.nytimes.com/2008/05/22/nyregion /22shrink.html.

12. Ron Rhodes, *What Happens After Life? 21 Amazing Revelations about Heaven and Hell* (Eugene, OR: Harvest House, 2014), 69.

13. Exactly why twelve angels are stationed at the twelve gates, which are inscribed with the twelve tribes of Israel, and why the twelve foundations are inscribed with the twelve apostles, is a mystery. See Rhodes, *What Happens After Life?*, 70–71.

14. The Greek word for "healing" in Revelation 22:2 is *therapeia*, from which we get the English word *therapy*. The basic idea of *therapeia* is "health giving." Since there will be no sickness or death in heaven (21:4), it's best to interpret the word as the promotion of well-being. Notice, however, there's no mention of the tree of the knowledge of good and evil. There's no need to test humanity in heaven. The redeemed already know of sin and its devastating effects and have been saved by the blood of Christ, who passed the test; they desire it no longer.

15. C. S. Lewis, *The Problem of Pain*, in *The Complete C. S. Lewis Signature Classics* (New York: HarperCollins, 2002), 428.

Chapter 3 Have Some People Already Visited Heaven?

1. "Dwight L. Moody Is Dead," *New York Times*, December 23, 1899, http://query.nytimes.com/mem/archive-free/pdf?res=9B04E1DA153CE 433A25750C2A9649D94689ED7CF.

2. "Near-Death Experiences: Key Facts," International Association for Near-Death Studies, accessed January 12, 2017, https://iands.org/images /stories/pdf_downloads/Key%20Facts%20Handout-brochure-small.pdf.

3. Gideon Lichfield, "The Science of Near-Death Experiences," *Atlantic*, April 2015, http://www.theatlantic.com/features/archive/2015/03 /the-science-of-near-death-experiences/386231/.

4. "'Heaven Is for Real' Hit Major Sales Milestone," *Christian Retailing*, December 11, 2014, https://web.archive.org/web/20141218031545/http://christianretailing.com/index.php/newsletter/latest/27680-heaven-is-for-real-hits-major-sales-milestone.

5. Alex Malarkey, as quoted in Dustin Germain, "'The Boy Who Came Back from Heaven' Recants Story, Rebukes Christian Retailers," *Pulpit & Pen* (blog), January 13, 2015, http://pulpitandpen.org/2015/01/13/the-boy-who-came-back-from-heaven-recants-story-rebukes-christian-retailers/.

6. Tyndale House Publishers' press release, as quoted in Ron Charles, "'The Boy Who Came Back from Heaven' Actually Didn't; Books Recalled," *Washington Post*, January 16, 2015, https://www.washingtonpost.com/news/style-blog/wp/2015/01/15/boy-who-came-back-from-heaven-going-back-to-publisher/.

7. Malarkey, as quoted in Germain, "'The Boy Who Came Back from Heaven' Recants Story."

8. J. Isamu Yamamoto, "The Near-Death Experience, Part Two: Alternative Explanations," *Christian Research Journal*, Summer 1992, http://www.iclnet.org/pub/resources/text/cri/cri-jrnl/web/crj0098a.html.

9. "Miracle Makers," *The Princess Bride*, directed by Rob Reiner (1987; Beverly Hills, CA: MGM Studios, 1999), DVD.

10. On Colton Burpo's descriptions of the Holy Spirit and God the Father, see "Frequently Asked Questions," Heaven Is for Real Ministries, http://www.heavenlive.org/about/faq.

11. Yamamoto, "The Near-Death Experience, Part Two: Alternative Explanations."

12. Dinesh D'Souza, *Life After Death: The Evidence* (Washington, DC: Regnery, 2009), 68.

13. Lichfield, "Science of Near-Death Experiences."

14. See Deuteronomy 18:10–13; Galatians 5:19–21; and Revelation 21:8.

15. See Rhodes, *Wonder of Heaven*, 241.

Chapter 4 Do Christians Immediately Go to Heaven When They Die?

1. Reinhold Niebuhr, as quoted in David L. Chappell, *A Stone of Hope: Prophetic Religion and the Death of Jim Crow* (Chapel Hill: University of North Carolina Press, 2004), 50.

2. Alcorn, *Heaven*, xix.

3. J. Sidlow Baxter, *The Other Side of Death: What the Bible Teaches About Heaven and Hell* (Grand Rapids: Kregel Publications, 1987), 22.

4. Jack Nicholson, as quoted in Rhodes, *Wonder of Heaven*, 26–27.

5. Tada, *Heaven: Your Real Home*, 201.

6. As quoted in Rhodes, *Wonder of Heaven*, 48.

7. Alcorn, *Heaven*, 57.

8. Charles Dickens, *A Christmas Carol* (New York: Barnes & Noble, 2005), 17.

9. Erwin W. Lutzer, *How You Can Be Sure You Will Spend Eternity with God* (Chicago: Moody Publishers, 2015), 9.

Chapter 5 What Will We Do in Heaven?

1. Mark Twain, as quoted in Archibald Henderson, *Mark Twain* (New York: Frederick A. Stokes Co., 1912), 109.

2. Mark Twain, "Tammany and Croker," in *Mark Twain's Speeches* (New York: Harper & Brothers Publishers, 1910), 117.

3. Isaac Asimov, as quoted in Alcorn, *Heaven*, 409.

4. G. K. Chesterton, *Orthodoxy* (Wheaton, IL: Harold Shaw Publishers, 1994), 61.

5. See Katy Sharp, "A Tour of the NFL's Loudest Stadiums," *SB Nation*, September 18, 2014, http://www.sbnation.com/nfl/2014/9/18/6257281/nfl-loudest-stadiums; and Kevin Lynch, "Seattle Seahawks Fans 'Cause Minor Earthquake' with World Record Crowd Roar," *Guinness World Records*, December 4, 2013, http://www.guinnessworldrecords.com/news/2013/12/seattle-seahawks-fans-cause-minor-earthquake-with-world-record-crowd-roar-53285/.

6. Tada, *Heaven: Your Real Home*, 64.

7. Alcorn, *Heaven*, 196.

8. See Luke 22:69; Acts 2:33; 7:55–56; Romans 8:34; Ephesians 1:20; Colossians 3:1; Hebrews 1:3; 8:1; 10:12; 12:2; 1 Peter 3:22; Revelation 3:21.

9. For more information on the millennial kingdom, see my book *Perfect Ending: Why Your Eternal Future Matters Today* (Brentwood, TN: Worthy Publishing, 2014), 137–60.

10. Jeremiah, *Answers to Your Questions about Heaven*, 32.

11. Sam Storms, as quoted in Alcorn, *Heaven*, 179.

Chapter 6 Do People in Heaven Know What Is Happening on Earth?

1. Though the Bible often refers to the body sleeping as a metaphor for death (John 11:11–14; Acts 7:59–60; 13:36; 1 Thess. 4:13), nowhere does the Bible speak of soul sleep. The Greek word translated "to fall asleep" is *koimao*, which comes from the same Greek word translated "to lie down." *Koimao* was used to describe someone who slept in a hotel

for the night and in the morning continued his journey. This is what happens to the believer's body at death. The body "sleeps" in the ground, while the soul gets up and continues its journey to heaven. See Jeremiah, *Answers to Your Questions about Heaven*, 12.

2. Warren Wiersbe, *The Wiersbe Bible Commentary: New Testament* (Colorado Springs, CO: David C. Cook, 2007), 1097.

3. See Joshua 15:8; 18:16; 2 Kings 23:10; Nehemiah 11:30.

4. See 2 Chronicles 28:3; 33:6; Jeremiah 19:6; 32:35.

5. C. S. Lewis, *The Screwtape Letters* (San Francisco: HarperSanFrancisco, 2001), 61.

6. See Matthew 7:13; 2 Thessalonians 1:8–9; see also 1 Corinthians 5:5; 1 Thessalonians 5:3; 1 Timothy 6:9.

7. On our endless worship of God see Revelation 1:6; 4:9; and 5:13. On the endless life of God see Revelation 4:10 and 10:6. And on the endless kingdom of God see Revelation 11:15.

8. James Joyce, *A Portrait of the Artist as a Young Man* (New York: Everyman's Library, 1991), 151–52.

9. Peter Kreeft, *Christianity for Modern Pagans: Pascal's Pensées* (San Francisco: Ignatius Press, 1993), 196.

10. Randal Rauser, as quoted in Rhodes, *Wonder of Heaven*, 144.

11. J. I. Packer, *Knowing God* (Downers Grove, IL: InterVarsity Press, 1973), 138.

12. J. I. Packer, "Hell's Final Enigma," *Christianity Today* 46, no. 5 (April 22, 2002): 84, http://www.christianitytoday.com/ct/2002/april22/27.84.html.

Chapter 7 Will We Know One Another in Heaven?

1. Erma Bombeck, as quoted in Charles R. Swindoll, *Improving Your Serve: The Art of Unselfish Living* (Nashville: W Publishing Group, 1981), 51.

2. Chart copyright © 1979, 2008, 2017 by Charles R. Swindoll, Inc. All rights reserved. Used by permission. The "Millennial Believer" section is not part of the original chart, and the opinions expressed in this section are the author's own and do not necessarily reflect the view of Charles R. Swindoll, Inc. or Insight for Living Ministries.

3. John Calvin, as quoted in Rhodes, *Wonder of Heaven*, 84.

4. See 1 Corinthians 15:12–19.

5. Luke 24:33 mentions that the two Emmaus disciples found the eleven disciples. However, since Thomas was absent at the time, the term "the eleven" is used in a technical sense to indicate the disciples as a whole.

6. Tada, *Heaven: Your Real Home*, 53.

7. Revelation 5:9 and 7:9 tell us that heaven is populated by people from every nation, tribe, and tongue, leading me to believe that we'll keep our racial distinctions in heaven.

8. Alcorn, *Heaven*, 290 (emphasis in original).

9. Ibid., 287.

10. Rhodes, *What Happens After Life?*, 107.

Chapter 8 Will Heaven Be the Same for Everyone?

1. See Ephesians 6:8; Revelation 2:23; Matthew 12:36–37; Luke 19:11–26; 1 Peter 1:17; Matthew 10:41–42; Luke 14:12–14; Luke 6:27–28, 35; Daniel 12:3; and Matthew 6:1–4 respectively.

2. Paul doesn't explain the spiritual significance of the precious metals and stones used in his illustration in 1 Corinthians 3:12. However, elsewhere in Scripture gold is typically used to indicate the glory of God, as seen in the tabernacle (Exod. 25) and the temple (1 Kings 6:21–32). Silver is the metal of redemption (Lev. 27). And though the precious stones aren't itemized, there are many other things Christians can do with their talents, time, and treasure to fulfill the great commandment to love God and others (Matt. 22:36–40).

3. Erwin Lutzer, *Your Eternal Reward: Triumph and Tears at the Judgment Seat of Christ* (Chicago: Moody Publishers, 2015), 51.

4. Norman Geisler, as quoted in Rhodes, *Wonder of Heaven*, 189 (emphasis in original).

5. William Barclay, *The Letters to the Philippians, Colossians and Thessalonians*, Daily Bible Series (Louisville: Westminster John Knox Press, 2003), 223.

6. Billy Graham, *Where I Am: Heaven, Eternity, and Our Life Beyond* (Nashville: W Publishing Group, 2015), 229.

7. John Walvoord, "End Times: Understanding Today's World Events in Biblical Prophecy," in *Understanding Christian Theology*, ed. Charles R. Swindoll and Roy B. Zuck (Nashville: Thomas Nelson, 2003), 1279.

8. Lutzer, *Your Eternal Reward*, 78.

Chapter 9 Who Will Be in Heaven?

1. See Leviticus 11:44–45; 19:2; 20:7, 26.

2. My book *Not All Roads Lead to Heaven: Sharing an Exclusive Jesus in an Inclusive World* (Grand Rapids: Baker Books, 2016) is dedicated to the exclusivity of Jesus Christ as the only means of salvation and way to heaven.

3. Lewis, *Mere Christianity*, 52.

4. On the exclusivity of Jesus as the source of salvation and means to heaven, see John 3:16; 11:25–26; Acts 16:31; Romans 10:9.

5. Charles R. Swindoll, *The Owner's Manual for Christians: The Essential Guide for a God-Honoring Life* (Nashville: Thomas Nelson, 2009), 229 (emphasis in original).

6. See Charles C. Ryrie, *Basic Theology: A Popular Systematic Guide to Understanding Biblical Truth* (Chicago: Moody, 1999), 37–38.

7. For a more in-depth discussion of what happens to children and the childlike when they die, see my book *Not All Roads Lead to Heaven*, 165–76.

Chapter 10 How Can I Prepare for My Journey to Heaven?

1. Warren Buffet, as quoted in Elliot Blair Smith, "Warren Buffet Signs Over $30.7 Billion to the Bill and Melinda Gates Foundation," *USA Today*, June 26, 2006, http://usatoday30.usatoday.com/money/2006-06-25-buffett-charity_x.htm.

2. George Marsden, *Jonathan Edwards: A Life* (New Haven, CT: Yale University Press, 2003), 51.

3. Jonathan Edwards, "The Christian Pilgrim," in *The Works of Jonathan Edwards*, vol. 2, ed. Edward Hickman (Edinburgh: Banner of Truth, 1974), 244.

4. Jonathan Edwards, *Jonathan Edwards' Resolutions and Advice to Young Converts*, ed. Stephen J. Nichols (Phillipsburg, NJ: Presbyterian and Reformed, 2001), 18–19, 24.

5. Winston S. Churchill, as quoted in James C. Humes, *The Wit and Wisdom of Winston Churchill: A Treasury of More than 1,000 Quotations and Anecdotes* (New York: HarperCollins, 1994), 25.

6. Adapted from Alcorn, *Heaven*, 457.

7. Henry David Thoreau, *Walden, or Life in the Woods* (New York: Everyman's Library, 1910), 80–81.

8. Ibid., 80.

9. John Greenleaf Whittier, "Maud Muller," in *The Poems of John Greenleaf Whittier* (Boston: James R. Osgood and Co., 1878), 206.

10. Bronnie Ware, "Regrets of the Dying," *Inspiration and Chai* (blog), November 19, 2009, http://bronnieware.com/regrets-of-the-dying/.

11. Audrey Hindle, "A Husband's Final Gift," as quoted in Robert Jeffress, *The Road Most Traveled: Releasing the Power of Contentment in Your Life* (Nashville: Broadman & Holman, 1996), 160–62.

12. As quoted in Charles R. Swindoll, *Living on the Ragged Edge: Coming to Terms with Reality* (Waco: Word, 1985), 358–59.

About the Author

Dr. Robert Jeffress is senior pastor of the 13,000-member First Baptist Church, Dallas, Texas, and a Fox News contributor. He is also an adjunct professor at Dallas Theological Seminary. Dr. Jeffress has made more than two thousand guest appearances on various radio and television programs and regularly appears on major mainstream media outlets such as Fox News channel's *Fox and Friends*, *The O'Reilly Factor*, *Hannity*, *Lou Dobbs Tonight*, *Varney and Co.*, and *Judge Jeanine*; ABC's *Good Morning America*; and HBO's *Real Time with Bill Maher*. Dr. Jeffress hosts a daily radio program, *Pathway to Victory*, that is heard nationwide on over eight hundred stations in major markets such as Dallas–Fort Worth, New York City, Chicago, Los Angeles, Washington, DC, Houston, and Seattle. His weekly television program can be seen in 195 countries and on 11,283 cable and satellite systems throughout the world, including China, and on the Trinity Broadcasting Network and Daystar.

Dr. Jeffress is the author of over twenty books, including *When Forgiveness Doesn't Make Sense*, *Countdown to the*

Apocalypse, and *Not All Roads Lead to Heaven*. Dr. Jeffress recently led his congregation in the completion of a $135 million re-creation of its downtown campus. The project is the largest in modern church history and serves as a "spiritual oasis" covering six blocks of downtown Dallas.

Dr. Jeffress has a DMin from Southwestern Baptist Theological Seminary, a ThM from Dallas Theological Seminary, and a BS from Baylor University. In May 2010 he was awarded a Doctor of Divinity degree from Dallas Baptist University, and in June 2011 he received the Distinguished Alumnus of the Year award from Southwestern Baptist Theological Seminary.

Dr. Jeffress and his wife, Amy, have two daughters, Julia and Dorothy, and a son-in-law, Ryan Sadler.

A PLACE CALLED
HEAVEN

Complete DVD Teaching Set

Teaching set includes . . .

» A hardcover copy of *A Place Called Heaven*

» The complete, unedited series on DVD

» A comprehensive instructor's guidebook, complete with answers to study questions and expanded responses to key points

DR. ROBERT JEFFRESS
Pathway
TO Victory

Pathway to Victory stands for truth and exists to pierce the darkness with the light of God's Word through the most effective media available, including radio, television, and digital media.

Through *Pathway to Victory*, Dr. Robert Jeffress spreads the Good News of Jesus Christ to a lost and hurting people, confronts an ungodly culture with God's truth, and equips the saints to apply Scripture to their everyday lives.

Our mission is to provide practical application of God's Word to everyday life through clear, biblical teaching and lead people to become obedient and reproducing disciples of Jesus Christ, as He commanded in Matthew 28:18–20.

ptv.org | 866.999.2965

 drjeffress

 @robertjeffress

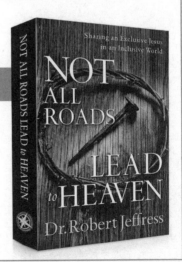